MILES OFF COURSE

SULARI GENTILL

A ROWLAND SINCLAIR MYSTERY

The Crime & Mystery Club
Harpenden
crimeandmysteryclub.co.uk

© Sulari Gentill, 2011

First Published by Pantera Press

A CIP catalogue record for this book is available from the British Library.

ISBN
978-0-85730-361-5 (print)
978-0-85730-362-2 (ebook)

2 4 6 8 10 9 7 5 3 1

Typeset by Avocet Typeset, Bideford, Devon, EX39 2BP
Printed and bound in Denmark by Nørhaven, Viborg

For more information about Crime Fiction go to @crimetimeuk.

The Rowland Sinclair Mysteries

To those with the courage to stay on course,
and those with the imagination to wander.

PROLOGUE

WAVE OF ABDUCTIONS TERRORISES SYDNEY'S WEALTHY

The grisly discovery of the remains of the Lindbergh baby in May last year, some months after the child had been kidnapped from its nursery, caused shock and outrage in the United States and across the world.

There is not a person in the civilised world who cannot feel for the anguish of Colonel and Mrs. Lindbergh, nor be repulsed by the brutality of the act.

The abduction of rich men's sons is not a new crime, and our part of the world is not immune from those who seek to extort money from the well-to-do with this sort of menace.

Sydney has in the past weeks fallen victim to a wave of suspected abductions.

In January, William Ainsworth of Ainsworth Textiles disappeared, as did Edward Carmichael of Carmichael and Sons Pty Ltd. Most recently Charles Wentworth—son of the industrialist, Sir Alfred Wentworth, and a prominent businessman in his own right—was seized in broad daylight by persons unknown.

Despite the best efforts of Superintendent Bill Mackay and his Criminal Investigation Bureau, not one of these gentlemen has been recovered. Police remain baffled and grave concerns are held for the lives of all three victims.

It is a stark reminder of the tyranny of the criminal that even the founding families of our fair city cannot feel safe in her streets. One can only wonder which family will be next to have a son snatched away.

The Sydney Morning Herald, 1933

1

"Norman Lindsay is a complete and utter bastard!"

Rowland Sinclair sat down and buried both hands in his dark hair as he vented his frustration. It had been a long day. He fell back and loosened his tie.

Milton Isaacs closed his book and rose from the comfort of his armchair to pour his friend a drink. He charged two glasses from the crystal decanters. The poet was nothing if not empathetic.

"What's old Norman done now?"

Rowland took the sherry and drained it in a single swig. He felt a little better. Perhaps intoxication was the answer. "Rosalina Martinelli."

"The model?"

Rowland simply groaned in reply, his temper exhausted by the trials of the day. The invitation to contribute a piece to the impending exhibition of classical figures at the Art Gallery of New South Wales had been an unexpected recognition of his work. A portrait artist, Rowland had acquired a quiet but growing reputation for his paintings of the female form. He was considered, by some, a protégé of Lindsay, though there were many who would say Sinclair had a lighter touch with oils, a greater finesse with the medium of paint. Rowland's nudes were somehow different, his work moved those it did not offend. He was a young man, and so he painted women as a young man would—with a kind of wondrous excitement that came out in the stroke of his brush. There was, however, nothing wondrous or exciting about the last few hours.

"What's the problem with Miss Martinelli?" Milton asked, refilling his glass. "She looked pretty enough to me."

Rowland's dark blue eyes flashed.

"Let's just say there's a reason why Lindsay was so damned happy to lend her to me… and it had nothing to do with being magnanimous. I swear I'm going to deck the old blighter when I see him next."

Milton smiled, intrigued. Rowland was most definitely put out. What on earth was wrong with the girl? Outwardly, Rosalina Martinelli was a very attractive young woman: blonde and fair-skinned despite her Mediterranean heritage, with the kind of gentle rounded figure that Rowland preferred. Of course she'd been dressed when Milton had seen her leave. Perhaps there was some hideous deformity hidden beneath the modest dress. How unfortunate.

"All right," he said. "Out with it. Is she missing a body part or does she have an extra one?"

Rowland choked on his sherry.

"God no… she's beautiful. She just can't model."

"Come on, Rowly." Milton sat down. "All she's got to do is take her jolly clothes off."

Rowland sighed. "No, she's also got to keep still—something of which Miss Martinelli is apparently incapable."

"Oh… fidgets, does she?" Milton looked more closely at Rowland. His hair was damp with perspiration, but the day was not that warm. "What on earth have you been doing, Rowly?"

"Miss Martinelli feels the cold," Rowland replied tersely. "Insisted I have no fewer than two kerosene heaters going full bore as well as the fire."

Milton laughed softly. He swirled his glass, apparently searching for inspiration in the movement of the amber liquid. "Her radiant shape upon its verge did shiver, aloft her flowing hair like strings of flame did quiver."

"Shelley." Rowland was neither soothed nor impressed by the recitation.

Milton owed his reputation as a poet to his ability to quote the works of the great bards at will, and without acknowledgement. It was unlikely that he had ever penned a line of original verse. It had become a tradition of sorts for Rowland to make the attributions that Milton blithely omitted.

"I've just wasted the whole sodding day," Rowland muttered.

"Chin up, old mate... there'll be something worthwhile in all the preliminary sketches—you couldn't have spent all your time stoking the fire."

Rowland shook his head. "Aside from the fact that Miss Martinelli was constantly moving and complaining about the cold in English, and somewhat more stridently in Italian, the room was so hot that the paint dried too quickly. I'll have to toss the entire canvas... there's nothing worth salvaging."

Milton was amused now. Rowland had studied languages at Oxford and had a reasonable understanding of spoken Italian, but Rosalina Martinelli had probably not known that. Still, Milton tried to be helpful. "Perhaps the studio is a touch draughty... why don't you try painting her here?" He glanced about the sun-drenched sitting room of the Grand Majestic suite. It looked out upon the lawns and gardenesque grounds of the Hydro Majestic Hotel,

Medlow Bath, in which they had taken up temporary residence for most of the summer. The suite was lavish and well lit, and the sitting room had a most agreeable outlook. Milton supposed that it would appeal to both Rowland and his model.

Rowland grunted. "I'm afraid Miss Martinelli is shy. She'll only pose with the curtains drawn in case the gardeners should peer in."

Milton chuckled. This was just getting better. "You could always let her go," he suggested. It was the obvious solution, but he doubted Rowland would take it. His friend was incapacitatingly civil, and it was difficult to sack a person politely.

Rowland looked pained. "Every time I broach the subject, she wails like a banshee. Apparently, she needs the income."

"So pay her." The cost of a model would mean nothing to Rowland, whose family fortune was vast enough to support his natural and determined generosity.

"I tried." Rowland's mouth twitched. He was starting to see humour in his predicament. "She's proud... refuses to take charity."

"Well you can't insult people, Rowly." Milton grinned. The poet, of course, had no misgivings about being the beneficiary of Rowland Sinclair's significant patronage. It was something they had both come to accept.

Rowland smiled now. He folded his hands behind his head and lay back in the couch. "I'm going to deck Lindsay."

"What are you going to do about the exhibition?"

"Lord knows. I'll have to paint her I suppose." Rowland was resigned.

"You can't use Ed?"

The young sculptress, Edna Higgins, had regularly modelled for Rowland in the past. His reputation owed much to the way he painted her.

Rowland shook his head. "She's not well enough yet, Milt."

Milton didn't argue. Edna was almost completely recovered, but Rowland was particularly protective of her.

"Ed's too thin at the moment anyway," Rowland added. "It won't paint well."

The dose of strychnine, which had nearly killed the sculptress just a few weeks before, had lingered in its effect upon her appetite. She had lost weight. Rowland still thought her beautiful, but the current slimness of her figure did not suit the style or subject of the impending exhibition.

Their current sojourn at Medlow Bath had allowed Edna to receive treatment. The Hydro Majestic offered guests the most modern hydropathic therapies. Rowland remained sceptical about the value of the various baths, wraps and douches, but his Aunt Mildred had been insistent that it would help Edna recuperate. It seemed Mark Foy, who had built the sanatorium, had been a friend of Rowland's father—apparently that settled the matter for Mildred, who revered her late brother. In the end Rowland had given in. It had been, at the very least, an opportunity to escape the worst of the Sydney summer.

"Where's Clyde?" Milton asked, reopening his book.

"He went out this morning looking for trees to paint." Rowland had never shared Clyde's interest in landscapes—he had neither the patience nor the talent for trees.

Clyde Watson Jones had, like Milton and Edna, lived as a guest of Rowland Sinclair for a number of years. A fellow artist, he and Rowland shared a love of paint and canvas, though they had come to their craft by way of vastly different circumstances. All the years that Rowland had spent at Oxford, Clyde had survived on the wallaby, moving from town to town, getting what work he could and sleeping wherever it was dry.

It was a quirk of fate, that while Rowland had been born into the most lofty social circles, he had little interest in the right sort of people. Indeed, the youngest son of the late pastoralist, Henry Sinclair, seemed determined to fraternise with scandal.

"Old Foy dropped off a few bottles of mineral water while you were working," Milton informed him, thumbing through the text for his place.

"Good Lord... you didn't try to drink it did you?"

Mark Foy was convinced that the mineral water he imported from Germany was some kind of miracle elixir and he encouraged all his guests to drink it regularly. He claimed the bitterness was proof of its medicinal potency. Rowland maintained that the water had been spoiled in transport.

"It's all right if you mix it with scotch," Milton advised. "Don't want to offend the old boy. He wanted to talk to you about those drawings, by the way."

Rowland sighed.

He'd been trying not to think about Mark Foy's drawings. Rowland had made the promise in return for the suite. The three superlative suites of the therapeutic resort, with their valets and personal cooks, had all been previously booked. Mark Foy had used his influence to ensure the Grand Majestic fell suddenly vacant. But he had wanted something from Rowland in return.

"Who does he want you to draw?" Milton enquired, smiling. It was not the first time that some respectable gentleman had requested a picture of his mistress to secrete beneath the marital bed. If it was drawn rather than photographed it could apparently be considered art, should it ever be discovered. Rowland usually declined such requests on artistic rather than moral grounds. Unlike most artists, he had the economic freedom to choose his subjects.

"Not who—what." Rowland shook his head. "Foy wants me to draw up plans for his tomb."

"His what?"

"His tomb. He wants to make sure that when the time comes, he's interred in a manner befitting."

"Is he ill?"

"No, just eccentric."

"What kind of tomb?"

"Well, Foy's rather taken with the pyramids."

Milton started to laugh. "You're not serious."

"I'm afraid I am. He's had an acre on the grounds marked out for it."

Milton sipped his scotch and mineral water and put his feet up on the upholstered footstool. "You know, Rowly, I think being idle has driven the upper classes completely bonkers."

Rowland nodded. "Yes, dangerous thing being idle."

There was a brief knock at the door, a perfunctory announcement of impending entry rather than a request to be admitted. Edna Higgins breezed in, pausing briefly to look through the open door of Rowland's makeshift studio. Her skin was rosy, her copper tresses still damp. She was noticeably thin, but otherwise she looked well and in good spirits.

"Hello, Ed," Rowland murmured, as she perched on the rolled arm of the couch. "How was your morning with Dr. Lindbeck?"

Lindbeck, the Hydro Majestic's resident physician, was a specialist in the hydropathic therapies offered at the resort. A small, wiry man who had a fondness for spats, he barked accented orders at the uniformed matrons as he supervised the treatments.

"Lovely, thank you. A hot immersion, a cold douche, a compression wrap and then another hot bath—I must say I've never before felt so extraordinarily clean."

"Are you hungry?" Rowland asked. "Shall I have Mrs. Murray cook something for you?"

Milton chuckled. "Rowly's trying to fatten you up for his own purposes."

Edna smiled. "Really? What purposes, Rowly?"

"He needs a model," Milton replied for him. "Miss Martinelli isn't working out," he added, in an exaggerated stage whisper.

"Oh that." Edna laughed. "I saw your painting when I came in— you can't blame the poor girl for that, Rowly. It's your palette. You've got far too much crimson in your flesh tones."

"I know how to mix paint, Ed. It's jolly impossible to get a reasonable skin tone when your model won't stop blushing," Rowland replied brusquely. "I could have painted her with undiluted scarlet."

"Oh dear, the poor thing. Whatever did you say to make her so uncomfortable, Rowly?" She poked the artist playfully.

"I think it was 'good morning'."

"I'm sure she'll settle down once she gets used to you. Modelling is not as easy as it looks you know," Edna was firm. "And you could be quite intimidating, I imagine."

"Me? How?" Rowland was genuinely surprised.

Edna thought back to all the times she had modelled for Rowland Sinclair. She remembered the clear intensity of his gaze, the blue eyes that seemed to leave her more than naked.

"It's the way you pose your models to look straight at you," she replied finally. "It's hard to hide any part of yourself from someone looking directly into your eyes. It takes a little getting used to."

Rowland snorted. "I have no idea what Miss Martinelli's eyes look like. She all but covered her face."

Edna smiled. "Come on, Rowly, be a sport." She put her hand on his arm. "I was very nervous on my first jobs too. I'll talk to her if you like—help her relax."

Rowland sighed. It didn't appear he had a choice.

Milton glanced at him and shrugged. It seemed Edna was adopting the hapless model as a personal crusade. It was better that Rowland give in now.

Rowland smiled faintly. Edna had not as yet met Rosalina Martinelli. It was very easy to be compassionate when you weren't standing in an overheated room with someone who complained about everything and couldn't sit still.

He waited till Edna had gone to tell the valet that they were ready for tea, before he muttered to Milton, "I'm going to deck bloody Norman Lindsay."

2

KIDNAPPED

―――――●――――――

LINDBERGH'S BABY
STOLEN FROM NURSERY

NEW YORK, Tuesday

The 19 months old son of Colonel Lindbergh and Mrs. Lindbergh was kidnapped from his home at Hopewell, New Jersey, on Tuesday night.

The baby was put to bed at the usual hour. Two and a half hours later somebody looked in the nursery and he was gone, clad in his sleeping suit. A wide search is being conducted by the police.

Mrs. Lindbergh discovered that the child was missing about 10 p.m. The nursery window was open and a frantic search of the house and grounds failed to reveal the infant, whereupon the police were notified, and the search immediately extended to New York and Pennsylvania, and will undoubtedly extend throughout the Eastern United States unless he is found by the morning.

It is assumed that the kidnappers, if they escape detection, will demand an enormous ransom.

The Canberra Times, March 1932

"Clyde, over here!" Rowland hailed his friend as Edna lined up her shot in the fading light.

Clyde Watson Jones approached with his easel folded over his broad shoulder. He carried a paintbox under his other arm. The wide-brimmed hat he wore when working outdoors cast a shadow on gentle eyes that had seen a different side of life. At thirty, Clyde was only a couple of years older than Rowland, but his face was etched with experience in a way that aged him. Of course Rowland Sinclair had seen his own trials—just not the kind that left a physical mark. Now, however, on the lush croquet lawns of the Hydro Majestic, hardship of any sort seemed very distant indeed.

Edna knocked Milton's ball away with her own and squealed in triumph.

Milton protested vehemently, calling the sculptress all manner of cheat.

Rowland glanced at Clyde. Edna notoriously and shamelessly bent the rules of croquet when it suited her. The artists had always let it go—it was just croquet after all—but Milton had known Edna since childhood. A kind of sibling familiarity prevented him from exercising any gracious tolerance in her favour.

"Any luck today, Clyde?" Rowland asked, as the other two proceeded to bicker.

Clyde put down the easel and handed over a large folder containing the sheets of cartridge paper on which he had been working. Rowland pulled out the series of watercolours. Clyde didn't often work with watercolours but they were convenient when one was lugging equipment any distance. He had wandered down to paint the Megalong Valley from the edge of the clifftops on which the Hydro Majestic stood.

Rowland studied the vistas that Clyde had created with muted washes of undersaturated colour. The effect was subtle, almost ethereal. His low whistle was wistful.

"This is smashing, Clyde… I'd forgotten how still and quiet trees were."

Clyde smiled. "Still and quiet? I take it Miss Martinelli was not the best model."

"A tree, she is not." Rowland glanced at Edna, who was still arguing with Milton. "I'll give you a hand taking this back to the suite," he said, replacing the paintings and grabbing the easel. He turned back to the warring croquet players. "We'll meet you at the restaurant for dinner."

They waved him away without pause.

As they walked back to the Grand Majestic suite, Rowland told Clyde of Rosalina Martinelli and his troubles. Clyde was sympathetic. Rowland worked intensely but he was not unreasonable.

"Ed's right though," he said. "She might get better. When is she sitting for you again?"

"Tomorrow," Rowland replied gloomily.

———————————————

At the suite, Rowland stowed the easel, while Clyde took a minute to wash up, collect his jacket and put on a tie. They were dining casually this night. Rowland waited in the darkened sitting room, wondering vaguely why Jarvis, the fastidious valet, had drawn all the curtains.

He stepped towards the window to remedy the lack of light. Even as he did so, he sensed it: the movement from behind him, another from the corner of the room.

There was no time to react—an arm locked about his neck. Rowland twisted, lashing out instinctively.

A hood was dragged over his head and pulled tight. He could see nothing, his breathing stifled by the sack. His arm was twisted painfully behind his back.

"Come quietly, Sinclair, and we won't have to break your arm."

Rowland's response was muffled by the hood, but it was less than co-operative. He swore again as his arm was wrenched further back. And then someone else joined the fray: Clyde.

Mayhem ensued amidst the crack of impacting blows and a great deal of profanity. The scuffle was fierce, confused. Rowland wrested free and pulled off the hood just in time to duck a swinging fist.

There were three intruders, hefty men in cheap suits. The settee crashed over as Clyde was thrown into it. Two men turned on Rowland again, striking without restraint and pinning him to the floor.

"Give over, you stupid toff!"

Rowland gasped as a heavy boot ploughed into his back. And then a second kick to the ribs.

"Enough already! I'm not carrying the bastard out of 'ere."

Clyde roared, launching himself at the closest intruder. Rowland struggled to help him.

The door to the suite flew open and Milton stood in the doorway—but only for a moment. The poet barely missed a beat—he knew a fight when he saw one—and launched himself enthusiastically into the scuffle.

The numbers were now even and the intruders seemed to be startled into retreat. They pushed past the bewildered staff at the door who had come to investigate this disruption to the sanatorium's advertised serenity.

"Mr. Sinclair, we heard... oh my Lord!" Once again, confusion seemed to reign.

In the ruins of the sitting room, Rowland helped Clyde upright. "You all right?"

"Fine." Clyde mopped his bloody nose with a paint-stained handkerchief. "You're going to have one helluva shiner though, mate." He looked critically at the bruise forming over Rowland's left eye. "Who the hell were those blokes? Bit game, burgling the place in broad daylight."

Rowland shook his head. "I don't think they were common burglars... they knew who I was for one thing."

Milton moved closer to him. "You don't owe money do you, Rowly? Those fellas looked like debt collectors, if you know what I'm saying."

"Don't be a flaming idiot," Clyde muttered.

Rowland understood what Milton meant. He had frequented enough of Sydney's gambling dens and sly-grogeries in his time to recognise the kind of men who inhabited Sydney's underworld. He shook his head.

"I don't owe anything," he said, as he rubbed his arm. "But they did want me to go with them."

By this time, there were other people pushing into the room, and Rowland was compelled to explain to the management what had happened to raise such a din and leave the suite in utter disarray. Edna also arrived to investigate why all the men in her party had left her waiting alone in the restaurant. Jarvis was found locked in a broom cupboard. It appeared he had been bound and gagged by the three intruders prior to Rowland's return to the suite. Inevitably the authorities attended to ask questions and take statements. And so, it was well into the evening when the battered men of Rowland Sinclair's party found themselves finally alone in the Grand Majestic suite with Edna.

Rowland loosened his tie and removed his jacket thankfully. He felt a little damaged and he was hungry. Milton handed him a glass of sherry. It would have to do. The dining room was closed now and Jarvis had retired early after his ordeal in the broom cupboard.

"So what's going on, Rowly?" Edna asked, perching as usual on the arm of the now righted couch. She looked from his bruised face to Clyde's swollen nose. "You were nearly abducted."

"Now let's not get carried away," Rowland said. Abduction sounded a bit hysterical.

"What else would you call it?" Edna challenged.

"Well, yes... I suppose... technically..."

"It's not beyond the realms of possibility that Rowly would be a target for abduction," Clyde said, frowning. "They could demand a whopping great ransom."

"From whom?"

"Your brother for one."

Rowland smiled. "I don't know that Wilfred would pay anything to get me back."

"Perhaps you should telephone him," Edna suggested. "Let him know what's happened. He might be able to..."

Rowland's eyes darkened. "I don't need Wilfred to rescue me quite yet, Ed."

"Oh don't be silly, Rowly." Edna reached over and patted his hand fondly. Rowland's relationship with Wilfred was invariably adversarial and Rowland instinctively resisted the control and interference of his elder brother. There were fourteen years between the two and the gap exacerbated the natural differences in their dispositions. Still, Wilfred Sinclair was an influential man and he would not tolerate any threat against his brother.

"Rowly can look after himself, Ed." Clyde spoke up with perhaps a little more understanding of Rowland's reluctance to seek his brother's help, unless absolutely necessary. Wilfred Sinclair cast a formidable shadow.

"So what do you propose to do?" Edna persisted.

They looked at her blankly. It had not occurred to any of them that they should do anything.

"The police have been called, Ed," Milton said finally.

"And if they come back?"

"What—the police?"

"No—the men who did this." Edna lifted her hand gently to the darkening bruise on Rowland's brow.

"We'll try to hang on to one—probably the best way to find out what they want with Rowly."

"But..."

"I'll be careful, Ed," Rowland assured her. He was touched by the sculptress' concern for his safety. He was not entirely nonchalant about the incident himself, but he didn't see what he could possibly do about it. There had been a spate of kidnappings in Sydney over the past couple of months. It seemed abduction had become fashionable among the criminal elements and the Sinclair fortune was not a secret.

And then something occurred to him. He dragged a hand through his hair. "I will call Wilfred," he said.

"Really?" Clyde was surprised.

"I'm not the only Sinclair... Wil needs to make sure Kate and the boys are safe."

Clyde nodded. He had not thought of Wilfred Sinclair's young family. The abduction and murder of the Lindbergh baby the year before had received worldwide coverage. The tragedy had made people like the Sinclairs understandably protective of their children.

Rowland stood to use the telephone. He dialled the exchange and had a call booked through to *Oaklea* near Yass, the family estate on which his brother resided. It was several minutes before he returned the receiver to its cradle.

"Wil's in Sydney on some kind of business," he informed them. "I told Kate to be particularly careful until he gets back... They'll be all right at *Oaklea*."

The Sinclair estate had long been well protected. Wilfred was both politically and commercially powerful—with that came enemies. Rowland had always believed his brother to be somewhat paranoid about security, but, in light of what had happened, perhaps it was fortunate.

He resumed his seat beside Edna. She still looked troubled. Her unease was a little contagious. Rowland rubbed his shoulder absently where his arm had nearly been wrenched from its socket. "I'll get hold of Wil tomorrow," he promised.

3

STUDY OF CIVILISED NATIVES

SOLUTION OF THE PROBLEM

By Daisy Bates

The natives coming out of the wilds will be an increasing menace as the years go by. The civilised native knows the power of the white man's law, but anything may happen with these wild creatures.

But there will be no solution of the native question, no cessation of exploitation or of broadcast misstatements to the detriment of our good name until some great Empire maker will take over the entire question and make it a "one man's duty of service" and carry on with his job to the end, above all politics and parties. No lesser man can do the needed work.

And I can think of no-one better fitted for the task than an English gentleman.

Brisbane Courier, 1930

The knocking at the door of the Grand Majestic suite was insistent. Rowland emerged from the room he was using as a studio. Jarvis had not as yet returned, so the suite was still without a valet. Clyde, who had been working in the parlour, reached the entrance first. He opened the door, cautiously at first, then flinging it wide as soon as he recognised the gentleman outside.

"Mr. Sinclair." He stood back surprised.

"Mr. Jones." Wilfred shook Clyde's hand and removed his hat as he stepped into the room.

"Wil—I've been trying to reach you." Rowland wiped the paint off his hand before he offered it to his brother.

Wilfred looked distastefully at Rowland's waistcoat, now smeared with Viridian blue, and adjusted his cuffs as he noted the rolled sleeves of his brother's shirt. His gaze stopped briefly on Rowland's bruised eye, but he made no comment.

"Rowly, it seems I've caught you at a bad time."

Rowland smiled. "I was just working…" He glanced anxiously back towards his studio as the noise from within became audible. Sobbing. It was unmistakable and impossible to ignore.

"And who may I ask is in there?" Wilfred demanded.

"Miss Martinelli… the model."

"Good Lord, Rowly, what's wrong with her?"

Rowland scratched his head. "She's a little emotional."

"What in the blazes did you do to her?" Wilfred glared at him.

"I didn't do anything to her!" Rowland replied, mortified and angered by the suggestion.

Wilfred stopped. "No… of course you wouldn't."

"I'll see if Miss Martinelli needs anything," Clyde said awkwardly. "Why don't you talk in the drawing room… it'll be… quieter."

And so the Sinclair brothers left Clyde trying to calm Rosalina Martinelli through the closed door of the studio.

"So, what are you doing here?" Rowland asked once he'd poured Wilfred a drink.

"I drove up to have a word with you."

Rowland was intrigued. It was more common for Wilfred to summon him to *Oaklea* than to seek him out. Obviously it was important. He handed his brother a glass of whisky.

Wilfred took a seat intimating that Rowland should do likewise. "You might remember that early last year we purchased a snow lease."

Rowland sat down. His brother was being liberal with his use of the word "we". Wilfred made all the decisions pertaining to the protection and expansion of the Sinclair fortune. Even if Wilfred had ever sought his input into their commercial dealings, Rowland would have struggled to feign interest. He did, however, vaguely remember some mention of leasing mountain country for the purpose of grazing stock.

"We've been driving cattle from our holdings at Nangus and Gundagai up to the lease during the summer," Wilfred continued. "There was some trouble last year... discrepancies in the numbers, so I sent a man up to look into it."

"Cattle?" Rowland murmured. "I didn't know we had gone out of wool."

Wilfred rolled his eyes. "We haven't. If you paid a modicum of attention to that which funds your lifestyle, you'd know that we've purchased a number of small cattle properties in the last few years. We combined the holdings to maximise economies of scale."

Rowland was beginning to lose interest. It seemed that Wilfred had tracked him down to lecture him on family finances.

Wilfred removed his spectacles and polished them with a handkerchief as he regarded his brother with the deep blue eyes that marked all the Sinclair men. "He hasn't returned—by all accounts he's vanished."

"Who?"

"The man I sent to investigate—I want you to go up there and look into it."

Rowland was a little bewildered. "Isn't this a police matter, Wil?"

"The authorities have taken the position that there's nothing unusual in this case."

"Why?"

"It's Harry, Rowly. I sent Harry. The authorities assume he has just gone wandering... as they do, I guess."

Rowland understood then. Harry Simpson was an Aboriginal man. His mother had worked for the Sinclairs at *Oaklea* and Harry had grown up on the property. About ten years older than Rowland, he was one of Wilfred's most trusted men. The Sinclairs had always been good employers. They took particular care of Harry.

"How long has he been missing?"

"It's hard to say. From what I can ascertain he hasn't been seen in about a week. One of the men he'd taken with him came back to let me know, but the dashed fool can't seem to tell me more than that Harry disappeared. As I said, I can't seem to get the police to take it seriously. That's why I want you to go."

"Of course," Rowland agreed without hesitation. "I'll set out tomorrow."

"We have several men up there already—you can call on them if you need to. You might need to take charge of them... Without Harry to keep them in line, God knows what they're doing."

Rowland looked up, alarmed. "What do you mean 'take charge of them'?"

"They work for us, Rowly. They're up there to do a job. I don't expect you to become a drover, just make sure the men are managing the stock properly."

Rowland wondered how he could possibly know if the stock were being managed properly or not, but he let it go.

"Where exactly am I going?" he asked instead.

Wilfred removed a folded map from inside his jacket and opened it out on the occasional table between them. He spent the next twenty minutes pointing out the boundaries of the Sinclair lease, and the major roads, villages and landmarks of the High Country. He described the planned routes of the Sinclair cattle through the mountain pastures.

"Base yourself somewhere near Kiandra," he said, marking the centre with a pencil. "You'll need to ask the men up there about Harry's movements."

Rowland nodded, refolding the map. "I'll find Harry," he assured his brother.

"Look Rowly," Wilfred leaned forward. "Harry would not leave the stock and the men without good reason. Something untoward must have happened. Be careful—from what I hear, the High Country is not entirely civilised... though I suppose that might suit you... but be careful nonetheless."

"On that point," Rowland started, remembering that he had been trying to get hold of Wilfred for other reasons, "you might need to be careful too." He proceeded to tell his brother about the intruders.

Wilfred frowned but he reacted calmly. "They knew who you were, you say?"

Rowland nodded. "It seems they had been waiting for me to return."

"And you are sure you have no idea who sent them."

"None at all, I'm afraid."

"Well, perhaps this would be a good time for you to get away. With a bit of luck you'll have this sorted in a couple of weeks. It's imperative you be back in Sydney by April."

"Why?"

"You have a board meeting," Wilfred informed him brusquely. "Dangars is meeting to vote on the Lister franchise—you'll need to be there."

"Oh."

Rowland had recently been appointed to the board of Dangar, Gedye and Company, a wool-broking firm in which the Sinclairs held a substantial shareholding. He did not pretend to possess any particular commercial insight, nor did he aspire to gain any, being content instead to allow his brother to guide any decisions he was called on to make. He trusted that Wilfred knew what he was doing. To Rowland's mind the board meetings were in any case a ceremonial formality—most of the business seemed to be done at the Masonic Club.

"These came for you." Wilfred handed his brother several envelopes. "They're from Mother. Apparently she's going to stay with Aunt Mildred till June."

Rowland nodded. The envelopes were not addressed to him but to his late brother, Aubrey Sinclair. Somehow in the grief that followed Aubrey's death, his mother had assigned him his brother's identity. She seemed to have forgotten the existence of her youngest son. Aubrey had been dead for seventeen years now... Rowland had become accustomed to it.

"When are you going back to *Oaklea*?" he asked.

Wilfred checked his pocket watch and stood. "I'm heading back to Sydney now—I'll catch the afternoon train and be home tonight... I suppose I'll see you at *Oaklea* tomorrow evening."

"Yes, I expect you will," Rowland replied, as he followed his brother out of the room. From Yass, near *Oaklea*, there was a road which followed the travelling stock route to Kiandra. It was probably the most sensible way to get up there.

"I'll have one of the Rolls ready for you to take up," Wilfred decided.

"No need—I'll take my car."

Wilfred regarded him coldly. Rowland's flamboyant Mercedes Benz had always been the subject of discord between them. An ex-serviceman, Wilfred maintained that owning a German automobile was somehow an act of disloyalty, a snub to their brother who had fallen in France. Rowland had been too young to see service. Perhaps this was why he saw it differently. He remained besotted with the motor car regardless of her dubious heritage.

The moment was broken by their growing awareness of chanting coming from within the studio. Clyde still stood helplessly outside the closed door. Rowland could just make out the Italian.

Wilfred Sinclair's brow rose. "What the blazes?"

Rowland sighed. "She's praying."

"Whatever for?"

"Forgiveness I think."

Wilfred shook his head. "Understandable, I suppose." He had never approved of his brother's determination to paint naked women; he approved of the women themselves even less. He put on his hat. "Perhaps this really would be a good time for you to get away."

Rowland smiled ruefully as he shook his brother's hand. "Quite."

He turned back to Clyde after he'd shut the door. He straightened his tie and braced himself. "I'd better go in and talk to Miss Martinelli."

Clyde stepped out of his way. "I'll pour you a drink."

Nearly an hour later, Rowland returned to the drawing room, having told Rosalina Martinelli that he had been unexpectedly called away. He had assured her, quite honestly, that his decision to delay, perhaps abandon, his painting of Eos, the Goddess of Dawn, had nothing to do with her, and quite dishonestly that he looked forward to working with her again. He eventually persuaded her to accept payment for the entire month, a sum which he quietly hoped would help her find another profession. After she left, he had glanced regretfully at the beginnings of his painting. Rosalina was undeniably lovely—a nightmare to paint but the results, however painfully extracted, were promising. He doubted he'd finish anything for the exhibition now.

Clyde handed him a glass of Pimms and lemonade as he sat down. Milton and Edna had returned and were seated on the couch expectantly. Apparently Clyde had informed them that something was afoot.

Rowland told them all of Wilfred's visit and of the disappearance of Harry Simpson.

"Since when do the Sinclairs personally chase their workmen around the countryside?" Milton asked.

"Harry's a good man," Rowland replied carefully. "Wil relies on him."

"Still, Rowly," Milton persisted. "He wouldn't be the first to just wander off."

Rowland was circumspect in his response. Milton was right. The Sinclairs had employed many native stockmen over the years and they had come to accept that sometimes even the best of them would wander… it was just their way. But something told him Wilfred was not overreacting. "Not Harry," he said finally. "He wouldn't just leave the men and stock like that… he's always let us know when he needed to go off."

"But why's Wilfred sending you?" Edna asked. "It's a little odd, don't you think, Rowly?"

"Not really. Harry lived on *Oaklea*, he saw service with Wil—aside from everything else they're good friends... they go fishing together."

Edna smiled faintly. Wilfred was a bastion of British traditionalism. It seemed an unlikely friendship, but both the Sinclair brothers appeared drawn to unlikely friendships. "He's an unusual man, your brother."

"You might say that."

"So when do we go?" Clyde asked.

Rowland was startled. "We... I didn't mean—"

"Of course you didn't," Milton interrupted him, "but we're coming anyway."

"The High Country's my old backyard." Clyde grinned. "You don't want to go up there without a local, mate. Folks up there take a little getting used to."

"Don't worry, Rowly, we'll look after you. It'll be a lark," Milton announced.

"But what about Ed—she's still not..."

"I'm fine," Edna protested, "and you are not leaving me behind. I'm jolly sick of baths anyway... I'm getting permanently wrinkled."

"Nothing like mountain air to fatten her up," Clyde added. "You should see my sisters."

Rowland shrugged. It probably wasn't such a bad idea. "We'll leave first thing tomorrow."

Clyde stood, and began rolling up his sleeves. "I'd better check over your car then," he said. "You coming, Rowly?"

Rowland rose enthusiastically. Clyde had once worked for a motor mechanic. He knew cars in a way that Rowland could only envy. Generally, the Sinclairs did not personally attend to their vehicles, but maintenance of the Mercedes was more an indulgence than a chore.

"Whoa, Rowly," Milton reminded him. "Don't you have to draft up some plans before we go? Old Foy's already been around this morning asking after them."

Rowland groaned. He'd forgotten about the plans for Foy's tomb.

Edna laughed. "Come on, Rowly, I'll help you draft something up." Milton had told her of the bargain between Mark Foy and Rowland Sinclair. It amused her, but then she was a sculptress and had worked on tombs before. To her, the request was not so odd. Indeed, the last few years had brought her many commissions for cenotaphs and memorials as each town across New South Wales honoured the men it had lost in the Great War. "Mr. Foy likes to sail, doesn't he?"

"I believe he founded the Sydney Flying Squadron."

"The what?" Clyde asked.

"It's a yacht club."

"There you go, Rowly—a nautical theme... this might even be fun."

Rowland sighed. He had given Foy his word. Maybe a nautical tomb would be slightly less daft than the pyramids.

4

GREAT TOMB NOT TO BE BUILT

---◆---

WAS TO HAVE COST £32,100
DIRECTION QUASHED

SYDNEY

A Sydney merchant's direction in his will for the erection of an elaborate £32,100 tomb in the Blue Mountains was quashed by Mr. Justice Hardie in the Equity Court today.

Mr. Foy, who died last year, aged 86, directed in his will that the tomb be erected on land he owned at Medlow Bath in the Blue Mountains.

He directed that the vault be built in a rock cliff with provisions for six coffins, that the floor be slabbed with thick billiard table slates and that the tomb be surrounded by an eleven foot wall with a strong iron barbed gate for the entrance.

The will also directed that an acre of land surrounding the tomb be fenced with two barbed wire fences inside the other, eleven feet apart to keep out trespassers. The space between the two fences should be planted with native shrubs.

The Sydney Morning Herald, October 1951

It was well after dark when Rowland Sinclair's yellow Mercedes pulled up at the entrance gates of *Oaklea*. They had been travelling since the early hours of that day. Even so, they had made a slight detour at the neighbouring farm to look in on the Gipsy Moth housed in its shed. Wilfred had purchased the *Rule Britannia* the previous year, along with the property itself. The land was consolidated into the Sinclair holdings and Rowland took enthusiastic possession of the plane. Now he had just to learn to fly.

Rowland and Edna had spent half the previous night designing Mark Foy's tomb. They had amused themselves for a number of hours working on plans featuring pyramids, giant fish and Biblical whales, challenging each other into producing greater absurdities, and they were consequently awake into the next morning trying to cobble their less fanciful drawings into something that looked like they had taken the project seriously. Even so, the final drawings featured marble mermen and a mausoleum which was set into the cliffs and resembled the hull of a yacht.

Lack of sleep had forced Rowland to initially share the driving of his beloved car, but by the time they had reached Yass he was once again behind the wheel. A small part of him was quietly convinced that the car preferred it that way.

The gates at *Oaklea* were locked, but Wilfred had left McNair, his taciturn one-armed gardener, to wait for his brother's arrival. McNair cursed as he fumbled with the chains and padlock. Somewhere in the string of profanity and grunts, Rowland made out the words "late" and "bloody daft". It seemed that McNair was unimpressed by Wilfred's tightening of security.

Rowland climbed out to help him with the gates, but in the face of the gardener's surly disposition, simply stood by. McNair had worked on *Oaklea* since returning from the Great War. He answered only to Wilfred, and for the most part ignored Rowland.

Edna giggled audibly from within the car, and McNair realised suddenly that there was a lady present. He fell sullenly silent and stepped back, signalling that they should drive through.

"Does he speak to Wilfred like that?" Edna asked, still amused, as Rowland climbed back into the car. The Sinclairs' staff were obviously very aware of the difference between Wilfred and Rowland. Regardless, few were so openly hostile.

Rowland laughed. "Yes... and more often."

"And Wilfred doesn't object?"

"I don't think it would matter if he did. McNair has his own way of doing things."

"Is he a particularly good gardener?" Edna was still looking to somehow explain this unusual level of tolerance.

"Good Lord no. He's constantly pulling out flowers to plant potatoes—drives Wil to distraction."

Clyde snorted. "Can't eat flowers, Rowly. Sounds like the old codger's got a bit of sense."

Rowland brought his Mercedes to a stop in the sweeping cobbled circuit in front of the *Oaklea* homestead. "It's more likely that McNair's suffering from a particularly belligerent case of soldier's heart," he muttered as he allowed the engine to idle.

"Oh, of course, the poor man," Edna said quietly. Too many men had returned from the war not quite whole, even if they still had all their limbs.

Clyde snorted. "Nonsense. It's common sense not shell shock. My folks used every square inch of ground we had to grow vegetables— only way to feed us all. It's only your lot that wastes good ground politely growing flowers."

Rowland laughed. "Flowers have their purpose, Clyde."

"I'll take a pound of potatoes over roses any day."

"And that," concluded Milton, "is why you can't get a girl."

They may have continued arguing over Clyde's romantic successes, or lack thereof, had not *Oaklea's* front door been opened to allow a small boy in pyjamas to hurtle out.

"Uncle Rowly, Uncle Rowly!" Six-year-old Ernest Sinclair jumped up and down on the spot excitedly until Rowland had alighted from the car. He stuck out his small hand. "Good evening, Uncle Rowly. Did you bring Lenin?"

Rowland bent to shake his nephew's hand. Lenin was Rowland's dog, a particularly ugly and ill-bred one-eared greyhound that Milton had rescued from the track. "I'm afraid Len stopped at home, Ernie."

Ernest's deep blue Sinclair eyes dropped in disappointment. Rowland swung the boy up under his arm. "Tell you what—you can catch up with Len at the Royal Easter Show—how's that? I'll talk your father into bringing you to Sydney with him."

Ernest squealed with delight. "That would be just splendid, Uncle Rowly."

"For pity's sake, Rowly, how am I supposed to say 'no' to him now!" Wilfred muttered as he came down the stairs to shake his brother's hand.

Rowland smiled. Wilfred was besotted with his sons—he was unlikely to have refused Ernest anyway. "Hello, Wil."

Wilfred looked over at Clyde and Milton who had just emerged from the car. "I didn't realise you were bringing company... Good day, Mr. Jones, Mr. Isaacs... Oh, Miss Higgins as well." Wilfred greeted his brother's friends politely if a little coolly. He pulled Rowland aside as the others were ushered into the house and Ernest was sent back to bed. "Blast it, Rowly! I'm sending you up to find Harry and sort things out, not to take your freeloading friends on some flaming holiday in the mountains."

Rowland bristled. "They thought I could use a hand. Damned decent of them actually."

"For God's sake, man, can't you do anything without your troupe of unemployed hangers-on!"

"I don't see that it's any of your business with whom I associate, Wil. I said I'd find Harry and I will. You can just…"

They were interrupted at that point by the gentle, elegant young woman who was Wilfred's wife. A couple of years younger than Rowland, Kate Sinclair wore the mantle of mistress of *Oaklea* a little nervously. She was very fond of her somewhat disreputable brother-in-law, and she adored her thoroughly respectable husband. She had become quite accustomed to their fiery relationship.

"Hello Rowly," she said, allowing him to kiss her cheek. "You boys aren't quarrelling already, are you?"

Wilfred glared at his brother. "No, of course not."

"You look lovely, Kate." Rowland noticed how glamorously she was dressed—best pearls and mink stole.

"Why thank you, Rowly," Kate said, glancing briefly behind her.

Rowland's eyes followed. A number of cars, black limousines, were parked on the far side of the circuit. "Oh, you have guests."

Kate smiled. "It's just a little dinner party—they've just arrived."

"I say, I am sorry Kate. I didn't realise. You get back to your party—we'll grab something in the kitchen and make ourselves scarce."

"Don't be silly, Rowly… you're not children," Kate replied before Wilfred could accept Rowland's offer. "You have time to wash up and join us for dinner. Wil was discussing business with the gentlemen anyway, so we won't be sitting down for at least an hour."

"Katie… that might not be—" Wilfred started.

"Nonsense, darling. Rowly and his friends are only here for one night—they can at least have dinner with us." Kate put a tender, persuasive hand on her husband's arm. "Everyone's been admiring my portrait—I'm sure they'll be delighted to meet the artist."

"I really think it would be better if Rowly and his friends just said goodnight... I'm sure they're rather tired. You can catch up with them all tomorrow, Katie."

"But everybody's already heard them drive up," Kate persisted. "Rowly's motor car isn't exactly quiet. If he doesn't join us for dinner now they're bound to think it terribly odd."

Rowland met Wilfred's eye. Well, this was awkward.

Wilfred sighed, exasperated. "Just hurry up and get changed," he snapped.

"I'll tell Mrs. Kendall to set four extra places," Kate added warmly.

They were taken to rooms by an upstairs maid while Wilfred and Kate returned to their guests. Rowland was directed to the room he'd occupied as a child. It was fortunate that they had come directly from Medlow Bath—they might not have thought to pack dinner suits otherwise. As it was, they had the more formal attire they'd worn to the regular concerts held in the Hydro Majestic's Casino Room.

Nevertheless, it occurred to Rowland as he showered and dressed that they would need clothes more suitable for the mountains. He'd have to at least pick up some overcoats in town before they set off. The last time he'd been to the High Country it was to ski—he remembered the weather in the mountains could be unpredictable and bloody cold even at this time of year. Dinner suits would probably not be adequate.

He had a few minutes to talk to Clyde and Milton on the landing while they waited for Edna.

"So who are we getting gussied up for?" Clyde asked, as he pulled at his bow tie.

"No idea, I'm afraid," Rowland replied. "But they're quite likely to be easily offended." He looked pointedly at Milton who was the most likely of them to give offence.

Milton grinned good-naturedly. "I get your meaning, Rowly old boy. I'll limit my conversation to the weather and the cricket... forgive me if I cannot speak definitively on these mighty things."

"Keats," Rowland smiled. "No need to speak definitively... just try not to start a fight—don't mention politics."

Edna emerged finally, struggling to secure a locket around her neck. The fact that she was wearing gloves was making the clasp difficult to manage. Milton took the jewel from her and closed the clasp in place.

"Thank you," she said brightly. "Shall we go down? I'm frightfully hungry."

"Well, that's a good sign," Rowland said as he offered her his arm. It may have been the gown, but she looked a little more like her old self.

Kate's dinner guests were all still in the drawing room with drinks and hors d'oeuvres. Wilfred's business had obviously been concluded, as the gentlemen had joined the ladies.

They paused at the doorway of the drawing room, taking in the impeccable society with whom they were about to dine. Kate sat upon the couch in conversation with two sophisticatedly coiffed matrons of about fifty. The first was sombrely but stylishly dressed in black, a fur shrug draped across her shoulders though it was not a cold evening. Despite being seated, she held her walking stick upright, clutching the pistol grip handle with both hands. Her face was tragic but controlled—a stoic mask. The second lady wore a pale pink gown, in a style unusual for someone her age. In the armchair was a younger woman, small, attractive and very chic. A tendril of smoke twisted up from the end of the slim bakelite cigarette-holder in her hand.

Wilfred stood with the men at the sideboard, recharging glasses.

Rowland heard Clyde laugh softly behind him. "Of course—who else would it be?" Then, "Just keep your mouth shut, Milt."

Rowland, too, recognised the younger man, handsome and brash in stance and manner. He had met Senator Charles Hardy Junior once before—at a rally in the main street of Yass. Wilfred had introduced them just before the anti-Communist mob incited by the senator had abducted Milton with the intent of tarring and feathering the poet. Rowland and Clyde had gone to their friend's aid and things had quickly become ugly. The incident might have ended very badly had Wilfred Sinclair not intervened to rescue his brother from the vigilantes that Hardy had stirred to action. And so now they were going to share dinner.

"Rowly, there you are." Wilfred motioned them in as he began to make introductions.

Apparently Senator Hardy had no knowledge of the actions of the outraged pack he had inspired. He was not in any way disconcerted by the presence of Milton Isaacs, and recognised neither his name nor his face. He greeted them all congenially.

Milton also performed admirably, giving no hint that he and the senator may ever have been at odds. Once, the poet might have been given away by the word "red" which right-wing extremists had branded on his forehead with silver nitrate. But the effects of the developing chemical had now faded enough to be almost invisible, and Milton had in any case taken to wearing a long fringe which hid what remained of the word.

"Well, well, the infamous Rowland Sinclair," Hardy said as he shook Rowland's hand.

Rowland's left eyebrow rose slightly as he wondered to exactly which particular infamy the senator alluded. There'd been a couple of awkward situations that had found their way into the headlines. He decided against enquiring.

"I'm afraid Kate's been singing your artistic praises," Wilfred said, motioning towards the painting which hung over the fireplace; a dramatic but touching work, in oil: Kate with Ernest asleep in her arms. Rowland had painted it over a year ago now.

Rowland's eyes met Hardy's. Clearly the senator had not been thinking of art. But graciously, Hardy accepted the opportunity to keep the conversation free of controversy and needless embarrassment. "Indeed, I have no doubt that Alice will not rest until she too is immortalised in paint."

Wilfred then introduced an elderly gentleman: Sir Earle Christmas Grafton Page. Rowland recognised him, though they had not met before. For most of the twenties, Earle Page had held the second highest office in the coalition government of the nation. That government had been defeated in 1929 and though the conservatives had been returned to power in '32, Lyons and his United Australia Party now held office in their own right. The support of the Country Party led by Page was no longer necessary and the direct influence of Page himself had been diminished.

The statesman had, however, featured in the papers earlier that year. The Pages had lost their eldest son to a lightning strike in January, and had retreated from public life. Indeed, Rowland was very surprised to see them at *Oaklea*.

Page greeted him sternly, as if he was reprimanding him rather than making his acquaintance.

"How do you do, Mr. Sinclair? It's a pleasure to finally meet you." He looked closely at Rowland, assessing him. "You weren't at Newington, were you?"

"No, sir—Kings initially, and then abroad."

"I see." Page, a surgeon, studied him as if he were some kind of perplexing symptom. Rowland stood his ground, but he was uncomfortable. "I've known your brother for a number of years—upstanding man—but I must say he's not spoken of you a great deal."

Rowland's lips twitched upwards. No doubt Wilfred felt the less said the better.

"And what is it that you do, Sinclair?"

"I paint."

"Rowly's with Dangar, Gedye and Company." Wilfred glared at Rowland.

"Oh yes... I forgot... the Dangars Board."

"Of course. Dangars. A fine establishment."

Wilfred briefly introduced Milton and Clyde as Rowland's colleagues and quickly moved their conversation to a discussion of the latest Lister diesel generator which was currently being imported by Dangars. It sounded too much like a board meeting to maintain Rowland's interest. He glanced towards Charles Hardy, who had escorted Edna over to meet the ladies. Judging by the refined laughter, the senator was making charming and witty introductions.

Wilfred nudged his brother's arm, directing his attention back as he introduced, or rather, reintroduced, a third man. Rowland had met Dr. Frederick Watson before. His property, *Gungaleen*, was between Yass and Canberra, which in loose terms, made them neighbours. If Rowland's recollection was correct, the good doctor was a writer of sorts, with a talent for ponderous referential texts.

"Dr. Watson, how do you do, sir?"

"Rowland," Watson returned, hooking his thumbs into the pockets of his waistcoat. "It's good to see you back at *Oaklea*. It's been a while since I've had the pleasure myself what with one thing and another."

"Freddy's just published a volume on constitutional reform," Wilfred said. "A very comprehensive work."

"I think you'll find the full title is *Constitutional Reform as the Basis for the Economic Reconstruction of Australia*." Watson rocked back on his heels beaming eagerly.

Rowland shifted uncomfortably.

Watson continued. "I'll have a copy sent over for you—a young man with your prospects should understand the issues… of course, I'm happy to discuss it with you at any time."

Commendably, Rowland's reaction was polite, though slightly less than enthusiastic.

"Capital idea," Wilfred approved. "Rowly has some business to see to, but I'm sure he'll be very keen to call on you at *Gungaleen* as soon as he's back—won't you, old boy?"

"Indeed," Rowland replied a little tensely.

"Come on, Rowly, we'd best get you a drink." Wilfred guided his brother away from the doctor. "The Watson girls have grown into very handsome young ladies," he said quietly. "It wouldn't hurt you to get reacquainted."

"Sod off, Wil."

Wilfred smiled faintly as he poured a whisky and handed the glass to Rowland.

Rowland glared at him. Wilfred knew full well that he detested whisky.

"Just try it, Rowly," Wilfred insisted. "It's jolly time you started to drink like a man."

"Well said, Wilfred." Earle Page was back.

Rowland left the whisky on the sideboard and poured himself a glass of sherry, ignoring them both. Wilfred had always considered his refusal to drink the malted liquor as a character flaw.

Page shook his head. "I say, we didn't see many sherry drinkers at the front, did we, Wilfred? Of course I don't know what old Fritz was drinking. It might well have been sherry." He looked Rowland up and down. "But I don't suppose you saw service did you, my boy?"

Wilfred started to look a little uneasy. "We didn't enlist children, Earle."

"Nonsense... I can't tell you the number of boys I patched up— some no more than fifteen."

Rowland glowered but he held his tongue. He had not been ten when the war started, but somehow he was marked by his lack of military service all the same. There was nothing he could politely do, but allow Page to rub his nose in it.

Page continued as if Rowland was not there. "You know, Wilfred, that fellow Menzies has been getting in Joe Lyons' ear—it seems he fancies his chances in the federal sphere."

"Yes, I heard." Wilfred was non-committal.

"I can't imagine he'll get far. It seems he didn't enlist either."

Now Wilfred looked distinctly irritated.

Rowland maintained a stony silence. He had no idea why this Menzies chap had not enlisted but he deeply resented Page's implication.

Kate joined her husband, suddenly. Perhaps she sensed the tension in that corner of the room. "Wil, you must stop monopolising Rowly. The ladies wish to meet your mysterious brother."

5

RIVERINA MOVEMENT

——◆——

Ridding Land of Communism

ALBURY (N.S.W.), Tuesday

Addressing a large meeting at Walla Walla, Mr. Charles Hardy Jun., leader of the Riverina Movement, said Fascism stood for individuality, and though he had been called a Fascist, he would prefer that title to one of Communism, which stood for disintegration and not rehabilitation. The question today was not one of getting rid of the Premier, but of ridding the land of Communism. There was too much preaching of class consciousness where the worker was supposed to be under the heel of the capitalist.

The Argus, 1932

The seating plan at the table of Mr. and Mrs. Wilfred Sinclair had been somewhat disrupted by the addition of so many extra guests, and the fact that the gentlemen now outnumbered the ladies. It did cause the hostess a little consternation, but it could not be helped. Rowland found himself seated between Ethel Page and Charles Hardy.

It was an interesting gathering. The senator was charismatic and quick with wit and compliments, which he showered upon all the ladies present, though Edna seemed to receive the lion's share.

Rowland watched Alice Hardy glance disdainfully at her husband on more than one occasion, but she seemed otherwise accustomed to the liberality of his attentions.

On the other side of the table, Watson referred repeatedly to his various publications bringing them into the conversation in a manner which was indirect and often quite inventive. It appeared there was no topic to which *The History of the Sydney Hospital, The Beginnings of Government in Australia* or some other of his weighty manuscripts, did not relate in some way worth a mention. For a while, Clyde, who was seated beside the literary surgeon, tried valiantly to steer the conversations away from Watson's tedious publications, but to no avail.

Mrs. Page regaled Kate with the benefits of securing a French governess; it seemed Kate was hesitant about relinquishing young Ernest to the care of a boarding school.

"He's just so small," she said, clearly reluctant.

"The other boys will be too," Wilfred said firmly. The Sinclair men had always gone away to school before they were seven.

Earle Page was expounding the details of the great hydro-electric schemes of North America, about which it seemed he had considerable and detailed knowledge.

Rowland noted with interest that Hardy, Watson and Page seemed to have little time for each other. Indeed, it was Wilfred who appeared to be keeping any exchange between them amiable. It was intriguing. Rowland wondered what business could have brought the three men to *Oaklea*. He was aware that, despite having never sought office, his brother was politically powerful. Perhaps it was Wilfred's political enemies who had accosted him at the Hydro Majestic.

In time, all the courses were complete, and the ladies retired to the drawing room while the gentlemen remained to smoke and drink brandy. Watson and Page produced pipes. Although Clyde usually rolled his own, on this occasion he followed the lead of his host and partook from the mahogany box of fine cigarettes which was placed on the table. Neither Milton nor Rowland smoked. Senator Hardy pulled a pipe from his jacket but he did not fill nor light it, seemingly content to simply chew the mouthpiece.

"Mustard gas... during the war," he confided when he noticed Rowland's glance. "Wrecked my lungs." Hardy sucked on the pipe and winked. "Still... don't like to be unsociable."

"Tell me Charles," Wilfred asked, as he lit a cigarette. "What does Campbell hope to achieve with this tour he's undertaking?"

Rowland looked up. Colonel Eric Campbell was the commander of the New Guard, a citizen's army which had at one time threatened a revolution in New South Wales. Somehow Rowland had found himself acting as a spy within the New Guard's ranks, a sequence of events which had ended badly and seen him exiled abroad for most of the previous year. Indeed, in some quarters it was claimed that Rowland Sinclair had attempted to assassinate Eric Campbell.

Charles Hardy glanced at Rowland curiously before he replied. The senator kept himself well informed. "Oh you know Eric," he said, unlit pipe clenched between his teeth. "He's quite happy to go halfway across the world to have his photograph taken with that Hitler fellow."

"Damned fool," Page muttered. "Courting the bloody Germans!"

Wilfred kept his eyes on Hardy. The senator had co-operated with Eric Campbell in the past.

"It's probably not safe to write Eric off yet," Hardy said cautiously. "Who knows what he may pick up in Europe. He's not a stupid man and," Hardy's eyes flickered just briefly back to Rowland, "there are still many men who will settle his scores."

Wilfred's voice was hard. "We'll just see how successful this tour to meet the leaders of Europe proves to be," he said quietly.

The conversation moved to more local politics. It was then that Rowland understood the commonality between Wilfred's guests; they were all secessionists: advocates of subdividing New South Wales into smaller states. He studied his brother who seemed to be directing the dialogue, subtly pointing out the benefits of an alliance of like minds.

Like Rowland, neither Milton nor Clyde attempted to contribute to the discussion in any way. Wilfred was polite but it was clear this was not a conversation into which Rowland or his friends were welcome. And so the three observed in silence as the establishment dealt with the nation's future.

And then things became awkward. It was Earle Page who first raised the issue of the Communists and with them the trade unionists.

"Of course you couldn't expect the red vermin to do anything but stand in the way of the nation's interests. They'll fight any secession to the last man."

Rowland stiffened. Clyde and Milton were both Communists and unionists. There was only so much he could ask them to tolerate in the name of civility.

In his condemnation of Communists, Page had an enthusiastic ally in Charles Hardy. "We've always had men more than ready to give the Bolshies a fight. They tend to be bloody cowards anyway."

Rowland glanced at Milton. The poet's eyes were darkening. Even easy-tempered Clyde looked tense. Wilfred cleared his throat warily.

Deciding on a peremptory exit, Rowland checked his watch and stood. Clyde and Milton followed suit.

"At the risk of being frightfully rude, I'm afraid I must ask you gentlemen to excuse us. We have another long trip in the morning, so we might just bid the ladies good evening and retire."

"Good idea, Rowly," Wilfred said, relieved. "You lads will have a rather early start to get yourselves organised."

Thus having been given leave to do so, they withdrew, pausing briefly in the drawing room to wish the ladies a good night. Edna remained, waving them away with a declaration that women did not tire so easily. Rowland smiled as he caught the tight purse of Ethel Page's lips.

"You know, Rowly, Hardy could have a point," Clyde said, as they climbed the stairs to the upper floors.

"What? About the Communists?"

"No—of course not. I mean about Campbell and the New Guard. They might still be looking to teach you a lesson."

Milton nodded. "Could be it was Guardsmen who came a calling at the Hydro Majestic."

"But Campbell's abroad."

"As the senator said—he still has men who do his bidding… and I reckon they'd still be smarting over what you did."

"It doesn't help that half of Sydney thinks you tried kill Campbell," Clyde added. "They won't have forgotten, mate."

Rowland shrugged, leaning back on the banister as they paused on the landing. "Maybe. Hopefully."

"What do you mean hopefully?" Milton folded his arms. "They nearly beat you to death, if you remember."

"I do. But if it's the New Guard, there's no need for Wil to worry about the boys."

"There is that," Clyde agreed. "But it doesn't get you off the hook, Rowly."

Milton grinned. "On the other hand, we can't be sure that it's anything to do with Campbell. Your brother seems to be running the country. I'd bet there's a few people who'd want the Sinclairs out of the way."

Rowland smiled. "Just Wil, old boy. I'm charming."

Although Rowland rose early the next morning, he arrived in the dining room to find Wilfred already seated with coffee and *Smiths' Weekly*.

"Rowly, good morning." Wilfred lowered his paper and looked over his bifocals. "Sit down and tell Mrs. Kendall what you want for breakfast. We need to talk about the logistics of this excursion of yours."

"Just toast and coffee, thank you, Mrs. Kendall," Rowland said, smiling at the plump motherly face of Wilfred's housekeeper.

"Nonsense!" Alice Kendall replied. "You'll be wanting a proper breakfast... just leave it to me—I know what you want." She bustled out of the room. "Just toast indeed!"

Wilfred sighed, audibly.

Rowland grinned. Mrs. Kendall seemed convinced he was still ten. He was aware it irritated Wilfred, but for him the housekeeper conjured the very warmest memories of his childhood.

"I'll drive into town and purchase what we need," he said. "We might be a bit pressed for luggage room, though."

"You can put some trunks onto the train to Tumut and have the mail truck take it up from there. Just make sure you're prepared for the weather."

Rowland poured himself a cup of coffee from the silver pot on the sideboard. "I'll telephone through to Caves House," he said, remembering the alpine guesthouse which had hosted his last skiing holiday. "We can stay there."

"You have the map of the lease boundary?" Wilfred looked to him for confirmation.

Rowland nodded and pulled the map from his jacket.

Wilfred opened it. "I believe the men are camped somewhere around here." He pointed out a section of the area known as Long Plain. "I'm a little concerned they won't know who the hell you are... Harry would have recognised you of course, but most of the stockmen were employed from Gundagai and Tumut."

"Who's in charge in Harry's absence?" Rowland took an artist's pencil from his pocket and marked in the area which his brother had indicated.

"A fellow called Moran. He'll be waiting for you tomorrow at the Rules Point Guesthouse—it overlooks Long Plain... pretty rough by all accounts, but the men like to drink there."

"Right then—if this Moran chap is expecting me, I shouldn't need a letter of introduction."

Wilfred paid no attention to his brother's flippancy. "I want you to look into things up there... There's something going on. It's why I sent Harry up in the first place."

"I'll talk to the men," Rowland assured him.

Wilfred met his eye. "Just you remember that these men work for us. Sack anybody you have to—we can always get more men."

"Sack them for what?"

Wilfred bristled. "I'm not sending you up there to make friends, Rowly... though being employed they're probably a bit beyond your usual social circle."

"Do you want my help with this or not?" Rowland asked coldly.

Wilfred sighed. "I'll have one of the trucks sent up with fuel." The words were grudging. Even just refuelling Rowland's German automobile went against the grain. "You might find that Fritz contraption is a little out of its depth in the High Country. You may be better off getting horses."

Rowland smiled faintly. He knew how to ride a horse but relying on the beasts for transport seemed unnecessary. "I'm sure my contraption will be fine, Wil. She's a damned sporting car."

Mrs. Kendall came in with Rowland's breakfast, a burgeoning tray of eggs and bacon, and toast cut into the strips he'd preferred as a child. She set it before him and hovered to ensure he ate.

"That'll be all, Mrs. Kendall," Wilfred said impatiently. "Rowly's quite adept with a knife and fork these days."

Rowland laughed. "Thank you, Mrs. Kendall, it looks delicious."

"I'll be baking today, Mr. Rowland," she said, ignoring Wilfred's dismissal entirely. "I'll make you a batch of shortbread. I'm that pleased to have you home."

When the housekeeper finally left the room, Wilfred broached the subject of security.

"Until this incident at the Hydro Majestic is cleared up I want you to take precautions."

Wilfred motioned towards a polished wooden box on the sideboard.

Rowland didn't need to look inside. He recognised the case. It held the service revolver Wilfred had given him over a year ago... ostensibly with which to shoot Communists. Rowland had never fired the gun, but he had been shot with it. He'd given the Webley back to Wilfred when he'd returned from abroad just months ago.

"I don't know, Wil."

"I presume you still have a licence for it," Wilfred disregarded his brother's obvious reservations. "Just make sure Miss Higgins doesn't get hold of it again."

Rowland said nothing. He doubted Edna would ever voluntarily touch a gun again. It was probably a good thing. In the end he agreed to take it—it was easier than arguing with Wilfred. Instead, he decided to question his brother in line with Milton's suspicions.

"This business at the Hydro Majestic wouldn't be connected to anything you're involved in, would it, Wil?"

"What do you mean?" Wilfred appeared a little affronted.

"I won't pretend to understand what you and the Graziers' Association are planning, but I gather last evening's soiree wasn't about catching up with old friends."

Wilfred smiled faintly. "You didn't enjoy my guests?"

Rowland shrugged. "Hardy seems a regular sort of chap. Watson's as dull as church and Page is an obnoxious prat."

Wilfred said nothing for a moment. Rowland waited for him to explode.

"Earle likes to exploit a man's weakness to gain the upper hand. It's how he came to power, and how he'll regain it I expect. Don't take it personally, Rowly."

Rowland did not reply. Lack of war service was apparently his weakness.

Wilfred put down his paper and sat back in his chair. "Earle has an interesting war record himself."

"I thought he made it abundantly clear that he served."

"He did—but on his own terms. He got himself released after a year, on the grounds that his practice could not survive unless he returned immediately." Wilfred's lips tightened. "Then he and Ethel took an extended tour of North America while the rest of us carried on." Wilfred took off his spectacles and polished them absently. "Don't let him bother you, Rowly. The Sinclairs did their bit, and not just when it was convenient."

Rowland was almost startled. This was the closest that Wilfred had ever come to talking to him of the war.

"I thought Page had retired from public life for a while."

"This was a private dinner party, Rowly, not a public engagement."

"You chaps aren't really going to try and carve up the state are you?"

Wilfred smiled now. "It is to everyone's advantage if Page, Watson and Hardy could work together despite their personal antipathy," he said calmly. "The call for new states is more than just sound, it is the common ground that will help build alliances that are in the national interest."

"So you were giving them a common cause so they'd play well together?"

"I didn't give them anything—I just highlighted areas of mutual interest."

For a moment Rowland considered his brother's words, and then he laughed. "Milt's right—you are running the bloody country."

Wilfred stared at him, his eyes penetrating, unamused.

Rowland returned to his breakfast. "I hope you know what you're doing, Wil."

6

MR. LYONS

Visit to Gundagai

GUNDAGAI, Friday

The Prime Minister (Mr. Lyons) will go to Gundagai on Monday to participate in the "Back to Gundagai Week" celebrations and will unveil a monument in memory of the pioneers at the five-mile camping ground, outside Gundagai. The ceremony will be followed by a civic reception and luncheon at Gundagai.

The monument has been erected on the old family camping ground of the bullock team days. Just behind the monument are the ruins of the old hotel known as Lazy Harry's, the centre of hectic scenes in bygone years. Among the pioneers who are still resident at Gundagai are a former driver of Cobb and Co.'s coaches and an old man who drove bullock teams when the nearest railway was at Liverpool.

The Sydney Morning Herald, 1932

Rowland emerged to find the household waiting around his Mercedes. Clyde had the hood up and appeared to be polishing the engine. Milton was posing with Kate and the children while Edna took photographs. Ernest looked quite bored with the process, whilst young Ewan smiled toothlessly from his mother's arms. Edna circled them, snapping from various angles. Photography had become her passion over the last year, despite Rowland's refusal to concede that it was art. Wilfred stood sternly at the bottom of the stairs, checking his pocket watch intermittently.

Preparations for their departure had been made with surprising speed and almost military precision. Additional clothing had been purchased from the gentlemen's outfitters in Yass and delivered to *Oaklea* before ten, and two extra trunks had been placed on the train to Cootamundra for dispatch to Tumut. Clyde had spent the early morning checking over the Mercedes, tuning the elaborate motor to perfection. Wilfred had insisted that towropes and chains be added into the contents of the trunk. Wilfred's revolver had been included as well. And Kate had insisted Edna take a couple of her own immaculately tailored riding habits.

Wilfred snapped his pocket watch shut. "For heaven's sake, Rowly, we've been waiting for fifteen jolly minutes!"

"Sorry." Rowland held up a basket. "Just popped into the kitchen."

"That'll have to go into the cabin with you," Wilfred muttered. "Nothing more will fit into the trunk with all that flaming paraphernalia you insist upon carting about."

Rowland paid no attention. He knew Wilfred was talking about his paintbox. He supposed it left less room for side arms.

"It'll only take you a few hours to get to Tumut, provided this contraption doesn't break down of course."

"Mercedes don't break down, Wil." Rowland placed the basket of Mrs. Kendall's shortbread onto the back seat and ran his hand soothingly along the tourer's canopy. "I wish you wouldn't talk like that in front of her—she's quite sensitive."

Wilfred glared at him. "You'd do well to stop in Tumut overnight."

"Why?"

"You don't want to get stranded on the road to Kiandra after dark. You'll be miles from any sort of assistance." Wilfred handed him a business card. "Call in at the stock and station agents' in Tumut and see if they know anything about Harry's movements."

Rowland took the card.

"I'll track Harry down, Wil. He might just have gone looking for good fishing holes."

"I hope so, but I doubt it." Wilfred's brow furrowed for a moment. "If there's anything else, I will send a message or phone through to Caves House. Remember, I'll need you back in April."

"Of course," Rowland said, somewhat unconvincingly.

Wilfred looked at his brother sharply. "Kingsford Smith has insisted he meet you before he'll admit you into this flying school of his. He'll be in Sydney for the Easter Show."

Rowland smiled. Clearly Wilfred didn't trust him to return simply for the Dangars board meeting. His brother had always been a careful man.

Rowland opened the passenger door. "We'd better get on then."

Edna clicked a final picture and embraced Kate farewell, before she raced Milton for the front seat. He was not a gentleman about it, but she was victorious anyway. Ernest cheered, and Rowland laughed. Wilfred shook his head, but he said nothing. Clyde closed the hood and adjusted the catches.

They completed their goodbyes and were soon cruising down the long driveway at *Oaklea*, waving madly at Ernest who chased the car to the gate.

Nestled into the lower slopes of the Snowy Mountains, Tumut was only a three and a half hour run from Yass. The temperature cooled noticeably as the road rose out of the Yass flatlands and into the hills. They stopped briefly en route near the township of Gundagai because Edna wanted to see the already celebrated monument which had been unveiled by Prime Minister Lyons a few months before. Rowland regarded the statue of a drover's dog curiously. He liked dogs, but it seemed to him an odd thing to bring the head of government to Gundagai. Perhaps Lyons liked dogs too.

Edna studied the bronze kelpie much more enthusiastically, noting features only visible to those in the trade. She had once collaborated with the dog's sculptor, Rusconi.

"Bronze isn't Frank's usual medium you know," she said, studying the detail in the form of the seated dog. "He creates his masterpieces with marble generally—mortuary monuments mostly—you must recommend him to Mr. Foy, Rowly... he'll need someone to carve those mermen we drew up for his tomb."

"Yes... of course... the mermen."

It was about three in the afternoon when they arrived in the Tumut valley. The town, built along a fast-flowing river, was a bustling mountain village which served as the immediate region's major centre. There were still several hours of light in the day.

Milton and the sculptress stopped at the railway station to check that their trunks had arrived on the train from Cootamundra and been duly dispatched on the mail truck. Rowland and Clyde set out to find the stock and station agent, whose office was in the main street.

A son of the neighbouring town, Clyde knew Tumut well, and was greeted heartily by many of the local citizenry. As a result they made somewhat halting progress, though they eventually arrived at the well-appointed shopfront of Mandelson's stock and station agency. They were shown into the office of the agent, a liberally proportioned man, who sat behind a desk littered with skewed stacks of carbon paper and a cross-cut saw.

Leonard Payne pulled the pipe from his mouth with his left hand and offered Rowland his right.

"Rowland Sinclair, Mr. Payne," Rowland said as he shook the man's hand. "This is Mr. Jones."

Payne laughed. "Mr. Jones indeed—I've known Clyde since he was a little tacker. How're your folks, Clyde?"

"Haven't had a chance to call in yet, Leo. We only just got here." Clyde shook Payne's hand with a warm familiarity.

"Capital people, the Joneses—salt of the earth," Payne said as he offered them seats. "I hear your brother's found work with the forestry."

"Really... which one?"

"Joe."

"Well, that's good news."

"Now, you didn't drop in to catch up on the news... what is it I can do for you gentlemen?"

"Actually, it is news that we're after," Rowland began.

"Harry Simpson." Payne interlaced his hands over the generous protrusion of his belly as he nodded sagely.

"Yes—you know him?"

"Came in once or twice for supplies and to hire a couple of extra men. I heard he walked off the job... they do, I guess."

Rowland ignored the last. "He hired extra men?"

Payne nodded. "Apparently he had to let a couple of fellas go— some of the boys don't like taking orders from his kind."

Rowland's brow arched upwards. "I see. Did he find the extra men he needed?"

"Couple of boys from Batlow signed up, but they didn't last long. Came back just after Simpson walked off."

"Who were they, Leo?" Clyde asked.

"Bumper Norris and the boy Henson."

Clyde nodded. He knew both men.

"What do you know about this chap Moran?" Rowland asked carefully.

"Ned Moran? Not much I'm afraid. Comes from near Talbingo I believe. That's about it."

A few more questions gleaned little more, and so they thanked the agent and took their leave.

They walked back to the car—Rowland was quiet, thoughtful.

"Leo seems to think your man walked off, Rowly," Clyde ventured.

"Perhaps he did," Rowland replied. "But it's not like him. Not without a word."

Clyde nodded. "Fair enough. What now?"

"We find Ed and Milt and we take a drive to Batlow."

"Batlow?"

"I'd like to talk to these chaps—Norris and Henson. I take it you are acquainted with them?"

"Yes, but…"

"It's less than an hour out of our way. We can head up to Yarrangobilly through Buddong Falls. I've been that way before—the road's quite good. We'll stay in Batlow tonight and you can introduce us all to your folks."

Clyde appeared distinctly alarmed.

Rowland laughed. "Clyde, old man, I think you might be ashamed of us."

"Of course not—well, maybe Milt—no, it's just… my mother is very set in her ways."

Rowland looked at his friend, amused. He had gathered that Clyde's mother was a formidable matriarch who disapproved of Clyde's lifestyle most vocally.

"She can't be as bad as Wil."

Clyde looked vaguely ill.

"Well, you can't not call in, since we're up here. She'll find out."

Clyde groaned. "Good Lord, you're right."

"Relax, Clyde. I assure you we can appear respectable."

"Mate, respectable is only the half of it. Mum's going to object to you for a whole bevy of reasons." He smiled ruefully. "You're just not our sort of people."

"No… I suppose not."

Clyde slapped his forehead. "God, how am I going to explain Ed?"

"I find it's best not to explain Ed," Rowland said, as he slipped behind the wheel of the Mercedes. "Don't worry… we'll win your mother over."

"Like we've won over Wilfred?"

Rowland stopped. Clyde had a point. "We'll make it a short visit."

7

MINES AND METALS

————◆————

COMPANY NEWS

Gold Mines of Australia, Ltd.
Gold Mines of Australia, Ltd., made a loss of £26,787... The director's report revealed that the company had abandoned operations at Batlow (N.S.W.) because values were proving irregular.

The West Australian, 1933

The swill had not yet begun when the yellow Mercedes pulled up at the Batlow Hotel. There was still over an hour till six, and so plenty of time for panicked drinking before the bar was formally closed to local patrons. Clyde Watson Jones' hometown had been founded in the gold rush. The creeks and tributaries of the area had been extensively worked by hopeful miners, but the rich strikes had become a distant memory. Batlow was a rapidly evolving orcharding district now, though the Depression had seen a resurgence in men willing to try their luck at fossicking.

Rowland climbed out and inspected his car. The road to Batlow was by no means the worst on which he'd driven, but it had been rough, gouged by heavy drays. He gave the grille a comforting rub. She'd held up well.

"Oh for goodness' sake! It's Clyde Jones!" A plump woman in a shapeless floral dress hurried up from the street, waving.

"Hello, Mrs. Merritt." Clyde all but hid behind the car.

"Well, haven't you moved up in the world, Clyde." Mrs. Merritt eyed the Mercedes and then moved her hawkish gaze to each of Clyde's friends in turn. Rowland and Milton tipped their hats politely but the matron did not wait to be introduced. "Must run. Your mother will be so thrilled to see you." She bustled off, periodically turning her head to look back at them.

Clyde groaned.

"Who's that?"

"The local exchange telephonist. The entire district will know I'm here in a matter of minutes."

They checked into the Batlow Hotel. A proud modern building, its new brick construction contrasted with the surrounding weatherboard cottages and shopfronts. Clyde struck up a conversation with the publican, a Mr. Davis, who, like nearly everybody else they'd encountered, seemed to know him. He rejoined them just as Edna descended the stairs.

"Rightio, Rowly, shall we go find Norris and Henson? Old Davis reckons they'd both be in the billiard hall about now."

"What about Ed?" Rowland rubbed the back of his neck. The country observed the conventions of gender segregation a little more strictly than Sydney, and billiard halls were not generally places where ladies were welcome. The sculptress would no doubt take the saloon in her stride, but the patrons of the hall could well be disgruntled.

"I'm more worried about Milt," Clyde replied glancing at the poet's green velvet jacket and purple cravat. "Walking in with him might get us killed."

Rowland nodded—he was inclined to agree. Even in Sydney, Milton's elaborate sense of style could raise eyebrows. Here it would probably raise more.

Milton preened, pushing Clyde aside to access the hall mirror and adjust his cravat just so. "Let us make a memorable entrance then, gentlemen." He grinned, clearly complimented by the possibility that his attire might offend the locals.

"How about you take Ed to the Refreshment Rooms over the road… we'll join you as soon as we're done," Rowland suggested.

Milton was unmistakably offended, but in the end he relented and agreed to remain behind, though not without an appropriately outraged and indignant speech.

"It's just this once, Milt," Rowland said, by way of apology. It did seem rude to hide the poet. "I need to get these chaps to talk to me… We don't want to make them feel… underdressed."

Clyde snorted.

Milton held his arm out for Edna, his chin raised imperiously. "Fashion is what one wears oneself. What is unfashionable is what other people wear!"

"Oscar Wilde." Rowland smiled. "Flaming appropriate."

The billiard hall seemed to stop in silence when Rowland and Clyde walked in. The locals scrutinised them, squinting through air that was thick with cigarette smoke in a hall that was, in any case, dimly lit. Finally someone shouted, "Clyde, what the hell are you doing here?" and the general buzz resumed.

Clyde returned the greeting and soon both he and Rowland were armed with drinks. He pointed out Norris and Henson, shooting balls on the far table. Both were tall men, long limbed and lean. They played with intense concentration in shirtsleeves, rolled to the elbow.

"Bumper, Pete—what's news?" Clyde took Rowland over and introduced him.

Bumper Norris put down his cue. Peter Henson wiped the chalk off his hand and offered it to Rowland.

"Sinclair, you'd be—"

"Yes."

"Simpson worked for you then?"

"He's one of our men."

"You blokes got a minute?" Clyde said. "Rowly needs to know what went on up there."

Bumper Norris raised a single brow. "You came all the way up here after Simpson? What's he done?"

Rowland met the man's eye calmly. "As I said, he's one of our men. I just want to find him."

Norris shrugged. "What do you want to know, Mr. Sinclair?"

"Anything you can tell me… about Simpson… where he could be…?"

Norris picked up his cue again. "No idea what happened to Simpson. Didn't seem a bad bloke for an Abo, though some of the lads thought he was getting a bit above himself."

"I see." Rowland's jaw tensed slightly. "And did they give him any trouble?"

"I take it they had done… but he sorted it. Sacked a couple of blokes—that's when Pete and I joined the gang."

"But you left?"

"Didn't fancy working for that Moran," Peter Henson muttered. "Moran's boys didn't welcome outsiders—they've been droving together for a while."

"Still, it was a job," Clyde said, frowning. "Don't tell me you fellas haven't noticed the bloody Depression."

Norris and Henson exchanged a glance. "Heard the forestry was looking for men."

"So you just quit?"

"Didn't fancy Moran," Henson repeated, as he lit a cigarette.

"Why?"

Norris shrugged once more. "Dunno really. Tell you what though, Simpson didn't like him much either."

"They argued?"

"Not really—you could just see it. Simpson kept his thumb on Moran. But they was like two dogs on ropes, if you know what I mean."

Rowland nodded.

"Simpson went out by himself one day… didn't say where he was going… didn't come back."

"How long did you and Pete stick around after that?" Clyde asked.

"Four or five days—it became clear Simpson weren't coming back. Moran decided he was the boss and we didn't fancy him."

"Why?" Rowland persisted.

Again Norris seemed evasive. He shook his head and returned to the billiard table. "Just didn't fancy him."

Clyde tried. "Come on, Bumper, a bloke doesn't walk out of a paying job because the boss ain't pretty. Nobody was asking you to marry him."

Norris did not look up from the table. "Rack off, Clyde."

Peter Henson glanced at Rowland and then back to Clyde.

"I might get another round," Rowland decided. "What are you chaps drinking?"

He left Clyde with them and took as much time as he possibly could purchasing drinks from the small bar. When he returned to the table Clyde tossed him a cue.

"Come on, Rowly, let's show these blighters how to play."

The game was quick… because Clyde threw it. Apparently they were just playing to be polite. They left Norris and Henson gloating over the minor victory and walked round to the Refreshment Rooms on Pioneer Street where they found Edna and Milton and a mound of scones.

"Did they tell you anything?" Rowland asked Clyde, as they joined the sculptress and the poet for tea.

"Not a great deal. They think Moran's involved in something— they're not sure what. The way Pete tells it, Moran made life bloody difficult for your man Simpson—reckons Simpson got jack of it and walked off."

Rowland stirred his tea. "Maybe." He frowned slightly. "Seems I'll have to look closely at what this Moran fellow is doing. Did they say what exactly he was up to?"

"No." Clyde propped his elbows on the table. "Those blokes aren't precious Rowly… and they need the work. Sounds to me like Moran scares them—enough for them to walk off the job rather than stand up to him."

"You could just sack him," Milton suggested, as he spooned jam generously onto his scone.

Rowland sipped his tea. "I could, but I want to find Harry first. And if I sack Moran, I'll have to find someone to bring the cattle back in before the winter."

Clyde nodded. "Play your cards carefully, mate. The hills are a law unto themselves."

Rowland checked his watch. "What say I run you home, Clyde?

If we leave now you can have dinner with your family. We'll come and get you on our way out tomorrow."

Clyde hesitated.

"We could come too if you like," Edna said, wiping a stray spot of cream which had somehow found its way onto her nose. "I'd like to meet your family, Clyde. I'm sure they're curious about us."

Milton laughed. "Of course they are. They have a right to know who you're consorting with."

Clyde began to look a little panicked.

"We'll introduce ourselves tomorrow when we collect him," Rowland interceded. "It wouldn't be polite to descend on the Watson Joneses unannounced."

Milton rolled his eyes.

Clyde stood hastily. "Yeah okay, let's go Rowly. I'll see you two tomorrow."

———————————   ———————————

Rowland entered the dining room of the Batlow Hotel, just as Milton and Edna were being shown to a table. He removed his hat and joined them. Clyde's parents farmed a modest soldier settlement block just out of town. He had dropped Clyde at the gate with the assurance that they would pick him up early the next day. As he pulled away an unreasonable number of children spilled out of the simple cottage to gawk at the departing yellow Mercedes.

The hotel must have been booked out that night for there wasn't a spare table in the dining room. The establishment was now closed to locals so Rowland presumed the diners, mostly men, were commercial travellers or itinerants of some sort.

Milton duly produced a map and they studied the route they would take the next day.

"I fear the road may get a bit rough for a while about here," Rowland murmured, pointing, "though we should make Caves House by lunch."

"Where are we meeting Mr. Moran?" Edna ignored the map and studied the menu. It was a set meal, but there was a choice of sweet—apple crumble or stewed quince.

"Rules Point." Rowland moved his finger slightly on the map. "It's just a little way from Caves House. We can pop down after lunch." He glanced at the sculptress. She looked well but he was conscious that they had cut short her convalescence. "But I can meet Moran on my own, Ed. I gather Rules Point is a rather rustic establishment."

Edna smiled. "I'm perfectly well, Rowly. Mr. Moran doesn't sound entirely trustworthy or pleasant, I don't think you should go alone."

"He works for me," Rowland reminded her.

"We're coming with you anyway. A man as important as you should have an entourage."

"Now you're just being ridiculous."

"We should really order? What does quince taste like?"

8

BLACK COAT PROFESSIONS

WOULD-BE PRIME MINISTERS
WOULD MAKE BETTER BLACKSMITHS

In his review of the work of the year at the Horsham (V.) High School, the headmaster (Mr. L. R. Brookes) described as folly the notion of thousands of parents that their boys should be trained for the "black-coat professions."

Mr Brookes said "I would warn the ambitious mother against the inclination to make her pet son a Prime Minister or a High Court judge, when he would make a far more efficient farmer, blacksmith or orchardist. That is why I say – 'intelligently' guide the youngsters."

The Mercury, 1933

The cockerels were still crowing when the motor car approached the long drive of *Greenhills*, the block Clyde's parents farmed. A boy casting grain to the chickens, and another who was splitting wood, immediately downed tools and pelted up to the Mercedes in bare feet, jumping onto the running board.

"Nan! Look at us, Nan!" they shouted, waving towards the house. "Bruce get up here before he stops… keep driving Mister, Bruce ain't had a ride yet."

Rowland was just about to swing the motor car around the cottage so that Bruce, who had emerged from the henhouse with a basket of eggs, could have his ride, when a small woman ran out of the door beating a pot with a wooden spoon. Clyde came out after her.

Rowland could see her lips moving, but with the roar of the engine, the children yelling excitedly in his ear and the clatter of the spoon against the pot, her words were lost. She didn't look pleased.

He brought the engine to idle and turned it off.

Clyde yanked the boys from the running board. "Mum's going to skin the two of you," he muttered. "Sorry, Rowly." He opened the door for Edna.

"Wasn't there another one?" Rowland asked, slightly concerned that he'd accidentally run down a boy in the bedlam of children and chickens.

"Bruce was smart enough to make himself scarce as soon as he saw Mum with her fighting face on." Clyde looked pointedly at the two boys who stood sheepishly beside him.

The smaller of them shrugged. "I reckon it was worth it... Blimey, it's a ripper of a motor."

Rowland smiled as he slid out from behind the steering wheel. "Your little brother's got taste, Clyde." He was always pleased to hear the Mercedes given her due.

"Oh these scallywags aren't my brothers—they're my sister Mary's kids—Mum keeps an eye on them when Mary's working. This here's Tom, and that's young Frank."

Milton vaulted out of the car with such flourish that the boys looked like they might applaud.

Clyde glanced cautiously over his shoulder. "She's stopped beating the pot," he said quietly. "It might be safe to introduce you."

"Lead on."

By the time they reached her, Clyde's mother had relinquished the pot, returned the wooden spoon to the pocket of her pinafore apron and was smoothing the tendrils of greying hair which had escaped the tight knot on her head. She gave her grandsons a look that sent them scampering back to their chores, and regarded Rowland with a straight back and square shoulders.

A young woman had now also emerged from the little house. Her face was a very rounded version of Clyde's, a smiling nervous presence in her mother's shadow. Clyde hastily introduced his mother and his sister, Eliza.

"Mr. Sinclair." Mrs. Watson Jones nodded, glaring at her daughter who had dropped into an awkward half-curtsey. "Our Clyde has spoken of you often. It's very kind of you to call." She moved her eyes to Milton and then Edna. Her expression did not soften. "You'd better come in then, I've just put the kettle on."

"I don't think we'll have time..." Clyde started.

"Nonsense, Clyde," Edna was already following his mother into the house. "We have a few minutes, don't we, Rowly?"

"Er—yes, of course."

The cottage was very warm. The table had been covered with a starched white tablecloth and set for tea, and the kettle was boiling on the hotplate of a small cast-iron Metters stove. The crockery was simple and a perfect teacake sat in the middle of the table beside a plain vase crammed with roses and lavender.

"Ma's got out her wedding linen for you," Clyde whispered. He sighed. "Rowly could I have a word?"

"There'll be enough time to talk to Rowly later," Edna said quietly. "Your mother's gone to so much trouble."

The room was smaller for the fact that there were now so many assembled within it. The walls inside were essentially unadorned except for a picture of the Madonna and a crucifix. Rowland wondered briefly about the absence of Clyde's artwork.

Young Frank squeezed into the room with an armload of wood, which he deposited into a makeshift bucket fashioned from a kerosene tin. The adults sat down at the table.

"I'm afraid Clyde's father is away at the moment," Mrs. Watson Jones murmured. "It's a shame… if we'd known you were coming,"—she paused to swat Clyde about the head—"Joe would have liked to meet you." She brought a large enamel teapot to the table and proceeded to pour.

"This trip was somewhat spur of the moment, Mrs. Watson Jones," Rowland offered in Clyde's defence, as Milton poorly restrained a smile.

Mrs. Watson Jones sniffed as she cut cake. "Still, it is good of you to come, Mr. Sinclair. I can't tell you what a comfort it is to know that at least one of my boys has regular work."

Rowland's brow arched slightly. Clyde worked hard on his painting and got the occasional commission, but it was a stretch to call it regular work.

Clyde met his eye uneasily.

"I've always told my boys to find a good employer and to work hard and be loyal. The world hasn't changed so much that a good, loyal worker isn't valued. Do I speak the truth, Mr. Sinclair?"

"Er… indeed."

"I can assure you, Mr. Sinclair, Clyde knows what a good employer he's found in you, and you'll not find him wanting in diligence, or good character." Mrs. Watson Jones refilled Rowland's teacup.

"Mum…" Clyde protested desperately.

Rowland kept his face unreadable. Apparently Clyde worked for him.

Milton broke the silence. "Clyde's always been an impeccable character."

Eliza giggled, stifled it quickly and glanced anxiously at her mother.

Mrs. Watson Jones regarded Milton and Edna sharply. "Do you both work for Mr. Sinclair, too?"

Edna smiled winningly. "Oh, it seems everybody works for Rowly."

Mrs. Watson Jones frowned, clearly unamused by the response.

"I assure you, Mrs. Watson Jones, Clyde is a most valuable… employee. I couldn't… do… without him." Rowland wondered what exactly it was that Clyde was supposed to do for him.

"I must say we'd never heard of a gentleman employing a man just for such a thing."

Milton turned away to cough.

Rowland looked to Clyde for help.

"Some would call it a sinful extravagance,"—Mrs. Watson Jones was warming to her subject—"to have a man on call for such a thing."

Clyde spoke up. "I told you, Mum, Mr. Sinclair is very particular about his motor and not every garage knows what to do with a car like his."

Rowland relaxed—a mechanic. Clyde was masquerading as his personal mechanic for some reason. He should probably help. "I've never met anyone who knows as much about motor cars as your son, Mrs. Watson Jones."

Their hostess smiled faintly. "Our Clyde was always tinkering when he was a boy, took my clock apart I don't know how many times. We never expected he'd make it his living, he was so keen to go into the Church…" She sighed heavily and Clyde rolled his eyes. Mrs. Watson Jones pressed her lips together. "I'm afraid Clyde may have become too fond of his creature comforts now." She looked accusingly at Rowland.

The awkwardness was broken by the entry of a young man, who by features and stance was obviously a Jones.

"Jim!" Clyde exclaimed with 'thank God' in his voice.

The man put down the swag he'd been carrying over his shoulder.

"Clyde, I was hoping you'd be here. Oh…" Jim took in the crowd around the table. "Mornin'."

Clyde introduced his brother.

"Well, Mr. Sinclair, most pleased to make your acquaintance." Jim shook Rowland's hand enthusiastically. "That's a mighty fine motor car you have out there. We don't often see Jerry cars out here. She'd put a few noses out of joint I expect."

"Every now and then," Rowland admitted.

"Well, she's a fine machine regardless. You mind if I have a gander under the hood?"

"Not at all."

"Come out and have a look now, Jimbo. We should make tracks anyway, Row… Mr. Sinclair," Clyde said, seizing the opportunity to make a graceful exit.

Rowland glanced at his watch. "Perhaps you're right." He stood. "Mrs. Watson Jones, thank you for your hospitality—it's been a long overdue pleasure to meet you. I feel privileged to count your son among my… staff."

There was a clatter of chairs as they all rose and thanked their hostess. Clyde embraced his mother who spouted last minute advice over his broad shoulder.

"You work hard, keep your hands and mind clean. The good Lord hears even wicked thoughts, don't be getting ideas above your station... and you remember that Sundays are for God."

"Oh, Clyde gives him Mondays and the occasional Thursday as well." Milton chuckled.

Eliza inhaled sharply and glanced apprehensively at her brother.

Clyde ignored the poet and put a reassuring arm about his mother. "Don't worry, Mum, I drop into St. Augustine's regularly."

Rowland smiled. Clyde had stepped out with Augustine Mitchell the previous year... though she was hardly a saint. Still, he had no intention of blowing his friend's cover, they all had their convenient subterfuges.

They dribbled out of the humble, shingle-roofed cottage and Clyde opened the Mercedes' bonnet. The shoeless boys once again left their chores to join Jim in gaping and exclaiming at the engine in a manner that quite endeared them to Rowland. He didn't hurry them.

Mrs. Watson Jones was directing proceedings as Milton and Edna argued over how best to secure a crate of apples from the Joneses' orchard to the running board.

"Rowly, come here a minute." Clyde beckoned Rowland quietly whilst his mother was preoccupied. "Jim's heard something about your Mr. Moran."

Rowland looked expectantly at Clyde's brother. "You know Moran?"

Jim shook his head. "Nah—never met him... only know what I heard. Peter Henson told me Clyde had been asking about Moran so I figured I'd let him know."

"What did you hear?"

"Moran's been meeting with Patrick O'Shea."

"Who's he?"

"He holds the snow lease next to yours, Mr. Sinclair. Has property around Tumbarumba."

"Do you know why he's meeting with Moran?"

"Not a clue... but men like Patrick O'Shea don't often sit down with their own workers—let alone someone else's."

Rowland bit his lip thoughtfully. Moran was looking more and more dubious and yet there was no tangible accusation with which to confront the man. "Thanks, Jim. Would you keep your ear to the ground? If you hear anything, just send word up to Caves House—I'll reimburse the telegram."

Jim grinned. "Sure, Mr. Sinclair, I'll let ya know."

A few further farewells, another box of apples and a jar of plum jam later, they pulled away from the cottage and turned the pointed grille of the Mercedes towards the High Country.

9

THERMAL SPRINGS

———◆◆———

YARRANGOBILLY CAVES, Friday
The Minister added that Yarrangobilly was situated in a valley
surrounded by precipitous limestone cliffs and beautiful
timbered country with several limestone caves open for public
inspection. The beauty of the formations was unsurpassed
elsewhere in the Commonwealth. The thermal spring
discharged 30,000 gallons of crystal clear warm water each
hour. At a temperature of 82 degrees the water flowed into a
bathing pool which was constructed for public use.

The Sydney Morning Herald, 1927

Caves House sprawled into the side of the mountain, a grand
vestige of Federation civility against the rugged country that
loomed around it. The limestone caves that attracted holidaymakers
and honeymooners to the area were just a short stroll away, as were a
myriad of mountain streams which offered the gentlemanly sport of
fly-fishing to the well-to-do occupants of the guesthouse.

Rowland noticed the Hudson truck, which had brought their
extra baggage from Tumut, parked outside. He could see his own
monogrammed trunk still strapped to the truck's tray and wondered
why their belongings hadn't been taken in and unpacked. It was
just a fleeting thought. It would all be taken care of as soon as they

checked in. He glanced at his watch: 11 o'clock. They'd have time to get settled and take a leisurely lunch before making the short trip back up the main road to meet Moran at Rules Point.

The polished foyer of Caves House provided a welcome respite from the bracing chill outside. A generous open fire warmed the wood-panelled reception. Rowland and Clyde went to the counter whilst Milton and Edna decided, despite the cold, to take a turn about the gardens.

Rowland introduced himself to the manager. "I believe we have a reservation."

The manager was a diminutive man, and completely bald. The only hair on his head sat under his nose in a small square moustache. He fingered his collar nervously. "I am afraid, Mr. Sinclair, sir, that we are… regrettably, completely booked out. We have tried to reach you…"

Rowland stared at the man blankly. "Do you mean to say you haven't any rooms?"

"I'm afraid not, sir. We had expected one of our guests to leave today but he's decided to stay on, with his entourage."

"Well then," Rowland said, "it is this other guest and his entourage, who have overstayed their reservations and are consequently without rooms."

"I'm afraid that the senator is a regular patron, sir, and is accustomed to a certain indulgence."

"Good Lord, man, isn't there something you can do?"

"I've taken the liberty, sir, of making a reservation for you at the Rules Point Guesthouse. The proprietress, Mrs. Harris, advised that she had two rooms available."

"*Rules Point!*"

"I can assure you, Mr. Sinclair, it's a perfectly sanitary establishment, even if it doesn't have the refinements that Caves

House is able to offer its guests. I'm sure you'll be comfortable there until we are able to accommodate you."

"Splendid... sanitary." Rowland glared at the hapless manager until an eager cry diverted his attention.

"Rowly? It can't be... Can it be Rowly Sinclair?"

Rowland and Clyde turned simultaneously.

A gentleman stood behind them. He wore a riding jacket and breeches with impeccably polished black boots—the ensemble was completed with a top hat and a silver-handled riding crop, wedged under his armpit. His complexion was extraordinarily pale, though his face was flushed red.

For a moment Rowland frowned and then, finally, he responded. "Good Lord, Humphrey? Humphrey Abercrombie! What the blazes are you doing here?"

Abercrombie's face broke joyously, and he hastily removed his glove to offer Rowland his hand. "I say, old man, what a delight, what an unexpected pleasure! You're the last chap I expected to see in this godforsaken place."

Rowland shook Abercrombie's hand, while the man effused, rushing to fully express his happiness at their reacquaintance.

Then Rowland remembered the formalities. "May I introduce my good friend, Mr. Clyde Watson Jones. Clyde, Mr. Humphrey Abercrombie."

"It's actually the Honourable Humphrey Abercrombie, should you wish to correspond with me," the gentleman said, smiling diffidently.

Rowland blinked. "Humphrey and I were at school together."

"Kings?" Clyde asked, offering Abercrombie his hand.

"Heavens no." Abercrombie seemed aghast at the idea. "Rowly and I were chums at Pembroke House. Somewhat a family tradition, fine education of course."

Clyde nodded. "Of course."

"What brings you here, Humphrey?" Rowland asked.

"Mama thought it would be good for my constitution to get away from the city for a spot of fishing. We'd not long arrived in Sydney and with one thing and another…" Abercrombie trailed off. "I say, Rowly, are you staying here too? I've just checked in myself, what a splendid coincidence." The Englishman's smile broadened further and he nodded excitedly.

"I'm afraid not, Humphrey. It appears there are no rooms at the inn… this inn anyway."

Abercrombie gasped. "Why that's outrageous! I'll have a word Rowly. Of all the colonial cheek!"

Rowland glanced uneasily at Clyde as Abercrombie prepared to berate the management. "Thank you, Humphrey, but I think we're simply out of luck—can't be helped."

"But this is just preposterous. I won't have my old chum treated in so off-hand a manner."

The manager—present for the entire exchange—was clearly affronted. "I assure you, Mr. Sinclair, if there was anything I could do to—"

Rowland nodded. "I understand, Mr… Wilson," he said, reading the name on the brass plate on the counter. "I'm sure Rules Point will be more than adequate. Thank you for arranging it."

"Royal's Point? Well that sounds rather super. Perhaps I'll check out and join you…" Abercrombie stuttered.

"Rules Point," Rowland corrected. "I think you'll find Caves House is a great deal better appointed. There's no need for you to give up your rooms."

Abercrombie seemed quite put out. "I say, Rowly, this cock-up is damned inconvenient. It would have been jolly to catch up and reminisce about the old days at Pembroke." The Englishman nodded emphatically as he spoke of the school.

Rowland shifted uncomfortably. This was awkward.

"You know, old man, I have an entire suite to myself. I'm sure you could have the second bedroom…"

"Thank you, Humphrey, but I think I'd better stay with my party for now."

Abercrombie turned on the unfortunate manager. "I'll have you know this is exceedingly unsatisfactory—just appalling! I shall be speaking to—"

"Rules Point is just a few miles up the way," Rowland said hastily. "I'm sure we'll have plenty of opportunity to catch up. In fact why don't you join us for luncheon, Humphrey. I'm sure Mr. Wilson will be able to accommodate us in the dining room at least."

"Of course, Mr. Sinclair," Wilson said gratefully. "We are terribly sorry about this regrettable mix-up, sir, and I'm sure Caves House will have rooms for you in just a few days."

"So what do you say, Humphrey? Will you join us for lunch?"

"Oh I say, may I?" Abercrombie's voice lifted with his face.

"Certainly, old man." Rowland tried to sound more enthusiastic than he felt.

"Capital! That's just splendid Rowly—we'll have a jolly time… it'll be just like the old days back at Pembroke!" He beamed enthusiastically. "The shenanigans we got up to…"

Rowland's face was controlled. He returned to the manager. "Mr. Wilson, would you be so kind as to arrange for our trunks to be taken up to Rules Point, whilst we are at lunch."

"Certainly, sir, and shall I arrange for your motor to be refuelled?"

"Yes, I suppose you'd better."

"I say." Abercrombie looked down at himself. "I'd better change if we're sitting down for lunch. I'll just be a few minutes... By George, it is quite marvellous to see you again..."

And so they left Wilson and Abercrombie, and strolled towards the dining room. Milton and Edna had apparently determined that it was too cold to appreciate the gardens and were already seated. Clyde called for drinks while Rowland explained both the change of accommodation and the imminent arrival of the Honourable Humphrey Abercrombie.

"He was certainly happy to see you, Rowly," Clyde murmured. "Remarkably happy..."

Rowland laughed. "I suppose I should be offended that you find that so extraordinary, but Humphrey's always been a bit keen."

"He seems eager to relive your school days."

Rowland frowned. "I can't, for the life of me, see why—he had a terrible time of it."

"Really?" Edna regarded him curiously. "Why?"

Rowland shrugged. "Poor fellow was prone to cry easily if I recall." He winced as he remembered. "Making Humphrey cry became a bit of sport, I'm afraid."

"You didn't..." Edna started.

"No, we Colonials didn't have the easiest time either."

"That's disgraceful!"

"It was a boarding school, Ed—they tend to be savage."

"And so you and Mr. Abercrombie were friends?"

Rowland grimaced. "I suppose."

"What do you mean by that?"

"Not long after I first arrived at Pembroke, I came across a bunch of lads tossing something into one of the school ponds." Rowland shook his head. "I thought it was a dog. Of course I've always liked

86

dogs and I was a bit of a hothead back then, so I picked out the biggest of them and belted him."

Edna gasped putting her hand over her mouth in surprise. "And that was Mr Abercrombie?"

"Not quite… Humphrey was in the pond. It wasn't a dog. There was a bit of fuss of course, and we were all hauled before the Headmaster. At some point I must have fished poor Humphrey out of the pond."

"So you saved him?" Edna smiled.

"The pond was only three feet deep, Ed."

"But you rescued him nonetheless." Edna seemed determined to cast Rowland as a hero.

"Humphrey seemed to think so. Stuck to me like wallpaper paste after that—I couldn't get rid of him. Always seemed to need rescuing. In fact, there were times I wanted to throw him back into that pond."

"And now he's joining us for lunch," Milton said unhappily.

"Well, the poor chap seemed so disappointed we weren't staying—it seemed the right thing to do."

Milton snorted. "Yes, of course… courtesy."

Edna beamed at Rowland. "What a gallant and noble way to begin an acquaintance."

Rowland laughed. "I don't know about gallant and noble, Ed—I really thought it was a dog. I haven't seen old Humphrey in years and to tell you the truth I'd forgotten all about him. I wonder what he's doing here."

"A spot of fly-fishing, apparently," Clyde offered.

"Long way to come to fish," Milton replied. "Don't they have trout in England?"

"Yes, it is a trifle odd… Humphrey was never a particularly intrepid chap."

The conversation was cut short at that moment by the arrival of its subject. Rowland made the introductions.

"Oh I say," Abercrombie bumbled uncomfortably as he shook Milton's hand.

He stared openly at the long-haired, flamboyantly dressed poet, his eyes lingering on the small Soviet badge on Milton's velvet lapel. Milton held his gaze boldly, amused.

Rowland sighed. The conservative circles to which he still had admittance, and to whom his friends were occasionally introduced, invariably reacted in this way. Humphrey Abercrombie was just particularly inept at disguising his unease.

If the Englishman's response to Milton was tense, Edna seemed to frighten him outright. Abercrombie was visibly unnerved. His chin dimpled and he stammered desperately.

Edna, whose sympathies had been elicited by the image of the unfortunate boy in the pond, attempted to soothe the situation.

"How lovely that you could join us, Mr. Abercrombie. Rowly mentioned you've only just arrived in New South Wales?"

Abercrombie glanced panicked at Rowland, who was becoming progressively more convinced that inviting the man to lunch had not been one of his better ideas.

"A couple of weeks ago... beastly trip," Abercrombie mumbled as he realigned the cutlery before him on the table.

"What have you been doing with yourself, Humphrey?" Rowland asked. "I had expected to see you around the place at Oxford." He hadn't really. He hadn't thought of Humphrey Abercrombie.

"I should say you didn't! The Abercrombies are Cambridge men, have been since Adam was a boy." The Englishman now launched into an expansive monologue detailing the links between his family and Cambridge. He seemed to overcome his discomfort and his speech became infused with force and fervour.

Rowland watched him with interest, as he was reminded of the schoolboy who had once been his annoying shadow. Abercrombie was taller, but otherwise had changed little in the years since they had last met. His mannerisms were still familiar—the exaggerated gesticulation, the overloud voice and compulsive straightening of cutlery that was not askew.

"And so, naturally," Abercrombie concluded, "like my father and grandfather before me, I left Cambridge with a fine degree in the classics."

Milton was clearly bored. "So what exactly does one do with a degree in the classics?"

Abercrombie looked at him with a kind of incredulous disdain. "My good man, the empire is run by classicists—there is not an arm of government or commerce in the realm that does not value a man trained in the classics."

Milton's mouth twitched.

"What brings you here, Humphrey?" Rowland asked before the poet could respond in a manner that he suspected would be less than polite.

Abercrombie's face darkened. He blinked several times and moved the cutlery once more. "A passionate entanglement, I'm afraid."

Rowland cleared his throat, wondering how he could change the subject. He didn't really want to know about Abercrombie's entanglements.

Edna broke the silence. "And you followed her all the way out here? Why, Mr. Abercrombie, what a romantic gesture."

Abercrombie seemed startled, as though he had forgotten Edna was at the table, but he did respond to the sympathetic note in her voice.

"No, no... the Lady Wilberforce is in the midst of the London Season. The affair finished in disappointment, I'm afraid. It was perfectly ghastly to tell you the truth."

"Oh, I am sorry. We all know what it is to be disappointed in affairs of the heart."

Milton laughed out loud, Clyde snorted and even Rowland smiled. It was unlikely that Edna had ever been on the disappointed end of an affair.

Abercrombie, however, was comforted. It seemed he was keen to talk of his amorous misfortune and his earlier nervousness was forgotten. "I was, I must tell you, dear lady, completely heartsick. Lady Wilberforce trifled with my affections and callously cast me aside."

"I'm afraid I don't understand why that brings you to the other side of the world," Rowland said.

"Well, the whole business was publicly humiliating. The unhappy incident played havoc with my nerves." Abercrombie pulled a silk handkerchief from his breast pocket and blew his nose. He stopped to adjust the cutlery. "I wasn't sleeping or eating—lost interest in life entirely. The Abercrombies have always been sensitive, you see. Mama thought the change of climate would be good for the both of us and we could return after all this ridiculous fuss about the wedding had subsided."

"Wedding?"

"Lady Wilberforce's," Abercrombie sniffed. "She's accepted some abominable American."

They paused while the waiter took their orders, a process slowed by Humphrey Abercrombie who made exacting enquiries about the ingredients of various dishes. It appeared the Englishman had several food allergies.

Now that he had broached the subject of Lady Wilberforce and her rejection of him, Abercrombie was intent on sharing every detail of the tragedy with his old friend, and the three others he had just met.

His introduction to Lady Wilberforce, her multiple virtues and excellent connections took them through the entree. His courtship of the young lady featured during the main course. Then dessert was a sombre episode, in which Abercrombie recounted how the Lady spurned his declarations, gently at first, and finally in a manner that he could no longer mistake as coy. Edna commiserated politely. The men met Abercrombie's heartbroken unburdening with pained silence. Rowland recalled ruefully that the Englishman's stiff upper lip had always wobbled somewhat.

"So you came out to Australia," Rowland said finally.

"My dear Rowly, I can only put oceans between me and the source of my anguish," Abercrombie replied, his eyes moistening.

"Cheer up, old boy," Milton said, leaning back in his chair. "Plenty of girls here."

Abercrombie began to look nervous again. By now the table had been cleared so there was no cutlery to straighten. He ran his fingers on the table linen instead. "I daresay that's the least of my problems right now."

Again there was a momentary silence. Abercrombie regarded them all expectantly, impatient for someone to enquire further. Eventually Edna took pity on him and asked, "Is there something else the matter, Mr. Abercrombie?"

"I should say there is," he replied. He looked about the room anxiously and rubbed the tablecloth more rapidly. He did not lower his voice, speaking instead in a high and hysterical tone. "There is someone trying to kill me."

10

… all the cracks had gathered to the fray.
All the tried and noted riders from the stations near and far
Had mustered at the homestead overnight,
For the bushmen love hard riding where the wild bush
horses are,
And the stock-horse snuffs the battle with delight.

A.B. Paterson, *The Man from Snowy River*

Clyde coughed and Milton drained his glass, hastily.

Edna glanced around the dining room—whether she was scanning for potential assassins or just trying to avoid the eyes of those at her table, was unclear.

Rowland gazed calmly at Humphrey Abercrombie. "You don't say… how terribly inconvenient."

"I assure you, Rowly, I am deadly earnest!"

"Steady on," Rowland calmed the Englishman. "Who is trying to kill you?"

"Well how should I know? If I knew who it was I'd simply have the fiend apprehended."

"What makes you think your life is in danger?" Rowland asked instead.

"I'm being followed," Abercrombie said hoarsely. "Ever since I arrived in the colony. And on Tuesday evening last a black saloon tried to run me down in the street."

"Which street?"

"Macquarie—outside the Australian Club if you please."

"In the centre of Sydney? You're lucky it was just the one."

"What do you mean by that?"

Rowland smiled. "Just that the traffic on Macquarie Street is fairly hair-raising at the best of times."

"No," Abercrombie insisted. "This automobile swerved in my direction. It was only the intervention of my man Michaels that saved me."

"Your man?" Clyde asked.

"Yes, Michaels, my valet."

"Oh… yes, of course." Clyde glanced at Rowland. The fashion amongst the English upper classes of keeping personal manservants had never been embraced in Australia. Rowland had once said it was because Australian men—however well-heeled—did not require nursemaids.

"Why would someone want to kill you, Mr. Abercrombie?" Edna asked gently. She could see that the men thought Abercrombie ridiculous. She felt sorry for him.

"I'm sure I don't know. It could be the Bolsheviks—the Abercrombies have always been the targets of political espionage."

Milton laughed outright. "I hear Stalin has it in for classicists."

"On several occasions since," Abercrombie continued, "I have been aware of black automobiles."

Rowland's brow rose sceptically. The vast majority of Australian cars were black. He was beginning to wonder if the Englishman was suffering from some form of hysteria.

Abercrombie put his face in his hands. "I must say, Rowly, it's a crying shame that you are being cast out of this establishment. It would be a comfort to have an ally when it seems there are enemies in every corner. Are you sure you won't stay and…"

"I really do think I'd better accompany these chaps to Rules Point," Rowland said quickly. "My overseer, Moran, is expecting me, and I do need to speak with him. We'll be back here as soon as rooms become available." He checked his watch. "You will have to excuse me. We'll need to be getting away soon and I should telephone Wil and inform him of our change of plans. I might just leave you lot to look after Humphrey…" He looked pointedly at Milton as he stood.

When Rowland returned he was noticeably preoccupied. Edna looked at him enquiringly but she didn't ask. It would keep until they managed to extricate themselves from Humphrey Abercrombie's company, which was a task in itself. The Englishman had a very nervous disposition and he seemed to regard Rowland as some form of champion. Eventually he allowed them to leave for the car, which Wilson had had refuelled and brought round to the entrance.

Edna put her hand on Rowland's arm as he held open the passenger door. "Rowly, what's wrong? Did Wil say something?"

Rowland waited until she had seated herself. He leaned on the door. "*Woodlands* has been broken into," he said.

"Bloody hell—when?" Milton asked, outraged. Although the Woollahra mansion belonged to the Sinclairs, Rowland's houseguests had lived there long enough to be personally affronted by the violation.

"The evening before last… while we were at Kate's dinner party, I suppose. Unfortunately, Wil didn't receive word till yesterday."

"Did they take anything?"

Rowland shook his head. "They scared the wits out of the staff and made a bit of a mess, but that's about it. Wil's sent Mary to stay with her sister for a while—apparently she was quite distraught."

"They didn't hurt her?" Edna said, horrified.

"No, just frightened her I think. It seems they were looking for me."

"The goons from the Hydro Majestic!" Clyde slapped the tourer's canopy.

"Possibly. They extracted from Mary that I'd gone home to Yass. Wil's increased security at *Oaklea*, in case they turn up there."

"Should we go home?" Edna looked at Rowland with concern.

Rowland shook his head. Wilfred had wanted him to return too. "They don't know where I am. I figure I'm safer here than at *Woodlands* or *Oaklea*." He slipped behind the steering wheel. "With any luck the police will have sorted it all out by the time we get back with Harry."

"Do they have any idea what these blokes want?" Milton asked.

"Just me apparently—that's all they told Mary in any case."

"What do you think?"

Rowland smiled faintly. "I don't know… I have a couple of enemies, but these blokes seem persistent. Most of the people I offend are not so committed."

Edna frowned. "I don't like this, Rowly."

"It's not ideal," Rowland agreed as he gunned the engine. "But so far all they've managed to do is terrorise my housekeeper."

The Rules Point Guesthouse overlooked Long Plain, the vast fertile plateau which had been divided into what had become known as snow leases—generous tracts of Crown land which were leased for summer and autumn grazing. The guesthouse was a rustic construction, with a high pitched roof of corrugated iron. A wide verandah surrounded the main wing, around which were clustered smaller structures including a well, stables and, of course, the amenities. Rowland glanced at the last dubiously. He'd become accustomed to plumbing.

A round yard had been erected close to the guesthouse, with a rough bush fence which straddled the trees. There were a few horses within the yard. Several stockmen perched on the fence, and followed the yellow Mercedes with slow, hat-shadowed eyes.

Rowland parked beside a pale-barked snow gum and they climbed out into the chilly day. Edna pulled her coat tighter. It was hard to believe it was just March.

"Winter comes early here, doesn't it," she said, shivering.

Clyde laughed. "This isn't winter, Ed. This isn't even cold for up here."

They were welcomed warmly on the doorstep by a very large, quite elderly woman, who introduced herself as Mrs. Harris.

She bustled them in to the fireside. Despite Rowland's concern that the establishment would prove to be on the rudimentary side of rustic, the guesthouse was neat and inviting. It was not opulent, or even stylish; more homey than fashionable. The easychairs were well-worn and draped with patchwork quilts and knitted blankets. The hearth had been scrubbed and the mantel was set with framed photographs and little china figurines.

"I'm afraid you gentlemen will have to share a room. We're quite full with the Sports Day on Saturday."

"The Sports Day?"

Mrs. Harris beamed, her round face creasing upwards. "Oh yes, it's quite the occasion, my word! Folks come from all over to watch and take part in the events. There's a dance afterwards... you're really in for a treat, my word you are."

She showed them to their rooms. Each boasted four beds, although Edna had a room to herself. Like the rest of the guesthouse the bedrooms were furnished simply in a manner that was more comfortable than impressive. There was a wardrobe on either side of the window, and a washstand in the corner with a large pitcher of water and towels. Each room had a door which opened onto the verandah. The bathrooms were, as Rowland had noted earlier, external.

"We light the fire under the water tank every afternoon so that there's ample hot water for everyone, my word there is," Mrs. Harris assured them. "Now would you care for a cup of tea? I've just baked a butter cake."

"Thank you, Mrs. Harris, but I'm meeting an associate in the bar this afternoon. We might just wait in there for him."

Mrs. Harris looked at Edna. "All of you?"

"I might have that cup of tea, Mrs. Harris," Edna said, smiling briefly at Rowland. There was no need to start out by upsetting their hostess.

And so they parted company. Edna disappeared with Mrs. Harris, chatting happily about the upcoming Sports Day and the other guests of Rules Point. The gentlemen retired to the bar to wait for Moran.

As it was, they didn't have to wait all that long.

The bar was crowded, being the only establishment with a liquor licence for miles. A few dogs had crept in behind their masters and lay unobtrusively at the base of bar stools or under tables. Milton, or more likely his attire, received a few sideways glances but generally the patrons appeared used to guests from the city. Rowland ordered drinks and asked the barman to let them know when Moran walked in, which he did just a few minutes later.

A thin and weathered figure, Moran's hat slouched low over his eyes. He wore a long riding jacket, split high at the back to accommodate the saddle. He went straight to the bar, ordered a whisky and slammed it down. Rowland waited, watching as the stockman made enquiries of the bartender. Moran straightened when he realised Rowland was already there, and removed his hat as he made his way to their table.

They stood.

Moran's eyes, now visible, moved slowly from Rowland to Milton and Clyde.

Rowland put out his hand. "Mr. Moran, Rowland Sinclair."

Moran shook his hand silently. His face relaxed into a broad smile that showed more gold than teeth, and Rowland introduced Clyde and Milton.

"Pleased to meet you gentlemen," Moran said as they sat down. "I'm just sorry you had to come all the way up here. I told that other Mr. Sinclair that we've got your mob in hand, sir. We'll bring them in as planned, even short-handed. There was really no need for you to come."

"Except for the fact that Harry Simpson is missing," Rowland replied evenly.

Moran shrugged. "Oh, Simpson... His kind do that, don't they? Somethin' in their blood."

"I understand that you and Harry didn't necessarily see eye to eye."

"That's just gossip... those fellas from Batlow, I s'pose. Me and Simpson had our differences. The High Country ain't like drovin' on the flats. He was a bit arrogant your Mr. Simpson—seems he forgot who he was at times."

Clyde and Milton recognised the hardening of Rowland's gaze, the very slight flex of his jaw, but Moran did not.

"Are you saying he forgot he was in charge? Because as I understand it, Mr. Moran, we put him in charge."

Moran looked at him. "Naw, you mistake me, sir. I had no problem with Simpson, but you pay me to look after your mob. Sometimes I had to point things out to Simpson and he didn't take that kindly. He was a bit high and mighty, considerin'..."

"Considering what?"

"Considerin' we were all there to do the same job."

Rowland took a breath. "When did you last see Simpson?"

"About ten days ago. Had breakfast and he went off to check the Eastern boundaries."

"And he didn't return?"

"Nope. After a day or two, I rode down to Caves House and had them call the other Mr. Sinclair and send a telegram to the agent in Tumut. A couple of blokes quit, but all in all we've been managin' pretty well. We'll start to bring the mob in after the Sports Day. It's been a tough season... we've lost a few head... but so has everyone else."

For a moment Rowland said nothing, and then, "Where are the men now?"

Moran smiled, a little embarrassed. "With the mob. Some of them are comin' in for the Sports Day," he said. "Most of the stockmen ride in for it," he added defensively. "It's only a day and it can get awful dull up here."

"Well I certainly wouldn't begrudge you that, Mr. Moran," Rowland replied. "We might come out with you after the Sports Day. I'd like to talk to the men myself, see if any of them saw anything."

"It'd be a waste of time, if you don't mind me sayin', Mr. Sinclair. None of the boys saw nothin'."

"Still, I'd like to have a look around myself. If you're short-handed we may even be of some use."

Moran laughed loudly at the notion.

Rowland was mildly affronted but outwardly he didn't react.

"Well, sir," Moran said finally, "if you're determined, I can't stop you comin' out, but I gotta warn you: the boys ain't used to tourists, you may find them a bit rough."

"I'll take that risk, Mr. Moran."

11

WANTED, a Protestant Governess, to proceed to Yass. One who is capable of instructing two young children in a good English education, with the piano. Excellent references must be given. By applying to Mrs. H. Sinclair, *Oaklea*, will receive further particulars.

The Sydney Morning Herald (Classifieds), 1897

Edna sat contentedly at the sturdy kitchen table, drinking sweet black tea and eating rich butter cake. Mrs. Harris and her fellow proprietress, a Mrs. Bruce, bustled about with news and gossip. Both women had a largesse that matched their physical size; they were baking for the upcoming Sports Day. Judging by the rotation of trays being placed into the Metters stove, quite the crowd was expected. While they mixed and rolled pastry and fed the firebox, they regaled the young woman from the city with stories of stockmen and guests, laughing often and loud, their great soft bellies jiggling with mirth.

A couple of very young poddy lambs were settled in a basket by the stove and got up to explore occasionally, wandering a few feet on their awkward spindly legs before they were shooed back.

Edna absorbed the warmth of the kitchen and the company. She smiled, picturing the two elderly women in sculpture, smooth round shapes polished to a gentle sheen. Clay she thought, not bronze—

there was something earthy about the old girls. She would pit-fire the sculptures so that the figures would be baked like the biscuits which filled the house with their aroma.

"I'll just put in another roast for supper, Mrs. Harris," Mrs. Bruce said, as she took the last tray of biscuits from the oven. "With three extra gentlemen we'll be wanting at least another leg."

"Yes, my word, Mrs. Bruce." Mrs. Harris checked the soup simmering on the stove top. "Miss Brent will be wanting her tray as usual, I suppose."

"Yes, I'm afraid so. She's still eating in her room."

"Oh dear, is she unwell?" Edna asked.

"Oh no. My word, she's as healthy as a horse!" Mrs. Harris laughed, her enormous girth bouncing gently. "Our Miss Brent is a writer… working on her latest book. Very committed she is. Why she's been here for weeks and we've barely seen her."

"Brent?" Edna tried to place the name. "I don't think I've heard of her. Is she very famous?"

Mrs. Harris looked at Mrs. Bruce and Mrs. Bruce looked back. The pause was just a breath too long.

"No, no… not at all." Mrs. Harris decided. "You won't have heard of her, my word."

"What is she writing?"

"Something about a monkey, I believe."

Rowland, Clyde and Milton enjoyed the benefits of the bar for a while after Moran had left, and so were in that congenial state just beyond complete sobriety when they returned to Edna. It was nearly suppertime by then and so they joined the rest of the guests in the dining room where the waitress brought them generous plates of the fare which Edna had watched being prepared. Over roast lamb and potatoes they told her of Moran and their plans to go out to where the men were camped.

"We'll have to get horses." Clyde poured more gravy over his plate. "There're no roads," he added, as Rowland began to protest. "You don't want to have to abandon your car because she gets bogged or worse, Rowly."

"No, I suppose not. I'll speak to Mrs. Harris and try to arrange something."

Edna beamed. "When are we going?"

Rowland halted. He had actually expected, hoped, that Edna would stop at the guesthouse. He mentioned that.

Edna cocked her head to one side. For a moment, Rowland dared to believe she was considering it. Then she laughed. "No, I think I'll come."

"Ed…"

"I'm not made of glass, Rowly. What happened, happened, I'm all right now." She glared at him, challenging him to tell her otherwise.

Milton glanced at Clyde. They had both known it would be only a matter of time before Edna rose against Rowland's protectiveness. It had never been in her nature to take a back seat, however safer that seat might be.

"Ed, we may have to stay out there a couple of nights. It's a camp of men…"

Edna spoke quietly, a bit too fiercely. "I've never been afraid of men, Rowly."

"Come on, Ed," Milton said. "Be reasonable." He suspected that Edna was trying to prove something to herself more than to Rowland. Still, the sculptress had very nearly died.

Rowland met Edna's eyes, a little uncertainly. He knew Edna would never tolerate any compromise of her independence, however well-intentioned, but that bastard had nearly killed her.

Edna's face softened. She put her hand on Rowland's arm. "Dear Rowly, it's so sweet of you to worry about me, but I'm well now. I've got to get back to being me."

Rowland groaned, but he relented. Edna was not one who'd wait meekly to inherit the earth, and he would never change her. Apparently she was determined to treat this excursion like a trail ride. "Tremendous."

She rewarded him with her most enchanting smile. "Good. That's settled then."

"So it seems."

They retired to the guest lounge after dinner, which initially was crowded with other guests. Clyde and Milton joined a card game with a couple of holidaymakers. Rowland sat by the fire with his notebook, drawing Moran from memory—the sun-lined face, the shadowy eyes. He hadn't come to a decision about Moran, but he was not predisposed to like him. He wondered if he should just sack the man and hire a new crew to muster the cattle... but the fact remained that finding experienced cattlemen this late in the season might not be easy, and he still had nothing specific to prove that Moran was not simply doing his job.

"Are they worth a penny?" Edna sat down and poked him from his reverie.

He smiled. "No—nowhere near that valuable."

She looked over at his notebook. "Is that Mr. Moran?"

"Yes."

"They're interesting, aren't they," she whispered, "the people up here. They make me want to work." She told him quietly of her plan to sculpt their hostesses. "If I use the right oxides I can turn the clay rosy in the pit... can we dig a pit at *Woodlands?* Will it upset the neighbours?"

Rowland laughed. "We'll say we're barbequing—it's very fashionable at the moment."

Edna giggled and, curling up on the couch beside him, chattered about her plans for a series of figures based on the rotund ladies of the Rules Point Guesthouse. Rowland drew them as she talked and then Edna showed him how she would simplify the images for her sculptures, choosing the lines that best conveyed the solid softness, the maternal comfort, of the women. They must have been so engaged for a while as, when they thought to notice the room again, most of the other guests had retired. Clyde and Milton were still playing cards though it was just the two of them now.

Rowland checked his watch. It was nearly midnight. He was just about to suggest they turn in when one of the bedroom doors creaked open. A woman walked out into the dark hall. She was small, with an extraordinary amount of grey hair piled in a bouffant knot on her head. It looked heavy. She emerged from the room muttering, "The words, where are my words?"

Rowland nudged Edna and nodded towards the woman.

"Oh that must be the writer, Miss Brent. She's writing a book about monkeys." Edna raised her voice. "Hello Miss Brent. Would you care to join us?"

Sarah Brent turned and squinted into the lamp-lit room. She stepped towards them. The gentlemen stood hastily.

In the light, the writer looked to be on the wrong side of fifty. Her frame was diminutive, her face unremarkable except for the masses of hair which were loosely tied up around it.

"Hello Miss Brent, I'm…" Edna extended her hand, but the woman was not paying any attention to her. Sarah Brent stared at Rowland as if she were looking at some kind of apparition. She turned abruptly and scurried back into her room, leaving them standing bewildered in the lounge.

"What the devil was that?" Milton asked.

"A writer apparently."

Then Sarah Brent was back. She held a card in her hand, and she looked from it to Rowland repeatedly. "You… who are you?" she asked.

Milton moved quietly to peer over her shoulder at the card. It was a photographic postcard, the kind servicemen had sent back from Egypt in the Great War. He recognised the soldier in the picture.

"Well, I'll be blowed, that's Rowly's brother! What are you doing with a picture of Rowly's brother?"

Rowland stiffened, surprised. This was most odd.

"Brother?" Sarah Brent started. "You can't be Wilfred?"

"No, madam, I'm Rowland Sinclair. I'm Wilfred's youngest brother."

Edna approached the writer. "Miss Brent, would you mind if I…?"

Distractedly, Sarah handed her the postcard. Edna too recognised it—a similar picture of Aubrey Sinclair had always graced the mantelpiece at *Woodlands*. Though he was now several years older than Aubrey had been when the photograph was taken, the image could easily have been of Rowland Sinclair. Edna handed the postcard to Rowland. He glanced at it and then turned it over. Aubrey had signed it with love. Now Rowland was confused. He had no doubt that his late brother had had sweethearts, but Miss Brent seemed a bit old for that.

"You knew my brother?" he asked.

Sarah Brent seemed finally to gather herself. Her lips pressed into a tight smile. "Your brother... well, isn't this a peculiar thing?"

She stepped a little closer to Rowland. "I knew both your brothers many years ago." She sat in an armchair, leaning forward with her elbows on her knees as she continued to study Rowland. "How old are you, Mr. Sinclair?"

"Twenty-eight," Rowland replied carefully as he returned to the couch.

"Well there you go then—it was all before you were born."

"What was?"

"I took a situation as a governess on a property near Yass in 1897," the writer said, without taking her eyes from Rowland. "Both circumstance and research really. Two little boys: the elder, a funny solemn child called Wilfred, and Aubrey, my beautiful laughing baby." Her eyes became misty. "I was fond of Wilfred—he was away at school a lot, of course. I loved Aubrey like he was my own."

Rowland looked down at the photograph again: Aubrey posing in front of the Sphinx. "You kept in touch?"

Sarah Brent smiled. "I'd write and visit. Your dear mother was very kind to let me do so. Aubrey was such a bright little boy; he grew up to be such a handsome decent young man. I was very proud of him."

Rowland was at a bit of a loss. He'd had governesses too, before he'd started school, but they were just vague memories. He had no idea what had become of them after they'd left his parents' employ. He didn't think any had ever tried to keep in touch. And yet, here was this writer, still carrying a picture of Aubrey some seventeen years after he'd died.

"You're aware that Aubrey..."

"Yes, of course. I was volunteering at a hospital on the Serbian front then." Sarah took a handkerchief from her pocket and dabbed her eyes and wiped her nose. "So many boys... Wilfred found one of my letters amongst Aubrey's belongings and wrote to me. It was so very kind..."

For a moment there was silence, none of them sure what to say, and then Sarah Brent spoke again.

"Tell me, is Wilfred well? I take it that he returned."

Rowland nodded. "Yes, Wil came back. He's well. I must telephone and tell him that I've run into you..."

"No! You mustn't do that. I'm incognito you know."

"Oh... really?"

"Wilfred will never have heard of Sarah Brent." The writer was adamant.

Rowland had no doubt she was right. "Who would he know you as?"

"I think I was calling myself Sarah Frankling then."

"I see." Rowland was beginning to think the writer quite bizarre.

"What's in a name? That which we call a rose by any other name would smell as sweet," Milton offered solemnly.

"Shakespeare," Rowland muttered, then realised that the niceties had to this point been ignored. "Miss Brent, may I introduce, Messrs Milton Isaacs and Clyde Watson Jones. And this is Miss Edna Higgins."

Sarah Brent, as she was now calling herself, sat back in her armchair. "And what brings you all to Rules Point? Have the Sinclair fortunes changed? I would have expected you to be holidaying at Caves House, at the very least?"

Rowland was mildly unsettled by the directness of the enquiry. "We are inspecting stock we have grazing on a snow lease up here," he said. "It's rather convenient to ride out from Rules Point."

The writer's eyes sparkled. "Well that sounds most agreeable! I was born in Talbingo, you know, grew up in the saddle, a child of the bush. There's nothing so exhilarating as riding in the mountains."

Edna smiled. "See, I told you, Rowly. Mr. Sinclair thought it would be too rough for me." She poked him playfully.

Sarah Brent's mouth tightened. "Did he indeed?" She fixed Rowland with a steely gaze. "How very patriarchal of you, Mr. Sinclair. I would have hoped a man your age would have been less inclined to oppress the women in his acquaintance under the guise of concern!"

"I was just…"

"Oh yes, you cloak it all in civility and consideration, but it all amounts to the same thing—the unjust, unconscionable pursuit of power over women and the denial of a woman's basic right to self-determine!"

Rowland looked for help. Milton grinned and even Clyde's mouth twitched. But only Edna came to his defence.

"I've been ill," she said, squeezing Rowland's hand. "Rowly was just being sweet—he didn't want me to overdo it."

Sarah sat back into the chair. "Oh I see. Well there is nothing so good for convalescence than a ride in the clear mountain air. I'm sure this excursion will do you the world of good. A ride on the plains sounds delightful indeed, struggling as I am with this novel." She sighed. "The words are elusive at this time, when I'm so nearly finished."

Rowland, if truth be told, was a little afraid of saying anything now. Milton and Clyde were also conspicuously silent. It was up to Edna.

"Oh dear, I do hope we haven't disturbed you too much. Have you written many books?"

"A few. Of course I've always had to fight the patriarchal conspiracy to find publishers. I've written under male names, travelled the world in search of more progressive attitudes... every time I met a like-minded gentleman, he'd spoil it all by wanting to marry me!" Sarah Brent pointed at Edna, her gaze intense. "That's how they do it, Miss Higgins. They enslave you with matrimony— you take their name and lose your self."

Edna nodded solemnly. Rowland got up to find a drink. Milton beat him to the decanter of sherry on the mantel. Sarah Brent moved into Rowland's place on the couch next to Edna and the two fell into earnest conversation. The writer engaged the sculptress with warnings and tirades against the suppression of their gender.

Rowland glanced at Clyde and Milton. It was clearly time to retreat gracefully.

12

OUR MOUNTAIN WONDERLAND

YARRANGOBILLY

After a hearty meal at Caves House a party was formed and conducted by Mr. Bradley through the Jersey Cave. Much might be said in praise of Yarrangobilly Caves as to their excellence and wonders, but it will be a long time before these caves will be in the public favour like far-famed Jenolan, owing to the accessibility of the latter. It would be unfair to compare or even to criticise Yarrangobilly Caves, as they scarcely bear any resemblance to the more northern limestone caves. But the writer thinks that the natural scenery without and the famous trout streams in the district will do much to place Yarrangobilly in public favour.

The Sydney Morning Herald, 1932

Rowland sprinkled salt liberally over his eggs and bacon. "Where's Ed?"

"Still sleeping, I believe," Milton replied. "She was up most of the night with that writer woman."

Rowland sighed.

Clyde agreed. "This could be ugly."

Milton elected to change the subject. "What do we need to do today, Rowly?"

"We'll have to get horses from somewhere I expect, and whatever supplies we need to stay out there a couple of nights."

"Got any idea where?"

Clyde spoke up. "We can collect horses and saddles at Long Plain Homestead."

"What's Long Plain Homestead?"

"Well, it's a homestead on Long Plain. It's not too far from here. The chap who runs it keeps horses for hire. The road out to it is rough but we could drive it. We'll leave the Mercedes at the homestead and take horses from there."

"You're sure he'll have horses?"

"He always used to—I'll check with Mrs. Harris to be sure. He's a cranky old bugger—he won't miss you for the hire, Rowly."

Rowland smiled. Clyde's concern for his finances had always been greater than his own.

Milton looked around at the congested bustle of the dining room. Stockmen were already starting to come in for the Rules Point Sports Day. "Looks like every man and his dog is going to be here tomorrow."

Rowland buttered his toast. "You have any idea what this Sports Day is all about, Clyde? I assume they're not talking about tennis?"

Clyde laughed. "No, I think it's more of a rodeo—buck jumping, horse races, gambling and a lot of drinking. Apparently there's a supper dance afterwards in the stables."

"Good thing we have dinner suits with us, then." Milton dusted the crumbs from his cravat.

Clyde lowered his voice. "Look, Rowly, today may be a good time to ask around about your man Simpson. Every stockman within cooee will be coming in—someone's bound to have heard something."

Rowland nodded. "I was just thinking that. We might even find out what Moran is up to... if he's up to anything."

Edna came into the dining room just as they finished breakfast and so they lingered over coffee as she ate. It seemed the mountain air had reinvigorated the sculptress' appetite. Rowland studied her. She was definitely less angular. The gentle curves that so suited his brush had returned. He wondered if he could start a new painting for the exhibition of classical figures—there might still be time if they found Harry Simpson quickly. He started to play with ideas and poses. Edna was more than Aphrodite, the goddess of love... perhaps he could paint her as Pentheselia the warrior queen, or Atalanta who sailed with the Argonauts...

Edna looked up from her breakfast. She smiled, recognising the intense focus, the darkening of the blue in his eyes. "Stop painting me, Rowly," she said. "I'm eating."

Rowland came back to the present. "Sorry."

"Do you suppose we'll have time to go down to the caves today?" she asked. "I thought since we have a couple of days..."

"I don't see why not."

"Oh good. I've wanted to see the limestone formations for years. Do you remember Marriott Spencer?"

"No."

"I took a few sculpture classes with him at Ashton's. I'm surprised you don't remember him. He'd lost his right hand—had a hook in its place."

"And he taught sculpture?" Rowland had met Edna at the Ashton Art School in the late twenties. He couldn't recall any hook-handed sculptors, however.

Edna poured a cup of tea. "Yes, he had a rather interesting technique."

"I'll bet."

"He sculpted with hot wax... dripped it to create the form. Apparently he was inspired by the limestone formations in these caves; his work was so wonderfully fluid."

"Sounds like a glorified candle," Clyde grunted.

Rowland laughed.

Edna rolled her eyes. Painters could be frustratingly conventional.

"We'll go as soon as you finish breakfast," Rowland said. "We can ask after Simpson when we come back."

Edna's face fell. "Oh Rowly, I'm sorry, how selfish of me. I know you're keen to find Mr. Simpson. We don't need to go to the caves— it was just a whim."

Rowland shook his head. "It's fine, Ed. I daresay these chaps aren't just going to open up to strangers. Better to wait till they've had a chance to get a bit lubricated."

Milton grinned. "You'll just have to entertain yourself this evening while we do a spot of research in the bar."

Edna brightened. "That works out well then. I promised Sarah I'd read her manuscript later today."

"Sarah...? Oh Miss Brent!"

"Yes, she's very interesting." The sculptress was characteristically enthusiastic. "She's lived abroad and met all sorts of people. Banjo Paterson proposed to her once. She was a great friend of Henry Lawson too."

Milton laughed. "Don't be too impressed, Ed. Old Lawson would befriend anyone who bought him a drink—his best work was scribbled on the back of beer coasters."

"At least he wrote something," Clyde murmured.

Milton ignored him.

"So it's settled," Rowland said. "We'll spend the morning down at the caves, and the rest of the day in the bar." He hesitated. "I don't suppose we should invite Miss Brent to join us? At the caves I mean, not the bar."

Milton swatted him. "Must you be so bloody civil? The woman's a harridan!"

"That's very kind, Rowly," Edna intervened, "but I think Sarah's helping Mrs. Harris with all the food for the Sports Day. She worked as a cook in England, and it seems there'll be all sorts of people here tomorrow."

Rowland was clearly relieved.

Edna leaned over to Rowland and spoke quietly. "You should chat with her if you can though. She corresponded with Aubrey for years... I gather they were quite close."

Rowland smiled. To Edna it was wistful.

"Did you know Aubrey wrote?"

Rowland shook his head slowly. He had been eleven when Aubrey was killed. He had loved his brother, but Aubrey was a mystery to him. There were so many people who knew Aubrey Sinclair better than he.

"Sarah encouraged him." Edna rubbed Rowland's hand gently. "She thought he showed great promise."

"Miss Brent told you all this?"

Edna nodded. "Last night. I think she was quite unnerved by you—how much you look like Aubrey. She wanted to talk about him."

Rowland said nothing.

"Ask her about him," Edna said. "Don't let her scare you; she's really very sweet."

"I'm not scared of her," Rowland protested.

"Of course you're not."

The yellow Mercedes pulled into the grounds of Caves House for the second time in as many days. The limestone caves were just a stroll from the hotel. Rowland spotted the senator whose decision to stay on had affected their reservation. Of the generation that still favoured the top hat, the elderly statesman stood straight backed at the top of the steps. Milton pointed out the primped and painted young blonde in his shadow. "Bet that's not his wife."

Rowland and Clyde looked over. The old senator seemed very happy indeed. Milton laughed. "At least we were turned out for a good cause."

Wilson, the manager, spotted them from the steps and hurried over. "I say, Mr. Sinclair, I'm glad I caught you, sir."

"Mr. Wilson."

"I thought I should tell you, sir, there were some gentlemen here yesterday—I'm afraid I—"

"Rowly, I say Rowly old man!"

Abercrombie. The Englishman trotted to join them. Just a half-step behind him was an elderly gentleman in a black suit and bowler.

"Miss Higgins." Abercrombie tipped his tweed fedora and introduced the man in the bowler as his valet, Michaels. The valet greeted them politely and said nothing more.

Rowland's brow flickered upwards briefly as he glanced at the plus-fours and herringbone jacket ensemble which attired his old friend. Perhaps Abercrombie was planning to golf.

"What a splendid happenstance to see you all again," Humphrey stuttered. "Have they sorted out this dreadful cock-up with your rooms then?"

Wilson cleared his throat. "I might catch up with you a little later, Mr. Sinclair. There is a matter about which I'd like to make you aware."

"Certainly Wilson, I'll stop by your office before we make our return to Rules Point."

Wilson nodded and retreated haughtily back up the steps.

"So they haven't sorted out your rooms?" Abercrombie sniffed.

"Afraid not, Humphrey. Miss Higgins wished to see the caves."

"I say, that's not a bad idea. I've heard the formations are quite something to see. I might come along if I may."

"Of course, Mr. Abercrombie." Edna sent the Englishman into a crimson flush with her smile. "We'd be delighted to have your company... what's that?"

Rowland squinted at the sky as the rattling hum of an airborne motor grew louder. The Tiger Moth was losing altitude, swooping low enough to allow them to spot a package being tossed from the cockpit. It fell into the scrub behind Caves House.

"What the...?" Rowland started.

"Oh, I say, this is too bad!" Abercrombie tapped his walking stick on the ground indignantly. "He's missed again! Michaels, you'll have to go foraging in the wilderness for my papers again."

"Your papers?"

"Yes, Mama has the London *Times* dropped off when she can get a copy in Sydney. Keeps one in touch with civilisation, don't you know. What say, Rowly, I expect you'd love to get your hands on a copy of the *Times*."

Milton started to laugh.

"Seems a lot of trouble for a newspaper, Humphrey," Rowland murmured.

"We mustn't forget that we're Englishmen, Rowly."

"Rowly's not English, Mr. Abercrombie," Edna corrected. "He was born here."

"We're all of us, British, Miss Higgins," Abercrombie replied stiffly.

Rowland cleared his throat.

Milton kept laughing.

Abercrombie motioned to his valet. "Off you go then, Michaels." He waved his hands vaguely in the direction of the trees. "You'd better get along and find it... Don't worry, I'll be all right."

They watched the elderly valet set off into the bush.

"Perhaps we should help him." Clyde looked after Michaels, a little concerned.

Abercrombie shook his head. "No, no, Michaels is quite the resourceful fellow. Shall we see these caves then?" He offered Edna his arm, hesitantly, forcing a nervous smile.

Milton shook his head, and they fell awkwardly into step on the narrow path that led down to the Glory Hole Cave.

"I am glad to have run into you, Rowly," Abercrombie said, craning his neck back. "There is a matter that I really must speak to you about."

"Indeed."

"I fear my life is in danger, Rowly."

Rowland smiled but so briefly that Abercrombie failed to notice. "Why do you say that, Humphrey?"

"Some unsavoury characters called by Caves House yesterday. That fellow, Wilson, had to show them to the door. I presume that's what he wishes to discuss with you."

"Why does he want to discuss it with me?"

Abercrombie's eyes moved fleetingly to Milton and Clyde. "Perhaps he believes you might know them."

Rowland gathered that Wilson had come to some conclusions about the company he kept. "What makes you say these fellows were unsavoury?"

"They had that look, Rowly."

"That look?"

"Yes, that look… a criminal countenance. Clearly ruffians."

"I see, and that's why Wilson showed them to the door?"

"No. I understand they were making insistent and impertinent enquiries."

"About what?"

"About the guests!"

"I say, enquiries… that is dangerous!" Milton exclaimed. "Spot of bother, what!"

Rowland elbowed the poet sharply but Abercrombie thought he'd found a sympathetic ally.

"It's been most distressing. I didn't sleep a wink last night for fear I'd be murdered in my bed."

"What makes you believe these men meant to harm you, Mr. Abercrombie?" Edna asked.

"Isn't it obvious, dear lady? They were enquiring to ascertain whether I was on the guest list."

Rowland looked skyward. "What did these gentlemen look like?"

"I very much doubt they were gentlemen, Rowly. Badly tailored suits are all I recall. Most undesirable."

"Nothing quite as sinister as an ill-fitting jacket," Milton muttered, adjusting his own. "Some people just have no—oww!" He stopped short as Clyde swatted him.

They had, by this time, arrived at the mouth of the cavern known as the Glory Hole. Its entrance was arresting, a classical and colossal arch. A large hole in the high roof of the cavern let in light with the kind of structural theatricality that made one stop short. Edna was in awe.

The temperature dipped dramatically when they entered, and Edna buttoned her coat and detached herself from Abercrombie's arm. She walked ahead, into the darkness of the smaller winding caverns away from the dramatic entrance. Her eyes wide, she gazed at the formations around them. The cave was gently lit so that the delicate straws and shawls of limestone glistened. Edna's mind conjured figures and movement in the shapes.

"I say, look at that!" Abercrombie exclaimed behind her as he pointed at one of the thousands of stalactites. "It looks just like a carrot!"

Edna sighed.

"How on earth do they get power down here?" Milton was certain that he had not heard the harsh hum of a generator on the walk down.

"Hydro-electric system. The wheel's in the Rules Creek."

"And that's enough for all the lights?" Milton was surprised.

"Powers Caves House as well, I believe," Clyde replied.

Milton whistled. "Who would have thought?"

There were a few other visitors to the caves that morning and so they milled amongst the loose crowds admiring the limestone formations.

"Careful!" Rowland caught Edna's arm as she slipped on the damp rock walkway. He glanced dubiously at the prettily heeled shoes she was wearing. "I hope you're not planning to ride a horse in those, Ed."

She smiled up at him. "Of course not. Kate insisted I take her riding boots... they're in my trunk somewhere. She gave me her riding habits too—they're rather splendid."

"I'm sure."

"It's lovely down here, isn't it, Rowly? Quite magical. The Glory Hole was—"

Edna gasped as the cave plunged suddenly into darkness. The blackness was absolute, it seemed to press down upon them. Rowland pulled the sculptress to him as the cavern rang with screams and the crowd began to jostle.

"Rowly, Rowly—help me!" Rowland felt hands clutch frantically at his shoulders and wrench him back. He tried to regain his balance by reaching for the rail but in the darkness he missed it, and crashed onto the slippery path, taking Edna with him.

Then Abercrombie fell on top of them. "Rowly, help me! They've come for me!"

Rowland twisted his head away as the Englishman grasped at his face. "For the love of God, Humphrey!"

"Rowly, it's you, thank heavens."

Rowland pushed the body he assumed was Abercrombie's away. "Ed—are you all right?" She was still in his arms... well, he hoped it was her.

"I'm fine, Rowly," Edna lifted her face from Rowland's chest and laughed. "I fell on you. Are you okay?"

"Never better."

"Ssshhhh, they'll hear us, Rowly." Abercrombie's face was somewhere close enough for Rowland to feel his breath. "Quickly, Rowly, this way... before they find me, old man." Abercrombie tugged at his arm.

Rowland ignored him. "Milt, Clyde?"

"Right here, Rowly, where the hell are you?"

"Down here—get Ed off me will you?"

"Are you sure?" Milton's voice. Rowland could hear his smile.

"Just help her up."

Edna was lifted to her feet. Fumbling briefly, Rowland found Clyde's hand and tried to pull himself up too, but Abercrombie held him back. "No, Rowly, get down. I think I can see a way out before they find us. They're here, I tell you, they're here!"

Rowland grabbed the lapel of Abercrombie's jacket and dragged the terrified Englishman up with him.

Bodies crushed against them in the blackness.

"They're here! There's a murderer in here!" Abercrombie was near hysterical. Predictably, his declaration started a panic within the cave and soon they were nearly deafened by a cacophony of distress and fear which bounced and echoed against the cavern walls. The shoving and jostling began in earnest as people scrambled to escape.

"Ed?"

"We've got her, Rowly." Clyde's voice.

"I can't see a thing," Rowland shouted in the general direction of the voice, his grip still firmly on Abercrombie's lapel. An elbow caught him in the stomach as someone pushed past. There was a crack. It was louder than the screams, the sound nearly physical in its impact. At first, it startled everyone into shocked silence and then the panic intensified. Abercrombie pushed Rowland to the ground. There were many others there now.

Abercrombie started to pray. A few people joined him. Rowland might have shot the Englishman himself if he'd been armed.

A beam of light cut through the darkness. Then another. The caretaker had arrived with torches. "Calm down now, folks, there's nothing to worry about. Just a bit of a problem with the lights. No harm done. Now if you just follow me—careful now—there's no need to push folks!"

13

ELECTRIC LIGHTING AT YARRANGOBILLY CAVES

The Hon. C. C. Lazzarini, Chief Secretary, had intended visiting Yarrangobilly Caves at the coming week end for the purpose of officially switching on the electricity to the Caves. Afterwards it was his intention to motor to the Hotel Kosciusko, via Kiandra and Adaminaby to open the summer season of golf, trout fishing and other Alpine pastimes for which Kosciusko is so well known. In view, however, of his necessity to remain in Sydney at the present juncture, Mr. Lazzarini has been reluctantly obliged to cancel the arrangements for his official tour. Arrangements for the public to view the Yarrongobilly Caves by electric light will not be delayed. It is the intention of the Minister to perform the official opening ceremony at a later date.

Queanbeyan Age, 1926

Rowland used his hat to slap the grit of the cave floor off his suit. Abercrombie sat on the low stone wall trembling and mopping his brow with a silk handkerchief. Rowland was too annoyed to speak to him.

Edna adjusted her hat back into place, but having been protected from the ground by Rowland's body, she was otherwise unsoiled. "Well, that was a little alarming."

"Do you think it was a gunshot?" Clyde asked, keeping his voice low in the wake of the recent panic.

Rowland shrugged. "Hard to tell. Maybe."

"Of course it was!" Abercrombie exploded. "My life is in danger, I tell you!" He looked around. "They could still be here…"

Rowland sighed.

Everyone was out of the cave now, essentially unhurt. A few people reported seeing apparitions, but according to the caretaker that was not an unusual reaction to the complete darkness of the caves. "The mind plays tricks when yer eyes ain't no use."

The crack, which may or may not have been a gunshot, was, however, not an hallucination—unless it was one shared by every person in the cave. A telephone call had been made from Caves House through to the Kiandra courthouse for police assistance, but it was unlikely that any sort of constabulary would arrive soon.

Shocked visitors milled around the entrance while the caretaker assured them that there was nothing to worry about and that lighting would be restored to the caves as soon as possible.

Rowland's attention was caught by a smartly dressed man who was speaking with the caretaker a short distance away. He strode towards them. "Babbington? Charlie Babbington?"

The man turned, his face creasing into recognition. "I say, Sinclair, fancy seeing you up here!"

Milton, Edna and Clyde left Abercrombie, still complaining, and joined Rowland who was shaking the hand of Charles Babbington.

Rowland introduced the various parties. "Charlie works at Dangars."

Babbington looked a little pained. He lifted his nose and sniffed indignantly. "I have the pleasure of serving with Mr. Sinclair as a director on the Governing Board of Dangar, Gedye and Company."

"Yes… Of course. Sorry, old boy… I didn't mean to suggest you actually worked."

"Quite all right, Sinclair—a mere slip, I'm sure."

"What brings you to the caves, Charlie?"

"My good lady's from the area—a little place called Tumbarumba, no less!" Babbington laughed loudly, shaking his head as if the name of his wife's hometown was beyond belief. "I'm doing a bit of fishing while she visits her relatives."

"You were in the cave then, when—"

"Yes, that was rather a spot of bother, wasn't it? I've just been telling that caretaker chap about our new Listers. I daresay this sort of inconvenience could be avoided with a proper diesel generator. I say, Sinclair, are you planning to attend the April meeting? I could take your apologies…"

"No need, Charlie. I'll be back in Sydney by then."

"Well if you find you'd like to stay on longer…" Babbington glanced fleetingly at Edna, "I'll be at Caves House for a couple of weeks."

Rowland cleared his throat. "Terribly decent of you, Charlie, I'll bear that in mind." He looked back at Abercrombie who was still sitting woebegone on the low stone wall. "We'd better get Humphrey back to Caves House—he's had a rather trying morning. Will you join us for luncheon, Charlie?"

"Thank you, Sinclair, but no." Babbington flipped open his pocket watch and checked the time. "I have some business to attend to, I'm afraid."

"Some other time then." Rowland offered Babbington his hand and they took their leave.

"What's worrying you, Rowly?" Edna whispered, having noted the slight furrow of his brow as they walked back to Caves House.

He smiled as she hooked her arm through his. "Nothing really. Just never known Charlie to be so easygoing about my attendance at board meetings. It's rather strange—he's a bit of a scorekeeper generally."

Milton nudged him. "Perhaps he's doing a bit more than fishing himself."

Rowland smiled. "I wouldn't have thought it of Charlie. He's somewhat inhibited."

Milton shook his head. "Nope, he's up to no good, he's trying to get you on side by getting you out of a board meeting."

Clyde grinned. "He's worked Rowly out then."

"Wil's adamant I be at the April meeting."

"Why?"

"No idea, but I'm sure he'll tell me."

"Mr. Babbington could just be trying to be congenial," Edna suggested. "Not everybody has a sinister motive, Rowly."

"Sinister? Of course it's sinister." Abercrombie had heard her last words. "Surely this morning's events are evidence that my life is in danger."

"He might have a point, Rowly," Clyde murmured. Rowland was not prone to overreact at the best of times, but he seemed particularly dismissive of Humphrey Abercrombie's predicament.

Rowland exhaled slowly. "Perhaps a spot of lunch will make a course of action clearer."

"Of course, luncheon..." Abercrombie visibly cheered at the suggestion, and the implication that some action would be taken. His step quickened. Rowland's did not.

"Righto, Rowly, what gives?" Clyde demanded, as they sat down in the dining room which was already abuzz with conversation about the blackout at the caves. Humphrey Abercrombie had departed to don fresh clothes, apparently unable to countenance eating in his morning attire.

"What do you mean?"

"You seem a little unconcerned about your friend's safety. He's a bit of an old woman, but given the shooting…"

"We don't know that it was a gunshot," Rowland replied. "I imagine sounds amplify and resonate in the caves."

"Still…"

Rowland leaned back in his chair and rubbed his brow. "Sorry, you're right… it's just that Humphrey's always been completely paranoid, convinced that danger was just round every corner."

"Was he wrong?"

Rowland smiled. "Not always… but then it's not entirely surprising that the odd person wants to kill him, is it?"

"The caves, this incident with the men in bad suits," Clyde persisted, "surely it's more than a coincidence."

Milton glanced up from his menu card. "Clyde's right, it is more than a coincidence though I don't know that it has anything to do with the Honourable Lord Abercrombie. I think we should be more worried about Rowly."

"Me?"

"Why?" Edna asked, alarmed.

"Well, these chaps in the cheap suits—they sound like the goons that tried to take Rowly at the Hydro Majestic."

"A lot of men wear cheap suits, Milt." Clyde glanced briefly at his own rather worn jacket. "Particularly these days."

"Still, they were asking about the guest list—they might have been trying to find out if Rowly was here."

"And the caves?"

"Maybe it was a bungled attempt to snatch him there."

"I think we're getting a bit carried away," Rowland murmured. "I'll tell Humphrey to chuff off back to Sydney. He's only going to work himself into some kind of hysterical breakdown here."

"Poor Mr. Abercrombie," Edna said softly. "But what about you, Rowly? Maybe we should head back as well."

Rowland's eyes darkened a little. "We will, as soon as I find out what happened to Harry."

Edna touched his sleeve. "You're really worried about him aren't you?"

"Yes."

"You don't think…?"

"I don't know… God, I hope not. I hope Moran is right and he just walked off."

Humphrey Abercrombie strutted into the dining room at that point. He had swapped his plus-fours for the smart tweed suit, and made his way quickly over to their table. He dropped his face into his hands as soon as he'd sat down. "Not a constable in sight!" he said. "A man is nearly murdered and the authorities still haven't arrived."

"What man?" Rowland barely masked his impatience.

"Why me, of course."

Rowland pushed his hair back from his face and paused a few seconds before he answered. "Perhaps you're right, Humphrey. It might be prudent to head back to Sydney as soon as possible."

Abercrombie's face lightened. "Do you really believe so, Rowly? One doesn't like to seem like one isn't—"

Milton couldn't help himself. "Courage, poor stupid heart of stone, or if I ask thee why, care not thou to reply, she is but dead and the time is at hand when thou shalt more than die."

Abercrombie blustered, confused.

"Lord Tennyson." Rowland turned back to Abercrombie. "What Milt is trying to say is that there doesn't seem any other sensible course of action, considering there've been so many attempts on your life."

Abercrombie's face lifted further. "You may be right, Rowly." He nodded emphatically. "There's no point being foolhardy, as you say. Clearly these fiends will stop at nothing."

"Clearly."

"But I say, Rowly, we've only just renewed our acquaintance." He seemed quite disconcerted. "Why don't you return to Sydney as well? What do you say? Let's jolly well leave this godforsaken place to the savages."

"I'm afraid I have some business to attend to first," Rowland said quickly. "I'll look you up as soon as we get back."

Abercrombie pouted. "I don't know that I'll be much safer in Sydney on my own. Perhaps I should stay here until you're ready to go too. I could help you with this business of yours... help you deal with this chap Moran."

"I really think it's best if you go." Rowland reached into his pocket and pulled out a card. He scrawled a name on the back and handed it to Abercrombie. "When you get back, call on the Sydney Police Headquarters. Ask for Detective Sergeant Delaney—he's an old friend of mine—I'm sure he'll be able to help."

"But..."

"Trust me, Humphrey," Rowland said firmly.

Abercrombie sighed. "Very well, Rowly, if you're determined to exclude me from this expedition of yours."

"I am," Rowland said, a little brusquely.

Abercrombie returned sulkily to his meal.

Milton leaned over to Rowland. "Delaney's going to kill you."

It was late afternoon by the time they returned to the Rules Point Guesthouse. After an initial period of petulance, Abercrombie seemed to buoy and became quite celebratory. Luncheon turned into rather an extended affair peppered with reminiscences. Rowland had been inclined to truncate the conversation but Milton had refilled Abercrombie's glass and encouraged the Englishman's revelations about life at Pembroke House. Consequently, it was well past three by the time they managed to extricate themselves, promising to catch up with Abercrombie in Sydney. Once back at Rules Point, Rowland realised he hadn't gone to see Wilson, but since he was now aware of the incident about which the manager wished to speak to him, he decided it was probably no longer important.

Crowds had started to come in for the Sports Day. The perimeter of the guesthouse blazed with campfires, around which sat the men who couldn't be accommodated within the hotel. The atmosphere was already boisterous and loud.

"Looks like things are warming up." Milton grinned, as he observed a clearly inebriated young stockman riding a horse out of the bar onto the verandah. Mrs. Harris followed him brandishing a broom to a chorus of cheers and laughter.

"I'll just walk Ed to her room," Rowland said, as he watched the ruckus. "I'll meet you chaps in the bar if you like."

Another stockman was hurled out of the bar to applause.

Milton laughed. "Don't be too long—we might need you."

Despite the commotion centred around the bar, the accommodations maintained some order and decorum. The sitting room was crowded with women and children as well as the more consciously respectable men. Rowland was much relieved. He was beginning to worry that leaving Edna alone amongst so many wild drunken stockmen would be ill advised. There seemed, however, to be some kind of respectful line drawn through Rules Point dividing the High Country cattlemen from the more sober patrons.

"Are you sure you don't mind?" Rowland started, as they stood by the door to Edna's room.

"Of course not, Rowly." Edna smiled. "I promised Sarah Brent I'd read her manuscript, remember? I'm quite looking forward to it— I'm sure it will be brilliant."

"What about dinner?"

"I'll have something in here, I'll be fine." She stopped and regarded him sternly. "You will be careful won't you, Rowly? Don't let Milt get you boys into a fight—you know what he's like."

Rowland laughed. "We'll keep him in line. Enjoy your book, Ed."

Getting into the bar proved to be quite the feat. It was full, as were the men within it. If it were not for the fact that Milton was in the middle of a recitation—Wordsworth, though he failed to mention that—Rowland might never have found his friends in the overcrowded room.

"Rowly!" Clyde grabbed his shoulder as he pushed past.

Milton was, to Rowland's surprise, playing to an appreciative crowd who encouraged his rendition with raised glasses.

"Keep at it, son. You ain't no Banjo Paterson but it's not a bad little ditty."

Rowland shook his head as Clyde handed him a beer. "Who would have thought?"

Clyde quietly pointed out the gangs of men who mixed around the room: those who had come in from the snow leases, those who were locals of sorts, and transients who had arrived just for the Sports Day. The distinctions in attire, stance and hygiene were sometimes subtle, but they were a map to where each man belonged.

"Have you seen Moran?" Rowland asked, scanning the room.

"Afraid not. Barman says he was in here earlier, but he took off."

"Makes it easier to ask around, I suppose," Rowland sipped his beer. Inebriated applause broke out as Milton finished reciting an ode to the daffodil. It appeared the men of the High Country liked flowers.

A sudden clatter of chairs and startled swearing took the attention from the poet. Men jostled to retreat from something near the door. Milton, who'd been standing on a chair, was knocked from his makeshift podium, and landed in an ungainly heap. Rowland and Clyde pushed forward towards him, only to freeze. The snake was within striking distance of the poet and it did not seem inclined to withdraw.

14

COUNCILS AND RABBITS

The risks some men will take to help a fellow man in distress were fully demonstrated at Adelong recently, when Mr. August Eichorn offered to allow himself to be bitten by any snake the public liked to bring along, providing a fair collection would be contributed to assist M. Broadhurst who is crippled for life, the result of an accident at Burrenjuck some time ago.

Mr. Trude succeeded in bagging a monstrous black snake, one of the red-belly species, and Mr. Eichorn offered to wager fifty pound that the reptile would kill a rabbit immediately after it had bitten him. Needless to say there were no takers, as it is well known, and has been proved several times, that that species of snake will kill six or seven rabbits in succession.

The monster was unbagged and put to Mr. Eichorn's arm, which it struck and hung to for several seconds in mid air, then dropped to the ground. There was a scatter among the people and none were able to bag the reptile, but the Professor hopped down off the box and bagged the brute before he attempted to treat himself.

Then he simply rubbed some of his remedy over the bite, got an onlooker to slightly lance each puncture, tied a handkerchief for a few minutes round the wound, and squeezed it a few times, then released the ligature again; again applied his remedy and went off apparently all right, and was knocking about town for the remainder of the evening.

Queanbeyan Age, 1920

The bar fell into a confused hush as Milton stared at the poised serpent.

"Don't move," Clyde warned.

There was a click as someone cocked a shotgun from atop the bar.

"For God's sake…" Milton started.

"Don't shoot! She's one of mine." A man stepped towards Milton. He was tall, his limbs long. A smart brown suit was tailored to his lean frame. The waistcoat was hung with a number of gleaming medallions, which jangled when he moved. His beard was grey and untamed, and seemed to have accumulated all manner of twigs and leaves. He held up a hand for quiet. "Just relax, son," he said to Milton.

Milton didn't look exactly relaxed, but he didn't move.

The man squatted, sweeping his hand slowly from side to side. The snake's head followed, its glittering eyes caught by the movement. The bar remained hushed, expectant, mesmerized.

Milton cursed and rolled as the old man sprang and snatched the snake by the tail, holding it at arm's length. The reptile writhed uselessly, harmless now.

"Good on yer, Aug!" The cattlemen cheered as the man coiled the snake into a tackle basket and promptly closed the lid.

Rowland pulled Milton up. "Are you all right?"

Milton straightened his cravat before he answered. "No harm done. Good thing the old blighter knows how to catch a flaming python." He walked towards the old man, who was still fastening the buckles on the basket, with his right hand extended.

"Thank you, good sir. You have both talent and timing. Who may I say is my saviour?"

The man grinned broadly, revealing blackened gums set with crooked teeth.

"Professor August Eichorn," he said, shaking the poet's hand. "Don't you pay Gladys no mind. She's curious is all."

"Gladys?"

Eichorn patted his basket. "Highly strung, the brownies… beautiful, but they can be temperamental."

Unsure of how to respond, Milton introduced his friends.

"I take it Gladys is your… pet?" Rowland ventured.

Eichorn laughed. "Struth! Blimey, don't be daft, son. She's a brown snake not a bloody cat!"

"Yes, of course." Rowland stared dubiously at the tackle basket which Eichorn hung on his belt.

"Gladys here's a working girl, star of the show really."

"The show?"

"Eichorn's Deadly Dancing Snakes."

"They dance?"

Eichorn grinned again. "In a manner of speaking… gotta watch more than your toes, of course."

"You been bitten often?" Clyde asked.

"I've been bitten plenty, it's a real crowd pleaser." Eichorn reached inside his jacket. "Of course I've had this." He held up a bottle. "Eichorn's Snakebite and Blood Poisoning Cure—excellent for bites and stings of all kinds; bruises, abrasions, bumps and scratches; cures irritations, sores, burns and ulcers; perfect for the treatment of strains, sprains, breaks and aches. Been using it every day of my life."

"You drink it?"

"No son, you apply it topically."

"Well then, I guess I should buy you a drink, Professor Eichorn." Milton took the bottle for a closer inspection.

"I wouldn't say no to a whisky," Eichorn said quickly.

"Allow me," Rowland said, knowing the usual state of Milton's finances.

"I'll have a Scotch in that case," said Milton. "We couldn't let the professor drink alone now, could we?"

Rowland laughed. "No, we couldn't do that."

By the time Rowland returned with a bottle of whisky, Milton had acquired several bottles of Eichorn's miracle elixir. "These might come in handy if we're going bush," he claimed, as he held up the bottles.

Eichorn looked Rowland up and down, noting the superior cut of his suit. The snake handler's eyes moved to Milton—velvet jacket, crimson cravat and hair which hung well below his ears. "You boys don't look like cow chasers..." He glanced at Clyde. "Well you could be, but you two..."

"We're just up here looking for a bloke," Clyde said smiling.

"Who?"

"Chap by the name of Simpson. He works for Rowly."

"Simpson... hey, he wouldn't be a blackfella would he? Big bloke..."

Rowland sharpened. "Yes, that could be Harry. Do you know him?"

Eichorn nodded enthusiastically. "Ran into him in Corryong a couple of days ago, came to a couple of shows."

Rowland's eyes narrowed. "Corryong? Did you talk to him?"

"Briefly, said he was going to follow the river, look for work. Those blackfellas love their rivers."

"And when exactly was this?"

"Three... no, four days ago."

Rowland shook his head slowly but he said nothing. They talked with Eichorn for a while longer and then moved into other conversations. The cattlemen, however, were guarded and they learned nothing more about Moran or Simpson.

"Well, what do you think, Rowly?" Clyde asked, rolling a cigarette. They had retreated to the verandah which was only slightly less crowded than the bar. It was cold but the air was clearer. Milton had stayed inside, sharing Wordsworth with the High Country once again.

"I don't know." Rowland leaned against the rail. "Eichorn seems to be the only one willing to talk to us, but I don't know."

"You think Simpson might just have walked like Moran says?"

"Not unless there's something else going on with him." He shook his head again. "I can't see it."

Clyde put the cigarette between his lips and struck a match. He didn't press Rowland. For some reason the Sinclairs had an unusual faith in this particular worker. Who knew? Rowland Sinclair was his best friend, but Clyde did not pretend to understand the upper classes. They were, at best, odd.

"We might have more luck tomorrow, at this Sports Day," he said finally. "I take it you're still intent on riding out with Moran?"

"Yes."

Clyde placed his elbows on the rail. "Okay then. Perhaps you'd better bring that gun your brother gave you."

Rowland looked at him askance. "We're not going into the Wild West, Clyde.'

"Don't you believe it, Rowly, don't you believe it."

Edna checked over her shoulder before she knocked quietly on the door. It was very late. From the sounds of it, the bar was still lively, but the rest of the house was quiet. She had still been reading when she heard Milton's voice in the hall. She'd waited a while in case they'd roused anyone else before she'd left her room for their door. Having lived with these men for years now, she was less circumspect about the propriety of visiting their quarters than she might otherwise have been.

She put her finger to her lips when Rowland opened the door and slipped in. He'd removed his jacket and his tie was draped loose around his neck, but he was otherwise still dressed, as were Milton and Clyde. Not that it would have concerned Edna, but she was aware that they were not at *Woodlands House*, and she had no wish to upset Mrs. Harris.

"Ed," Rowland whispered, surprised she was still up. "What are you doing here?"

"I couldn't sleep," she said, taking the only chair in the room.

"Miss Brent's novel?" Rowland glanced at the manuscript in her hands.

Edna sighed. "I'm afraid so."

Milton took the sheaf of papers from her, reading the title aloud. "*My Brilliant Monkey*... less than inspiring. What's it like?"

Edna grimaced. "Oh Milt, it's terrible. Simply awful. That's why I'm here really." She regarded them all with her most becoming and appealing smile. "I was hoping you'd read it."

"Don't say anything, Rowly," Clyde said quickly. Then to Edna, "No."

Edna gazed straight at Rowland. "Please."

"Not a word, Rowly," Milton pushed in front of him. "Why would you want us to read it, Ed?"

"Sarah indicated she would like to talk about it tomorrow."

"With you, presumably, not us."

"But I thought you might be able to find something good about it. I can't just tell her it's awful!"

Milton flicked through the manuscript, his interest obviously piqued. "What exactly is so terrible about it?"

"Well, for one thing, the monkey's annoying, not brilliant at all."

"The title's easy enough to change."

"The characters all have ridiculous names."

"Exotic monikers have always been popular, Ed."

"The story rambles, I'm not sure it makes sense."

Milton exhaled. "For God's sake, Ed, I don't know what you think we can tell you."

Edna turned her smile back towards Rowland. "It's just that Rowly's so polite... I thought he might know how to phrase..."

Clyde laughed. "You want Rowly to help you with a courteous lie?"

Rowland took the manuscript from Milton. "I'll read it," he said, checking his watch. "It doesn't seem that long, I'm sure there's something praiseworthy about it."

Edna sprang out of her chair and hugged him. "Thank you, Rowly."

Milton shook his head. "You're shameless."

Rowland laughed. "It's all right. The monkey sounds rather intriguing." He thumbed through the pages. "I'll read it now. You'd better get back to your room, Ed. We haven't got time for scandal at the present."

15

NIBBLING AT THE PARKS

It is not surprising that the proposal to lease the corner of Hyde Park fronting on Elizabeth and Liverpool streets to a private concern which will adorn it with a buck jumping arena has already met with strong criticism.

There are many in Sydney who view with alarm the continual encroachments on the city's open spaces. Buck jumping shows are a most excellent form of entertainment, but they have their proper place, and that place is not a park which has been reserved in the middle of Sydney as a lung for the city and is an oasis in a desert of bricks and mortar where our citizens can take their pleasure. In this particular case it has been argued that the public will suffer no real prejudice.

The Sydney Morning Herald, 16 December 1920

The morning of the famous Rules Point Sports Day broke clear and cold. The frost was so thick that one might have mistaken it for snow. The cattlemen and the hotel staff were up before dawn preparing for the day's events. Breakfast was served in the dining room and as a buffet on the verandah to feed the men who were camped outside. Courses had been marked for the races and dozens of horses were being prepared in the vicinity of the hotel.

Rowland Sinclair was in his car discussing Sarah Brent's manuscript with Edna. Unfortunately, she had not been wrong in her original assessment of the work.

"Sarah's very excited about it," Edna said. "Apparently she believes crime fiction could be her genre."

"What did she write before?"

"I don't know... she's incognito, remember. She could be Agatha Christie for all we know."

Rowland's eyebrow arched dubiously. "That, I very much doubt."

"I'm glad you read it, Rowly," Edna confided. "I was really worried that I was missing something, that it was a work of literary genius but I was too obtuse to see it."

Rowland laughed. "You're far from obtuse, Ed."

"Do you think it'll be published?"

Rowland shrugged. "We're artists, Ed, what would we know about books?"

"So what should I tell her... should I just be honest?"

"Lord no! Lie as though your life depended on it!"

Edna looked relieved. It was not in her nature to be disingenuous, but neither did she want to hurt Sarah Brent.

Rowland smiled. "What's the worst that could happen? Some crazy publisher might decide to inflict it on the unsuspecting public, but that would hardly be your fault."

Edna giggled. "I suppose not."

Milton climbed into the car behind them. He shivered, rubbing his arms vigorously. "What are you two doing out here?" He noticed that Edna held the manuscript. "Oh that—you were right, Ed, it was dreadful."

"You read it?" she asked, surprised.

"Rowly read bits of it aloud."

"Why?"

"We wanted to know why he was laughing."

"We'd better get back," Rowland said a little guiltily. "We might have better luck finding news about Harry today."

Milton said nothing for a moment. "You don't think he was in Corryong then?"

Rowland rubbed the back of his neck. "I can't see Harry at a snake show."

"Why would Eichorn lie?"

"I don't know." Rowland turned to face the poet. "Harry always had a thing about snakes—he wouldn't approve of their being harassed for public entertainment."

Milton frowned slightly. "Are you sure, Rowly? Eichorn's story fits with what Moran was saying. Maybe your man Simpson just walked."

Rowland shook his head. "There's something wrong. Not quite sure what yet, but I'm going to find out."

Milton regarded him intently as he sat back. "Good enough. Let's go make some friends then."

———————————   ———————————

The horse races were run first. A course of about four furlongs had been marked out from Long Plain, finishing at Rules Point. Entry into the event required that each participant provide his own horse. The atmosphere was already one of a country fair. The gathering of stockmen was now diluted with spectators—the well-heeled holidaymakers from Caves House and locals—ladies and children, as well as men. Rowland found that having Edna in tow made the cattlemen quite friendly, but then, they were not interested in talking to him.

Clyde introduced Rowland to Lawrence Keenan, who managed the Long Plain Homestead. Keenan was an elderly gentleman who had a reputation for being willing to do anything for a price. He was a wily negotiator whose voice was none too quiet. He sized up the cut of both Rowland Sinclair and his suit, and decided the young man was not in need of a discount for the horses he wished to hire. Rowland was not concerned about the cost, but Clyde felt the need to intervene on principle. Aside from the issue of compensation, Keenan was unhappy with their plans to take Edna with them.

"The High Country is no place for women," he warned. "The huts ain't no gentrified country inn... all right for a bloke but it's not somewhere I'd be takin' my young lady! How's a pretty lass like this going to be sleepin' in a swag... in a camp full of men... it's just not right... not proper."

"Mr. Keenan!" Sarah Brent emerged suddenly onto the verandah in an apron, with a wooden spoon still in her hand. She pointed it at Lawrence Keenan. "Who, sir, are you to tell Miss Higgins what she can or cannot do? Who are you to curtail her freedom of movement simply because she is a woman? How dare you, sir! Miss Higgins is as entitled to the High Country as any of these gentlemen. Why should she be denied the glory of the mountains on the basis of her gender? For shame, sir! Miss Higgins shall make this excursion! Indeed I shall accompany her!" She fished a small purse from the pocket of her skirt and took some notes from within. She pressed them into Keenan's leathery hand.

"But Miss Brent..." Rowland started.

She held up her hand. "No, Mr. Sinclair, I have observed that you are a generous man, but I have always paid my own way." With that, she turned on her heel and returned to the kitchens.

Keenan folded the bills and placed them into the pocket of his dusty jacket. "My price has just gone up by two shillings a horse."

"What?" Clyde was outraged. "Why?"

"You boys are taking a bleedin' suffragette into a cattlemen's camp. To my reckonin' the horses are going to have to find their own way back." The old man laughed, but he maintained the inflated hire fee. "It's all about risk, boys. You're lucky I'm not insistin' you buy the nags. Those is my terms—take it or leave it."

"Done," Rowland said quickly, before Clyde could protest again. "You'll make sure we're equipped with everything we need?"

Keenan grinned. "I'll even throw in a shotgun." He jerked his head towards the kitchen. "You might need it."

"How the hell did that happen?" Clyde murmured, as Keenan moved on.

Rowland shook his head. "I don't know. Do you think he was serious about the gun?"

"Take yours in case he wasn't."

The buck jumping was staged in the large yard on the flat land beside the hotel. It was a popular event for both participants and spectators. The rules were quite simple: the entrant was required to remain on his mount for as long as possible and avoid being killed. So far that day everybody had managed to observe both rules to a greater or lesser extent.

Milton was leaning on the rail watching enthusiastically.

"What do you think, Rowly?" he asked, as a call was made for contestants. "Should we have a go?"

"Don't be an idiot, Milt. Rowly couldn't do that," Edna answered for him.

"Why not? He can ride a horse."

"Polo ponies, not wild horses. He'll break his neck."

Rowland looked out at the brumby which had just been led into the ring. It was a fine looking animal, well-proportioned with a glossy coat. It wasn't quite as large as the horses he was used to riding, but already its nostrils flared and its ears were back. He was mildly irritated that Edna assumed he'd come to grief, though she seemed quite content for Milton to enter the event. He removed his hat and his watch and handed both to the sculptress. "Hold on to these, will you, Ed?"

"Rowly you're not—" Edna turned to him alarmed.

Rowland smiled, aware that he was reacting a little childishly… but still, it was a matter of pride. He had ridden some bloody flighty polo ponies in his time—he knew how to stay on a horse.

Milton, too, was startled. He had not really expected Rowland to accept his challenge.

Clyde, who had always considered himself the most sensible of the three, rolled his eyes. Even so, he did not try to dissuade his friends.

Edna on the other hand was not so judicious. Unfortunately she succeeded only in setting their resolve to try their luck in the ring.

Rowland went first. The stockmen who watched him mount seemed more than a little amused that someone would attempt to ride in a three-piece suit. Admittedly, Rowland felt a little overdressed for the task at hand, but he was not inclined to change clothes for the few seconds he would be on the horse.

Lawrence Keenan was apparently the judge of the buck jumping events. He studied Rowland critically for a moment and called him a few names under his breath. "I don't do refunds, you know," he said. "You get yourself killed, them horses are still hired as far as I'm concerned. It won't be the first time I've collected payment from a dead man's pocket."

Rowland ignored him and listened to Clyde's last-minute advice. "Just watch your hand, Rowly. You want a good grip, but it's better to come off than break your hand trying to hold on."

Rowland nodded. Clyde's warning was that of a fellow artist. They needed their hands. He climbed up onto the rough stall. The mare was larger than the one he'd seen before. Her name was Gunpowder, but then he supposed that one would be unlikely to name a bronco Peaches.

"Good luck, Rowly."

The gate flung open. For a heartbeat there was nothing and then the mare exploded into the yard. She pig-rooted and bucked at least two dozen times in the ten seconds that Rowland managed to stay on. He came off in rather spectacular fashion, crashing into the fence at the end of a skid. Still, he landed well and most of the damage was done to his jacket. He dusted himself off as he straightened his tie. He was oddly exhilarated now that it was over, and in truth a little surprised that he had stayed on so long or ended up intact. He accepted the applause with a polite nod to the crowd.

The general opinion was that the toff from Sydney had done remarkably well, all things considered. Clyde was impressed, Edna relieved. Rowland climbed out of the yard to join them as Milton climbed into the stall.

The poet had removed his cream jacket and retied his cravat into a flamboyant silk kerchief.

"He might need his jacket," Rowland said, as he glanced at the torn shoulder of his own. He would have a tremendous bruise anyway. Shirtsleeves were unlikely to give Milton a great deal of protection.

The gate was opened. Milton's horse was more volatile than the last beast. It bucked and twisted as if it was trying to bite him. Rowland watched in a half-flinch expecting it to end brutally very soon. It didn't. The horse failed to throw Milton at all. Indeed the poet won the buck jumping.

Rowland was astounded and ecstatic, as was Clyde. Edna was happy but less surprised. "Milt was always entering the buck jumping at Hyde Park—he's quite good, isn't he?"

"Hyde Park? There was buck jumping in Hyde Park?"

"Every Sunday."

Milton's triumph and Rowland's respectable performance at the event had an additional unforeseen benefit. In the rounds of congratulatory drinks that followed, the stockmen seemed more willing to talk of Moran and Simpson.

Michael Schulz worked a lease out near the Currango Homestead. He was a squat man who, despite his name and a distinctly Eastern European accent, insisted that he was an Irishman. Since the war, it was not uncommon for those of German origin to pretend to be Swiss or Danish, but Rowland thought Irish was a bit optimistic. Regardless, Schulz was forthcoming about Moran.

"Dere was talk—desecration of da graves, fights, shenanigans of dat sort." He crossed himself. "Mine God! Dat was before Simpson. I hear on da wind dat he was trying to sort out Moran's crew."

"Have you heard what happened to him?" Rowland asked hopefully.

"Simpson? Whisked away by da little peoples as we say in de old country."

Admirably, Rowland managed not to laugh.

"Dat snake-handler says he was in Corryong," Schulz added.

Rowland nodded. "He told me."

"I'll tell yer dis for free, young'un." Schulz checked over his shoulder. "From what I hear of Moran and his boys, it would not make me surprised if your man Simpson is dead."

16

ON THE TRAIL TO YARRANGOBILLY

Two Girls and Three Horses on a 140-Mile Trek

Camping out on the open spaces and tethering the horses in the freezing wind was not at all a cheerful prospect. Then a house came into view just beyond the hut, and inquiries elicited the astonishing and delightfully welcome information that we were only two miles from Rules Point; our, as we imagined, still distant goal! Greatly elated, we pushed on in the gathering gloom till suddenly loomed up a gate labelled "Rules Point Hotel". Here, in spite of our outlandish appearance, we were hospitably received and obtained accommodation for ourselves and our steeds without question.

The Sydney Morning Herald,
Women's Supplement, March 1933

The Sports Day Ball at the Rules Point Guesthouse was a large and eclectic affair. There were at least a couple of hundred people in attendance. Many had made the trip up from as far as Adaminaby, Tumut and Batlow. The formality of dress varied. Some wore traditional ballroom attire, others were less extravagant, but even the saddlesore stockmen made some attempt to be more presentable.

Rowland unbuttoned the jacket of his dinner suit. The main festivities were being conducted in the garage and it was quite warm as the crowd milled and danced to a band of accordians, violins and a piano, which had been carted up from Caves House.

Milton and Edna were on the floor, foxtrotting in the arms of locals. Rowland hadn't been able to get near the sculptress since she had joined the dancers. Her dance card had filled quickly and, at times, the competition for her attention flared dangerously.

Clyde handed him a drink. Rowland spotted Moran making his way towards them. The stockman wore a jacket and tie and seemed to have groomed himself somewhat. He offered Rowland his hand. "Mr. Sinclair, sir, I hear you done well on Gunpowder this afternoon."

Rowland smiled. "I managed to hang on for a bit."

"Well that's better than many."

"We'll be collecting our horses early tomorrow, so we'll join up with you and the men as you ride past Long Plain Homestead."

Moran's face tensed. "So you're still set on coming out?"

"Yes, we are. In fact we'll be bringing Miss Higgins and Miss Brent with us."

"Yer joking, ain't you? You can't be bringin' women into a stockmen's camp. The boys ain't gonna put up with that."

Rowland's eyes darkened. "I'm not joking, Mr. Moran. Perhaps you'd better warn the men that the ladies will be joining us. You might also like to tell them that I will not hesitate to sack any man who gives any sort of offence to Miss Higgins or Miss Brent."

"But you can't…"

"I believe I can and I intend to."

Moran's mouth twisted as if it was all he could do not to swear at Rowland Sinclair. Perhaps it was, for he turned on his heel and stalked away in disgust.

Clyde sipped his beer as he stood beside Rowland. "He could be trouble, Rowly."

Rowland nodded, his eyes still flashing. "Mr. Moran has a hard time remembering that he works for me."

Clyde nudged him. "Wilfred would be proud. I might have to talk to Moran about joining a union."

Rowland looked startled for a moment, and then he laughed. It wasn't like him to be so high-handed, but Moran rubbed him the wrong way. "They'll probably get over this no women thing once they see Ed," he said wryly.

Clyde took another sip of beer. "True... but then there's Miss Brent."

"Mr. Sinclair! Mr. Sinclair, I'm so glad I found you, my word!"

Rowland turned to the red breathless face of Mrs. Harris.

"What can I do for you, Mrs. Harris?" he asked, offering her his arm in case she should faint.

"The Arnolds boy just rode up from Caves House." She clutched his arm, wheezing a little. "Your brother's been trying to reach you. I'm afraid there's some terrible emergency."

Rowland stiffened and took the note she held out to him. The message said only that there had been an accident and that Wilfred Sinclair needed to speak with his brother as a matter of urgency.

Rowland's voice was calm. "Thank you, Mrs. Harris." He ran his hand absently through his hair. "I'll drive down to Caves House and telephone Wil now." He didn't wait for her response.

"Would you please inform Miss Higgins and Mr. Isaacs of where we've gone?" Clyde called to Mrs. Harris as he followed Rowland out.

They wasted no time in getting to the car, but driving out of Rules Point proved to be a challenge as there were now many cars, and the odd horse-drawn vehicle, parked in rather haphazard and congested rows. Rowland engaged the supercharger as soon as he pulled onto the road and the Mercedes roared towards Caves House.

The carpark outside the hotel was all but empty. The headlamps of the Mercedes illuminated a black Chevrolet, but otherwise it appeared that all the guests had gone to Rules Point for the dance.

Rowland jumped out with the car idling, leaving Clyde to cut the engine once it had cooled. Rowland moved quickly towards the reception at the front of the building where he would find the manager and a telephone. He was worried. Wilfred was not predisposed to sending alarmist messages for no reason. The entrance stairs were badly lit and it was quite late. Rowland nearly ran into the man before he noticed him.

"Excuse me..."

The figure answered with a punch that sent Rowland to the bottom of the stairs. Two men were there to meet him. One winded him with a kick to the ribs while the other pressed the muzzle of a gun to his temple.

"Not a sound." The command was whispered directly into his ear as they dragged him roughly to his feet.

The figure from the top of the steps walked down and shone a torch into his face. Rowland blanched in the bright light. "You're coming with us, Sinclair. It'd be a lot less trouble to just shoot you, so don't tempt me."

"Who the hell are you?" Rowland doubled over as he took a fist beneath the ribs once again.

"You don't speak. Last warning." The man lit a cigarette and in the glow of the match Rowland glimpsed his face. He was fair. A telltale T-shaped scar on his cheek spoke of razor gangs, but he wasn't familiar. "Now we're going to get into my Chev like gentlemen, and we'll go for a little ride."

Rowland said nothing. The muzzle of the gun was now pressed into the arch of his back. He was still unsure what was going on, but it was clear he was in trouble. Instinctively he knew that getting into the car was something to be avoided at all costs.

They pushed him past the Mercedes toward the black Chevrolet. One of the men broke off to walk around the car to the driver's side. Rowland saw his chance. Feigning a stumble, he dropped away from the line of the gun. In what seemed like the same moment a sizeable rock was flung at the man holding the weapon. He reeled as it struck him in the head. There was a clatter as the gun was dropped and Rowland threw himself towards it. The horn of the Mercedes blasted repeatedly. Caves House stirred in response. Rowland struggled on the ground with two men, the third started the engine of the Chevrolet. A shot— and then the men were scrambling. Apparently neither had fired.

"Rowly, get down!" Clyde's voice. "I'll blow these bastards away." Another shot for good measure.

The wheels of the Chevrolet screeched and the two men abandoned their attempted abduction and jumped onto the running board as the car accelerated out of the driveway.

Clyde knelt beside Rowland, a revolver in his hand. "You all right, Rowly?"

Rowland rolled over gingerly and wiped the blood from his lip. "Is that my gun?"

"Yeah… you probably shouldn't keep it in the trunk, it's not all that secure."

Rowland coughed, still a little winded. "Lucky it was there though. Thanks, Clyde."

"Don't mention it, mate."

Clyde stood and offered Rowland his hand. By now people were spilling tentatively out of Caves House. Wilson, the manager, reached them first. Rowland told him briefly what had transpired and why they had come.

"There was no call from your brother, sir. I've been manning the office all evening."

Rowland was relieved. That, at least, was something. Kate and the boys were probably fine.

Wilson dropped the beam of his torch to the blood on Rowland's dress shirt. "Shall I call you a doctor, sir?"

"No thank you, Wilson. I'll be fine. I could use a drink though."

"Certainly, sir. Why don't you come inside, and we'll see if we can't find some ice for your jaw."

They proceeded inside where Wilson offered them brandy and spoke anxiously of calling the police. "I don't know what the senator's going to say about all this," he said. "One doesn't expect a respectable establishment to require the attendance of the police."

"There's probably no point in calling them now," Rowland suggested. "Report the incident in the morning—three men in a black Chevrolet. The boy who delivered the message to Rules Point, Arnolds I think, should be able to give them a description. I'll stop in at Kiandra and talk to them when I get back."

"We're still going to the camp?" Clyde asked, surprised. "Rowly, don't you think...?"

"We'll only be gone a few days, Clyde. It seems that they know I'm at Rules Point so it's probably not a good idea to stay there anyway."

Clyde snorted. "You're going to be a stubborn blue-blood about this, aren't you?"

"I believe I am."

"Well then, there's no point trying to make you see sense."

"Absolutely none."

Clyde exhaled, resigned. "You may be right. Those bastards look like they're from the city. They're unlikely to saddle up and follow us onto the plains... but maybe you should at least talk to the police before we go."

"Wilson can tell them everything I know."

Wilson agreed without hesitation, keen to avoid the attendance of the police at his hotel. The gunshots were bad enough, but luckily most of the guests were still at the Rules Point dance.

Rowland put down his brandy and checked his watch. "I might call *Oaklea* if I may, just to make sure..."

"Of course, Mr. Sinclair." Wilson hastily moved the telephone on his desk closer to Rowland. "I'll just leave you to it, sir."

Rowland spoke to the exchange telephonist, and booked a call to *Oaklea*. It was several minutes before they rang back and connected him. He spoke and then argued with Wilfred. Clyde left the room to smoke as the words became heated. Eventually the Sinclair brothers stopped arguing, and Rowland joined his friend in the foyer of Caves House.

"Wil didn't call—there wasn't any sort of accident, thank heavens. It seems as though it was just a ruse to get me out here on my own... I presume they didn't count on you."

"Did you tell Wilfred?"

Rowland nodded. "He overreacted of course—wants me to come back to *Oaklea* now." Rowland smiled. "I think he plans to call in the army."

"If anyone could..." Clyde muttered.

Rowland rubbed his brow thoughtfully. "We might be wise to tell Wilson and Mrs. Harris that we're heading back to Sydney, just in case these blokes make enquiries again."

"What about Sarah Brent?"

Rowland groaned. He'd forgotten about the writer. "I'll speak to her when we get back to Rules Point… explain…"

Clyde laughed and backed away. "You're on your own, mate."

Rowland's interview with Sarah Brent did not really go as well as he had hoped. For one thing, he had neglected to change his blood-splattered shirt before he went to find her. She was immediately suspicious.

"I must say that Aubrey would never have slunk back to Sydney like a whipped puppy over some minor altercation."

Rowland bristled at the reproach.

"I don't believe Wilfred would either. What are you not telling me, Mr. Sinclair?"

Rowland offered to reimburse her for the money she had already paid Keenan, whom he doubted would refund it.

"No," she said, folding her arms defiantly. "I don't accept for a moment that you are going back to Sydney, Mr. Sinclair. You are not changing your plans and nor will I be. I don't require you to tell me what trouble you're in—gambling debts I expect, I've seen the way you and your friends play cards—but I do intend to ride with you tomorrow, regardless."

He tried to change her mind.

Her mind was unchangeable.

In the end he gave up. Sarah Brent was tenacious if nothing else.

He returned to the garage as the musicians announced the last dance. Edna claimed him for the final waltz, demanding to know what had happened. Rowland told her of both the encounter at Caves House and Sarah Brent's insistence on riding out with them, as they cut across the dirt floor. The latter, he recounted somewhat ungraciously.

Edna laughed. "Poor Rowly." She frowned slightly as she ran her hand over the bloodstains on his shirt. "We're going to have to be more careful though. If Clyde hadn't been with you…"

"I've always been taught to be cautious," he murmured.

"But you haven't learned so well, darling."

He led her into a turn, smiling. "Keenan's giving us a shotgun, remember?"

17

ON THE LAND

FARM AND STATION
THE SNOW LEASES

It would appear that the Department of Lands is fully alive to the importance of preserving the snow belt for the use of stock owners generally in time of scarcity of feed, and that for some years past the interests of the public in this matter have been as closely watched as is possible under the existing circumstances.

The Sydney Morning Herald, 1914

Rowland waited by the Mercedes with Milton and Clyde. It was early and many of the cattlemen camped around the guesthouse were still sleeping off the previous evening's festivities. Clyde was busy under the hood, tightening and checking.

Michael Schulz was up early too, striding about the verandah singing some Irish folk ballad in his thick Germanic accent. Rowland watched him, pondering the cattleman's suggestion that Simpson could be dead. He tensed at the thought, suppressing it before it could take hold. He was worried though.

Milton nudged him. "What's wrong?" Rowland's anxiety had not escaped him. "Are you having second thoughts?"

"About what, Milt?"

"About carrying on as if we didn't know you were being hunted by some gang of thugs."

"No. I'm not particularly worried about that."

"One wonders why not?"

Rowland polished the chrome mascot of the Mercedes with the sleeve of his jacket. "They've already been to the Hydro Majestic and *Woodlands*. There's no reason to believe I'll be any safer in Sydney... Anyway, they seem more out of their element here than we are, and, regardless, I still have to find Harry."

"Simpson... so that's what you're fretting about. You think that joker Schulz could be right? That he's dead?"

Rowland didn't respond. He railed inwardly against Milton voicing his own unspoken fears.

"Leave it, Milt," Clyde said from under the hood. He straightened, wiping his hands on a rag. "Rowly's right. He's as safe up here as anywhere else—probably safer. If Simpson's found some kind of trouble, he'll need our help regardless of what half-cocked gang is trying to bag a Sinclair."

Milton studied Rowland thoughtfully. "Fair enough. Just don't go wandering off anywhere, will you, Rowly? I'd hate to miss a fight."

Edna and Sarah Brent emerged from the hotel. The writer lugged a large carpetbag. Edna left hers at the top of the stairs confident that one of the men she lived with would insist upon carrying it anyway. Rowland was the first to oblige. Milton tried to take Sarah's bag but she would have none of it, refusing in a manner that made the offer seem discourteous.

Rowland glanced admiringly at Edna. The sculptress occasionally wore overalls when she was working, but he'd never seen her in trousers before. The curves of her figure were definitely returning and the fitted breeches of Kate's riding habit suited her.

"You look pretty, Ed," he said quietly, as he lifted her bag into the trunk.

Edna looked at him nervously. "I feel a bit naked."

He smiled, amused that Edna should feel more naked when she was actually wearing clothes. She had always modelled for him without the slightest hint of self-consciousness. "Either way, you look pretty."

Sarah pushed between them and put her own bag into the trunk. The writer wore a long gathered skirt. Apparently she planned to ride side-saddle.

They piled into the Mercedes. Sarah Brent called Edna into the back seat so that they could discuss her manuscript on the ride out from Rules Point to Long Plain Homestead. Clyde and Milton both squeezed into the front with Rowland so that there would be plenty of room in the back for the writer and her extraordinary volume of hair.

Long Plain Homestead was well constructed. Some of the original shingles had been replaced with iron sheets. The roof was sharply pitched to prevent the accumulation of snow and its red brick chimneys were substantial. A lean-to beside the house was stacked to the roof with split logs, and the stables were larger than the homestead.

Rowland brought his car to a stop inside the stables. Keenan was already there, saddling horses. He'd allocated them strong animals, obviously bred for the mountains, and launched into instructions for the care of the steeds as soon as Rowland alighted from the car. A swag was secured behind each saddle as well as an extra blanket. Keenan had also equipped them with lanterns, ropes, canteens, soap and various other essentials. For each of these acts of consideration he charged Rowland an exorbitant premium. But he did throw in an old Enfield shotgun.

"She pulls to the right a little," Keenan warned, as he strapped the gun to the pack on the back of Clyde's horse. Rowland had already slipped Wildred's revolver into his own saddlebag.

"If you forget to secure the horses, they'll find their own way back and you'll have a long walk," Keenan continued brusquely. "And whatever you lose, you've bought."

"Understood," Rowland replied. "Now my car…"

"If you're wanting me to keep the cats off her," Keenan grumbled, "I'll not be responsible for what the bush rats do to your fancy upholstery."

Rowland glanced back at his beloved Mercedes in alarm. What the hell were bush rats?

"You look after the car, Laurie," Clyde growled. "Rowly's already funded your old age."

"You're getting a bit above yourself, Clyde." Keenan looked from Clyde to the car. "All right, I'll keep an eye on 'er… but you lot had better take care of me horses."

And so it was with some misgivings that Rowland left his car in Lawrence Keenan's reluctant care and rode out with the others. "She'll be right, Rowly." Clyde placed a reassuring hand on his shoulder. "Laurie's a cantankerous old bugger, but he's all right."

Moran and the three stockmen who had come across for the Sports Day rode through about a half hour later. Moran appeared to have forgotten his earlier hostility and was, if anything, congenial. He led an extra horse which carried provisions to replenish the camp's supplies. He was particularly conciliatory towards the ladies.

"Just let me know if you'd like to stop awhile, ladies," he said, smiling. "It's quite a ride. The Sinclair lease is one of the farthest from here, just before Blue Waterholes."

Sarah Brent sniffed. "You'll find, Mr. Moran, that Miss Higgins and I are more than capable of keeping up. I was born in the mountains, you know, and in the saddle when I was just months old."

The other stockmen Moran introduced as Jacob Crane, Bob Fisher and Clancy Glover. They were unsmiling men who spoke only when absolutely necessary, and even then the speech was terse and impatient as if the conversation was keeping them from some other matter of greater importance. Rowland spoke with them anyway. He started with Crane. "Did you work with Harry Simpson, Mr. Crane?"

Crane uttered a barely audible grunt that sounded vaguely affirmative.

"Do you have any thoughts on what happened to him?"

"He took off."

"And why would he have done that?"

Crane shrugged. "In their blood ain't it? Can't turn him into a white man just by makin' him boss... damn fool thing to do."

"Crane!" Moran brought his horse up alongside. "You may wanna remember that we all work for Mr. Sinclair."

Crane glowered at Rowland. "Didn't mean nothin', Mr. Sinclair."

Rowland shrugged it off. "Was he seen at all, afterwards?" He turned his head to Moran, remembering what Clyde's brother had told him. "The neighbouring lease belongs to O'Shea, doesn't it?"

Moran nodded warily.

"Did you ask him if he'd seen Simpson?"

"Never met O'Shea or his men. They keep to themselves."

Rowland's face did not betray him, did not reveal that he knew this to be untrue. Why was Moran hiding his association with O'Shea?

They stopped to water the horses at one of the small streams which networked the plain. Their canteens did not yet require refilling as the day's chill had kept thirst at bay. Many of the streams were just trickles, narrow enough to jump. Occasionally it was necessary to walk the horses through the cold water.

"Rowly, look!" Edna pointed excitedly. A lone young stallion appeared on the plain ahead. The muted sunlight glistened on its glossy black coat as it lifted its head, alert but unafraid. It studied them for a moment before turning and heading on, picking its way in a jagged line across the ground. Moran pulled up his horse.

"Bog," he said. "The brumbies know how to get through it, but we'll have to ride round. Could lose a horse if we get stuck." He turned his mount west and motioned them to follow. The detour took them on a wide berth around the boggy ground. They picked up the fence line again and rode along it to the gate and, in doing so, rejoined the trail. Sarah Brent rode beside Edna, explaining her book.

"But what made you choose a monkey, Sarah?" Edna asked. "Have you owned one yourself?"

"No, of course not," the writer replied. "The monkey, Percy, is the key to the underlying message of the novel. It symbolises the selfish frivolity of the upper classes. A victim of fashionable excess, taken from his natural environs to be paraded for the amusement of the idle rich, and yet the hero of this tale."

Edna bit her lower lip and nodded sagely. "Yes, of course. I suppose that's why they had to bring the monkey."

"Of course they had to bring the monkey!" Sarah replied. "Percy is a simian metaphor for the best and worst of humankind." The writer became quite fierce. "Mysteries, as a rule, have no claim on literary subtlety, but one does not need to lower one's intellectual standards simply because the genre has been underwritten in the past."

Rowland thought he'd better help Edna. He pulled up his horse till they caught up. "Miss Brent, I was hoping to have a word with you."

She looked at him intently. Her face softened. "About Aubrey?"

Rowland let his horse fall into step beside hers. "You seem to have known my brother much better than I did."

The writer sighed. "Perhaps. He had a prodigious talent, you know. I tried to guide it."

"Miss Higgins mentioned that. I didn't know he wrote."

"Oh yes." Sarah shook her head sadly. "He might have been great if he'd survived, and if he'd been willing to mix outside his comforts."

"Outside his comforts?" Rowland was a little puzzled.

"To test his character amongst the working classes—to truly understand people, one must walk in their shoes. I suggested he adopt a cover and go into service, but I'm afraid he did not take the idea seriously."

"And going into service would have…?"

"Given him a perspective outside the privileged one to which he had been born. Not all artists are born to struggle, Mr. Sinclair, but struggle we must if we are to truly unleash and then realise the potential of our talent."

"I see."

Milton laughed loudly from a little distance behind them. Whether his mirth was unrelated, or whether it was the idea of a Sinclair in service that amused him, was hard to determine.

"There are hardships other than poverty, Sarah," Edna said quietly.

Sarah Brent agreed. "Yes, there is of course gender, but being a woman is not something one can experience if one is not born to it."

Rowland said nothing. The conversation was getting dangerously close to the subject of gender equality once again.

The ageing writer looked sharply at Rowland. "You really had no idea that his muse was literary?"

"I was a child when he died. It was not something he confided in me."

"Yes, of course. It's a pity. You may have understood one another."

Rowland nodded. It was more than a pity.

"I believe I have one of Aubrey's manuscripts among my things in Sydney. He sent it to me for critique just before he enlisted."

Rowland looked at her, unsure of what to say.

Sarah paused in thought for a moment. "I could send it to you if you would like to have it."

Rowland cleared his throat. "Yes… I would like to have it… very much."

"I should have sent it to your parents when he died, I suppose, but I wasn't sure what Aubrey might have wanted, and I was abroad myself…"

"I'll have it copied and returned to you," Rowland offered. The manuscript had after all been entrusted to the writer.

"No, Mr. Sinclair, you send me the copy. Your family should have the original written in dear Aubrey's own hand. Your mother would find comfort in it, I'm sure."

Rowland's eyes clouded just faintly. Elisabeth Sinclair's mental health had never recovered from her middle son's death. Even now, she refused to accept it, preferring instead to forget the existence of Rowland so that she could call him "Aubrey". He was unsure what she'd do if faced with Aubrey's manuscript. In the end, "Thank you," was all he said.

18

Nothing else has its "TRIPLE HEALING" powers

It stops Pain ... It Cleanses ... It Heals

EICHORN'S AMAZING ANTISEPTIC

Eichorn's Antiseptic is the amazing prescription of August Eichorn. For 25 years it has proved positively the most remarkable healing remedy and strongest antiseptic known to science. It contains previously unknown herbal properties for neutralising toxins, or blood poisoning and all septic organisms, it even neutralises the venom of the most poisonous snakes, including death adders. Highly Concentrated. Used in Dilution. Eichorn's Antiseptic is most economical in use.

SPEEDY ACTION

Eichorn's Antiseptic is unequalled in the rapidity with which it heals. You positively feel it heal. From the moment you apply it, it stops the pain and begins to drive out all impurities. Use Eichorn's Antiseptic for all septic wounds, cuts, sores, grazes, for all treatment of poisonous bites, boils, ulcerated or septic throats, mouths or pyorrhea.

MAIL COUPON
FOR GENEROUS SAMPLE PACKAGE

"Healing in Every Drop"

Australian Women's Weekly, 1933

It was late afternoon by the time they first sighted the modest hut on the Sinclair lease. It stood, or leaned, beside a couple of very large boulders and an old snow gum which had seen better days. Originally built in the last decade, successive gangs of stockmen had added to the structure over the years. Named Rope's End, the hut was by no means as elaborate as its counterpart on Long Plain from which they had collected the horses. It was the most basic of buildings, constructed of split logs and ripple iron. There was a lean-to for firewood and another which housed saddles and equipment as well as a dozen cattle dogs on chains. The other four men who made up Moran's crew sat around a large fire pit outside the hut.

Moran and Rowland rode up first and dismounted.

Moran made the introductions. "These here are the Cassidy brothers: Joe, Blue, Andy and the big one's Lofty. Boys, this is Mr. Sinclair... he owns the lease."

The four men looked Rowland up and down for a moment and then laughed.

"Yeah, and I'm the king of bloody England," Joe Cassidy said, grinning.

Blue Cassidy removed his hat to expose a shock of citrus-coloured hair. He bowed to his brother. "Your majesty..."

"Fellas..." Moran started.

Joe Cassidy slapped him on the back. "Come off it, Ned, this bloke doesn't even look as fancy as that joker you brought out here with his snake bite potion." He looked at Rowland. "What are you selling, mate?"

Rowland was caught a little off guard. "Actually, I'm not..."

The rest of the party caught up and approached the hut. Joe looked up, squinting at Milton who had chosen to ride across Long

Plain in a green velvet jacket and crimson cravat. "Jesus, Mary and Joseph… you've brought the whole flaming gypsy caravan with you!"

Rowland looked back at his companions and sighed. Milton perched on his horse adjusting his cravat as if he were posing for some heroic painting; Edna was beautiful, but in Kate's riding habit she did look like she was embarking on a fox hunt; and Sarah Brent, riding side-saddle with greying wisps of her crowning glory blowing out on the wind. As a group they did conjure images of fortune tellers and crystal balls. He could see Joe Cassidy's point. Only Clyde looked vaguely like he belonged on Long Plain.

Rowland offered Joe Cassidy his hand. "Rowland Sinclair, Mr. Cassidy. I'll be happy to introduce the caravan once they dismount."

Cassidy looked at Moran who nodded slowly. Rowland's hand was extended. The stockman shook it reluctantly. His manner darkened. It seemed he may in fact have preferred it if Rowland had some snake oil to sell. His brothers likewise lost their good humour with the realisation that the man who owned the lease was among them.

Joe Cassidy did not ask what Rowland was doing on the plain and when he spoke to him next, his voice was surly and brittle. "You'll have to give us a minute to clean out the hut… weren't expectin' no visitors."

"Of course," Rowland replied evenly, as he surveyed the hard unkempt men before him. He was beginning to get an idea of the hostility Harry Simpson had faced as overseer. There was something going on here. Wilfred had sensed it; so obviously had Harry. They'd have to be careful.

Moran's men scrabbled around inside the hut. Milton grinned as they all heard the clink of bottles being collected amongst poorly restrained cursing. Rowland smiled too. He didn't expect there was much to do at Rope's End once the livestock had been seen to.

They led the horses down to the stream, which ran not far from the hut, and allowed them to drink as they waited for the stockmen to finish their housekeeping. Sarah Brent was in excellent spirits and chattered happily about the importance of the High Country in the identity of the nation.

On their return, Moran showed them inside the hut. Though it was basic, Rope's End was large. There were two rooms, but the opening between them was so wide that they might as well have been one. The walls had been lined with old newspapers to plug the gaps between the timbers, and the ceiling was a canopy of hessian sacks. The floor, also constructed of split logs, was uneven. A stone fireplace took up one entire wall. A mirror and a green enamel medicine cabinet were propped on its mantel behind a kerosene lamp and several bottles of Eichorn's Snakebite and Blood Poisoning Cure.

"I'm afraid the ladies won't find much by way of creature comforts here," Moran murmured.

"Don't be concerned, Mr. Moran—we won't be staying long," Rowland replied. "I just want to have a look around, see if I can't pick up Simpson's trail somehow."

Moran's eyes narrowed. "If you don't mind me sayin', Mr. Sinclair, I don't follow."

"What do you mean, Mr. Moran?"

"With respect, sir, I've worked for folks like the Sinclairs for years. They're lucky if they even know who works for them."

"Your point, Mr. Moran?"

"Why is it that you come out here personally to look for Simpson?" Moran flicked the bumper of his rolled cigarette onto the floor and stepped on it. "Makes a man wonder if it's because the Sinclairs trust Simpson, or because they don't."

"What exactly are you suggesting?" Rowland's voice was calm, almost casual, but his eyes flashed threateningly.

"See, I've gone after men myself, Mr. Sinclair. It was never to do 'em a good turn."

Rowland put his hands in his pockets as he stared hard at the stockman. Moran was serious. Shaking his head, Rowland looked away and laughed. "Believe me, Mr. Moran, there is no price on Harry Simpson's head."

Moran's lip curled. "Then what are you doing here? What's Simpson to you?"

Now the edge was apparent in Rowland's voice. "It doesn't really matter, does it? The fact is I'm here and I intend to find Harry Simpson."

Moran grunted. "It'll be dark soon," he said. "We might see about supper and settle on some sort of sleepin' arrangements." He walked out of the hut.

Rowland watched him go, still a little shocked by Moran's presumption. Clyde and Milton moved to stand by him.

"What do you think that was all about, Rowly?" Clyde asked.

"I don't know."

Milton spoke ominously. "You watch him, Rowly."

"Not just him," Rowland muttered, as he looked out of the open door to all the men in his employ.

Lofty Cassidy it seemed was the camp's cook. He set to work adding ingredients to a large camp oven which sat on the coals of the fire pit. Sarah Brent bombarded the stockman with suggestions and advice. Lofty grumbled sourly under his breath but otherwise tolerated her input.

The stockmen who had ridden in with them ate in sullen silence, and then busied themselves with the horses. Blue and Andy Cassidy were friendly to no-one but Edna, and to her, excessively so.

Edna found their attentions unsettling, but she tried to be pleasant in the face of their crude charm. There was something devious about these men. She was aware that Rowland was within arm's reach, watching her, though he seemed to be engrossed in whatever it was he was drawing. Milton also hovered nearby talking to Sarah Brent. Perhaps for these reasons she did not feel vulnerable.

"Would you care to take a stroll, Miss Higgins?" Blue Cassidy suggested. "The plain can be really pretty at sunset."

"I'm a little cold actually—I might stay near the fire."

"I could fetch you a blanket," Andy offered.

Blue laughed. "Only way you'd get a good sort in your blanket, Andy!"

Rowland looked up from his sketchbook. His eyes glinted angrily. But Edna smiled.

"Did you gentlemen work with Mr. Simpson?" she asked brightly. They were here to find Harry Simpson—perhaps she could help.

"Yeah, till he took off," Andy replied.

She leaned forward, her elbows on her knees, and whispered conspiratorially. "What was he like, really? I take it that Mr. Moran didn't like him."

Blue grinned, his gaze lingering below the sculptress' neckline. "Moran's used to being the boss... he don't like being told what he can't do."

"Oh." Edna's eyes widened as she looked up at Blue Cassidy. "What could Mr. Simpson want to stop him doing? Was it dangerous?"

Andy interrupted, clearly disgruntled that his brother was getting more attention. "Simpson just liked sticking his black nose into other people's affairs. That can be dangerous up here."

"Oh, I see."

"Course, you'll be safe with us, Miss Higgins." Blue winked at her. "But you'll want to stay real close."

"What do you think happened to Mr. Simpson?" Edna asked, looking about her nervously.

"Shot through," Andy said, moving a little closer. "Lot of places a man can get lost on the scrub leases... even if he didn't cross onto anybody else's land there's more than four thousand acres on the Sinclair lease for a man to disappear into."

"Simpson knew his way around the scrub, but I guess they do," Blue added. "I reckon the bludger's still here somewhere, waitin' till we've done all the work." Blue seemed incapable of lifting his eyes to Edna's face.

In the periphery of her vision Edna could see Rowland, ready to intervene.

"What exactly is it you gentlemen do out here?" she asked, glancing reassuringly at Rowland.

Blue got between Edna and his brother. "We look after Sinclair's... I mean *Mr.* Sinclair's cattle, and keep an eye on the bogs in case any get stuck. We brand any calves..."

Edna nodded encouragingly. "Is that difficult, poor creatures."

Andy laughed. "They get over it pretty quickly and your Mr. Sinclair wouldn't thank us if half his mob got mistook for the neighbour's cattle."

"We'll be beginning to round them up in a few days." Blue obviously felt the need to offer more information than his brother.

"And is that dangerous?"

Andy winked. "Naw, not really. We'll start putting salt on the ridges to call them out and then we'll round them up from the outer pastures into the closer ones. It can take a couple of months to get them all... then we work out whose cattle we've got—that's where the brands come in handy."

"You might want to stay for the muster, after Sinclair's headed back," Blue suggested. "We'd look after you." He put his arm around her. Edna stiffened. Andy also pushed in beside the sculptress. She removed his hand from her leg. He put it back.

Rowland stood. "Ed," he said, offering her his hand. "I believe Clyde's sorted out something in the hut for tonight. Shall we go and see if it's satisfactory?"

Edna took his hand gratefully and stood. "If you'll excuse me, gentlemen."

Blue Cassidy got to his feet, annoyed, and glowered at Rowland.

Rowland returned his gaze coldly. "Why don't you go ahead, Ed. I need to have a quick word with these gentlemen."

"Rowly..." Edna started, and then thinking better of it she turned and walked into the hut. Milton broke away from Sarah Brent and joined Rowland.

"Is there a problem, gentlemen?"

Andy stood at his brother's shoulder. "Problem's not ours, Sinclair."

Moran stepped into the circle. "What the hell are you boys playing at? We work for Mr. Sinclair." He shoved Blue Cassidy. "You two go make sure all the branding gear is ready for tomorrow. Fisher saw some cleanskins near Flannagan's Waterhole."

Still glaring murderously at Rowland, the Cassidy brothers retreated.

"They don't mean nothin', Mr. Sinclair," Moran muttered. "Been up here without a break for three long months, a man forgets his manners."

Rowland did not take his eyes off the Cassidys. "I meant what I said, Mr. Moran. I won't hesitate to sack any man whose manners I find wanting... regardless of how long he's been up here."

The other cattlemen watched on dourly. Rowland was aware he and his friends were outnumbered.

Sarah Brent stood by the hut's door beside Edna, her arms folded fiercely. Clyde stepped out.

For a while there was nothing as Rowland and Moran stood silently against each other.

Moran surrendered. "I'll speak to them, sir. You won't have any more trouble." He turned and walked towards Blue and Andy Cassidy.

"Come on, Rowly." Milton put a hand on his shoulder. "Let's go see how we're going to sleep tonight."

"With one eye open, I expect," Rowland murmured.

19

THE BOGONG HIGH PLAINS

AN UNEXPLORED PLAYGROUND

On Dungey's Track a few miles below the plateau there is a hut and there is another at the foot of Mount Fainter on the Tawonga Hack while at different parts of the plateau itself there are three huts. These huts are the property of the farmers who lease portions of the high plains as cattle runs but they are always available to travellers.

The Argus, 1926

Inside the hut, Clyde had sectioned off a corner of the second room with a blanket. "Ed and Miss Brent can sleep in there," he said. "We'll put our swags just outside."

Rowland glanced out the window as the last of the natural light was lost. He could see Moran and his crew gathered about the fire. He groaned, angry with himself. "I don't know what I was thinking bringing you ladies out here," he said. "I'd send you back to Rules Point now if it wasn't dark…"

Edna touched his arm. "Rowly, you're overreacting." She waited till he was looking at her. "They were just a little forward, that's all."

"It's not just that, Ed." He smiled. "I have no doubt you could have put Andy and Blue in their place, but to tell you the truth I'm not sure how long it'll be before they mutiny outright."

"Don't be ridiculous!" Sarah Brent lost patience. "We are not on the high seas, Mr. Sinclair. I know it's fashionable for Sydneysiders to regard the country as some uncivilised wilderness but you will find the stalwart people of the mountains are as law-abiding and reasonable as their city counterparts."

Rowland blinked. "I beg your pardon…"

"These men work for you. Treat them with a modicum of respect, acknowledge their worth as men of skill and endurance in this most rugged part of our great nation. Of course they'll be hostile if you come down here threatening to sack them. If you'd spent any time in service you would understand the inherent integrity of the working man."

"Miss Brent, perhaps you don't understand…"

"What I understand, Mr. Sinclair, is that you and Mr. Moran are carrying on like two young bulls in a paddock. It is tiresome to watch and quite preposterous on the eve of a muster! It's very late in the season to be testing your horns against the men who will bring your stock in."

Rowland stared at the writer in disbelief. Milton was trying not to laugh. Clyde had more sense than to get involved.

Edna spoke up. "Rowly doesn't really care about the mustering, Sarah—not really. He's looking for Mr. Simpson."

Sarah Brent's eyes narrowed. "Then why are you and Mr. Moran at odds?"

Rowland looked out at Moran arguing with the Cassidys. "I'm not sure, Miss Brent. Perhaps he doesn't want me to find Harry."

"So what do you plan to do?" Sarah Brent folded her arms again. "As far as I can tell, all you've been doing is putting people off-side."

Rowland's jaw tensed. He didn't want to fall out with Sarah Brent, but the woman was a shrew. "Do you have any suggestions, Miss Brent?" he asked.

"I do indeed. Suppose you speak to Mr. Moran and let him know that you are not here to review how he deals with the cattle. Let him get on with the mustering while you search for this Mr. Simpson of yours. Though why you'd think Simpson would linger here like some stray cat, I don't know."

Rowland leaned back against the wall, biting his lower lip pensively. "I think you and Edna should go back to Rules Point tomorrow. Clyde, would you mind escorting the ladies on their return?"

Clyde didn't have time to respond before Sarah Brent exploded in protest.

Edna simply said she wasn't going. Rowland toyed with the idea of insisting.

"Rowly," Milton caught his attention whilst Sarah was still loudly refusing to be dictated to by a man who was neither a relation nor had authority over her. Rowland followed Milton's gaze to the door. Moran was standing in the frame with his men behind him.

Sarah Brent halted her invective. Moran smiled broadly, his gold teeth gleaming in the light of the kerosene lamp.

"Mr. Sinclair," he said, stepping aside to allow Blue and Andy Cassidy forward. "These fellas have somethin' they wish to say."

The Cassidy brothers held their hats in their hands like errant children. "Miss Higgins," Andy started. "Me and Blue's sorry if we offended you earlier. We were outta line but we really didn't mean nothin'…" He lifted his head and said loudly, almost shouting. "We'd be grateful if you'd see fit to accept our apology."

Edna's eyes flickered just briefly to Rowland, before she smiled. "Of course, gentlemen. There was no harm done."

"Look Mr. Sinclair," Moran spoke up again. "We all seem to have got off on the wrong foot. The fellas were just a bit surprised to see you, is all. We're just tryin' to look after your mob the best we can."

Rowland replied carefully. "I appreciate that, Mr. Moran."

"The boys and me are riding out at first light tomorrow to put out the salt blocks." He smiled again as he looked around at the hut. "So the homestead will be all yours for a few days. We'll camp in the caves while we're working the boundary."

"I didn't know there were caves on the lease," Rowland said. "Are you sure they'll be adequate if the weather turns?"

"We'll be fine, Mr. Sinclair, and it'll give you gentlefolk a few days to enjoy the mountains without us ill-mannered cattlemen." He clouted Andy over the head with his hat as he said the last.

Rowland nodded. Perhaps he'd misjudged these men. God forbid Sarah Brent was right. "As long as we're not throwing you out, Mr. Moran."

"Not at all, Mr. Sinclair."

Rowland sighed. He tried appealling to this newfound goodwill. "Do you blokes have any idea what happened to Harry Simpson?"

There was a general mumbling and then Clancy Glover answered for them all. "Sorry, Mr. Sinclair—he just took off. Rode off and didn't come back." A chorus of agreement.

Rowland gave up. "Very well then." He checked his watch. It was still reasonably early. "What do you chaps do of an evening?"

"We put the Cassidys in frocks and we dance," Crane replied curtly.

Rowland met his eye. "As entertaining as that sounds, how about we play cards instead?"

Crane smiled faintly. "Do you mind if we drink?"

"Insist upon it."

20

THE WOMAN'S WORLD

WANDERING WITH PAINT BOX AND PALETTE

Art does not usually run in families unlike blue eyes or freckles, and there is a special interest in the remarkable talent of Miss Nora Heysen, daughter of South Australia's greatest artist. Her self-portrait, which has just won the Melrose portrait prize in the Society of Arts Federal exhibition, shows strong individuality of treatment. Miss Heysen studied for several years under Mr. P. Milliard Grey at the School of Fine Arts.

The Advertiser, 1933

The stockmen proved to be rowdy company. Once it was established that Rowland was not going to demand sobriety, Moran produced the bottles he had brought in from Rules Point, from behind a stack of firewood. The stockmen drank with a singular commitment. Apparently, it had been a fortnight since they had last restocked and the camp had been dry for several days. Perhaps it was fear of an extended prohibition that had made the stockmen so hostile to the presence of their employer.

They were, however, less than extraordinary card players, and Rowland and his companions had to be careful that they did not take every hand. Lubricated, the men became lively and even friendly.

Rowland and Clyde created a subtle buffer between Edna and the stockmen, in case the alcohol made them too forward once again. Sarah Brent retired behind the blanket with a kerosene lamp to write in her diary, a thick leather-bound journal in which she wrote in what appeared to be a shorthand code.

"We'll leave the magic stew behind for you tomorrow," Lofty Cassidy said congenially.

"The magic stew?"

"In the camp oven. Just add a few spuds and whatever's in the rabbit traps to it each day and you'll never reach the bottom... it's been feeding us all for weeks now." The stockman laughed at the look of horror on Rowland's face.

Milton nudged Rowland and grinned. "Close your mouth, Rowly, your silver spoon may fall out."

Clyde was similarly unperturbed. "The flavour really improves after a few days," he assured Rowland, who was now convinced they would all die of disease within the week.

True to their word, and despite a late night of drinking, the stockmen were up before dawn the next morning. Clyde and Rowland rose with them and helped saddle and pack horses by lantern. The dogs, now off their chains, ran excitedly amongst the steeds as they sensed the impending departure. With the first light of day, the men who worked the Sinclair snow lease rode into the hills.

Clyde turned to Rowland. "The Sinclair brand's a flying 's', isn't it, Rowly?"

Rowland nodded vaguely. "I think so."

"One of those horses—the black gelding they were using as a pack animal—has a Sinclair brand."

Rowland shrugged, wondering what his friend was getting at. "So they're using Sinclair horses—they do work for us."

Clyde frowned. "As a rule, stockmen have their own horses, Rowly... and none of the others are Sinclair animals—I checked."

"What's on your mind, Clyde?"

"Simpson would have ridden a Sinclair horse, wouldn't he?"

"You think that could be Harry's horse?" Rowland rubbed the back of his neck.

Clyde nodded. "It wouldn't be particularly surprising if..."

"If they hadn't said Harry had ridden away," Rowland finished for him.

Clyde nodded. "I should have said something before they left."

"It's probably fortunate you didn't. They're carrying guns."

"I noticed," Clyde frowned. A shotgun probably had its uses in protecting stock from wild dogs and dingoes, but the weapons he'd caught sight of were handguns.

They threw a couple more logs on the last glowing embers in the fire pit and stared silently at the growing flames.

"So what do you reckon, Rowly?" Clyde asked finally, as he took cigarette papers and a tin of tobacco from his breast pocket.

Rowland dragged at his hair. "Maybe there's a reasonable explanation for Harry's horse... Perhaps it threw him and came back to camp of its own accord."

"It's a horse not a pigeon, Rowly."

Rowland smiled. "Still."

Clyde sighed. "No—you're right."

"There is something going on though," Rowland said. "Do you think you could find your way to the next lease?"

Clyde nodded, lighting his cigarette on the fire. "It shouldn't be too hard. Why?"

"Thought we might go and speak to the men working O'Shea's—they may have seen Harry or know something."

Clyde drew on his cigarette. "Not a bad idea. O'Shea's Hut isn't that far from here, maybe an hour or so on horseback... if we can get Milt up."

Rowland looked back towards Rope's End. It was silent. The others were obviously not yet awake. He checked his watch—it had only just gone past six. "Let them sleep," he said. "We can be back before midday." He took his sketchbook out of his jacket and proceeded to scribble a note.

Clyde yawned. "I'll get the horses ready then." He glanced at the camp oven which still hung over the fire pit. "You're sure you don't want some breakfast before we go?"

Rowland grimaced. "No."

O'Shea's Hut was situated in a long valley, sheltered from the winds by sharp rises on either side and conveniently near a small stream on which a water wheel had been constructed. It was not quite a homestead but it was a great deal less rustic than Rope's End. There were two chimneys on the hut—a large flue of stone which identified the fireplace and a second smaller chimney. The lean-tos were well stocked with firewood, bags of flour, alcohol, and other supplies. Stockyards and cattle runs had also been erected near the hut, but they were currently empty. A freshly slaughtered beast was hanging by a chain from the branch of an old stringy bark.

"These blokes are well set up," Clyde murmured, as they rode up.

Rowland agreed. "It does seem rather more civilised than Rope's End."

There were only two men in the hut, the others having ridden out to check on the cattle. Rowland introduced himself and Clyde, and

183

O'Shea's men cautiously invited them in and offered them a drink. The inside of the hut was also well appointed. A sturdy table for dining; a cast iron, potbellied stove, as well as the fire; and an Astor radiola, apparently powered by the waterwheel.

"Lou Merrick, Mr. Sinclair." The solid, bearded stockman shook Rowland's hand vigorously. "Me mate's Hans Iverson."

"Pleased to make your acquaintance, Mr. Merrick. Mr. Iverson." Rowland greeted each man in turn.

"Sinclair? Say, you're not the fella who buck jumped in his wedding suit?"

Iverson looked Rowland up and down and concluded that he was indeed. His face creased with amusement. "Would have made it easy to lay you out, I guess."

"Lay me out?"

Merrick grinned. "Most folks figured they'd be burying you after the buck jumping."

Clyde chuckled.

"You were at Rules Point I take it?" Rowland smiled.

"Naw, but word travels fast up here. What can we do you for?"

"I seem to have lost one of my men, Mr. Merrick. I was hoping that you might have seen him."

"Simpson."

"Yes."

"We heard he'd done a runner. That snake fella, Eichorn, reckons he saw Simpson in Corryong."

"Did you run into Simpson while he was out here?" Clyde asked.

"We don't really do much socialising."

Rowland smiled again. For some reason an image of the Cassidy brothers in evening gowns came too easily to mind.

"That's probably a good thing, Rowly," Clyde said, settling into an easychair with his coffee. "If your crew saw this place they'd start to think the Sinclairs weren't doing the right thing by them."

Rowland nodded. "It's certainly what I'd be thinking."

Merrick seemed gratified. "Mr. O'Shea used to muster his own cattle once, and he ain't forgotten. We don't see him no more, of course, but he insists that the men are looked after proper... makes 'em loyal. You wouldn't find any of my boys wandering off the job."

"Indeed." Rowland gave no sign of his annoyance with the widespread insistence that Simpson had walked away.

"So how many head are you carrying up here?" Clyde asked with a sideways glance at Rowland.

Merrick smiled smugly. "Two thousand."

"Blimey—how big's the lease?"

"A thousand acres, give or take."

They talked for a while longer of cattle and feed, and other aspects of animal husbandry which Clyde seemed to understand much better than Rowland. In time Merrick checked his watch pointedly, and spoke of the dog fence that he intended to work on that day. Hint taken, they thanked Merrick and Iverson for their hospitality and remounted for the ride back to Rope's End.

"Rowly, how big's your lease?" Clyde asked as they rode.

"About four thousand acres I believe."

Clyde was surprised. "How'd you manage that? I thought there were limits."

"I didn't manage, Wilfred did. The Sinclair holding is, so I'm told, made up of a number of leases. Wilfred applied for the extra land in my name to get around the restrictions."

"You know, Rowly," Clyde continued thoughtfully, "Moran said last night that they expected to count out less than a thousand Sinclair cattle in the muster."

Rowland nodded, remembering the conversation vaguely. "Maybe that's what Wil meant about the numbers being off..."

They rode in silence for a few minutes.

"So what now, Rowly?" Clyde asked finally.

Rowland shook his head. "I don't know. Other than this supposed sighting in Corryong, Harry seems to have bloody well disappeared." He stared towards the horizon clearly frustrated. "Perhaps we should be asking after him in Corryong."

Clyde frowned. He didn't for a minute think Rowland was serious about looking for Simpson in Corryong, but they weren't having much luck here.

Perhaps because they were both unsure of what to do next, their conversation turned instead to other matters. As always when he was in need of distraction, Rowland's mind went to art. Clyde's thoughts were quick to follow and soon they were deep into a discussion of Nora Heysen, whose first solo exhibition had caused a sensation in Sydney that year.

"Nora could win the Archibald one day." Rowland had met the young South Australian briefly. They had a common love of portraiture, although Rowland had a preference for nudes.

"She is good," Clyde agreed, thinking appreciatively of her work. Nora Heysen was barely more than twenty and yet it was already clear that she was within that tiny circle of artists who could achieve greatness. To Clyde's mind, Rowland Sinclair was similarly talented, though possibly not driven enough to ever join the artistic elite.

"Are you planning on finishing your painting for the classical figures exhibition?" Clyde's voice was painstakingly casual. "The one of Miss Martinelli?"

Rowland hadn't thought of the model in some time. "Only if I don't have to use her again."

"It's hard to finish a piece like that from memory," Clyde mumbled, "and it was coming along so well."

Rowland's brow rose. "You think I should get Rosalina Martinelli to pose for me again? Clyde... she's impossible."

Clyde reddened, and smiled self-consciously. "We all have to suffer for our art, Rowly."

"Not that much." For a time neither said a word.

"Have you forgotten all the weeping and praying?" Rowland asked finally.

"You can't hold a moral upbringing against her, Rowly."

"Why not? It's damned inconvenient."

Clyde shrugged. "I'm just saying, she's rather pretty."

Rowland stared at him. "Why don't you ask her to model for you then?"

"I'm not really interested in her as a model." Clyde sighed, coming clean at last.

Rowland laughed. "All the more reason to ask her to model for you, I should think."

Clyde looked ahead. "That would be highly unprofessional, Rowly." He smiled. "Besides, I think I'd rather be the shoulder she cries on."

Removing his hat, Rowland wiped his brow with his forearm. "She does do rather a lot of that, Clyde old man." He shook his head in disbelief. Clyde had always been the most level-headed of them. "Are you sure? You might find her moral upbringing more inconvenient than I did."

Clyde sighed again. "Quite possibly. But Cupid's arrows don't always fly straight."

"Cupid's arrows? Good Lord, you sound like Milt!"

Clyde looked startled. "You won't mention this to Milt, will you? He'd never let me..."

"No, I won't tell him."

"And you'll re-hire Miss Martinelli?"

"Falling in love with models is rather a bad idea, Clyde."

"She won't be my model."

Rowland groaned. "She's Catholic at least. That should make your mother happy."

Clyde grinned. "Thanks Rowly. You're a mate."

"So it seems."

Clyde's romantic ambitions thus sorted, the conversation moved to more technical subjects. Rowland had been experimenting with the palette knife over the summer. The resultant work was softer and more textured. It suited his style and he was quite intrigued with its possibilities. Clyde was committed to his brushes, insisting that he had no desire to become a plasterer.

It was in the midst of this good-natured debate that they first noticed the smoke.

21

BURNS AND SCALDS

———◆———

In burns of the first degree pain is most quickly relieved by an application of bicarbonate of soda, made into a paste with a little water, laid thickly on the skin, and kept in place by a sterile piece of flannel or cotton cloth. Healing may be hastened by an application of picric acid, for first aid use, or of the tincture of the chloride of iron.

The treatment of a burn of the second degree consists in the application of melted paraffin with thin sheets of cotton. Before this is done the blisters must be opened, the fluid being allowed to run away, but without removing the outer layer of skin. The application is to be renewed every day, or every second day as it becomes loosened.

A burn of the third degree, and even one of the second, if extensive, calls for management by a doctor, for general as well as local treatment is necessary in such cases.

Gippsland Times, 1930

"What the devil?" Rowland stood in the saddle and squinted towards the smoke. It was clearly more than the output of the fire pit.

Clyde kicked his horse into a gallop. Rowland followed suit. The smoke thickened, a billowing column churning skyward. Rope's End came into view. It was ablaze.

The horses baulked but Clyde and Rowland urged them on and brought them up to the burning hut in a cloud of dust and panic.

"Rowly!" Edna screamed from near the door.

Rowland slipped off his mount and ran to her. He seized Edna in his arms, forgetting himself in his relief. It was short-lived.

"Rowly, Milt's still in there."

"Mr. Isaacs! Mr. Isaacs!" Sarah Brent shouted into the window. It was impossible to see anything through the smoke.

Rowland released Edna. They didn't waste any further time. Clyde gulped air and entered the hut bent low as the flames engulfed the roof. Rowland dived in after him. The room was black with smoke. Rowland stumbled first on the body facedown in the middle of the floor.

"Clyde!" He kept one hand on the body and reached for Clyde with the other. A beam crashed down somewhere in the hut. Rowland could hear Edna scream outside. The heat was intense, it seemed to suck the air from their lungs. There was no time for anything but a blind frantic lunge for the door, dragging the body between them. They pulled Milton clear of the hut, and collapsed beside him, coughing black soot and choking for clean air.

Edna knelt beside Milton. She rolled him over, calling his name. Sarah Brent loosened the unconscious poet's cravat. Clyde was still coughing. Rowland was on his knees, gasping.

Sarah Brent took charge. She held Milton's head in the crook of her arm and dribbled water from a canteen onto his blistered lips. At first, nothing, but she persisted. Eventually, wondrously, Milton gagged and spluttered, and finally he swore.

Edna smiled faintly, reassured by the spontaneous profanity. She passed the canteen to Clyde and Rowland, concerned now for them.

They watched, bewildered, as Rope's End burned to the ground. The fire did not spread—the area around the hut was too bare to provide passage away from its source. In time, the roar of the flames subsided and Rowland was able to make his hoarse, scorched voice heard. "What happened?"

"A log rolled out of the fireplace and caught." Edna stared at the remains of the hut. "Milt went back in with a blanket to try and put it out."

Milton winced as Sarah Brent poured water over the burns on his left hand and wrist. "I knocked over one of the bottles of Eichorn's Snakebite Cure that were on the mantel," he rasped. "Bloody thing exploded." He brought his good hand gingerly to the back of his head. "I must've knocked myself out when I fell."

Clyde raised himself onto his elbows. "That was a close shave, Milt."

Rowland nodded. "Next time just let the place burn."

"Well, it did anyway," Sarah Brent said curtly, tearing some of the fabric from her voluminous skirt to make bandages.

Rowland dragged himself to his feet and offered his hand to Clyde. "If you ladies can take care of Milt, Clyde and I had better go and catch the horses." He spotted the two saddled animals not far away. "Then we'll work out what to do."

⸻ ⸻

As it turned out, Clyde and Rowland were able to retrieve only four of the five horses they had hired from Lawrence Keenan. They took those animals down to the creek for watering before tethering them to a tree.

They returned to find Milton sitting up, demanding the return of his cravat.

Rowland put down the pail of water he had brought up from the creek and sat on a log.

"How's Milt?" he asked Sarah Brent, because she seemed to know what she was doing.

"He should be seen by a doctor as soon as possible," she replied, wrapping strips of soaked cloth around the poet's blistered hand.

"Can he ride?"

"I'm fine," Milton muttered, straightening.

"The burns will probably be more painful in a while," Sarah Brent said, frowning. "But he should be able to stay on a horse."

"We're down one horse," Clyde said. "And it's too long a ride for one horse to take two of us."

"Mr. Isaacs needs to see a doctor as soon as possible." Sarah was insistent.

"What if we do this?" Rowland glanced from the horses to his companions. "Clyde, you and Miss Brent ride back to Rules Point with Milt. Ed and I will take the other horse and ride for O'Shea's. It's just over an hour away. I'm sure they'll give us shelter for the night."

"Shouldn't you send Ed back?" Clyde asked. "I could stay with you."

Rowland shook his head. "The weight of the two of us would be too hard on the horse. There isn't much of Ed at the moment." He glanced at Sarah Brent and continued hesitantly, fully expecting to cause the writer offence. "I'd be happier knowing you were escorting Milton and Miss Brent... just in case."

The writer bristled momentarily, but she said nothing.

Rowland moved on quickly.

"Once you get back to Rules Point, send someone back to us with an extra horse, just in case O'Shea's men don't have one spare."

Clyde nodded. He could see the sense of Rowland's plan. He checked the position of the sun. "Fair enough. If we move quickly, we'll get most of the way before dark. We don't want to be stuck out overnight without swags."

"We're lucky the saddles weren't in the hut." Rowland walked over to his horse and pulled his riding coat from the pack behind the saddle. He'd worn it that morning so it had survived the fire. The day wasn't yet too cold, but the weather in the mountains was highly localised and temperamental.

"Take this," he said, pushing the riding coat into the saddlebag of Milton's horse. Sarah Brent seemed to have a shawl but Milton's overcoat had obviously been in the hut.

"What about you and Ed?" Milton protested.

"We don't have as far to go."

Rowland and Clyde saddled and checked the horses, and refilled the canteens, while Sarah Brent and Edna tried to protect Milton's injuries for the journey. For the moment the poet did not seem too bad, but he was unusually quiet.

"Look, Clyde," Rowland watched the poet, anxiously, "as soon as you've made sure Milt's all right, would you get in touch with your brothers?"

"Why?"

"I need some men I can trust. They'd know the locals. I want a dozen men up here to look for Harry. I'll pay whatever wages they want."

Clyde snorted. It was clear Rowland hadn't made the Sinclair fortune. "Okay. I'll send word to Jim. I'm sure he knows a few blokes who would be glad of a job. What about Moran's crew?"

"I haven't decided if I need to sack them yet, but I don't trust them to look for Harry."

Clyde nodded. "Fair enough." He glanced back at the smouldering hut. "They're going to get a surprise when they come back."

"That won't be for a few days. Hopefully by then we'll have sorted this jolly mess out."

They helped Milton into the saddle, and tethered his horse to Clyde's. The poet's hand was too painful to grip the reins properly.

Edna said goodbye a little tearfully. "You look after Milt," she entreated Clyde. "I'm not sure he should be riding."

"I'll be all right," the poet said slowly. "I won the buck jumping, remember?"

22

CATTLE BRANDS

———◆———

SINGLETON

The stock inspector, Mr. G. R. Freeman, has reported that a circular has been received, proposing to alter the position of brands on large stock, especially of cattle. The proposal originated with the Tanners and Leather Association, who pointed out that there was a loss in the value of hides to the amount of £100,000. He was of the opinion that if the branding were altered, and an increased price for hides given, not one penny would go into the pockets of either the breeders or fatteners of cattle. There was not the least doubt that the best place to brand a beast was on the cheek, but this could be only done when a calf. When cattle were branded high on the body it was much easier for an owner to pick out his cattle when looking through a mob.

The Sydney Morning Herald, 1912

Edna sat rather forlornly on the log bench as Clyde, Milton and Sarah Brent rode from sight.

Rowland sat beside her. "He'll be all right, Ed. Milt'll dine out on this for years."

"I hope so." Edna sighed. "At least Sarah is with him... she worked in a hospital during the Great War."

Rowland was comforted by the reminder.

"She was just an orderly… but still, she might have picked up a thing or two…"

Rowland looked down and laughed. "I'm sure she did."

Edna studied him critically. She pulled a few flakes of ash from his hair. "If we're going visiting, perhaps we'd better wander down to the creek and clean ourselves up a bit."

Rowland glanced at the sculptress. Her creamy skin was streaked and her hair stood out in every direction. Even so, she caused the breath to catch in his throat. "You look fine, Ed."

She patted his knee. "You look like a chimney sweep."

And so they paused to make themselves presentable. The stream water was clear as glass, but icy, and Rowland was reminded of his fondness for hot and cold plumbing. Still he was grateful to wash the sticky smoke residue from his face and neck. His suit had seen better days, but they were not calling on the king.

Rowland wondered briefly if Moran and his men had spotted the smoke. He supposed it would depend on where exactly they were. He had been quite surprised when they had returned to work, having expected Moran's crew to try harder to persuade him to abandon his search.

Edna somehow emerged from fifteen minutes of streamside grooming looking entirely kempt, if a little windswept. "After the Hydro Majestic, I never thought I'd miss hot baths again," she admitted, rubbing her arms against the creeping cold. Kate's riding habit was the height of chic, or it had been when Edna had first put it on, but it was not really made for the highland chill.

Rowland mounted and sat well back in the saddle so there would be room for Edna in front of him. He pulled her up and put his arms around her to hold the reins. In that way he protected her a little from the wind.

The ride to O'Shea's Hut was slow going. They stopped often, conscious that carrying two adults would test the endurance of any horse, but the trail was not unpleasant and Edna and Rowland had never found it difficult to be in each other's company. The way was relatively flat, though the trail wound with the erratic paths of the mountain streams. On occasion they came across small mobs of cattle sleek on the grasses of Long Plain. Once they spotted brumbies. The wild horses roamed the High Country and had never known farrier or stable, blacksmith or brush, and yet they were as handsome as any horse Rowland had seen.

As much as he tried to ignore it, Rowland was very aware of Edna as they rode—on the saddle before him she may as well have been in his arms. But he was a gentleman, and he kept his mind on the task at hand. Still, he was conscious of having to do so.

They were still out of sight of O'Shea's Hut when they heard the cattle—the strident lowing of beasts being handled. For some reason Rowland reined in their horse.

"What's wrong, Rowly?" Edna could feel his body tensing behind hers.

"I don't know. Probably nothing." Merrick hadn't mentioned that they were bringing cattle into the yards. It was too early to do so—there was still at least two months before the snow season—and Rowland distinctly recalled Merrick talking about spending the day working on a dog-proof fence. "Ed, would you mind terribly if we walked up the hillside a bit and came down behind those trees?" He pointed out the route.

"Whatever for?"

"Well, if we go that way, I can have a look at what they're doing before we ride in. It's probably nothing, but I'd rather like to check."

She sighed and leaned back against him. "Okay... sleuth all you like, as long as someone feeds us soon. I'm starving."

Rowland smiled. "Sorry, it won't take long. I just have this feeling."

He took the horse off the trail and into the scrub. The undergrowth was not particularly thick and so it was not a difficult path despite being steep in places. As they got closer, they dismounted and led the animal instead. Rowland stopped at a spot where they could see down into O'Shea's Hut and its surrounds. There were at least sixty head in the yards. Large healthy beasts, with gleaming hides. The cattle were being pushed into the series of roughly constructed yards. A fire roared in a pit beside a rudimentary crush. Several men, on horseback and on foot, went about their business.

Rowland cursed.

"What is it, Rowly?" Edna asked, whispering already.

Rowland pointed. "That's Moran, and there's Lofty. I'm not sure but I think those men could be the Cassidys."

"But what are they doing here?"

"I have no idea." He tied the horse to a tree. "I'm just going to get a bit closer and see what they're up to."

"Okay, let's go."

"Maybe you should stay here."

"Why?"

"Well, you could always go for help if this turns out to be a bad idea."

Edna shook her head. "I haven't a clue how to get out of here, Rowly. I'd get hopelessly lost and die of exposure... or starvation, or..."

"All right, but we're just going to have a look... just so we know if we need to get out of here." He stroked the horse's muzzle. "Won't be long, old girl."

Quietly, without any sign to the sculptress, he slipped his hand into his saddlebag and removed his revolver. Edna didn't like guns. There was no need for her to know he had one in his pocket.

They made their way carefully down towards the hut, emerging from the scrub behind the yards. Crouched low, they were unseen and unnoticed. Rowland followed the perimeter of the yards to the runs into which the cattle were being herded. At the end of the run was a single small pen, within which the cattle were being contained one at a time. Ropes were used to hobble the animal and keep it still. Moran and Joe Cassidy stood by the fire pit with Merrick.

Merrick was shouting at Blue Cassidy who sullenly flung a branding iron back into the coals. "We're going to have to shoot that one you bloody moron! I told you to be careful... if it's not exactly in the right spot it'll be obvious what we're doing!"

"Settle down, Lou." Joe Cassidy came to his brother's defence. "There're plenty of bloody cows."

Rowland looked carefully at the cattle in the run. They had already been branded—a flying 's'—the Sinclair brand. He watched as Blue Cassidy tried again. The stockman took the glowing iron from the fire and approached the rump of the cow which had been put into the holding pen. Blue raised the iron and brought it down quickly, burning directly over the old brand with a simple red hot circle. The animal bellowed and kicked.

Edna could see Rowland's jaw harden. The dark blue of his eyes glinted furiously as he gazed at the beast Blue Cassidy had just branded. She grabbed his hand to get his attention.

"What are they doing?" she whispered.

"They're amending the brand, placing an 'o' over the flying 's'," he replied tightly. "It turns the Sinclair brand into O'Shea's."

"They're cattle stealing?" Edna said, shocked.

"I believe that's what people call it."

Edna watched in dismay as the rebranding continued. Rowland now looked more disgusted than anything else.

"Rowly, what are we going to do?"

He turned back towards her, his face grim. "Dropping in is probably out of the question," he said. "We're going to have to get out of here and hope like hell that the poor bloody horse doesn't die of exhaustion before we find shelter for the night."

Edna nodded. It would be dark within a couple of hours but they really didn't have any other option.

A sudden crack exploded over the noise of cattle and men and echoed through the valley. Edna tried to suppress a scream but she didn't quite manage it. Rowland barely flinched—from where he was, he could see Joe Cassidy with the stockwhip. Only Moran seemed to hear Edna's cry and alone moved to investigate.

"Ed, go now!" Rowland whispered. "I'll be right behind you."

Realising she'd exposed them, Edna did as he asked. Rowland took the gun from his pocket and flicked the safety. He pushed himself back against the rail, still crouching as he waited for Moran to come around the run. He didn't wait long.

Moran caught sight of Edna as she darted away from the yards, scrambling towards the scrub. Before he could raise a shout he felt the hard, cold muzzle of a gun in his ribs. Rowland Sinclair's voice was in his ear. "I'd stop right there, Mr. Moran."

Moran froze. "The boys will mow you down as soon as you get off the first shot, Sinclair."

"I'd just worry about that first shot if I were you."

"Drop the gun, Sinclair." Blue Cassidy emerged with a pistol.

Rowland eyed the gun. He decided to call the stockman's bluff. "I think you're more likely to miss than I am, Cassidy," he said, poking his own revolver into Moran's back.

"Blue..." Moran started nervously.

A scream and Edna's furious cursing from the scrub. The sculptress had been caught.

"Let her go!" Rowland demanded, keeping his gun on Moran.

"Drop the gun, Sinclair, or we'll brand her like one of your flaming cows."

Rowland wasn't sure if they were serious. He couldn't, wouldn't, take the risk... and he wasn't about to shoot a man in the back anyway. Slowly, Rowland pulled the gun away from Moran and tossed it to the ground. "Don't hurt her."

Moran turned and punched him. As Rowland reeled back against the rail, Moran picked up the gun he had dropped. Andy Cassidy dragged Edna, kicking and screaming, back to the yard.

"What the hell are you doing here, Sinclair?" Moran demanded.

"I could ask you the same thing."

Lou Merrick turned on Moran. He swore at him for a while, until Moran lost patience and threatened to shoot him.

"I thought you took care of this," Merrick spat. "What happened to your blokes from the city?"

"I don't know," Moran replied. "Just shut up and let me think." He moved back to Rowland. "Where are the rest of your people, Sinclair? The old witch and the ponce with the neckscarf?"

Rowland said nothing.

"Don't make me hurt the girl, Sinclair, because believe me, I will... or perhaps you'd like to see your brand on her pretty little rump."

"I sent them back down to Rules Point," Rowland replied, glancing at Edna.

"Why?"

"Rope's End burnt down."

"Why didn't you and the girl go with them?"

"We lost a horse. We thought we could borrow another from the chaps at O'Shea's."

"Bloody terrific!" Merrick exploded. "Their friends will be here looking for them in a couple of days."

Moran remained calm. "They won't find them." He motioned to the Cassidys. "Tie them up and put them on horses. Tell Lofty to bring the forge."

Clyde reined in his horse, motioning Milton and Sarah Brent to continue along the rough road. The Chevy Capitol was well and truly bogged, all four of its wheels embedded in the mud, up to the axle. Three men stood around the radiator arguing. They were clearly glad to see him. Clyde didn't dismount.

"You fellas a bit stuck?" he called.

"Can you pull us out?"

Clyde squinted at the man. Flashy pin-striped suit, white hat, brogue shoes now covered in mud. Clearly from the city. Nobody who was a local, or even had the advice of a local, would even consider bringing a motor car out here.

"Where are you blokes headed?"

"Bloody nowhere at the moment. You gonna pull us out or not?"

"I think you're too far gone," Clyde said carefully. "It'll take more than a horse to pull the Chevy out. We have to get back... we'll send someone for you with a truck, or a pair of bullocks."

The man swore.

Clyde moved his horse on warily. "We're only an hour or so from Long Plain Homestead, it won't take long." He kicked his steed into a trot before the man had an opportunity to insist. Milton's horse was pulled along and Sarah Brent urged her own to keep up.

They were half a mile down the track before Clyde slowed.

"What the hell?" Milton asked, wincing. The jarring pace had been hard on his injured hand. "What's going on, Clyde? We could have got them out if we'd hooked up all the horses. Twenty minutes and..."

"Indeed, Mr. Jones. Your reluctance to give aid to a stranded traveller is nothing less than discourteous and contrary to the tradition of the country!" Sarah Brent was not impressed. "I trust you had a good reason for being so rude."

Clyde looked anxiously back up the road. "Those are the blokes that jumped Rowly at Caves House." He scowled at the sun, now nearly one with the western horizon. "We'd better get moving," he said. "They're stuck for the moment but I want to get back to Rowly before some more courteous stockman pulls them out."

23

THE NORTHERN GOLDFIELDS

The Chinese have finished exhuming the bodies of their countrymen, or rather those they intend to take up at the present time, and have left our graveyard in a most disgraceful state. I visited it today, and found six graves left open, with the piles of earth upheaved alongside. The graves, or rather large holes (for they have been re-opened to twice the size) are half full of water, and in some a number of gin bottles are floating alongside the rags taken from the coffins.

Maitland Mercury, 1928

Rowland and Edna had been on horseback for an hour or so, their hands bound in front of them as Moran and Andy Cassidy led their mounts. They were following the faintest of trails which picked through trees into the O'Shea lease. A ravine appeared unexpectedly in a heavily wooded area. The stream was fast moving and the walls of the valley which led down to it were steep and rocky.

Edna caught Rowland's eye and smiled briefly. She wanted him to know that she was all right. They hadn't hurt her. They had been rougher with Rowland, of course, but even so... She hoped it meant that the stockmen didn't intend to kill them.

Lofty Cassidy had galloped ahead with Clancy Glover, and so when they came upon the rough camp at the bottom of the ravine, there was already a fire blazing under the breath of the bellows. The shadows were lengthening and it was cold, but there was still light.

The area appeared to have been prospected at one time. Wooden sluices and races were visible in abandoned disrepair. The only vegetation in the cleared camp was a half-dead tree growing quite near the stream, around which was a long thick chain. The chain appeared to disappear into the valley wall.

Moran pulled on it. "Get out here, Jackie. You've got visitors."

For a moment there was nothing and Moran pulled again. "Get out here!"

Edna watched as a man emerged from what must have been a cave in the ravine wall. He was a black man, large—taller even than Rowland but broad and solid. His waist was generous and it was only the sheer breadth of his shoulders that caused his torso to taper. He walked slowly, hampered by the iron attached to his ankle. Stopping before Rowland's horse, he raised his face. An untrimmed beard hid his jaw but it was hard to miss the intense blue of his eyes, a cobalt gaze so like the one that Edna had known for years.

"Well, here's your man, Sinclair." Blue Cassidy reached over and shoved Rowland hard.

With his hands bound in front of him, Rowland was unable to right himself and fell out of the saddle, hitting the earth with an ungainly thud.

Simpson reacted angrily. "Leave the kid alone, you bastards!"

"Mind your mouth, Simpson!"

Rowland rose to his knees. "It's okay, Harry."

Simpson helped him stand. "Bloody oath... *gagamin*... what're you doing here?"

Rowland smiled, relieved to find Harry Simpson, but embarrassed to be doing so as a prisoner himself. "Glad you're not dead, Harry."

"We haven't time for flaming reunions," Moran snapped. "Shackle them and let's get out of here."

"What... even the girl?"

"Of course the bloody girl, unless you're willing to shoot her."

Apparently they were not, and so Lofty Cassidy got to work heating iron to shackle them to the tree alongside Simpson. Lofty was an efficient smith and the process did not take long. Edna did not struggle. It did not seem wise in the presence of red hot metal.

Rowland simmered silently, furious—the way Andy Cassidy looked at Edna made him uneasy. And so he did not resist as he was chained to a tree like a dog.

Once they had all been shackled, Rowland was searched and divested of his wallet and his pocket knife. Blue Cassidy also found the artist's notebook in his jacket's inside pocket. He flicked through the pages slowly.

"Hey, you're not a bad drawer, Sinclair. Bloody hell!" He whistled and glanced at Edna as he found some old sketches Rowland had made for the painting of a nude. Rowland tried to snatch the notebook back but Blue jerked it away gleefully and continued turning the pages. "Oi, Boss, look at this... it's you."

Moran strode over impatiently and studied the sketches Rowland had made of him after their first meeting. He tore them out. "I'm flattered Sinclair, but I had better hold onto these."

Blue Cassidy tore out the sketches of Edna and stuffed them under his shirt. "It'll keep me warm," he said, laughing as he threw the dishevelled notebook back at Rowland.

"Rowly..." Edna watched him smoulder. "Just let him have them," she whispered.

Lofty cut the ropes which bound Edna and Rowland's hands. "The chains are long enough to let you into the cave, and to the stream if you need to drink," he said.

Glover flung a hessian sack onto the ground. "There's enough tucker in there for a couple of days. One of us will be back when it runs out." He grinned. "Couldn't let the boss starve, could we?"

Rowland glowered at him in return.

Andy Cassidy sniggered and walked over to nudge Rowland. "Cheer up, Sinclair." He nodded at Edna and winked. "It'd be right cosy if there wasn't three of you... still she might..."

That was too much for Rowland. He punched Andy in the mouth.

Moran and Blue Cassidy stepped in. Lofty dragged his brother to his feet.

Seizing Rowland by the throat, Blue raised his other fist. "Why I ought to..."

Harry Simpson grabbed the stockman's arm. "Leave him be," he growled.

Blue Cassidy responded by swinging at Simpson. Rowland started after Cassidy and Glover jumped into the fray.

For a moment it seemed that shackled or not, there would be an all-in fight, and then Moran pulled Blue and Glover away. "We haven't got time for this. Just get on your bloody horses and let's get outta here."

Blue swore at Rowland, but he mounted. Moran's men rode out of the ravine just ahead of the last light.

Rowland watched them go, still fuming.

Harry Simpson sighed as he spat blood and gingerly touched his split lip. "So, what are you doing here, Rowly?"

"Can't you tell? I'm rescuing you."

Simpson laughed and clipped Rowland playfully on the side of the head. He left his large hand on Rowland's shoulder.

Edna looked on quietly, intrigued, unaware that she was shivering. Rowland took off his own jacket and placed it around her shoulders as he introduced Harry Simpson to the sculptress.

"Delighted to meet you, Miss Higgins," Simpson said, taking the hand she offered him. "Though I'm real sorry you've been dragged into this... this unfortunate mess."

"I'm very pleased to know you, Mr. Simpson." Edna gazed thoughtfully into the familiar blue of his eyes. "Rowly's been rather worried about you."

"Has he just?" Simpson pulled at the long chain which secured them all to the tree. "What say we get into the cave? It's not posh, and it's crawling with swallows among other things, but it's warmer than out here."

"Capital," Rowland said, somewhat unenthusiastically. He squatted to test the chain. "How strong's this chain, Harry?"

Simpson shook his head. "I'm still here."

They walked the few yards to the valley wall. Edna and Rowland had been shackled along the same length of chain that secured Simpson. There were several yards of chain between them and enough length overall to allow them all to enter the cave without losing slack. The entrance to the cave was narrow and steep, and they had to slip into it in single file. It opened into a large cavern. Edna found Rowland's arm as they stumbled. The darkness was close, oppressive. The only light came from the glowing embers of a fire which Simpson stoked and coaxed into a brighter flame. There was sufficient draught to prevent the cave being filled with smoke so there must have been openings further up. In a while their eyes adjusted a little and they could make out the cave's interior.

The cavern was not empty. Its walls were lined with baskets and boxes, a few hessian sacks, some waggas and swags. Edna gasped as her eyes fell upon a stack of what looked like coffins.

Simpson looked up from the fire. "Oh yes, sorry, I should have warned you. Moran's gang's been using this place to store things."

"Coffins?"

"They're not for us," Simpson assured her. "The Cassidys have been digging up Chinese graves near the old goldfields."

"Whatever for?"

"Some people say the Chinamen bury their gold with their dead."

"So they've been digging people up?" Rowland was horrified.

"Afraid so. They got all these from the ravine… apparently there were a whole bunch of Chinamen prospecting out here at one time."

Edna gulped. "Are the bones…?"

"Try not to think about it," Simpson advised.

Rowland rubbed his brow. "What the hell aren't these chaps up to?"

"You know about the cattle stealing then?"

Rowland nodded. "Are they on O'Shea's payroll?"

"Can't prove it, but why else would they brand our cattle as O'Shea's?"

"So this is all about stealing cattle?" Edna sat on a stump which had been placed close to the fire and rummaged through the sack that Glover had left them. She extracted a tin of Arnott's biscuits.

Simpson shook his head. "They're just filling in time with the rebranding. They're treasure hunting."

"They're what?" Rowland asked, from where he was poking around among the boxes cluttering the wall.

"I've checked those, Rowly," Simpson said. "There's nothing in there that'll help us break these chains."

"What treasure, Mr. Simpson?" Edna asked.

Simpson grinned. "You met Clancy Glover?"

Edna nodded.

"Well it seems Clancy had a great uncle or something who rode with Ben Hall."

"Ben Hall, the bushranger?" Edna asked through a mouthful of milk arrowroot biscuit. She passed the tin to Simpson.

"Apparently." Simpson helped himself to a handful of biscuits. "Rowly, there really isn't anything there… Anyway the story goes that Glover's uncle hid the proceeds of the Eugowra stagecoach robbery in one of the caves near Blue Waterholes."

"But Blue Waterholes is miles from here." Rowland was still rummaging through boxes.

"That's the interesting bit. Glover's stash has never been found… Clancy reckons he's got some family secret, that the gold was never at Blue Waterholes but out here. They've been hunting through every cave in the area the whole time they've supposedly been looking after the Sinclair herd."

"So they don't plan to kill us?" Edna said, taking another biscuit.

"No, they just want us out of the way till they find this gold. They're thugs, but probably not murderers."

"Comforting," Rowland murmured, as he began to check the baskets.

"Rowly, no!" Simpson dropped the tin of biscuits and leaped up. The chain snapped taut and he was stopped short. Edna was pulled off her stump. She heard Rowland curse and looked up to see him slamming down the lid of a large cylindrical basket.

Simpson unsnagged the chain and launched himself at Rowland and the basket, forgetting entirely that they were both connected to Edna who found herself on the cave floor. Simpson refastened the strap that secured the lid. "Damn it Rowly, I told you to leave this stuff alone!"

Rowland leaned back against the cave wall. His right hand was clasped over his upper left arm.

"Did it get you? Did it get you, Rowly?"

"Yes."

24

SNAKEBITES

HOW THEY SHOULD BE TREATED

To prevent circulation of the poison the blood circulation at the bite should be stopped at once if such a course is possible. This is done by applying a ligature at some point between the bite and the heart. It is a good plan to carry a length of about two feet of strong and fairly thick cord for use as a ligature. The bite should be thoroughly scarified by making a series of incisions an eighth of an inch or so deep across the punctures made by the fangs. The ligature on the limb will prevent extensive bleeding and what bleeding occurs will be useful in that it will carry some of the poison out of the wound. When the bite has been thoroughly scarified, permanganate of potash should be poured into the hand and rubbed well into the scarified wound. If permanganate of potash is not available the bite should be cut right out. This is done by pinching up the site of the punctures with the forefinger and thumb and severing the fold of tissue drawn up with sharp knife or razor. The wound should be then thoroughly scarified to induce bleeding and an attempt should be made to draw out the poison by sucking it with the mouth. The poison can usually be swallowed in small quantities without ill effects but it should be borne in mind that it may enter the bloodstream and cause injury if the person treating the bite has cracks or pores on the mouth or bleeding or unhealthy gums.

The Argus, 1931

Simpson acted quickly. He brought Rowland back to the fire and sat him down.

"Do you know which one it was?" he asked.

"You mean to say there's more than one?"

"Eichorn pays the Cassidys to collect snakes for his show... there's at least half a dozen in there."

"Well how the hell am I supposed to know which one bit me?"

"Give me your tie, *gagamin*."

Rowland removed his tie and handed it over without question.

Simpson ripped the sleeve from Rowland's left arm. The puncture marks were clearly visible on the biceps. Securing a large knot in the tie, he wrapped it around above the puncture wound, and reefed it tight. Then he slipped a thick twig under the tie and twisted it even tighter. Rowland winced, but didn't protest. He knew what snakebites meant.

Edna, having righted herself, knelt before him watching Simpson anxiously. Her eyes were large, distinctly panicked.

"I need something sharp," Simpson said, casting his eyes around the cave.

"They took my pocketknife," Rowland muttered.

"What about a pen? Or reading glasses?"

Edna reached into her pocket and removed a small Bakelite compact. Flipping it open, she slid out the mirror and handed it to Harry Simpson.

He nodded approvingly, and pressed it firmly against one of the fireside stones until it snapped into two jagged pieces. "Righto, Rowly, this might hurt."

"Might?"

"Just try not to move." Simpson clamped one of his large hands just above Rowland's elbow to hold the arm still and tried to incise the wound as quickly as he could. The fragment of mirror was not the ideal instrument for the purpose and the cuts were neither as clean nor as quick as they might have been. He had to try several times to ensure he had sliced deep enough.

"Bloody hell!" Rowland gasped.

"Sorry, Rowly." Simpson put down the mirror. "I'm afraid it's not over yet, mate. I've got to suck out the poison."

"You can't," Rowland said through gritted teeth.

"Got to be done, mate... I'll try to..."

"No, Harry. You can't suck out poison with a split lip." Rowland pulled his arm away. "You might as well stick your head into that jolly basket."

Simpson realised he was right. "Can you reach it yourself?"

"No, it's too far round." Rowland looked at Edna. Already he was having trouble focusing, but she seemed very pale. Her teeth were chattering. Whether or not it was from the cold was hard to tell. "Ed...?"

She nodded uncertainly. "I don't know how to..."

Simpson patted her shoulder. "Just place your mouth over the wound and suck out as much blood as you can—try not to swallow any."

Edna shivered, feeling nauseous after having watched Simpson incise the bite. But she didn't waste any time. She put her mouth over the wound and tried to draw the blood.

Rowland recoiled sharply and struggled to pull his arm away. He contained a profanity and groaned.

Edna shrunk back, her lips and chin dripping with his blood.

"Come on Rowly, give her a chance."

"She bit me!" he managed to get out.

"Oh God, Rowly, I'm so sorry." The sculptress was close to tears.

Simpson examined Rowland's arm. It was bleeding profusely. In her panic the sculptress had indeed bitten him... rather hard by the looks of it. Her teeth had cut deeper than Simpson had been able to with the mirror.

"Unconventional," he said, smiling kindly at the distraught Edna, "but I think it might have helped."

"Helped?" Rowland choked, as blood ran freely from the wound and down his arm.

"The blood will take the poison with it," Simpson said firmly.

Edna wiped the back of her hand across her tears, smearing blood over her face in the process. "I'm sorry, Rowly, I didn't..."

Rowland took her hand, regretting now that he hadn't been more stoic when she'd bitten him. His head throbbed.

Simpson stood, moving carefully so the chain didn't snag again. He took a bottle from a crate against the wall and pulled the cork out with his teeth.

"Believe it or not, I know people who swear by this," he said, returning to Rowland with the bottle of Eichorn's Snakebite and Blood Poisoning Cure.

Rowland sniffed the open bottle. It smelled of whisky, capsicum and eucalyptus.

"I'm tempted to let you take a swig of this first," Simpson murmured.

Rowland looked at the bottle dubiously. "Smells like something I'd clean my brushes with."

"Ready?" Simpson asked.

"Does it matter?"

"Guess not. If you're going to hold onto her hand," he warned, nodding at Edna, "be careful not to break it."

"You're hilarious." But Rowland released the sculptress' hand, just in case. She moved closer and wrapped her arms around him instead.

Simpson gripped Rowland's arm at the elbow again and gradually emptied the bottle over the wound.

To Rowland, Simpson could well have been pouring sulphuric acid. He was aware of nothing but the searing pain, the faint smell of Edna's rose perfume and the way she trembled as she held him.

When the bottle was empty, Simpson tried to stem the blood, using the shirtsleeve he'd removed earlier and a strip which he tore from a blanket.

Edna pressed a canteen of water to Rowland's lips while Simpson rolled out a swag.

"I'd put you closer to the fire, Rowly," Simpson said apologetically, "but I'm afraid you'll go up."

Rowland nodded, remembering vaguely the part Eichorn's snakebite cure had played in the incineration of Rope's End. His headache was getting worse and the fire seemed very bright. He fell back onto the swag and closed his eyes for a moment. Edna's hand pushed the hair back from his forehead. Her voice sounded far away.

"Good Lord, he's burning up."

Simpson's voice was calm. "We only need to worry if it was *warralang*... the brown snake."

"And if it was?"

Simpson hesitated and then answered honestly. "If it was, then his odds are still even."

"Even?" Edna choked. "You mean he could die?"

"Browns are nasty, but Rowly's a grown man." Simpson soaked another piece of blanket with water from the canteen. He handed the compress to Edna. "I've known men to survive... a couple of dogs too."

"Oh God." Edna's eyes welled and she looked away as she tried to control her tears.

"Hey," Simpson said gently. "It may not have been the brown. The others will make him sick for a while but…"

Edna wiped Rowland's brow with the wet cloth. She didn't trust herself to speak. Rowland seemed to be deteriorating so quickly. "So what do we do?" she asked finally.

"We'll just try to keep him comfortable—I'm afraid there's not much else we can do."

Rowland opened his eyes. "I can hear you, you know," he said weakly. "I'm not dying—Harry's overreacting."

"This might teach you to stop poking around where I've told you not to," Simpson said, moving to check the tourniquet. "I suppose some things never change…"

Rowland winced as the tie was adjusted. "You'll remove that before my arm drops off, won't you?"

"Stop complaining, you've got two."

Edna wiped the perspiration from his forehead once again. "You should try to sleep, Rowly."

Rowland looked up at the sculptress, the perfect contours of her face streaked with blood and tears. He reached up and wiped some of the drying red from her chin. "You're going to give me nightmares."

Simpson laughed. He handed another wet cloth to Edna. "Here, use this. There's the stream but none of us will be able to get out of this cave until Rowly can walk." He glanced at the leg irons.

Edna cleaned her face, while Simpson hung a billy over the fire. Her compact now gone, she had no idea if she'd successfully removed the gore.

Simpson grinned. "If you don't mind me saying, Miss Higgins, you're a very pretty girl without all the blood."

Edna smiled, stroking Rowland's hair absently. "Thank you, I don't usually wear red."

Simpson chuckled, handing her a tin cup of black tea. "Don't you worry too much, Miss Higgins," he said. "Rowly'll get through this…" He glanced at Rowland who seemed to have fallen asleep. "He was a tough little kid… didn't say much, but game for anything."

Edna looked up. Rowland rarely spoke about his childhood.

"Were you born on *Oaklea*, Mr. Simpson?"

He shook his head. "Not quite. My mother went away with the women when her time came but she brought me back to *Oaklea* pretty much straightaway. I grew up there. It's always been my home."

"You called Rowly *gaga… gagamin*."

Simpson didn't look up. "It's Wiradjuri. My mother was a Wiradjuri woman. She couldn't give me much, but she did give me language."

"What does it mean?"

Simpson giggled. A rich child-like chortle. It was both startling and endearing. "You know, Rowly used to think I was swearing at him." He shook his head still laughing. "I didn't realise till his pony threw him and he called it a useless bloody *gagamin*."

Edna couldn't help but smile at the obvious warmth of the memory. "You weren't swearing at him, then?"

"No, I wasn't."

Edna stopped pressing him. Clearly Simpson did not want to tell her what the word meant. She sensed that it represented something important and personal to both men. Rowland would tell her if she asked him, but she wouldn't ask him. She didn't need to.

"Did you and Rowly play together as children?" she said instead.

Simpson was plainly happy with the change of subject. "Afraid not. I'm a good ten years older than Rowly. I knocked about with Wil and Aubrey some. Rowly was just a bit of a kid, always wanting to tag along. We spent most of our time trying to get rid of him. That was all before the war, of course."

"Yes, the war." Edna stared into the fire. "I guess that changed everything... even for the Sinclairs."

Simpson nodded. "Especially for the Sinclairs."

"What was Aubrey Sinclair like, Mr. Simpson?"

Simpson smiled faintly. "He looked exactly like Rowly... like him in other ways too." He scratched his beard, and gazed at Rowland sadly for a while. "Aubrey was more noticeable, didn't play his cards as close."

"You miss him?" Edna said softly.

Simpson was unperturbed by her directness. "Yes, he was the kind of bloke that's missed."

"He was a writer," Edna said, picturing the young man who'd been lost to the world with his talents still secret.

Simpson looked surprised.

"You didn't know?"

"No, I just didn't know Rowly did. He's never mentioned it before."

"He only just found out." Edna put down the wet cloth with which she had been cooling Rowland's face and neck, and wrapped her arms about her knees. "It must have been awful for them when the telegram came." She remembered how the sight of the boy on his bicycle had become an object of terror in those years. Edna had known the boy who delivered the telegrams in her street; he had drunk himself to death in the twenties.

"I don't know, really. We were all serving. Rowly was the only one still around... poor kid. Mrs. Sinclair took it hard."

Edna nodded. She had met Rowland's mother and witnessed her inability to acknowledge her youngest son's existence. "My poor Rowly." Her voice was almost a whisper. "How horrible for him. *Oaklea* must have been such a desperately lonely house for a little boy on his own."

Simpson shrugged. "I've never been in the big house… but I don't s'pose it was a good place back then."

"Well, at least Rowly had his father," Edna said without conviction. Henry Sinclair had died before she had ever met Rowland, and she knew him only through the severe portrait which glowered sternly from the wall at *Woodlands*.

"Don't think the Boss took it much better than Rowly's mother," Simpson said, almost to himself, as he leaned back against a swag. "He was a hard man anyways. I reckon Rowly fought his own kind of war back here."

Edna put her hand on Rowland's, overcome by an impulse to protect him. But of course the war was a long time ago—Rowland was a man now. He mumbled restlessly in fevered sleep. She wiped his face with the cloth again. She had never thought Rowland secretive, but she realised there were many things he didn't talk about.

Simpson studied her. "If you don't mind me asking, Miss Higgins, are you the young lady who shot Rowly?"

"Yes." Edna frowned. "I didn't mean to," she added.

Simpson's eyes twinkled. "I figured that. Wil mentioned Rowly was keeping some interesting company."

Edna sighed. "Mr. Sinclair doesn't like us, I think."

Simpson's dark brow rose. "He doesn't approve of you… that's an entirely different thing."

Edna liked Harry Simpson very much. His relationship with the Sinclair brothers, though unusual, was unforced and natural, as was their loyalty to each other. The stockman had a certain unflappable peacefulness about his manner that was reassuring under the circumstances. As the hours passed and Rowland became more fevered, she needed that.

Edna stirred. The fire had burned down a little but it still cast a warm inconstant light on the cave walls. A deep, rhythmic rumble told her that Simpson too had dropped off. She was aware that the ground was hard but she was not particularly uncomfortable. Quietly, she brought herself to her knees, looking first to Rowland.

His eyes were open, bright and confused. He had thrown off the blanket; his hair was visibly wet with perspiration.

"Rowly," Edna whispered as she leaned over him. He was hot to touch.

"Ed?" He tried to sit up.

She stopped him, pushing him back down gently.

"What are you doing here?" he asked vaguely.

"Where else would I be?" She brushed the hair back from his forehead. "Do you remember what happened, Rowly?"

"What is wrong with your face?" he said, putting his fingers to a remnant smear of blood on her cheek.

"You don't want to know."

"Are you hurt?"

"No."

Edna was aware that her face was moving closer to his but it was not something she could stop. Rowland's chest was hot beneath her hand and she could feel the rapid beat of his heart.

His hand moved from her cheek to the back of her neck and he pulled her into him. The first kiss was gentle, almost reverent, as if she were made of the finest glass. The kiss of a man who worshipped her. The second was different, passionate and demanding. He drew her down strongly, insistently, his hand entwined in her hair. The kiss of a man who wanted her.

Edna pulled back, startled by both the intensity of the kiss, and the depth of her response. The closeness of it… how badly she wanted to stay, just to lie against him with her heart pressed against his. Quietly. Forever. For a second she looked at Rowland from the edge of complete surrender… and then the familiar fear—she couldn't do this without losing herself, and she would not. Instinctively she resisted.

Rowland would not let her go. His eyes were glazed. He pulled her back and kissed her again. She struggled. "Rowly, no!" She tried to writhe out of his grip. It tightened.

"Whoa, Rowly, what are you doing?" Simpson grabbed Rowland's arm and forced it away.

It was only then that Edna noticed Rowland was shaking. Within seconds he was convulsing. She watched in horror as Simpson forced a wad of cloth between Rowland's teeth and held him down. Rowland's eyes rolled back as his muscles spasmed. The chain jangled as the fit took hold. Despite his substantial bulk, Simpson battled to restrain Rowland.

Then finally it was finished.

Simpson removed the cloth. Rowland's body was limp, exhausted by the seizure.

Edna watched, unable to move, horrified by what she had allowed to happen, terrified by what had followed.

"Are you all right, Miss Higgins?"

She nodded, sobbing now. "I'm fine."

"If I thought Rowly knew what he was doing I'd… are you sure you're all right?"

"It wasn't Rowly's fault."

"I saw what he was doing, Miss Higgins. If he remembers it, he'll be mortified... and bloody sorry."

"I know, but it wasn't his fault." She moved back to Rowland's side, wiping at her tears with her sleeve. "Is he going to... is he...?" Edna choked on the question.

Simpson replied calmly. "The seizure's probably to do with the fever... I had a dog once who took a fit every couple of days—never hurt him." He checked the wound on Rowland's arm. "Had to shoot him in the end, but that was for something else entirely. Look, Miss Higgins, if you don't mind me saying, you look beat. Why don't you get some sleep?" Simpson settled himself comfortably beside Rowland. "I'll sit up with Rowly."

Edna was torn, aware of how tired she was—how much she wanted to retreat into her own mind for a while—but she was scared, afraid to take her eyes off the laboured rise and fall of Rowland's chest in case it stopped. Her lips were still seared with Rowland's kiss—the memory of it confused. She wanted to run away and she wanted to sink back into his arms. She needed to think. "You'll wake me if..."

"Of course." Simpson smiled. "I'll pull your chain."

25

A FIRE-LIGHTING HINT

Cinders soaked in kerosene make the best possible fire-lighters. It is a splendid idea to keep a little oil in an old fruit tin and each day to pop half a dozen fair-sized cinders into this. In the morning the cinders are taken out and used for starting the fire. No paper, and hardly any wood, will be required where the oil-soaked cinders are employed. Six or eight of these cinders are quite sufficient in an emergency to boil a small kettle, and this is a much cheaper way of getting hot water than putting the kettle on the gas. The actual amount of kerosene used is very trifling, far less than might be supposed. In fact there are no cheaper fire-lighters than cinders saturated in oil.

The Examiner, 1932

Rowland opened his eyes. It took him a couple of minutes to realise that he was staring at the ceiling of the cave. He could make out a bit of movement where the swallows nested in the crags. His mouth was dry, parched. Slowly he turned his head to check that his arm was still there. It felt hot, numb and painful at the same time. Simpson was sitting beside him in a half-doze.

"Harry," he said hoarsely.

Simpson started into full consciousness. "Rowly? How're you feeling, *gagamin?*"

"Do you think you could take this flaming tourniquet off now?" Rowland bit his lip as he tried to move his deadened fingers.

Simpson tested Rowland's forehead. The fever had subsided completely.

"I've already loosened it but your arm's probably swelled a bit. Can you sit up?"

"I think so, give me a hand."

Simpson helped Rowland to sit and when he had done that without any problems, Simpson removed the tourniquet. He watched Rowland carefully as the circulation returned to normal, and when nothing untoward happened, he relaxed.

"How long have I been out?" Rowland asked.

"Nearly a full day. You got through the worst of it a few hours ago."

"Rowly?"

Rowland turned as Edna looked up drowsily from the swag on which she'd been lying. At first he thought she looked frightened but then, she smiled and reached out.

Rowland squeezed her hand. "You've cleaned your face," he said, studying her. "Much better."

Edna breathed, clearly relieved.

Rowland's eyes lingered on her face. Despite the smile, her lashes were still clumped with tears. He frowned as he remembered her crying.

"Why am I wet?" he asked, noticing the dampness of his clothes and hair.

"Fever," Simpson replied, handing him a canteen of water. "Probably what saved you—I think you might have sweated out most of the poison."

"Charming," he said grimacing.

"How's your arm, Rowly?" Edna asked.

"Hurts like the blazes, but it's much better without the tourniquet." He drank from the canteen. "I'm famished. Did you eat all the biscuits?"

Edna found him the biscuits, stopping to unsnag the chain yet again. Rowland stared at the chain as she freed it.

"What now, Rowly?" Simpson followed his gaze.

"I may have an idea how we can get loose," Rowland said, picking the shortbread out of the tin. He felt a bit stiff, but essentially he thought he'd come out of the snakebite quite well.

"You won't be able to break the chain," Simpson said wearily.

"No, if it were possible you would have done it by now," Rowland said, glancing at the large stockman. "Milt said that snakebite potion of Eichorn's exploded when it fell into the flames."

"Milt exaggerates," Edna reminded him.

"Even so, it's flammable… certainly smells that way." Rowland rubbed his hair. "What if we set the tree on fire… burned it down? We could douse it with the snakebite concoction and set it alight."

Simpson shook his head. "That kind of fire would make the chain red hot… and we're shackled to it."

Rowland was not deterred. "But if we stood in the stream, the water would cool the chain before the heat reached us."

Simpson looked at him thoughtfully, clearly interested in the proposal. "We could end up setting the whole ravine alight."

"There is that," Rowland admitted. "But the camp is fairly well cleared except for that tree. We'd be unlucky." He looked at Simpson. "Do you know where we are?"

Simpson nodded. "Pocket's Hut is just a few miles from here, we could get help there… but it's rough country, Rowly."

"Our other option is to wait," Rowland replied. "God knows how long they plan to keep us here. Clyde will be back looking for us in a few hours... but out here..."

"I think we should try burning the tree," Edna said. "If nothing else, it might tell Clyde where to find us."

"We'll be standing in the stream for a while," Simpson warned. "The tree will take a few hours to burn to a stump low enough to get the chain off."

"We don't need to stand in the water," Edna said confidently. The sculptress understood about heating metal. "We only need to put enough of the chain between us and the tree, in the water. It just has to cool before it reaches us."

"Are you sure?"

"I think so. We can always walk into the stream if it gets hot."

Rowland smiled. He'd always admired Edna's gumption. "Shall we light this thing up then?"

Simpson shook his head. "For God's sake, Rowly, you're not lighting a bloody Aga. You can't go out and just toss a match. We'll need to build a fire at the tree's base—it'll take a bit of work."

Rowland shifted impatiently. "The sooner we get started..."

"Rowly, darling, you were very ill just a few hours ago," Edna said softly.

"I'm quite well now... really." He looked round at the two of them. "I've sweated out the venom, or it wasn't the brown snake in the first place... headache's gone, I can see all right, my arm hurts but that's to be expected. You did bite me..."

The world outside the cave seemed bright though the day was overcast. The wind slapped at their faces with icy hands.

Rowland turned up the collar of his jacket, which Edna had returned to him. Although the shirtsleeve had been torn off his injured arm, it had been bandaged with strips of blanket and was consequently the warmest part of his body. Edna was wearing her blanket like a plaid cape. Only Simpson was reasonably attired against the cold.

They hobbled down to inspect the tree. It was only a few feet from the stream and may in some seasons have been partially submerged. Perhaps that's what had killed it.

Rowland squatted on the bank and splashed his face and neck, gasping with the shock of the frigid water. Still, he felt better for it. He rubbed the dark stubble on his jaw. If they didn't get out of here soon, Simpson wouldn't be the only one sporting a beard.

"What do you think?" he asked Simpson, who was looking closely at the tree.

"It might just work, Rowly. I'd say a good part of it's hollow. It mightn't take as long to burn down as I thought."

"We're going to have to carry the chain with us once we get it off the tree," Edna said, frowning at the long length of linked iron. It would be heavy.

"Not far," Simpson assured her. He pointed. "There's another small cave about there. They took everything they thought could help me escape over to it."

"What things?" Edna asked.

"Tools mainly—a couple of shovels, an axe, picks... If we can get to it, we'll be able to break the chains."

Rowland was pleased. It had occurred to him that ploughing through the undergrowth still shackled together would present a challenge.

Simpson gathered the odd bit of driftwood and kindling, pulling both Rowland and Edna with him. He took the supply of firewood which had been placed beside the cave and piled that too at the base of the tree. Rowland could use only one arm, but Edna was both learned and efficient on the subject of building fires. She advised Simpson on how to stack and layer the fuel to concentrate the heat around the trunk. They went back into the cave to retrieve the crate of Eichorn's Snakebite Cure. Simpson kept one bottle back.

"What's that for?" Rowland asked suspiciously. Much of the previous night was confused and hazy, but he remembered the application of Eichorn's Snakebite Cure all too clearly.

Simpson grinned. "This might have saved your life, Rowly."

Rowland was unconvinced. He said so. Somewhat bluntly.

Regardless, Simpson slipped the bottle into the pocket of his jacket.

At sunset they poured the rest of the crate into the hollows of the tree and doused the base. Edna took control and insisted they retreat as far as possible along the stream. She ran the length of the chain through the water.

"How are we supposed to light it from here?" Rowland asked.

"I have an idea," Simpson said, heading back to the firepit and dragging Edna and Rowland with him via the chain. He stretched out towards the fire and extracted a burning faggot.

"Would you like to do the honours, Miss Higgins?" He offered the flaming branch to Edna.

"Good Lord, don't give it to Ed," Rowland warned. "Her aim's abysmal."

"That's hardly fair!" Edna protested.

"You shot me," Rowland reminded her.

"It's very ungracious of you to keep bringing that up."

Simpson threw the torch himself.

Rowland blanched and Edna put her hands over her face as the tree caught and exploded into flame.

Simpson cheered, and put his big arm around Rowland. "How's that for aim, Rowly?"

Rowland laughed. "Hell of a blaze though," he said, sizing up the flames. "Moran and his boys will be back if they notice."

Simpson shook his head. "It's too dark to see the smoke. If one of them happens to spot the flames they won't do anything till morning anyway... They're usually well and truly pickled by now."

"How long do you think it'll take?" Rowland asked, as he watched the tree which was now engulfed.

"A couple of hours at least. Make yourself comfortable, mate..."

And so they sat there by the edge of the stream. The fire threw enough heat that they were not cold despite the evening chill. Simpson took the opportunity to unwrap the bandages around Rowland's arm and wash out the wound.

"You don't want it to get infected, Rowly," he said, as he poured the icy stream water over Rowland's arm. "Had a dog once with this tiny little nick on its paw... got infected and we had to shoot it in the end." He sighed. "Bloody good dog too."

Rowland craned his neck to look at his arm. It was slightly inflamed and bruised, but other than the gash Simpson had incised, and the impression left by Edna's teeth, it didn't look too bad. With any luck Simpson wouldn't have to shoot him any time soon.

It took most of the night for the tree trunk to burn down to a level that would allow them to simply lift the chain over the stump, then another half-hour of pouring water over that part of the chain to ensure it was cool enough to lift without injury. All in all they were free before dawn.

They clambered, still shackled together, towards the cave in which Moran's men had stored the tools. It was about a hundred yards away and reaching it in the dark was a stumbling challenge. It took Simpson several minutes to smash through the chains with an axe, and then more carefully to remove the shackles entirely.

"Right." Simpson glanced up at the lightening horizon. In the daylight the smoke from the now smouldering tree stump was obvious. "Let's get going before Moran turns up to investigate the smoke."

"How long will it take us to get to Pocket's Hut?" Rowland asked, as Simpson passed swags out from the cave.

"Not sure, at least a day..." Simpson slung two swags over his shoulder. "Can you take one, Rowly?"

Rowland nodded, taking the third swag on the shoulder of his good arm. They gave Edna a canteen and what food remained.

"Shouldn't we take more water?" Edna asked. The single canteen seemed a paltry supply for the three of them.

"There're streams all over this country," Simpson reassured her. "You don't want to be carrying any more than you have to... we have a fair way to go." He glanced at Rowland and frowned. "If you have trouble with the swag, Rowly, toss it. We'll make do."

"I'm fine," Rowland muttered. "We should get going. O'Shea's Hut is only about an hour's ride from here. They could be here any moment."

Simpson agreed. "This way."

Clyde dismounted, and signalled for the others to do likewise. He'd brought six men with him; the other six had already started to search for Simpson... or his remains. Despite Rowland's refusal to seriously consider the possibility, Clyde thought it likely that the Sinclairs' head stockman had perished. For some reason Rowland, and it seemed, Wilfred, had a loyalty to the man that was hard to fathom. Still, to Clyde's mind, the ways of the landed gentry were often odd.

Milton and Sarah Brent were safely back at Rules Point. Clyde had stayed just briefly before he set out to do as Rowland had asked.

He could hear several voices within O'Shea's Hut, and there was a number of horses tethered outside. Clyde smiled. If anything could bring cattlemen back to the home pasture it would be the presence of Edna.

The door was opened, to Clyde's surprise, by Moran.

"What are you doing here?"

Moran's eyes narrowed slightly. "The hut burnt down, didn't it? We were worried about you all... figured you would have tried to get to O'Shea's."

Clyde nodded slowly. It seemed reasonable, but still he was uneasy.

"Where's Rowly—Mr. Sinclair?" Clyde asked, scanning the room.

"You mean he's not with you?" Moran's voice was startled.

"We lost a horse and had an injured man," Clyde said alarmed. "He and Miss Higgins came here."

Merrick rose from the easychair. "Well, they didn't arrive. We haven't seen them, have we boys?" He looked around at the men in the room, who all nodded and murmured in a show of consensus.

"This is terrible!" Moran exploded. "This is not friendly country for a couple of city kids lost on their own."

"I doubt they're lost," Clyde said, a little irritated by Moran's reduction of Rowland and Edna to children. Neither was he convinced by the stockman's apparent show of concern.

"I guess the boys and I better go look for them." Moran sighed. "They're bound to be somewhere between here and Rope's End. Why don't you wait at Rules Point, Mr. Jones? My boys know this country. We'll find them."

"We might as well join the search while we're here." Clyde's response was guarded. He'd caught a glimpse of something pinned to the wall behind the Cassidys. He recognised the drawing—he had seen the painting which Rowland developed from it, but this was not the time to show his hand.

"Fair enough," Moran said congenially. "Why don't we split up? We'll cover more ground."

Clyde agreed. "We might head back to Rope's End... or what's left of it. Maybe they found trouble on the way here."

"Righto." Moran seemed satisfied with the proposition. "We'll fan out from here."

And so an uneasy agreement was reached. Clyde took his leave, and his own men, to begin the search for Rowland Sinclair and Edna Higgins.

26

FIRST AID TO THE INJURED

———————◆———————

WHAT TO DO TILL THE DOCTOR COMES

[By the late Dr. W. Gordon-Stables]

BANDAGES AND BANDAGING

We can dispense with prettiness when doing up an arm or
leg; what we want is real utility, and the bandage so fixed
that it will not get loose and fall down—come off, as it were.
If there be any prettiness or dandifying to be done the doctor
himself is the man to do it, and if you have been successful
in the application of the bandage he will not mind if it be a
little untidy.

The Register, 1929

Rowland rested his head back against the smooth bark of the
snow gum. They had been trudging through the scrub for
hours now. Simpson had finally allowed them to stop for a while.

"Hope you know where you're going, Harry," Rowland said, as
Simpson built a fire.

"I'm keeping well away from the trails in case Moran's boys are
looking for us," the stockman replied.

"They've probably decided to let us die hopelessly lost in the wilderness," Rowland sighed.

"We're not lost."

"So you keep saying."

"You can't always go places directly, Rowly. I had a dog once, lazy blighter, always went in a straight line... was trampled by a cow in the end—had to shoot him."

"You've had a lot of dogs, Mr. Simpson," Edna said, sitting beside Rowland.

Rowland smiled. "They don't seem to last long though, Harry."

Simpson threw a stick at him. "Don't be smart, Rowly! I like dogs."

"Do you think Mr. Moran knows we're free yet?" Edna asked, rubbing her arms. Now that they had stopped, it was cold.

"They might," Simpson replied. "Hopefully they think their time is better spent finding Glover's gold than us."

"You know," Rowland said regretfully, "I do believe I forgot to sack them."

"I didn't," Harry Simpson replied. "It was how I ended up chained to that tree. When I realised they were rebranding my cows, I went straight in and sacked them..." He shrugged. "Probably wasn't all that well thought out, really."

"I didn't fare much better," Rowland admitted.

Simpson handed him the hessian sack which Glover had left them. It still contained some biscuits, and a box of sultanas.

"If I had a rod, I'd catch us something better than this." Simpson poured water from the canteen into a billy and added a generous fistful of tea. "Some of the best fishing in the country here."

When the billy had boiled he swung it in a circle to settle the leaves and set it off the fire. "Give it a couple of minutes to cool."

Rowland looked critically at the sky. It had turned a greenish grey. "We might not have a couple of minutes, Harry." The clouds had gathered with extraordinary speed.

Simpson glanced up and nodded. "You're not wrong, Rowly." He frowned. "Try and drink some tea." He wrapped the empty hessian bag around the billy and handed it to Edna. "We're about to get wet."

The rain, when it started, was an inundation. There was no introductory drizzle, just an immediate downpour. It seemed to fall in icy, almost horizontal, sheets, making it difficult to see. Very quickly the ground became slippery and they were soaked. Rowland pulled Edna to him as they stumbled after Simpson.

Despite its ferocity, the deluge was not expended. The rain became hail and the landscape was soon netted with rivulets and streams.

They ploughed on through the mud, trusting that Simpson knew where he was going.

The hut was small, a rudimentary construction that appeared so unexpectedly that Rowland was still surprised when they staggered through the door and stood dripping and shivering on the uneven floor of the single room.

"Damn it!" Simpson began building a fire in the stone fireplace. A stack of dry wood and kindling had been left on the hearth.

"Where are we?" Rowland asked, as he removed his sodden jacket.

"Lonesome Hut," Simpson replied. "Only really used in emergencies."

"Like now," Edna shivered. "We're lucky it's here. I'm so cold..."

"Maybe," Simpson replied, frowning.

Rowland pulled a blanket from his swag. Rolled up in the oilskin, it was only a little damp. He handed it to Edna and knelt beside

Simpson who was coaxing a flame from smouldering kindling. "What's wrong, Harry?"

"This is the closest hut to the cave," Simpson said, pulling back as the fire caught and jumped suddenly. "If Moran's men are looking for us, they'll check here. I wouldn't have brought you here if there'd been any other shelter nearby."

"Oh." Rowland glanced upwards as the hail pounded and clattered on the iron roof. "Hopefully this storm will slow them too. We'll leave as soon as it eases."

Simpson piled logs upon the fire. "Let's try and get as dry as possible in the meantime," he said.

They rolled out the swags and removed as many wet clothes as decency would allow.

Edna laughed at Simpson's obvious embarrassment as she removed her sodden breeches under the blanket. Rowland placed them with the steaming jackets and muddy socks before the fire. He watched the sculptress thoughtfully as she tried to wring the water from her hair. She'd wrapped the blanket chastely about her body. The firelight cast her in a warm, gentle light that gave her beauty an earthy timelessness—like a Degas, her figure seemed to emit its own glow. He wondered briefly if his notebook was too wet to allow him to capture her.

All the while he listened closely for any sign that the storm was letting up. There was none. It seemed the rain had set in.

"How far are we from Pocket's Hut?" Rowland asked, sitting as close to the hearth as he could without scorching himself.

"Five miles maybe," Simpson said, keeping his eyes on the fire and averted from Edna.

Rowland smiled. "Good Lord, Harry, I didn't think you could blush."

Simpson regarded him sternly and poked him in the chest. "A man cannot help but wonder why you're not blushing, *gagamin*."

"He used to." Edna laughed as she combed her fingers through her hair. "The first time Rowly painted me, he was completely crimson!"

Simpson chuckled.

"How's your arm?" he asked Rowland, still unwilling to let his eyes anywhere near Edna.

"It's not getting any worse," Rowland lied. He was doing his best to ignore the pain, but he was well aware of it.

Simpson inspected the rough bandage. Rowland's arm was bruised from shoulder to elbow, swollen and clearly tender. "We can get you a doctor as soon as we get to Pocket's." He tested Rowland's forehead. "You're a little warm. Perhaps you and Miss Higgins should try to catch some shut-eye. I'll keep watch and wake you as soon as the rain clears."

"I'm fine, Harry," Rowland murmured, though he did stretch out on the swag.

Edna moved closer to the fire to check her clothes. She turned them over to dry the other side and sat huddled in the blanket beside Rowland. It was only close to the fire that it was not cold and even then the side of her that was not facing the flames became quickly chilled.

"I wonder if Clyde got Milt and Sarah back all right." She bit her lip anxiously.

"Of course he did." Rowland wondered vaguely how she could manage to smell like roses after all the rain and the mud. "Clyde's probably back looking for us by now."

"He'll go to O'Shea's Hut... What if they...?"

Rowland put his good arm behind his head. "Clyde will bring a few blokes with him. How many men can they possibly shackle to a tree?"

"With any luck, the fact that your friends are poking around will keep them from going back to the cave to check on us," Simpson said thoughtfully. "If the rain doesn't let up soon we'll be stuck here till morning. We don't want to risk being stuck in the open at night."

Rowland stirred as Simpson prodded him with his foot. Edna roused him more gently, shaking his shoulder.

"Rowly, wake up."

The rain had stopped. It was quiet and dark, but for the fire which Simpson had kept fed through the night. Rowland sat up. "Time to go?"

"The sun will be up soon," Edna replied.

Rowland was a little surprised that he'd slept so soundly and for so long.

Edna handed him his jacket, now dry. She was dressed. "It's no wonder you were tired," she said, as he gingerly inserted his injured arm into the jacket's sleeve. "Poor darling, you've had a terrible time of it."

"Rubbish—you're getting soft, Rowly," Simpson said, as he re-rolled the swag. "We want to leave at first light."

"You're still worried that Moran could find us?"

"Nah, I'm just hungry."

Rowland smiled. "Fair enough."

Simpson put out the fire and restocked the logs which had been beside the fireplace from the woodpile outside, and they left Lonesome Hut as they had found it, ready for the next person who needed shelter from the inclement and unpredictable mountain weather. The rain had left the ground soft and, in some places, quite boggy. The trek was increasingly arduous and it was very cold. It wasn't long before the glistening undergrowth had soaked them anew. Rowland grabbed Edna's hand to keep her from sliding down the steep incline. A little way further up the slope, Simpson cursed.

"Harry?"

Simpson climbed up onto a rock and looked grimly out over the valley. "They're coming."

Rowland clambered up beside Simpson. Half a dozen men on horses were picking their way through the scrub, following their trail.

"It'll be dead easy to track us with all this bloody mud," Simpson groaned.

"Can we outrun them?"

"They're on horses, but in this country it might not be an advantage. Either way we're going to have to try."

They set out now with urgency, moving as quickly as they could through the dense scrub. Though they did what they could to keep their tracks invisible, it was an impossible task. The mud and fragile undergrowth kept a faithful record of their passing. Despite the cold, Simpson was sweating as he led them. In the interests of speed they discarded the swags and blankets and committed themselves to reaching help before nightfall.

They came over the rise, hopeful that they had increased the gap between themselves and the horsemen.

Rowland saw the movement in the distance ahead of them first.

"Harry!" He got down, pulling Edna with him.

Simpson cursed quietly. "They must have split up and come round."

"So what do we do now?" Rowland craned his neck around the pale grey trunk of a snow gum.

"This way." Simpson motioned for them to follow. They moved slowly at first, keeping down, trying to avoid any undue noise, but then they heard the shouts.

"Over there!"

They ran out of instinct more than reason, a wild panicked scramble to escape. Of course they could not outrun horses. Rowland pushed Edna before him as they climbed a steep incline in the hope the horses would be unable to follow. Simpson grabbed the sculptress' hand and pulled her up.

"Rowly, come on!"

"Gotchya, you bastard!" Rowland heard Blue Cassidy's voice just a split second before the rope fell around his shoulders and pulled tight. He was dragged over, his injured arm taking the impact of the fall. For a moment he could do nothing but swear, and then he rolled, struggling to free himself from the rope. Simpson came back for him. The others arrived—Glover, Moran and three more Cassidys. Simpson dragged him up, refusing to give in, and then they heard the unmistakable click of a shotgun being cocked.

"So what the hell are we going to do with them, now?" Blue Cassidy barked at Moran.

Moran didn't respond, glaring at Rowland from behind the double barrel of a shotgun. Glover and Andy Cassidy had also trained firearms upon them. Rowland glanced uneasily at Edna. This was not good.

"You've backed us into a corner, Sinclair," Moran said finally. "If you'd just stayed put, you would have walked away from this eventually. Now we don't have much of a choice."

"Look Moran, you don't need to…"

"Shut the hell up!" Moran shouted.

Blue Cassidy pulled on the rope still around Rowland's arms. Rowland gasped as it tightened on his wound. Simpson grabbed the rope and pulled it from Cassidy's grip, nearly unseating him in the process.

"Why you…" the stockman started.

"Leave it!" Moran ordered sharply. He pointed the shotgun at Simpson. "Get the rope off him," he said.

Warily, Simpson loosened the loop and pulled it over Rowland's head.

Moran reached into his saddlebag and took out a gun— Rowland's gun. He tossed it to Glover. "Load it."

"Why?" Glover asked.

"Because you're going to use it to shoot Sinclair and the girl."

Edna gasped, reaching instinctively for Rowland. He pushed her behind him. She was shaking. He didn't feel that steady himself.

Moran's crew reacted with alarm.

"You want him to do what?"

"You can't be serious…"

Moran raised his hand for silence. "I'll shoot Simpson, we'll leave Sinclair's gun in his hand. Sad story… ungrateful blackfella turns against his employer, takes the poor blighter's gun and shoots him and his girl." Moran leaned forward in the saddle, obviously pleased with himself. "Of course we were forced to shoot the murdering bastard for fear of our own lives. Everybody knows what happens when one of his kind goes bad… sadly it was too late for Sinclair and the girl."

"You're flaming crazy!" Rowland put his good arm around Edna and pulled her into him. "No-one's going to believe that."

"I think they just might—there'll be no living witnesses to tell them otherwise."

"Just a bloody minute," Glover said, looking down at Rowland's revolver. "Stealing and kidnapping is one thing but you're talking murder... I ain't no murderer."

"You do this and you'll all swing," Rowland promised. He was angry.

Edna's eyes were fixed on the gun, her face pale with terror. "Oh God, Rowly..." He held her tightly.

"Load the gun!" Moran snapped at Glover. The Cassidys said nothing, dumbfounded. Glover began to load the revolver.

Simpson spoke. His voice was unnervingly calm. "You know, shooting a blackfella is one thing, you could even get off with the right jury. But shooting a woman and a Sinclair... they'd hunt you down."

Glover stopped.

Moran pointed his own weapon at Simpson. The click was faint as he cocked it.

The shot was deafening.

27

STATION, FARM AND GARDEN

NOTES AND COMMENTS

5 February

Details of the issues of two very important pastoral companies operating in Australia, the Australian Estates and Mortgage Co., the New Zealand Loan and Mercantile Agency Co., have been revived. Our cable messages gave a digest of both, and also the information that the issue had been over-subscribed. The Australian Estates and Mortgage Co. owns a large number of pastoral property in New South Wales and Queensland, and important sugar interests in the latter state. It also possesses a valuable pastoral agency business.

The Queenslander, 1927

"Harry!"

Rowland pulled Edna down and turned towards Simpson in the same movement. There was no blood. Simpson had recoiled but that was all.

Another shot.

"What the…?" Glover dropped Rowland's gun and looked for the source of the shots. Moran wheeled around. The Cassidys turned their horses in a chorus of expletives.

"Sinclair's mine, you bastards—get in line!" The shout came from the trees and was accompanied by more blasts of the shotgun.

Another voice, different from the first. "Drop the guns, fellas, or we'll blow your ugly bloody heads off!" A series of similar sentiments, more profane, different voices.

Now Moran and his men began to panic. They shot wildly into the trees.

Simpson knelt beside Rowland and Edna, blanching with each shot. "Who else is trying to kill you, Rowly?"

"I don't know," Rowland replied. Edna's face was buried in his shoulder.

Moran made the decision to flee. Glover and the Cassidys followed.

"Now's our chance," Simpson urged. "Let's go."

They scrambled towards the incline, heading back in the direction of Pocket's Hut, but not for long. A man on horseback cut them off and then others emerged from the scrub behind them.

"Where the hell do you think you're going?" Lawrence Keenan rested his shotgun across his saddle and pointed at Rowland. "That's two horses you owe me for, not to mention this little expedition... and let me tell you, Sinclair, my time don't come cheap!"

Rowland stared at him, truly bewildered, and then he recognised one of the other horsemen. "Jim!" He hailed Clyde's brother, still confused, but now cautiously relieved.

Jim Watson Jones smiled broadly. "Can't tell you how glad we are to see you, Mr. Sinclair. There are about fifty men out lookin' for you people."

"But you'll be paying for those horses before you pay anyone else," Keenan grumbled. "Else I'll sell that fancy rattletrap for scrap."

"Take it easy, Laurie," Jim said, still grinning. "Mr. Sinclair will see you right."

"Of course I will," Rowland muttered. "Just keep your bloody hands off my car…"

"Actually, I meant the other Mr. Sinclair," Jim said, climbing down from his horse.

"Wil?" Simpson interrupted. "Wil's here?"

Jim nodded. "Clyde sent a message back a couple of days ago when he didn't find you at O'Shea's. Mr. Sinclair came straight up with about a dozen of his own men. He hired whoever else was able and willin'."

"I see." Rowland let go of Edna and offered Jim his hand. "Thank you, you arrived in the nick of time."

Jim took the offered hand and motioned to a number of his men to dismount. "You all right to ride, Mr. Sinclair?" He nodded at Rowland's arm. The wound had reopened in the scuffle and blood had now soaked through the lining and sleeve of his jacket. Rowland hadn't noticed. But now that it was pointed out…

"I'll be fine. But do you have enough horses?"

"Not for you," Keenan bellowed. "The way you lose them, even King George wouldn't have enough flaming horses for you."

"We're only a mile or two from Pocket's Hut," Jim replied, ignoring Keenan. "The fellas will be right to take Shanks pony from here and Mr. Sinclair will be anxious to see you."

———————   ———————

Pocket's Hut was a rambling building of tin and timber. It looked more like a homestead than a hut, and was of a different ilk to the rustic shanties in which they'd recently sheltered. An enamel sign at the gate read "Australian State and Mortgage Company". The house and sheds were surrounded by well-tended gardens. The naked branches of stunted fruit trees bordered the house garden, which boasted a large vegetable patch, currently fallow, among the thorny rows of dormant roses.

There were several motor cars outside the main house. Rowland recognised Wilfred's dark green Continental. There was another Rolls Royce, black and immaculate, amongst a variety of trucks.

"Mr. Clapton's the manager here," Jim said, as they rode in. "That's his motor... usually just brings it out to go fishing."

"They've found them!" Someone shouted from the verandah. Very quickly many hands emerged to help them dismount and take the horses.

Wilfred Sinclair walked out of the house. He did not move with unbecoming haste but neither did he waste any time in reaching them. He greeted Simpson warmly while Rowland was still dismounting.

"Harry! Thank God!"

Simpson grinned. "Hello Wil. Sent the kid to rescue me then?"

Wilfred sighed. "Rowly has his own way of doing things." He turned to Rowland and shook his hand. "Good Lord, where's your tie?"

Rowland told him where to go, and Simpson laughed.

"I say," Wilfred noticed the blood on the sleeve of Rowland's jacket. "Don't tell me that Miss Higgins shot you again?"

"I did no such thing!" Edna was affronted.

Wilfred had the good grace to withdraw the remark. "Of course not, Miss Higgins, I do beg your pardon."

"Rowly might need a doctor, Wil," suggested Simpson.

"Yes, I rather think he might. What on earth happened to him?" Wilfred addressed Simpson as if Rowland was not there.

"Poor bloke was bitten... twice."

Wilfred took them into the main house. It was most comfortably furnished, a charming if not elegant country home. The main living room had been timber lined and had electric lighting. Clapton, the manager, expressed his concern and his gratification that they had all been recovered. Rowland gathered that Clapton had served with Wilfred in the Great War. It wasn't hard to imagine—there was a certain militaristic neatness and order to the man.

Wilfred directed Rowland to a chair by the fire. "Clapton, would you mind telling Maguire that we require his services?"

"Maguire? What's he doing here?" Rowland asked, sinking thankfully into the easychair. Wilfred's ability to produce the surgeon never ceased to amaze him. It was as if he carried Maguire in his back pocket.

"I received word that you'd managed to burn down Rope's End," Wilfred said tersely, "and that someone had been hurt in the process. I thought it might be a good idea to bring Maguire with me. Of course I didn't realise it was just that long-haired buffoon."

"How is Milt?" Rowland inquired, as Maguire strode into the room.

"Some nasty burns, but he'll be shipshape given time. He was blithering like a damn fool, but your brother tells me that's the normal state of affairs." The surgeon regarded Rowland disapprovingly. "Take off your jacket."

Maguire removed the rough bandage and inspected the damage. "Hmmph, infected—looks like some kind of wild animal attack..."

Simpson chuckled. Edna stood next to Rowland's chair, mortified.

Clapton went to the sideboard and poured drinks from a series of decanters. He looked a little uncertainly at Simpson. Wilfred took a glass and handed it to Simpson. "Whisky still your drink, Harry?"

Simpson nodded and accepted the drink. "I suppose I'd better tell you what's been going on," he said, settling into an armchair.

"I'll ask Mrs. Evans to prepare some refreshments, shall I?" Clapton said. "Better get word out that we've found them, too."

"The authorities..." Rowland murmured, preoccupied with what Maguire was doing to his arm. "Moran..."

"Rowly's right," Simpson agreed. "Moran and his gang are still out there doing God knows what... we'll need to notify the police."

"I'll make a telephone call," Clapton assured them and left the room to put things in order.

"So what happened, Harry?"

Simpson recounted the events as he understood them, telling Wilfred about the rebranding of Sinclair cattle, and the unlikely quest for Glover's gold.

Wilfred's face hardened. "So O'Shea is part of this?"

"You can't tell me he didn't know what his men were up to."

"So this character, Moran, is working for O'Shea?" Wilfred asked.

"Doubt Moran and his boys would do anything for nothing, Wil. The cattle stealing isn't what they're here for though—they were just earning a few extra quid while they were looking for this blasted gold."

Wilfred sipped his drink. "And where the devil have you been, Harry?"

"Moran imprisoned me at an abandoned gold dig. I'd been there for well over a week when Rowly and Miss Higgins arrived."

Edna told them the series of events which found her and Rowland chained to Simpson at the cave.

Wilfred shook his head. "So what happened to Rowly?"

"He was bitten by a snake, probably a brown," Simpson replied. "I had to incise the bite with a piece of broken mirror, which is why it's such a mess," he added.

Edna looked away.

Wilfred glanced at Rowland who inhaled sharply as Maguire scraped at the ragged edges of the wound with a scalpel. "That's his arm you're carving, old chap, not some flaming roast," Wilfred muttered with something that verged on sympathy.

Maguire gave no sign that he had even heard.

Wilfred looked back to Simpson. "You're jolly lucky you and Miss Higgins didn't end up chained to a dead man."

Simpson was thoughtful. "You know I had a dog once, who killed chickens… tied the dead chicken round its neck for a day or two, didn't go near the chickens again."

For a moment they stared at him mutely as he smiled over his whisky, obviously pleased with the memory of his own ingenuity.

"Oh…" Edna gasped finally, horrified by the image of the poor dog wearing a dead chicken as a collar, and its tenuous association with Rowland's corpse.

Wilfred smiled. "I remember when you did that," he said. "Rather unsightly, but I must say it worked."

Rowland pulled his arm gingerly out of the sling to knot the tie Wilfred had lent him. The shirt was also Wilfred's, though he wore his own suit which had been cleaned and pressed while he slept. Grimly, he forced the minor movement required to secure the Windsor knot. Maguire had lectured him at length about infection, gangrene and amputation. But Maguire was a surgeon—probably more likely to remove a limb than to develop any sort of bedside manner. Still, his arm was noticeably less painful in the sling.

Fed, bathed, rested, shaved and now properly attired, Rowland was feeling rather well. He was anxious to finalise matters, to see that the gang of present-day bushrangers who had worked the Sinclair lease were captured and brought to justice. It was six in the morning. For all he knew Wilfred had already taken care of it.

Rowland made his way into the dining room in search of his brother. Wilfred was there, taking breakfast and reading *Smith's Weekly*.

"Good morning, Rowly—sit down, the cook will appear again in a minute I expect."

"Did you bring that up with you?" Rowland asked, nodding at the newspaper. It was dated the day before.

"The paper? No, apparently some chap flies over and drops papers into these outposts... made a drop yesterday."

Rowland thought briefly of Humphrey Abercrombie. He wondered how his neurotic old friend was getting on in Sydney.

"Have they found Moran and the others?" Rowland asked once the cook had taken his request for breakfast.

Wilfred poured him a cup of tea. "Afraid not. They seem to know this country well—it may take a while to catch them... if we ever do."

Rowland leaned back in his chair. "Blast!"

Wilfred studied him. "You found Harry—that's the main thing... we'll catch them sooner or later."

"The thugs that jumped me at Medlow Bath and then at Caves House Moran knew about them. Apparently he had expected them to accost us at Rope's End."

Wilfred nodded. "I believe Mr. Jones found them bogged en route, but they'd gone by the time he'd returned."

"It doesn't make sense, Wil. Why would Moran want me jumped at Medlow Bath before I even knew we had a snow lease? How would he even know I existed?"

Wilfred nodded slowly. "I must say you have a point."

"Unless we find Moran and get it out of him we're still none the wiser as to what these chaps want."

"So these thugs could still have you in their sights?"

"I suppose so."

Wilfred stirred his tea frowning. "I want you back at *Oaklea* until this is cleared up."

Rowland shook his head. "No, I can't."

"What do you mean you can't?"

Rowland smiled. "Wil, I know you think I do nothing with my time but play cards, but I have work to do. I could still get something finished for the classical figures exhibition."

"What about your arm?" Wilfred pointed his teaspoon at the sling.

"I only need one to paint." Rowland waved his right hand.

"I suppose it makes no difference which one you use… but you can paint at *Oaklea*."

"Do you really want me and my models working at *Oaklea*?"

Wilfred hesitated.

"I'll be careful," Rowland promised. "I'll speak to Detective Delaney. If these chaps are from the city, the Sydney police may have an idea what's going on." He met Wilfred's eye with a completely straight face. "Perhaps I'm not the only artist they've tried to snatch."

Wilfred bit. "I doubt very much that what you call art has anything to do with it! Unless, of course, the fathers of those poor girls you disgrace on canvas have banded together…"

"Disgrace on canvas?" Rowland grinned. "Sounds uncomfortable."

There was nothing in Wilfred's face that could be mistaken for amusement.

The cook came in with Rowland's breakfast. Wilfred checked his pocket watch. "I have a meeting this morning. Once it's finished, we'll have to ransom that Fritz contraption of yours from that mad old pirate."

"You've met Mr. Keenan then?"

"He is of the opinion that you did not take due care of his animals, and has unilaterally imposed certain financial penalties."

Rowland started on his eggs and bacon. He may have been inclined to protest, but Lawrence Keenan's belligerent arrival had saved them from being shot. As long as the old man hadn't damaged the Mercedes, Rowland was happy to pay him whatever he wanted.

"With whom are you meeting then?" Rowland asked.

"O'Shea." Wilfred's eyes narrowed.

"Shouldn't the police...?"

"They'll deal with Moran and his thugs. I'll sort the rest out with O'Shea."

Rowland let it go. He had no doubt that O'Shea had more to fear from Wilfred. His brother could exert much more than just the full force of the law.

28

LISTER SHEEP-SHEARING MACHINERY

———◆———

A two-stand portable shearing and crutching outfit complete with the well-known Fairbanks-Morse 'Z' kerosene engine can be seen at the company's exhibit in the machinery hall. Many of the largest sheds in Australia, in fact, throughout the world, are Lister fitted, and over 20,000 stands of Lister shearing machines are at work in Australia.

The Register, 1924

Rowland had barely finished breakfast when the housekeeper came in to say that there was a gentleman to see him. Clapton had apparently accompanied Wilfred to his meeting with O'Shea. Hoping that it was Clyde, Rowland stepped into the drawing room.

"Babbington! Hello... what are you doing here?" Rowland greeted his fellow Dangars director with blunt surprise.

"Just paying my respects, old man. I heard you'd been found. Jolly pleased to hear it."

"Quite pleased myself," Rowland replied carefully, unsure of how much Babbington knew.

"I say, you've been injured." Babbington was looking at the sling.

"Not seriously. I thought you might have headed back to Sydney by now."

"I will be quite soon; I was hoping to have a chat about the Lister vote."

"The Lister vote?" Rowland invited Babbington to take a seat.

"It was all in your board papers."

"Yes, of course." Rowland tried to remember what he'd done with the papers.

"As you have no doubt read, Dangars holds an option over the Lister franchise."

Somewhat deceitfully, Rowland nodded.

"The option must be exercised by the first of April or it lapses and Lister is free to sell its licence to the highest bidder."

"I see."

"The fact of the matter is, old chap, I don't think Dangars is in a position to take up the option. I've been through the books... the company has not the financial strength to take on such an investment."

Rowland was curious. To his recollection Babbington had been a great champion of the Lister pumps and generators. "I was of the impression that you were rather excited by Lister."

"This has nothing to do with the quality of Lister products, Sinclair. There is no demand at the moment... Dangars has so far survived the financial downturn but we cannot continue as if it were still the twenties."

"So you don't want Dangars to exercise its option?"

"Precisely. It's the only rational path." Babbington leaned forward, his elbows on his knees. "Can I count on your support, Rowly?"

"I'll have a look at the board papers... again... and I'll talk to Wil."

Babbington studied him. "May I speak plainly?"

"Please do."

"I understand that Wilfred has been... an invaluable mentor since you joined Dangars, but I believe that you are now ready to trust your own judgement. Your brother is a very capable man, but he is from a world where loyalty dictates decisions of business. That world has changed… we cannot simply support Lister to our own detriment. That is why young men like you bring an essential objectivity to the board. Can I urge you, Rowly, to step outside your brother's directive in this matter and act in the best interests of Dangars."

"It's always been in the best interests of Dangars for me to take Wilfred's advice," Rowland said coolly, not entirely sure if he should be offended, but feeling irritated nonetheless.

Babbington took a measured breath. "I too have an elder brother, Rowly. I have always respected his opinion, valued his experience, but there came a time when I became my own man, and I like to think he respected me for it."

"I'm very happy for you, Babbington."

"I have always considered you to have a great future in business." Babbington stood. "I look forward to seeing you make your own mark on the commerce of the nation."

"Indeed." Rowland stood too, glad that Babbington seemed to be leaving. It was all rather odd. "I'll walk you out to your motor," he said, holding open the front door.

It was later that morning when Edna stepped out, restored after rest and breakfast. Rowland and Harry Simpson were both leaning on the rail which surrounded the verandah, deep in earnest exchange. There was a closeness to the conversation, a confidence between the two men. Rowland's face was in his hands. Simpson spoke quietly, his shoulder squared up against Rowland's, their backs to the house.

Edna's smile faded as she approached them. "What's wrong?"

Rowland did not look at her.

"Miss Higgins," Simpson said uncomfortably.

"Good morning, Mr. Simpson. What's the matter with Rowly?"

"I've got to go see a man about a dog." Simpson replaced his hat upon his head, nodded to Edna and left.

"Maybe we should follow him," Edna said, as she took Simpson's place at the rail. "See if we can't save that poor dog."

Rowland smiled, but still he seemed unable to meet her gaze. To Edna, who was accustomed to his eyes upon her, it was unsettling. A flutter of panic as she wondered if he'd remembered. She forced courage and asked again, "What's wrong, Rowly?"

Finally he looked at her.

"Harry told me, Ed—what happened in the cave." The words came in a rush of remorse. "God, I'm so sorry…"

Edna moved backwards just slightly, startled by the fact that he should be ashamed. "Why did he… What did Mr. Simpson tell you, Rowly?"

Rowland turned to face her now. "That he woke up to find me forcing myself on you." He flinched as he said it. "I'm sorry, Ed, I truly apologise. I don't know why… I would never…"

"It wasn't your fault, Rowly."

"There's no possible excuse…"

"You were delirious, you had no idea what you were doing."

"I…" He stopped.

"Do you remember?"

He shook his head. "No. I don't."

Edna placed her hand firmly on his arm. "Rowly darling, stop. I won't have it. It wasn't your fault. I should have been more careful… you were very ill."

"I couldn't have been that flaming ill if I was…"

Edna shoved him. "For pity's sake, Rowly, it wasn't your fault. It was mine."

He almost laughed. "You tried to ravish me then?"

She smiled, and reached up to turn his face towards hers. Wistfully, she remembered what it was like to kiss him. "Stop looking like that. Nothing's broken."

"Are you sure?"

"I've forgotten it, and you can't remember it at all."

29

WOMAN'S WORLD

———◆———

By CLIO

...it is interesting to see how a writer recently on the vexed question of manners, sums up the position. He takes for his text a delightful little half-page in a recent "Punch", showing an up-to-date governess in the shortest and skimpiest of garments, cigarette in mouth, sprawling on a sofa, and a pretty little pupil making the pathetic request, "Oh, Miss Gazzleton, do tell us a story about the time when there were ladies and gentlemen and not old beans and things." The writer says that a hundred years or more ago the manners of the English upper class were coarse, and now they are merely vulgar, which, so far, is an improvement.

The Mercury 1922

Rowland looked up from his notebook as Wilfred and Clapton walked in. Edna was coiled on the couch beside him with the paper, reading aloud the articles that caught her eye or amused her. It was a moment before she noticed they were no longer alone. She unfurled her legs and sat up hastily.

Wilfred cleared his throat. "Miss Higgins." Removing his hat, he looked her up and down. "I'm pleased to see you've recovered from your ordeal," he said, with nothing but his actual words to indicate that he was in fact pleased.

"Why thank you, Mr. Sinclair." Edna smiled at Clapton who stood rigidly beside his guest. "Mr. Clapton has been most kind to accommodate us so well. Hot and cold running water seems positively miraculous after the last few days."

Clapton puffed, gratified, and nodded in acknowledgement. "Piped from a tank over a mile away, you know. We at Australian State and Mortgage have always felt that homestead living should not require one to abandon the conveniences of civilisation."

"An admirable sentiment, Mr. Clapton," Edna agreed.

"How'd it go, Wil?" Rowland asked. While he too appreciated the plumbing, he was anxious to find out how his brother had fared with O'Shea.

Wilfred frowned, glancing pointedly at Edna.

Rowland ignored him, but Edna stood. "I might take a walk about your garden, Mr. Clapton, if you'll excuse me gentlemen."

Rowland smiled faintly. Wilfred had an old-fashioned aversion to discussing any form of business in front of women. Edna's polite exit may have seemed deferential but Rowland had no doubt she would simply eavesdrop from behind the door.

"O'Shea and I have come to an acceptable arrangement," Wilfred said finally.

"That's it?"

"What did you expect, Rowly—pistols at dawn?"

"No... but..."

"I've hired most of the men who joined the search to see to things up here. We'll be cutting out a thousand head from O'Shea's herd. They'll need to be rebranded properly and we'll also need to rebuild the hut you burnt down."

"Any sign of Moran?" Rowland asked, electing to avoid an argument about who burnt down the hut.

Wilfred shook his head. "Afraid not."

"We'll keep looking," Clapton assured him. "The police are sending men up from Albury to continue the manhunt. I'll be taking a personal interest in it myself."

"More than happy to leave it in your capable hands, old man," Wilfred said, nodding. "We should get moving, Rowly. I'd like to reach Gundagai before dark and we have still to retrieve your paraphernalia from Rules Point."

Rowland sighed. Apparently his car and his friends were paraphernalia. "I'll get Ed," he said. As they had arrived at Pocket's Hut as fugitives with nothing but what they were wearing, there was no need to pack.

He left Wilfred talking to Clapton and stepped out onto the verandah. He expected to find Edna lurking nearby, but the verandah was clear. He found her eventually near the stables with Harry Simpson. Her arms were folded tightly across her chest and, even from a distance, Rowland could tell the conversation was heated. From her part at least. Simpson was scratching his head—he looked both abashed and amused. As Rowland approached, the exchange fell silent.

"What have you done, Harry?" he asked, grinning.

"You heading off then?" Simpson replied, nodding towards Wilfred's Continental which was idling at the front of the house.

"Yes... aren't you coming?"

"Naw... I've got cattle to muster."

"You're going back out?" Rowland was surprised, and uneasy. Moran had not yet been apprehended.

"The new blokes that Wil's taken on seem pretty sound, Rowly. That chap Jim Jones is a good hand. I want to finish the job."

"But Moran..."

"He won't risk coming in again," Simpson laughed. "Wil's summoned the Graziers' Association."

Rowland smiled. "Wouldn't underestimate them, Harry."

"I'm going to say goodbye to Mr. Clapton." Edna turned to Simpson and, after looking at him reprovingly for a moment, she held out her hand and smiled warmly. "I'm really pleased to have met you, Mr. Simpson. I do hope we'll meet again often."

Simpson took her hand in both of his. "Likewise, Miss Higgins. You look after yourself."

They watched Edna walk back towards the house. "So why was Ed dressing you down, Harry?"

"Miss Higgins believes I've been speaking out of turn."

For a moment Rowland was perplexed and then, "Oh, this is about the cave… No, I'm glad you told me." He frowned. "At least I could apologise, for what it was worth."

"I didn't tell you so you could feel bad, *gagamin*. Just thought you and Miss Higgins should talk."

"We did."

"And…"

"I apologised. She was gracious and insisted we never speak of it again."

Simpson sighed loudly and shook his head. Rowland's eyes were still on Edna as she stopped on the verandah to stroke a cat.

"Wil's convinced that girl's going to make a fool of you, Rowly."

"Yes, I know. He's probably right." Rowland dropped his eyes to the ground as he tried to explain. "Edna's got plans."

"They don't include you?"

"They don't include being Mrs. Sinclair."

Simpson shrugged. "Who could blame her?" He smiled broadly. "You know I had a dog called Edna once, bitzer, entirely untrainable... wouldn't sit, or come or stay... did just what she pleased..."

"Did you shoot her?" Rowland asked, not sure he wanted to know the answer.

"Naw... I loved her. Best dog I've ever had. She ran away one day..."

<hr>

The Rules Point Hotel was crowded with the men who had joined the search for Rowland Sinclair. They had come in from surrounding settlements and stations, for the promise of work or because they were sent by employers who had, for one reason or another, cause to do Wilfred Sinclair a favour. Some were staying on to work the Sinclair lease, others because Wilfred had opened the bar to all those who had assisted.

The Sinclair brothers and Maguire had called in first at Long Plain Homestead to rescue the Mercedes which Lawrence Keenan was holding as collateral. Keenan itemised at length the charges that made up the debt, complaining bitterly that he was forced to retrieve Rowland himself to ensure that he survived to settle the bill.

Rowland produced his chequebook and soothed the situation with his signature.

"I'll be glad to see the back of it," Keenan muttered. "Taking up half my shed, bloody Fritz contraption..."

Regardless, the old man had polished the automobile until she gleamed and, though a large ginger cat was evicted from the back seat, the car was pristine.

Despite his injuries, Rowland managed to drive his beloved car with Edna leaning in to operate the gearshift. Fortunately, the lurching, stalling journey, was not a long one and they arrived at Rules Point with both vehicles.

Milton and Clyde emerged from the bar to greet them with a train of well-lubricated spectators.

"Rowly, thank God." Clyde clapped Rowland on the back. He looked tired. "We were beginning to fear the worst... We found the cave but lost your trail in the rain."

"Two roads diverged in a wood and I, I took the one less travelled by."

Rowland looked down at Milton's arm, heavily bandaged to the elbow. "Good Lord, Milt, Frost isn't even dead." Milton usually only robbed the deceased. Rowland shook the grinning poet's good hand with his own as Edna threw her arms about Clyde.

"Cripes, Rowly, what have you done to yourself?"

"Snake... I'm fine."

"Well, it's certain you have the luck of the Irish!" Mick Schulz boomed. "Come, young'un! We'll have a drink to your good health."

A general roar of approval followed. It seemed that everyone was happy to drink to Rowland while a Sinclair was paying the bill.

Rowland glanced back at Wilfred, expecting his brother would be anxious to leave, but Wilfred was deep in conversation and waved him on. They seemed somehow to have acquired the status of heroes by virtue of being rescued, and even Edna was made welcome in the bar. Indeed she was plied with glasses of shandy before she even sat down and the seats about her were taken quickly. The feeling was high and festive, and the stockmen were keen to hear all. Though it seemed that Moran's duplicity was not quite a scandal by mountain standards, it was the subject of great interest.

Rowland gave his attention to a beer and allowed the story to be told by Milton and Edna. Between them the poet and the sculptress had all the necessary theatrical inclination to turn the tale into an epic of survival. Rowland spoke quietly with Clyde instead, giving his friend a slightly more accurate account of the events since they last parted ways.

Clyde in turn told him of the Chevy which had been bogged on the track between Long Plain Homestead and the charred remains of Rope's End.

Rowland shook his head. "Just who are they? There's got to be more to it than a bit of cattle stealing."

"Sarah!" Edna exclaimed, pushing her way out of the centre of the crowd and towards the door. Sarah Brent strode into the bar.

Rowland and Clyde stood hastily.

"Edna, my dear," Sarah said, clasping the sculptress' hands. "I was positively sick with worry for you. Of course I wanted to ride out with the search party, but the closed-minded fools would not hear of it... but that's by the by. I am so glad to find you safe and well."

"We're very grateful to you, Sarah, for all you did for Milt."

The writer shrugged dismissively. "I understand Wilfred is taking you all back with him."

"You've spoken with Wilfred?" Rowland asked. Wilfred hadn't mentioned Sarah Brent whilst they were at Pocket's.

"Of course... he was a little astonished to find me here. He's become the man I expected he would."

"I see." Rowland was unsure if her words were praise or censure.

"You must keep in touch, Sarah... Rowly, give Sarah your card," Edna said warmly. "You must come and see us in Sydney. Now that we have had such an adventure together we must be friends."

"Yes, Edna, I believe we must. I will see you all before long I expect. Now that my book is finished, I too am aching for home."

Sarah Brent took Rowland's card. "Indeed, I believe you may be able to help me with my book, Mr. Sinclair."

"Me?" Rowland asked, startled. He was fairly sure Sarah Brent's manuscript was beyond help. "I'm afraid I have none of Aubrey's literary talent, Miss Brent."

"No, I didn't expect you would, Mr. Sinclair," Sarah replied smartly. "Mr. Jones mentioned that you were something of an artist. The book will require a dust jacket and I think the internal pages could be enhanced with some illustration."

"Illustration?"

"Of the monkey, naturally. I have several ideas... You may need to procure a monkey. I'll outline my expectations properly when we meet in Sydney."

"I really don't think..."

"Rowly!" Wilfred beckoned from the door. He looked grim.

Rowland put down his drink, thankful for an excuse to leave the conversation.

"What's wrong, Wil?"

"Rowly, these gentlemen are from the Commonwealth Police Force—Special Detectives Murphy and Webster. It seems Mr. Moran was found this morning."

"Splendid." Rowland was pleased. Perhaps now they would find out what this was all about. "Have you had a chance to question him, gentlemen?"

"I'm afraid not, Mr. Sinclair," the first policeman said curtly. "Mr. Moran is dead."

30

BRITISH ITEMS

LONDON

In connection with the Communist propaganda scandal at the Oxford University, at a meeting of the Oxford Union Society, a motion of protest was introduced by the President of the University Labor Club against the extraction of a promise from two undergraduates and it was carried, by 216 to 92. Another motion was instantly submitted demanding a poll on the motion, which will be taken on Monday. One of the signatories to the petition was one of the undergraduates concerned in the promises.

Townsville Daily Bulletin, 1926

"Dead... how?"

"It appears someone shot him," Wilfred replied.

"Mr. Moran's corpse was discovered this morning, not far from Pocket's Hut." Detective Murphy's eyes were piercing.

"And the others?"

Webster replied. "No sign of them, sir. It seems Mr. Moran was alone."

"Perhaps one of his own men turned on him," Wilfred suggested.

"Maybe..." Rowland frowned. "He was pushing them pretty hard."

"I believe you own a handgun, Mr. Sinclair."

"Yes, I do."

"We'd like to check it if we could."

"I'm afraid that won't be possible, Detective Murphy. Moran took it from me at O'Shea's Hut. The next time I saw the gun was when Glover was loading it to shoot us."

"I see." Murphy made a note.

"Everybody up here seems to carry a gun," Rowland added uneasily.

Murphy smiled, a little too quickly. "Yes, sir."

"Why are the federal police interested in this, Detective?"

"That'll be all for now, sir. We'll be in touch."

Rowland fumbled in his jacket to find a calling card. "You can reach me at…"

"That won't be necessary, sir," Murphy interrupted. "We have quite the file on you… we know where to find you."

"Indeed." Wilfred glowered. Rowland was unsure whether it was at him or the Commonwealth officers.

In silence they watched the two men walk back out to a black Studebaker.

"Your gun's in the trunk of the Rolls," Wilfred said, as the Studebaker pulled away.

"Really? How'd it get there?"

"Harry gave it to me just before we left Pocket's. He picked it up after that chap Glover dropped it."

Rowland nodded. "Very tidy of him." There was no reason to bring Harry Simpson to the attention of the federal police. He studied Wilfred for a moment. "You don't know why the feds are interested in Moran, do you, Wil?"

"I haven't the foggiest idea." Wilfred removed his glasses and polished the lenses with his handkerchief. "Perhaps he's committed some crime in Canberra."

"Senator Hardy may know," Rowland prompted cautiously. "He could find out at least."

"Perhaps." Wilfred gave nothing away, but then he rarely did. "You've got enough to worry about without poking your nose into this, Rowly."

———————————————

It was late afternoon when they reached the gates of *Oaklea* after stopping overnight in Gundagai where Wilfred had spent the morning attending to some sort of business. McNair was once again on hand to admit them, but Rowland noticed the presence of three other men in the shadows. Wilfred had certainly taken no chances. Perhaps his brother knew more than he was revealing. Frowning, Rowland wondered whether the Old Guard was gathering once again, as they had the previous year when revolution had seemed inevitable. Clearly this was about more than cattle stealing. The involvement of the Commonwealth Police was an intriguing development.

"You're quiet, Rowly," Edna said, looking back at him from the front seat. Clyde had driven the Mercedes from Rules Point. "Are you in a lot of pain?"

"Not at all," Rowland replied. "I was just thinking."

"About what?"

"Just that I should talk to Delaney," Rowland said thoughtfully. "Unofficially, I mean. He may be able to tell us why the feds are interested in Moran…" His voice trailed off and he turned, distracted by a manic barking as they pulled up to the house. "That sounds like Lenin," he said, just before his ramshackle greyhound came into view.

Clyde parked the Mercedes and Rowland stepped out, falling back against the motor car as Lenin jumped up to greet him. "Take it easy, Len. What on earth are you doing here?" The dog responded with wriggling paroxysms of joy. Rowland laughed. "Settle down, mate."

Wilfred climbed out of the Rolls, and was very similarly greeted by his son. He swung young Ernest up into his arms. "I brought your bloody dog back from Sydney with me," he said.

Rowland was surprised. Wilfred had never shown any particular fondness for the dog. Indeed Wilfred often used the hound as another example of Rowland's propensity to befriend the ill-bred.

"Why would you bring him here?" Rowland asked, noting a new scar just above the one where Lenin's ear should have been.

Wilfred put Ernest down. "Go and tell your mother that we're back, there's a good boy."

Ernest set off obediently, stopping only to shake his uncle's hand and wave to the others who had by now alighted from the Mercedes. Once he was gone, Wilfred spoke again.

"It seems your dog made a nuisance of himself when *Woodlands* was broken into… Bit one of the intruders. They hit him with the butt of a gun."

Edna gasped, dropping immediately to her knees to embrace the battered greyhound.

Rowland's face hardened as he too knelt to inspect Lenin's head more carefully. Clyde and Milton clustered around the dog as well. Lenin whined happily, delighted by the attention.

"Why didn't you tell me?" Rowland asked.

"It's a bloody dog, Rowly," Wilfred said gruffly. "I was hardly going to send a telegram."

Rowland scratched Lenin's single ear. "You've pulled up all right, haven't you, old boy?"

Edna grasped Lenin's face and kissed his muzzle. "You're a hero, aren't you, Len?"

Wilfred shook his head and cleared his throat impatiently.

Kate Sinclair came down the wide stairs and Wilfred's attention was drawn away by his wife. Ernest trailed after his mother. He pulled on Rowland's sleeve. "Don't worry, Uncle Rowly, I looked after... Lenin." He whispered the dog's name as if it was a profanity. Rowland supposed that in his brother's house, it was.

"I knew I could rely on you, Ernie."

Ernest nodded solemnly. He leaned over to whisper again in Rowland's ear. "Daddy pats him when no-one's looking."

Rowland ruffled his nephew's hair. "I thought as much, mate." It was only then that he noticed the number of cars parked in the drive. Mostly Rolls Royces. A conservative collection of chrome and black.

"Say Ernie, who's here?"

Kate broke in before her son could reply. "Oh my, whatever have you done to yourselves?" Her eyes widened with horror at the bedraggled state of them. "This is terrible. Do come inside... Wil, you didn't tell me they'd been hurt. You shouldn't be standing out here... what in heaven's name happened up there?"

Kate shepherded them into the drawing room, called for tea and fussed. Edna apologised profusely for the state in which she would be returning Kate's riding habit.

"Don't be silly, darling," Kate said. "I'm just glad you're all right. What a frightful time you've had."

"Oh I'm fine," Edna said, smiling at her hostess. "It was poor Milton who got hurt, and then Rowly..."

For a time Rowland listened as his sister-in-law questioned Edna; concerned, kind and, as always, gracious. Tea was poured and plates of sandwiches and fruitcake were passed around. The nurse brought in Ewan Sinclair, who had just woken from his nap, and Ernest tried to teach his little brother to walk. He was not patient about it.

"Isn't your godson clever, Rowly?" Kate asked, as she watched her boys proudly.

"A genius," Rowland replied, as the child tried to stand once again.

He glanced out of the large bay window at the motorcade parked just outside. "Have you guests, Kate?" He suddenly realised that both Wilfred and Maguire had disappeared shortly after their arrival.

Kate nodded. "Senator Hardy and some other gentlemen. They've been waiting for Wil in the library."

"Hardy,' Rowland said quietly.

Kate smiled nervously and shrugged. Rowland didn't press her any further. It was unlikely she knew why Hardy was there, and even if she did, he wouldn't ask her to break her husband's confidence. He let it go and drank his tea.

It was nearly dark when Wilfred stepped into the drawing room. There was something in the set of his jaw that made Rowland wary.

"I'm sorry, Katie, we're not finished quite yet," Wilfred said, as Kate spoke of dinner. "You might go in to dinner without us I think. Rowly and I will have something later."

"Rowly?" Milton asked, stiffening. "What does Hardy want with Rowly?"

Wilfred ignored him. "Would you come with me, Rowly? I need a word."

Rowland put down his teacup, and stood. "If you'll excuse me."

He followed Wilfred towards the library. From the top of the long hallway, he could see that there was a man posted outside the door. It was all reminiscent of the meetings at *Oaklea* when the Old Guard was bracing for revolution. But surely that hysteria had now passed.

"What's going on, Wil?"

Wilfred turned on him fiercely. Startled, Rowland backed up.

"Just what have you been…"

The library door opened suddenly.

"I say, there you are." Senator Charles Hardy stepped out. "We were wondering what was keeping you."

Wilfred turned stiffly. He moved away from Rowland. "Charles, you remember my brother, Rowland."

"Senator Hardy." Rowland offered his hand.

Hardy paused just a moment before he took it. "Rowland… Good Lord, man, you look like you've been in the wars."

"I seem to have become accident prone," Rowland replied carefully.

"Shall we step in here?" Hardy invited them into the library as if it were his own house.

The library at *Oaklea* was a large masculine affair, oak-panelled and furnished with studded leather armchairs. The domain of the Sinclair men, Kate's renovations had been minimal here. A grandfather clock metered the tension as they walked in, the haze of tobacco smoke a testament to cloistered hours of meeting. The door was closed behind them.

Hardy introduced his colleagues. There were three: Middlemiss, who impressed Rowland as a peacock, vain, consciously posed in the leather armchair. David Drummond, the New South Wales Minister for Education sat on the Chesterfield settee. Some years ago he had made a futile attempt to enlist Rowland Sinclair in the junior farmers' movement. Rowland had been careful to avoid him since then. The third gentleman Rowland knew well—Michael Bruxner, hero of the Great War, Leader of the New South Wales Country Party and the Deputy Premier. They all remained seated, their manner formal and stiff. Maguire stood sullenly by the fireplace. Rowland glanced uneasily at Wilfred, aware now that he was about to be interrogated.

"What can I do for you gentlemen?" he asked, taking a seat though he had not been invited to do so. Rowland was not about to be bullied in his brother's home.

Wilfred took the chair beside him.

Hardy was the first to speak. "I understand you're on the Board of Dangar, Gedye and Company."

"I am." Rowland watched as Middlemiss extracted a cigarette from a decorative gold case. His face was soft, almost pretty, his lips too red. He sucked on the cigarette and exhaled in flamboyant rings of smoke.

"Capital organisation, Dangars," Hardy said, pacing the room. Clearly he was running this meeting. "One of our very best firms. Important to the prosperity of the entire state."

"Just get on with it, Charles," Wilfred said irritably.

Hardy dropped a file onto the desk. "Do you know what this is, Rowland?"

"How could I possibly know?" Rowland asked, annoyed by the senator's theatrics.

"This is just one of the files we have on Communist activity in New South Wales." Hardy sat on the desk's edge and looked down at him. "This particular file contains intelligence gathered on a Communist plot to undermine Dangar, Gedye and Company."

"Just how do the Communists propose to do that, according to your intelligence?"

Hardy continued to stare at him. "We have reason to believe that the Reds have infiltrated the board."

Rowland laughed.

"You find that funny, Mr. Sinclair?" Middlemiss asked sharply.

"Yes."

"Rowly…" Wilfred cautioned.

"Why do you find that funny, Mr. Sinclair?" Middlemiss leaned forward, dragging slowly on his cigarette.

"I know the board quite well, Mr. Middlemiss. I doubt any one of them has the imagination to be a Communist spy."

"For God's sake, Rowly!" Wilfred muttered.

"You're an artist, aren't you, Rowland?" Hardy smiled affably. "I suppose it goes without saying that you have an admirable imagination."

"What exactly are you suggesting?" Rowland demanded.

"Your brother mentioned that you were at Oxford. Is that right, Rowland?" Michael Bruxner, the Deputy Premier, spoke for the first time.

"Yes."

Hardy opened his file. "The High Commissioner advises that Scotland Yard has been looking into Communist cells at the better English universities."

Drummond pulled at his tie. "Can we assume you saw a lot of this Communist activity in your time at Oxford, Mr. Sinclair?"

"I saw a lot of things at Oxford, Mr. Drummond," Rowland said evenly. "Most of them were a good deal more alarming than the odd Communist."

"But you did know Communists at Oxford?"

Rowland glared at him. "Yes."

"Your friends, Mr. Sinclair…" Middlemiss waved his cigarette at Rowland.

"What about them?"

"They are not the kind of people one would expect a man of your breeding to associate with."

"What can I say... they're willing to overlook my breeding."

Wilfred cleared his throat.

"Rowly, this is a very serious matter," Michael Bruxner warned. "Any man found to be conspiring with the Communists to cause strife in his own country would be guilty of treason."

Rowland stood, angry now. "This is ridiculous. Just what are you gentlemen accusing me of?"

Middlemiss jumped instantly to his feet. "We're not finished, Sinclair." He grabbed Rowland's arm to emphasise the point and drag him back.

Rowland swore and recoiled as Middlemiss' grasp closed tightly on his wound.

Wilfred moved in. "Let him go, Freddie. I agreed to let you chaps talk to him, nothing more."

"Hell's bells, Wil... how are you going to get him out of this? We're talking about treason!"

Wilfred placed himself between Rowland and Middlemiss. "Choose your words carefully, Freddie."

"I think we should all calm down, gentlemen," Hardy asserted over the top.

"I'll say this once," Rowland gasped, wondering if Middlemiss had broken the stitches Maguire had inserted at Pocket's Hut. "I am not a Communist. Perhaps Stalin is fool enough to want a seat on the Board of Dangar, Gedye and Company, but he has not sent me to prepare the bloody way."

"But your friends," Middlemiss insisted. He moved to the desk and flicked through the file. "Elias Isaacs... well known to the police, possibly a dangerous insurgent."

For a second Rowland was perplexed. "Elias?... God, you mean Milton... he's a poet for pity's sake—they're all Communists."

Freddie Middlemiss shook his head. "Could it be you're so bloody arrogant you don't realise…?"

Rowland was thinking seriously about hitting him.

"Tell me," Middlemiss asked. "Does Isaacs take a particular interest in your work on the board of Dangars? Does he love to hear the detail of your meetings, the cut and thrust of business?"

Rowland stared at him, incredulous, convinced now that the man was an idiot. "I don't talk to Milt about Dangars."

"And why is that?"

"Because it's bloody dull!"

"So what do you and your Communist mates discuss, Sinclair?"

"Art mainly, women occasionally… not things that would interest you, Mr. Middlemiss."

Middlemiss reared, affronted. Bruxner tried to soothe matters.

"Rowland, it is in acknowledgement of the sacrifices the Sinclairs have made for King and Empire that we are here tonight. If you have found yourself involved with the wrong people then it is not too late to do the honourable thing. We can help you extricate yourself from this situation without embarrassing your good family."

Rowland had had enough. "Go to hell, Bruxner!" He didn't wait, shaking off Wilfred's hand and storming out of the library.

Kate and the others were at dinner when he found them in the dining room.

"Rowly, you're finished… I'll have Mrs. Kendall set a place for you."

"Don't bother, Kate, I'm not hungry." He was aware that his friends were staring at him. Rowland tried consciously to make his face relax. "I just came to say good night actually… I might turn in."

"Rowly darling, are you all right?" Edna's was not the only concerned face at the table.

He smiled briefly. "Yes, of course."

"Where's Wil?" Kate asked hesitantly.

"He's not quite done with his guests," Rowland hoped that his fury with Wilfred was not betrayed in his voice.

"You're sure you don't want to play a hand or two after dinner?" Milton ventured.

Rowland shook his head. "Don't play too late," he said. "We're leaving for Sydney in the morning."

31

HAND OF MOSCOW

———————◆———————

BEHIND BRITISH RIOTS
INSTRUCTIONS TO RED AGENTS
(British Official Wireless)

LONDON, March 10

A series of questions was put to Mr. Henderson (Foreign Secretary) in the House of Commons regarding the announcements made at Moscow that instructions had been issued by the Third International to its agents to organise strikes and riots in Great Britain and the British dominions and colonies.

One member asked whether the Foreign Secretary's attention had been called to the fact that last Thursday's unemployment demonstrations in Great Britain were organised by the Communist party on representations from Moscow.

The Sydney Morning Herald, 1930

Rowland dropped the bandage, startled by the knock on the door. Before he could answer, Edna entered, balancing a plate, generously but precariously piled with shortbread.

"Good Lord, Rowly, what are you doing?" she asked, closing the door quietly behind her and placing the plate on the dresser.

Rowland stood shirtless by the washstand with a bottle of iodine and various items from a first-aid box.

"I'm trying to change this flaming dressing."

Edna picked up the gauze roll from the floor. "Shouldn't you get Dr. Maguire to do this?"

"I can manage."

"Here, sit down… I'll do it."

For a while neither said anything as Edna fumbled with disinfectant and replaced the dressing and bandages. Rowland glanced at the finished product. "It's a bit lumpy," he murmured.

"Shall I get Dr. Maguire then?"

"No, it's fine, thank you." He slid his arm back into the sling. "You'd better go to bed, Ed. It's getting late."

"Eat something," she ordered. "Mrs. Kendall is very upset you didn't have dinner. She wanted me to steal this up to you."

Rowland smiled. "She must think I'm being punished." When he was a child, the housekeeper would soften his father's discipline with surreptitious plates of shortbread.

Edna studied him. "Are you going to tell me what happened, Rowly? What did Wilfred want?" she asked gently. "What's made you so angry?"

Rowland rubbed his good hand through his hair. He doubted Edna would let this go, so he told her who had been in the library… what they had wanted with him.

Edna listened in disbelief. "They think you're a Communist spy?" She giggled. "Why, Rowly, that's ridiculous. Are you sure they were serious?"

"I think they were willing to believe that I was being manipulated by Milt. Apparently he's some kind of criminal mastermind."

Edna fell back on his bed, laughing.

Rowland watched her, and his mood lifted a little.

Eventually, she sat up, wiping the tears from her eyes, and took his hand in hers. Her face became serious. "It's just silly, Rowly."

"I know, Ed."

"They can't have anything but their absurd theories or they would have arrested you, darling."

Rowland nodded. "I know that too."

She squeezed his hand. "Then why do you look so winded?"

He looked away from her. "I'm not winded, Ed—I've been called a Communist before. Just wish I'd decked that prat, Middlemiss."

Edna did not seem convinced. She may have said more but there was another knock on the door.

"Come in," Rowland called, expecting it to be either Clyde or Milton. It was not.

Wilfred strode into the room with Maguire at his elbow.

They both stopped short to see Edna perched on Rowland's bed. Rowland, who had not yet managed to put on his shirt, had no doubt his brother would view the scene as grossly improper. At this point, however, he was not inclined to care about Wilfred's moral sensibilities.

Edna smiled cheerfully. "Good evening, Mr. Sinclair. Fancy running into you here."

Faintly, Rowland smiled. He loved the complete unflappability of the sculptress. Not even Wilfred Sinclair could make her step backwards.

"Miss Higgins. I trust you've found your guest room comfortable."

"Why it's delightful, Mr. Sinclair. You have a very lovely home."

Wilfred cleared his throat. "Would you mind excusing us, Miss Higgins? I'd like to have a word with Rowly."

"Certainly, Mr. Sinclair." She released Rowland's hand and stood. "Goodnight gentlemen."

Rowland said nothing as the sculptress left. She took any improvement in his humour with her.

Maguire moved to check Rowland's arm.

"It's been done," Rowland said, standing to retrieve his shirt from the bedroom chair on which he'd tossed it.

"Rowly…" Wilfred started.

"Go to hell, Wil."

Wilfred glanced at Maguire and motioned towards the door. The surgeon left them alone.

Wilfred watched Rowland struggle with his shirt. "Rowly, I can understand you're upset but…"

"You didn't even warn me, Wil."

"I only allowed them to question you."

"They didn't question me, they accused me—and you just stood there." Rowland gave up wrestling with the shirt and threw it into a corner.

Wilfred sat down on the bed. "Rowly, you've got to understand that your lifestyle, your associations will raise questions…"

"Of course I realise that! I couldn't give a toss what Hardy and his well-connected buffoons think!" Rowland turned on his brother. "But you, Wil… How could you think that? I'm only on that flaming board because you insisted. Forget about bloody King and country, how could you think I'd betray you like that?"

Wilfred stared at him, jolted.

"Look Rowly, I have a responsibility to…"

"Would you just get out, Wil. I'm tired and there's really nothing more to be said."

Wilfred stood. "We can talk tomorrow, once you've cooled down."

They left the next morning. Wilfred was not there. Kate apologised, informing them that her husband had gone to Wagga Wagga at first light. Rowland frowned. Charles Hardy lived in Wagga Wagga.

Kate Sinclair put her hand anxiously on her brother-in-law's arm. "Wil wants you to wait for him, Rowly. He barely slept last night… he wouldn't have gone if he didn't really have to."

Rowland shook his head. "I need to get back, Kate."

Kate's eyes moistened. "You've really quarrelled this time haven't you?"

Rowland smiled. "As opposed to every other time?" He didn't wish to distress his brother's gentle wife. "I'll get over it, Kate. Don't worry."

Ewan, who had been crawling about his mother's feet, clung to Rowland's leg and used it to pull himself up. Rowland scooped his nephew into his good arm. Clyde had helped him re-bandage the other that morning, after Edna's efforts had completely unravelled in the night.

Ewan gurgled and bounced excitedly, and Rowland was forced to use both arms to hold onto him. "By George, you're a big lad," he murmured, wincing. "Ernie will have to be careful to stay on your good side."

Clyde took the wheel of the Mercedes for the drive back to *Woodlands House*. Being unable to drive didn't help Rowland's mood. Clyde approached the task with the same conscientious caution with which he did most things. Milton often said he drove like an old woman. While Rowland would probably not have expressed it in the same words, Milton did have a point. The trip back to Sydney would be a slow one.

Neither Clyde nor Milton had asked Rowland about their abrupt departure from *Oaklea*, or the cause of his barely concealed brooding. They had known Rowland long enough to leave it until he was ready to talk, happy to trust that he had his reasons. Rowland appreciated the space, but the unquestioning faith of his friends only put his brother's lack of it into sharper relief.

It was not until they reached the outskirts of Sydney that Rowland spoke of what had gone on in the library at *Oaklea*. Like Edna, Milton and Clyde seemed to find the notion more funny than anything else. Indeed, Milton was clearly flattered that he was considered a "dangerous insurgent".

"I always wondered what happened to your brother's crazy Fascist mates after Lang was dismissed."

"They went into parliament, I believe," Rowland said, shifting so that Lenin's bony legs didn't stick into his ribs.

"So, have they sacked you from the Dangars Board?" Clyde asked.

"No… I think only the board itself can do that," Rowland replied. "I'm going to resign anyway."

"You can't do that, Rowly." Milton was adamant. "It'll make you look guilty."

"I don't care."

"You're just wild with Wilfred, mate," Clyde said calmly. "As funny as the idea is, you don't want to be branded a Communist spy. Things could get ugly."

Edna knelt on the front seat facing Rowland and Milton in the back. "Clyde's right, Rowly. Being a Communist is one thing—being a traitor, another entirely."

"There's a car following us," Clyde informed them suddenly, as he checked the mirrors.

Rowland twisted round to see, recognising the black Studebaker not far behind.

Clyde engaged the supercharger. "Hang on."

32

JACK AND JOCK

In the well-known political school from which Messrs. Lang and Garden have graduated with almost equal honours, and to which in spirit, they are both believed to be loyal to this day, it is customary for the alumni to address one another as "Comrade", at least for ceremonial purposes.

Obedience to this unwritten rule formerly posed no hardship upon Comrade Lang and Comrade Garden. As, when gentle folk meet, compliments pass, so when these notable demagogues met there was a cordial exchange of the proper party honorifics.

Indeed, during a series of weary years Comrade Garden and Comrade Lang, fighting side by side, as they averred, for the fellowship of men and other exalted causes, made comradeship seem a frigidly inadequate term for the mutual love and strong community of purpose.

They were the David and Jonathan of New South Wales politics: and as though conscious of the fact that, between themselves, the word "Comrade" must thus have had altogether too formal a sound, they addressed one another, in private, if not always in public, as "Jack" and "Jock". It may be doubted whether, when Messrs. Lang and Garden were thus most closely associated, there was ever a nearer approach to the ideal of Tweedledum and Tweedledee in the politics of any country.

The Advertiser, 1936

The established serenity of Woollahra was shattered by the roar of the yellow Mercedes as it hurtled up the driveway of *Woodlands House* and then screeched to a stop. For a moment the motor car's occupants sat in silence.

"I think we lost them," Clyde said.

"That was bloody terrifying," Milton murmured.

"Don't be melodramatic, Milt," Edna said, adjusting her hat. "We don't even know what they wanted."

"I was talking about Clyde's driving... he's a lunatic."

"At least I lost them," Clyde retorted.

"Maybe not." Rowland rubbed his neck, which had taken quite a jarring as Clyde swerved and wove at speed through the traffic of Sydney. "I think that may have been those chaps from the Commonwealth Police—they know where I live."

"The feds? I thought... why didn't you say?"

Rowland laughed. "You were having such a good time, it seemed a shame to tell you..." Rowland looked over to the base of the mansion's grand entrance stairs. "What on earth is this?" The entire household staff seemed to be gathered there in formal rows.

He climbed out, shoving Lenin before him, and looked carefully. It was indeed his staff. He wondered what they were doing outside.

A prim, starched woman stepped forward from the head of a row. Rowland didn't recognise her.

"Mr. Sinclair, sir," she said, dipping into a quick curtsey. "I'm Agnes Carstairs. Mr. Wilfred Sinclair retained my services while Mary Brown is indisposed. Welcome home, sir. I trust everything will be to your liking."

"Thank you, Mrs.—oh, I beg your pardon—Miss Carstairs." Rowland glanced at the formal receiving line of servants. "I'm sure everything will be fine."

"Very good, sir." Agnes Carstairs lifted her chin. "I'll just have your luggage taken up and unpacked. Would you like to take tea in the conservatory, sir? I'm afraid the main drawing room is somewhat cluttered... but I did want to consult with you before throwing anything out."

Rowland blinked. The main drawing room was his studio. "Yes... the conservatory, smashing idea," he replied awkwardly. Although Mary Brown had clearly disapproved of the way he conducted himself, they were used to each other. She had been at *Oaklea* since before he was born. It seemed odd, vaguely adulterous, to have some other woman run his household.

And so they retired to the conservatory, where tea was poured from a silver service into fine Royal Doulton. *Woodlands* was, if anything, more immaculate than it had been under Mary Brown. Every surface had been polished to a glassy finish, every nook and cranny dusted. Most noticeably the staff went about their work in complete silence. It was not that Rowland remembered his servants being particularly chatty or noisy before, but he was aware of the silence now. It was a little unsettling.

Aside from meddling with his staff, it appeared that Wilfred had also installed security at *Woodlands House*. The gates were manned and guarded, and there were more men patrolling the grounds. A chap called Jenkins reported shortly after they arrived to inform Rowland of the precautions his brother had taken.

Agnes Carstairs brought in the post that had been delivered in the time he had been away. Rowland groaned as the neatly stacked envelopes were placed on the table beside him. "It'll be weeks before I get through this."

Milton handed him a tall glass of gin. "This might help, Rowly."

Rowland flicked unenthusiastically through the envelopes... then one caught his interest. There was no postmark—it had obviously been hand delivered. Dropping the rest of the mail onto the table, he opened it. He smiled.

"It's from Humphrey," he announced, as he read the meticulous copperplate. "It appears he got back to Sydney all right—still thinks someone's trying to kill him."

"Where is he staying?" Edna asked, walking behind Rowland's chair to peer over his shoulder.

"The Grace, though he's thinking of finding somewhere quieter. Apparently it's full of Americans."

"You should invite him here, Rowly," Edna suggested. "At least the poor man will feel safe with all this security."

Rowland grimaced. "I suspect that's what he's hinting at. His mother has gone to visit a cousin in Melbourne and so he is 'at something of a loss'."

Milton laughed. "His mother? Good Lord Rowly, what were you thinking knocking about with this bloke?"

Rowland sighed. "Mostly I was trying to ignore him."

"Don't be mean, Rowly," Edna chided. "The poor man doesn't know anyone here but you."

"Here we go..." Milton muttered.

"It'd probably do him the world of good to spend time with people his own age." Edna was persistent.

Rowland laughed. "You want me to invite him out to play?"

"We could take him out to some parties or to the races... perhaps he'd like to come to the Easter Show?"

"If he falls in love with Ed, we'll never get rid of him," Clyde warned, flicking open the paper and settling into an armchair.

"Yes, Rowly," Milton agreed. "Your houseguests never seem to leave, mate."

"He's not going to fall in love with me," Edna protested. "Mr. Abercrombie's still heartbroken over Lady what's-her-name."

"He writes that he's leaving Sydney at the end of the month," Rowland said, glancing at the letter again. He sighed. "It might be safe to ask the poor blighter to stay... I'll phone."

"You'll regret it," Clyde said from behind *The Sydney Morning Herald*.

"No doubt, but I can't have Edna thinking I'm mean."

Edna ruffled his hair fondly. "You're not mean, Rowly, you're really very sweet."

Milton shook his head. "You know, mate, there's something particularly sad about a hen-pecked bachelor."

Rowland returned to his mail. "Yes, I know."

Humphrey Abercrombie arrived the next morning, with Michaels and a half-dozen trunks. Rowland had forgotten about Michaels. Fortunately his new housekeeper took charge of the ageing manservant, finding him a room in a part of *Woodlands House* that Rowland rarely entered.

Abercrombie was installed in one of the more luxurious bedrooms. The Englishman was deeply and expressively grateful for the invitation; so much so that Rowland felt quite bad about his reluctance on the matter. Edna, it seemed, had decided to adopt the bumbling classicist as a cause of sorts and set about organising activities that would distract him from the conviction that his life was in danger.

To Rowland's recollection, Humphrey Abercrombie had always suffered under some kind of persecution paranoia. Admittedly, back when they were at school, it had not been entirely unwarranted. Perhaps the poor fellow had been permanently scarred by the experience.

Rowland avoided giving Abercrombie any reason for the extraordinary security at *Woodlands House*, having decided that his guest's imagined dangers did not need to be collaborated with evidence of real ones. Abercrombie seemed in any case disinterested in the reasons for the fortification. Perhaps he assumed that such precautions were in the ordinary scheme of things.

"I think he was more lonely than scared," Edna whispered when Rowland pointed this out. "This nonsense about being in fear of his life was just an excuse to come here, I think."

"Possibly," Rowland conceded.

"You know, Rowly…" Edna's eyes glittered with the excitement of a sudden idea. "We should have a party! It'll be a fabulous way to introduce Mr. Abercrombie to people who don't spend their lives in gentleman's clubs."

"A party?" Rowland hesitated. They had thrown parties at *Woodlands* before. They were far from staid affairs. "Don't you think our crowd might be a bit much for old Humphrey? He's not particularly intrepid."

"He just needs to come out of himself," Edna replied, sliding onto the couch beside him. Then she stopped. "Perhaps it's not such a good idea," she said, frowning. "It wouldn't be the best time for you to invite an entire crowd of dangerous insurgents into your home."

Rowland looked up. The sculptress had a point. The sympathies of the artists and performers in whose circles they moved were often very left-wing. There were probably a number of "dangerous insurgents" among them.

"Everybody seems to be watching you at the moment, Rowly," Edna said gently. "We should be careful."

Rowland's eyes darkened. He wondered what Hardy and his conservative inquisitors would think of a *Woodlands* party. He could almost hear Wilfred's fury. "They can't hang me for throwing a party, Ed," he said quietly.

"Rowly…"

"This Saturday, I think," Rowland smiled. "We can all go to church and repent the next day."

The preparations for Humphrey Abercrombie's introduction to the wrong crowd were, at Rowland's insistence, elaborate. After some discussion, an evening soirée was agreed upon, with a picnic supper and champagne on the lawns; jazz bands and dancing in the ballroom. The guest list was extensive and varied, and it was not entirely devoid of names from the better families of Sydney, many of whom were quite happy to attend Rowland Sinclair's scandalous parties, even if they would never throw such an affair themselves. Also invited were the more creative, occasionally quite destitute, acquaintances of the residents of *Woodlands House*.

"Are you sure, Rowly?" Milton asked, scanning the list. "Some of these blokes are on the crazy side of red… Good grief, you've asked Jock Garden…"

Rowland smiled.

"Are you throwing this party for Humphrey or for Wilfred?" Clyde asked dubiously.

"Who cares?" Milton laughed. "It's going to be one helluva gathering!"

"Still, Rowly, I don't know that Humphrey's going to cope." Clyde folded his brawny arms and shook his head. "The bloke spends two hours every morning writing to his mother."

Unexpectedly, it was Milton who came to Abercrombie's defence. "He might surprise you. I had quite a regular conversation with him yesterday—he seemed quite interested in the party... we might turn him into a comrade yet."

Rowland sighed, convinced Milton was exaggerating. "I'll keep an eye on Humphrey," he said. Then, realising he hadn't seen the Englishman all morning, "Where is he?"

"Ed took him to Manly... she thought he needed a bit of colour."

Rowland's brow creased. Abercrombie's initial shyness of women seemed to have dissipated where Edna was concerned.

"Excuse my intrusion, Mr. Sinclair." Miss Carstairs entered the room. She seemed put out, but then she had seemed thus since they arrived. "A Detective Delaney to see you, sir."

"Smashing... where is he?"

"I asked him to wait until I checked whether you were receiving visitors, sir."

"Oh... yes, I am. Tell him to come in."

Colin Delaney strode in shortly thereafter, clearly bemused by the unexpected increase in formality at *Woodlands*. He shook Rowland's hand warmly.

"Bloody hell, Sinclair," he said, grinning. "You can't seem to go two months without coming to the attention of the Bureau... Blimey," Delaney glanced at Milton and then back at Rowland, "I'm out of town for a few weeks and this is what happens!"

Rowland relaxed a little. Delaney hadn't been in Sydney. Rowland had been worried the detective was calling with a few words to say on the subject of the Englishman Rowland had directed to him. "You've come about the break-in here haven't you?" he asked hopefully.

"What else have you been up to?" Delaney regarded him sharply.

"Nothing at all." Rowland offered the detective a seat, and Milton poured him a drink. "So… this break-in, Col… what do you know?"

Delaney sighed. "Not a great deal I'm afraid. We're no closer to identifying the blokes who broke into *Woodlands*… or who they were working for."

"So you don't think this is a random snatch a rich bloke thing?" Clyde asked.

"Doesn't seem likely. They want Rowly particularly, for some reason."

"Well, we just have to apply our intellects to that reason to deduce both it and the perpetrator," Milton mused, pacing.

Clyde groaned and threw a cushion at him.

"Sorry, Col." Rowland looked at Delaney apologetically. "Milt channels Conan Doyle from time to time… it's some kind of elaborate tic."

Delaney smiled. "There was a time when Elias Isaacs would have been our prime suspect."

"What's changed?" Clyde asked dryly. "Don't tell me Milt's become respectable."

"I wouldn't go that far." Delaney swirled the whisky in his glass. "It's just that there are any number of reasons to snatch Rowly." He put down his glass, counting off on his fingers. "Between the New Guard, the Communists, Wilfred's political enemies and the usual gentlemen of Sydney's underworld, we have a few people who could be behind this… and now this connection with treasure-hunting bushrangers really has us pulling out our hair."

Rowland regarded the detective thoughtfully. "Why would the Communists want to kidnap me, Col? Word has it I've been one of them for a while now."

Delaney shrugged. "They'd know that you're not... you're not, are you?"

Rowland sighed. "No, I'm not."

Delaney leaned forward onto his knees. "The feds seem to think that Soviet spies are operating here."

"Soviet?" Rowland started to laugh.

Milton said nothing.

Delaney sat back in his chair. "According to our friends in the federal police, Communist spies are infiltrating our great bastions of capitalism on Moscow's orders. There are rumours about a Senate Enquiry or some such thing."

"Do you think there's something to it?" Rowland asked. It all seemed a bit fanciful.

"There's definitely something, but it's hard to tell what. Bit early for a witch hunt though."

"Don't you believe it," Rowland murmured.

33

IN THE NATIONAL GALLERY

BY F.S.S.

"Chaucer at the Court of Edward III" is one of the glories of
the National Art Gallery of New South Wales—its chief glory,
I should like to say… In his "Chaucer" there is another point
of contact of a more whimsical kind to the stranger, but not
unimportant to Brown, because it made each work of art a
monument to friendship.

The Sydney Morning Herald, 1931

The halls of the National Art Gallery in Sydney were, on this day, nearly deserted. Edna rocked gently back on her heels as she gazed at *Chaucer at the Court of Edward III*. The oil had been one of the first ever purchased by the gallery and was still the anchor of its European Art collection. Her own artistic tastes lay elsewhere, with the modernist school, but Humphrey Abercrombie seemed more at home with British realists like Ford Madox Brown. Still, the painting was not without its allure. The classical formality of its composition was almost sculptural.

Glancing at her watch, Edna looked around for the Englishman. He strolled over to her, beaming. "Dear lady, this is a simply superb way to spend a morning. An appreciation of art in the farthest outpost... who would have thought!"

Edna laughed. Humphrey Abercrombie was ridiculous, but so completely unaware of it that she could not take offence. She did not find him unpleasant company. His earlier nervousness seemed to have improved somewhat. It had been at least an hour since he had felt the need to duck behind a door and leave the room for fear of some imaginary assailant. In the beginning, Edna had dived out of sight with him, quite enjoying the drama of his paranoia, but very quickly it had become tiresome. Admittedly she had recognised some of the people from whom he insisted on hiding as Communists, but considering the number of people he avoided, at least a couple were bound to be from the Left. She'd tried greeting them cheerily to show him that there was nothing to fear, but whenever she turned to introduce him, Abercrombie had disappeared. She came to understand Rowland's impatience with the man. Fortunately, Abercrombie had seemed to settle down a little in the gallery and the last hour had been passed in relatively agreeable conversation.

Occasionally he gave the sculptress vague insights into Rowland's past.

"Rowly was never much good with figures," Abercrombie said, while professing his own proficiency in mathematics. "Always getting thrashed by the master..."

"Oh poor Rowly!"

"Yes, beastly man really. I tried to help Rowly with the subject, naturally, but he was hopeless." There was faint smugness about his smile.

Edna observed, intrigued. It seemed an odd thing to gloat over. "Rowly has other talents," she said.

"Yes... of course he does, capital fellow—a real Briton," Abercrombie blustered, startled. "I didn't mean to suggest... I have nothing but the most sincere admiration and affection for Rowly."

"I can see that." Edna laughed, pitying the man in his discomfort. "I just meant that Rowly seems to have got by quite well without mathematics."

"Yes, of course he has... people do, you see..."

"Rowly was always rather clever with languages, I believe."

"Yes, brilliant in fact." Abercrombie seemed keen to extol Rowland's virtues now. "The French master would applaud as he walked in!"

Edna giggled. "Really? That does sound a bit peculiar."

Abercrombie nodded. "Frenchman, you know. Mad Frog really."

There was a brief moment of silence during which Edna considered informing Abercrombie that her mother was French. In the end she didn't. "Shall we take a walk in the Domain, before we head back?" she asked finally.

Abercrombie offered her his arm. "I am at your disposal, dear lady."

Edna ran into the drawing room, breathless. Her hat was awry. Her dark copper tresses had escaped beneath it into stray wisps, and she was flushed.

"Ed!" Milton put down his drink. "What's wrong?"

"Mr. Abercrombie hasn't come back here, has he?"

Clyde looked up now. "No... why?"

"I've lost him." The sculptress sank wearily into an armchair.

"What do you mean you lost him?" Milton asked. "He's a man, not a purse."

"Where's Rowly?" Edna demanded with a note of panic.

"In the kitchens—he's inviting the staff to this party."

"Really?" Edna stopped, surprised and for a moment distracted. "What a lovely idea."

"Milt's actually," Clyde replied. "I think Rowly just wanted to see the look on that woman Carstairs' face."

Rowland walked into the room in time to catch Clyde's words. "Miss Carstairs has given her notice, I'm afraid." He smiled at Edna. "But the rest of the staff, with the exception of the cook, have accepted. I suppose I'd better hire some more staff to attend to the guests and whatnot. I should probably have thought this through…"

"Rowly, I've lost Mr. Abercrombie!"

"How could you lose him?"

"He's gone. I took him for a walk in the Domain and he ran away."

"Good Lord, Ed, he's not a puppy—what do you mean he ran away?"

"There were some men from the Party at Speakers' Corner—Mr. Ryan and his friends. As soon as he saw them, Mr. Abercrombie just turned and ran away."

"Did you look for him?" Clyde asked.

"Of course. He's vanished. Rowly you don't think there's anything to this notion that the Communists are after him?"

"More likely the bloke needs to be committed," Milton muttered.

Rowland was clearly leaning in favour of Milton's assessment. He retrieved his jacket and slipped it on. "I suppose we're going to have to find him now. He's probably got lost or some such thing."

"Rowly, aren't you supposed to be keeping a low profile until these kidnappers are caught?" Clyde reminded him. "That security bloke, Jenkins won't be happy with you wandering the streets. Milt and I could…"

"I'm not going to stay inside *Woodlands* for the rest of my life," Rowland replied firmly. "And we can't leave Humphrey out there."

"I'm so sorry, Rowly," Edna said.

"Heavens, it's not your fault, Ed. Humphrey's always been a bloody fool."

"We should take the Rolls," Milton suggested. "It's more discreet than your car."

"I'll call Johnston," Rowland agreed. Taking the chauffeur would make the search easier.

"Perhaps you should take your gun too, Rowly," Milton suggested.

Rowland smiled. "No thanks... somehow it always ends up pointed at me." He grabbed his hat. "Let's find Humphrey. We can have him committed after the party."

Johnston stopped the car outside the ornately-wrought iron gates at the entrance to the Domain. The afternoon was slipping into evening and the parklands were falling into shadow as they began to empty of polite society. The bedraggled figures of the men who would find refuge for the night in the rock walls of Mrs. Macquarie's Point trickled in through the gates.

The residents of *Woodlands House* set out on foot in search of Rowland Sinclair's missing guest. Edna took them to the place where she had last seen the Englishman.

"He ran that way," she said, gazing at the tree line as if she expected to see him there.

Rowland frowned. "I don't see how he could possibly be lost here." He turned to Edna. "Where exactly did you take him, Ed? Perhaps he went back to one of those spots in search of you."

They spent the next hour and a half retracing the route Edna and Abercrombie had taken. By the time they arrived at the neoclassical Archibald Fountain in Hyde Park, where the tour of Sydney had apparently begun, Rowland was becoming concerned. He glanced back at St Mary's Cathedral, just over the road from where they stood. He wondered if the Englishman would have sought refuge in the church. The gothic British grandeur of the building would have attracted him, if nothing else.

He waved to the others who were gathered near the fountain's bronze minotaur. "I'm just going to check St Mary's," he called, as he walked briskly towards the road. For a moment he thought he'd caught sight of Humphrey Abercrombie on the stairs of the cathedral. He quickened his pace, shouting "Humphrey!"

He didn't hear Edna scream, "Rowly!"

He didn't see the car until it was too late.

34

DANGAR, GEDYE
AND CO.

19 September 1932

Dangar, Gedye and Company Ltd reports a net profit of £22,951 for the year ended June 30, an increase of £205 over that of the previous year. In the previous report gross profit was given. It is not given in the present report. The distribution on ordinary shares is unchanged at 22 per cent (15 per cent dividend and 7 per cent bonus) requiring £16,875, preference dividend of 8 per cent accounts for £2912, and the balance, £3164, is transferred to reserve account with capital of £111,400, of which £36,400 is preference, and a reserve of £18,475, bank overdraft, sundry creditors, and provision for taxation is £38,111. In the previous balance sheet these accounts were given in three items, totalling £49,351. Assets amount to £182,401. Here, too, there has been consolidation of items, three against five previously given cash debtors and deposits amount to £68,687, stock in hand to £79,005, and property and plant to £34,709.

The Sydney Morning Herald, 1932

The Pontiac screeched to a stop just in front of him. The back door swung open before Rowland could react. He was only feet away from the barrel of the gun.

"Get in the car, Sinclair."

Rowland froze.

"Now, Sinclair! I'm bloody sick of chasing you around... I'll happily shoot you and be done with it."

Rowland recognised the fair brows and the T-shaped scar: the face he had seen by the flame of a match at the steps of Caves House.

A Whippet blasted its horn as it tried to get past the Pontiac.

"Rowly!"

Clyde yanked him back as Milton kicked the door shut. It closed hard on the hand that held the gun and the weapon was dropped amid screaming profanity. The tyres screeched again and the Pontiac roared away.

Rowland stepped back from the road a little stunned. Edna reached up to grasp his face. "Rowly, are you all right?"

Milton picked up the abandoned gun. He switched the safety back on. "That was close, Rowly."

Rowland nodded. "Yes... Thanks..."

"These blokes are bloody clowns, but they're flaming persistent," Clyde muttered. "We'd better get you back to *Woodlands* before they try again."

Edna put her hand on Rowland's arm. "Rowly darling, I know you think Mr. Abercrombie is a little hysterical, but is there a chance he might have been abducted?"

Rowland removed his hat and pushed back his hair. "Maybe," he admitted. "Perhaps I'd better talk to Delaney."

"Mary!" Rowland stood surprised at his own door. Mary Brown held it open. "What are you doing here?"

"I believe Miss Carstairs has given her notice, Master Rowly." The elderly housekeeper looked at him accusingly, and sighed. "I warned

Mr. Sinclair that this was not a situation for the faint-hearted. It's a fortunate thing I'm ready to resume my duties."

Rowland smiled. He was well aware that, at best, Mary Brown regarded his lifestyle, his friends, and many of his decisions, with a kind of martyred sufferance, but she had known him all his life. There were certain things that Mary had come to accept, however plaintively she sighed while doing so. "Are you sure you're well enough, Mary?"

"I am, sir, and not a moment too soon."

"Indeed, Mary. I'm pleased you're back."

"There's a gentleman waiting for you in the drawing room, sir. Apparently he's staying here."

"Abercrombie? You mean he's here?"

They charged into the drawing room. Humphrey Abercrombie sat by the fire with a glass of Scotch and a book. "I say, you're back. I wondered where you'd all got to."

"We've been out looking for you," Rowland said, a little too evenly.

"We were terribly worried about you," Edna chimed in.

"Oh yes, Miss Higgins." Abercrombie stood. "We lost each other when we were forced to flee from those Communist thugs in the park. I searched for you for hours, and then decided it'd be best if I just took a taxi back here. I came in just as your housekeeper was leaving. She informed me, to my overwhelming relief, that Miss Higgins had come back here and was now in your company, old boy."

Edna threw herself into the settee. "Well, I'm exhausted."

"I believe we could all use a drink," Milton muttered, as he unstopped various decanters.

Rowland nudged Edna over and sat down beside her. "How did you know the men in the Domain were Communists, Humphrey?"

"Aren't they?"

"Yes, but how did you know?"

"Well they were wearing those badges that they all seem so fond of... and I believe one of them was singing that appalling Communist anthem."

On cue, Milton began to hum "The Red Flag".

Abercrombie nodded. "Yes, that's the one."

Rowland stared at the financial statements before him. Columns and columns and columns of numbers... neat, clear and incomprehensible. He threw the pages down in disgust. It was a language he didn't understand.

The Dangar, Gedye and Company board meeting loomed the following Tuesday. In the normal scheme of things Rowland would not have paid nearly so much attention to his board papers. He had always expected that Wilfred, having ensured his appointment to the board in the first place, would guide his vote. It was an arrangement that worked well for both of them.

Decisions taken by the Dangars Board were usually unanimous. Indeed, Rowland wondered if a dissenting vote was considered impolite. The board members were all men of an ilk. Wilfred's ilk.

On this occasion, however, Babbington's entreaty at Pocket's Hut had alerted Rowland to the possibility that the meeting could be more contentious. He had no idea of Wilfred's position on the Lister franchise. They had not yet spoken a word to each other.

Rowland scowled unconsciously as his mind strayed to the meeting at *Oaklea*. He and Wilfred had their differences but he had always been loyal—to his country and to his brother. Surely Wilfred knew that. Being called a Communist didn't bother him. Being accused of treason was another thing altogether.

He looked up a little startled as Edna sat on the arm of his chair. He hadn't noticed her come in.

She peered over his shoulder. "What are you reading?"

He pointed to the large stack of papers on the side table beside his armchair. "Legend has it that you can assess the health of a company by reading these. I think one may need the Rosetta stone to decipher them however."

Edna stroked his hair. "Poor Rowly, how frightful."

"I've never been very good with figures," Rowland admitted.

Edna nodded. "Mr. Abercrombie told me."

"He did?"

"He was telling me about your sadistic mathematics master." Edna frowned, clearly disturbed by the story.

Rowland dismissed it. "They were all like that, Ed."

"It sounds like a frightful school, Rowly... quite Dickensian." She glanced defiantly up at the portrait of Henry Sinclair which glared contemptuously at her from the wall behind Rowland. "I can't understand why your father sent you so far away... to somewhere so awful."

"It wasn't that bad... and it wasn't my father, Ed." Rowland was amused by the way she was challenging a painting. "I was still in Australia when he died. Wil packed me off to Pembroke House."

Edna turned to face him, not in the least appeased. "That's horrible! How could he?" Rowland regarded her with a faint smile, as her tone darkened. "Why do you suppose Wilfred wanted you out of the country, Rowly?"

"I don't think it was anything sinister." He decided to explain before Edna's imagination ran away with her. "Wil had just come back from the war, my father died suddenly and my mother had been unwell since Aubrey was killed. I was fourteen. Wil probably thought I'd have an easier time, away from it all."

"But England, Rowly?" Edna was once again seized with the impulse to protect the child he had been. "You were already at boarding school... You could just have stayed at Kings."

Rowland's smile became sheepish. "Well, no actually. I'd been expelled by then."

"Really?" Edna seemed more impressed than scandalised. "Whatever for?"

Rowland shrugged. "Nothing particularly villainous. I started a bit of a poker club..."

"What's wrong with that?"

Rowland grinned. "Things were stricter back then and the headmaster was a clergyman—he took it badly."

Edna shook her head in amazement. "I can't believe you've never mentioned this before. You couldn't possibly have thought we'd think less of you for it?"

Rowland laughed. "No, I'm sure it will only raise me in Milt's estimation." He shrugged. "Wil went to such extraordinary lengths to cover it up for the sake of my reputation, that I just became accustomed to not talking of it, I suppose."

Edna's brow arched.

"What?" he asked.

"Just wondering exactly how many secrets you Sinclairs have."

"Good Lord, Ed, our family secrets are a good deal worse than my chequered schoolboy career."

"Rowly, old boy, there you are!" Humphrey Abercrombie strolled into the room adjusting the cuffs of a grey flannel smoking jacket. "I say, what's this?" He picked up the papers Rowland had discarded and flicked through them.

"Financial statements," Rowland said quite bitterly.

"What fun!" Abercrombie was excited. "Would you like me to go through them with you—relive the old days…"

"No, I would not," Rowland muttered. He looked again at the papers and sighed. "But perhaps you'd better anyway."

Rowland stared out the window into the grounds of *Woodlands House*. Jenkins had men stationed at various points and vantages. The gates were locked, manned by two men who checked everyone who came and went. It was a bloody nuisance.

Delaney had made some headway. Apparently there had been a spate of abduction attempts on prominent citizens in the last months. Indeed two businessmen had disappeared in the last week, though there was some suggestion that they had absconded for reasons of their own. The already stretched police force was now looking into a potential kidnapping ring at work in the Sydney area. Fortunately most of the targets to date were in a position to retain their own security against further attempts.

Rowland turned back to the Dangars papers which lay in a disordered heap on the table. Abercrombie had confirmed what Babbington had told him. The company's financial position was precarious. The numbers still made no sense to him.

35

PUBLIC INQUIRY

◆━━━━━━◆

ROYAL SOUTH SYDNEY HOSPITAL
DOCTORS' CONDUCT:
ADMISSION OF HORSEPLAY

An admission that there had been horseplay among certain of
the doctors at the Royal South Sydney Hospital on the night of
February 21, and that bedding had been damaged, was made
by counsel for the former resident medical superintendent
(Dr. E. J. Ryan) at a Hospitals Commission Inquiry which
began yesterday, The president of the hospital (Sir Joynton
Smith) said, in evidence, that Dr. Ryan had admitted to him
that he and two doctors had been "making whoopee".

The Sydney Morning Herald, 1933

"For pity's sake, Clyde!" Rowland was exasperated. "I only hired
her again for your sake... you could at least have spoken to her."

"I know. I just... she's coming back, isn't she?"

"Yes." Rowland groaned. He felt grey.

Between abduction attempts, supposed Communist plots,
Babbington's entreaties, Charles Hardy's accusations and the
ongoing coldness between him and Wilfred, Rowland was not
thinking clearly. He had turned to painting as he always did when
his mind was troubled. And Clyde had reminded him of his promise.

Rowland had hoped Rosalina Martinelli was no longer available to model but, as fate would have it, not only was Miss Martinelli willing to work, but she was able to do so immediately. Her technique had not improved, and though she professed to be enthusiastic, she had wept and prayed and complained through most of the session.

Surprisingly, the painting was coming along well, but it gave Rowland none of the clarity and calm that the brush and canvas usually delivered. To make things worse, when given this dearly bought opportunity, Clyde had become incapable of conversation. Rowland was sure that Rosalina had left convinced that his friend was either mute or simple.

"This looks bloody good though, Rowly," Clyde offered by way of compensation, as he scrutinised the work in progress—*Psyche Weeping on the Banks of the Styx*.

Rowland regarded the compliment suspiciously. Perhaps it was sincerity. More likely it was remorse. He sighed. The Dangars board meeting was impending, and the question of the Lister franchise was playing on his mind, as was Hardy's accusation that he was working to undermine the company. The safest path would be to speak with Wilfred. He sat down, resting his elbows on his knees as he looked up at his friend. Clyde was a sensible man. "What do you think, Clyde? Should I vote in favour of the Lister franchise?"

"Which way would Wilfred vote?"

"Not sure."

"You could ask him."

"I'm asking you."

Clyde laughed. "You know me, Rowly. I love machinery."

Rowland nodded. He and Clyde had that in common.

"And I'm from the bush," Clyde continued. "Can't see the country getting by without generators, pumps and whatnot. Every shearing shed I've ever worked had a Lister plant... Things are grim now but when they get better folks will start restocking and producing things again—and they'll need their machines."

Rowland studied him thoughtfully and then, suddenly, he smiled.

"What are you thinking?" Clyde asked.

"That you should sit on this board, not me." Rowland leaned back, relaxed. "You've made more sense in one minute than poor old Humphrey has in all the hours I spent with him and those bloody figures."

"Thank God," Clyde muttered. "Commercial contemplations don't suit you, Rowly... I don't think you're cut out for it, mate."

Rowland nodded. "You'll get no argument from me, Clyde old son."

Clyde smiled. "So now you just have to survive this party."

"What could go wrong?"

Clyde looked hard at him. "Rowly, you've invited every Communist you know, and half the police force, as well as our usual crowd—who aren't exactly quiet. And just to make things really interesting, you've asked 'society' to come too... it'll be a bloody miracle if there isn't a riot."

"Now you're being hysterical."

"Talking of hysterical, you might need to warn Humphrey that half the people he's been ducking and hiding from will be dropping by to welcome him to Sydney."

***

"Rowly, stop! What are you doing?"

Rowland dropped his brush, startled.

Edna pushed him away from the canvas. "You'll get paint on your dinner suit." She stopped to take in the painting.

The goddess, Psyche, knelt by a river, weeping. The scene was both dramatic and poignant. Rowland had captured not only misery, but a deep resentment and a faint pride in the face of his goddess. He had cast Rosalina Martinelli in the perfect classical role.

"Oh Rowly, this is heartbreakingly beautiful. I'm so glad you gave Rosalina another chance."

Rowland smiled. "I miss painting you, Ed."

She met his eyes and for a moment neither said a word.

"Don't be silly, Rowly," Edna laughed finally. "You can't be a chef with just one recipe."

"You look lovely." He changed the subject though he allowed his gaze to linger upon her. She wore a gown of palest green which just skimmed the gentle curves of her figure before floating to the floor. The neckline was scooped and daringly low, and if not for the long gloves she wore, the sculptress' arms would have been bare.

Edna curtsied. "Why thank you, sir. And you have just enough time to change your shirt."

"My shirt?" Rowland looked down. The pristine white of his dress shirt was marred by a large splash of Pthalo blue. "Damn! How did I do that?"

"One wonders," Edna murmured, as she picked up his brush and dropped it carefully onto the tray of his easel. "Have you seen the garden?" She smiled excitedly. "They've strung up lanterns, and put up the marquees. There are floating candles in the pond, and garlands of roses in the ballroom… It all looks magical, Rowly. I'll be rather sad to see it all taken down tomorrow."

Rowland smiled. "It'll all have to stay then."

She giggled. "Yes, that'd be very practical—you'd better go and change."

Rowland checked his watch. "You're right. Have you seen Humphrey at all?"

"He's still getting ready I believe. I saw Michaels coming in and out of his room with shoes and that sort of thing."

"I'll check on him after I change—prepare him a bit. It wouldn't do to have the guest of honour hiding under the table in terror."

As it was, however, Rowland had only just managed to find and don a dress shirt which had not been ruined by paint when the music started, and the first of his guests arrived. He then discovered droplets of colour on his waistcoat and was further delayed in replacing it. Consequently he was in a hurry when he stuck his head into Abercrombie's room. The Englishman was fussing with the lapel of a white mess jacket.

"Rowly!" Abercrombie beckoned him into the room. "Could I possibly have a word, old man?"

Rowland stepped in. "Yes, of course, in fact there was something…"

"I couldn't help but overhear you speaking with Mr. Watson Jones about this board matter of yours."

"Oh. Yes."

"I must say, Rowly, I'm surprised you would seek the counsel of a person so ill-qualified to advise you on a matter of such import."

"Indeed."

"Mr. Watson Jones is a capital fellow but I doubt he has anything more than a basic colonial education. It was, if you don't mind my saying, quite unfair of you to put the weight of a decision which could ruin a company on such unprepared shoulders."

Rowland regarded him silently.

"And the fact that you would dismiss my own advice after the hours I committed to assisting you... well... it's just too bad... too bad."

Rowland took a deep breath. "Look Humphrey, I didn't mean to offend you. I didn't realise..."

"Have you considered how Mr. Watson Jones is going to feel when his advice leads you to ruining Dangars and destroying your own reputation in business?"

"No, I can't say I had."

"Well, I'm not surprised. You're an outstanding fellow, Rowly, but I must say you've always been a bit oblivious."

"Oblivious? To what exactly?" Annoyance was challenging Rowland's initial reluctance to continue the conversation.

"Rowly! There you are!" Edna appeared at the doorway. "You must come down—everybody's arriving. Mr. Joynton Smith is demanding to know why you think you're Jay Gatsby all of a sudden." She grabbed Rowland's hand insistently.

Rowland allowed himself to be pulled away. He'd deal with Abercrombie's wounded feelings later.

The party seemed to have exploded immediately into full swing. Rowland's guests milled, appraising each other warily. His staff mixed gaily with those they had served and attended on other occasions. The small army he'd retained to serve at the party kept glasses charged and moved through the crowd with silver trays of dainty hors d'oeuvres.

Edna led him towards an elderly moustachioed gentleman who stood by the mantel, smoking a cigar and observing the room with a single monocled eye. The other was glass—a fact made obvious by contrast with the constant movement of its partner. Sir James Joynton Smith was the founder of *Smith's Weekly*, Wilfred's newspaper of choice. Whilst Joynton Smith loved his paper, the conservatively patriotic perspective of the publication had more to do with the man who now stood stiffly by his side.

"Sinclair!" Joynton Smith boomed. "You know Robert?"

"Mr. Packer—pleased you could make it." Rowland extended his hand.

Robert Packer shook it, but cautiously. He was ostensibly retired now but had been largely responsible for the success of *Smiths Weekly* in the twenties. He looked about him much as Rowland envisaged Wilfred would—with a kind of well-mannered horror. Rowland couldn't remember inviting Robert Packer.

"I insisted Robert come along," Joynton Smith said, his good eye twinkling. "Knew he'd enjoy your crowd."

Rowland smiled. The newspaperman was a notorious practical joker—he probably thought it would be funny to bring Packer to one of Rowland Sinclair's parties. "I hope you're right, James."

"You're with Dangar Gedye aren't you, Sinclair?" Packer asked. "I hear the board is at odds over this Lister franchise."

"You're well informed," Rowland replied, startled.

"Nothing wrong with a boardroom stoush, my boy," Joynton Smith said, slapping Rowland on the back. "What I'd give for something so simple at the Royal South Sydney."

Rowland looked at him curiously. Joynton Smith was the president of the Royal South Sydney Hospital Board, among others. "Problems?"

The old newspaperman sighed. "Bloody doctors are running riot."

"I had dinner with Charles Hardy last week," Packer interrupted. "Your name came up, Sinclair."

"The senator dined with my brother and his wife a couple of weeks ago," Rowland responded evenly. "I happened to be there."

"Indeed." Packer's tone was non-committal but his eyes were sharp, assessing.

"Rowly, there you are!" Milton put an arm about his shoulder. "You've got to circulate, old mate…"

Rowland introduced the poet, who had elected to enhance his dinner suit with a red brocade waistcoat and a boutonnière of Cootamundra Wattle.

"I'm sorry, gentlemen, I must steal Rowly away." He pulled Rowland aside and whispered. "Humphrey hasn't come down yet."

"Right." Rowland straightened his shoulders. "I'd better go and get him." He wondered if Abercrombie was pouting over the Dangars matter or was just so terrified by the sight of Communists that he had chosen to remain in his room.

Rowland ran up the staircase leaving Milton to play host in his absence. Abercrombie's room was on the third floor. Receiving no response to his knock, Rowland pushed the door open.

"Humphrey, it's just me…" The room was empty.

He made a quick search, even pausing to check under the bed. It seemed a ridiculous place to search for a grown man, but he vaguely remembered that Abercrombie had often hidden under beds and in cupboards when they were boys. He had been an odd child. And he seemed to have grown into an odd man.

The search yielded nothing.

36

MESS JACKET GAINING ON "TAILS"

For formal evening wear, the die-hards still retain their fond preference for the black dinner jacket or complete tails, but with those who prefer coolness with their formality, the white mess jacket has gained tremendous popularity. These jackets have about them a dash of their original Indian flavour when worn with the cummerbund, a bold sash of black silk about the waist. Two or more pert black buttons relieve the glossy white of the jacket. Such dress is correct on every occasion warranting tails or dinner jacket.

The Courier Mail, 1934

Initially, Rowland searched for Abercrombie, but in amongst greeting guests, the odd conversation and being dragged occasionally onto the dance floor by both old flames and potential ones, the quest became impossible. Despite Milton's fears, there was no real trouble that evening. At one point Jock Garden had taken exception to something Robert Packer had said, but Rowland had been on hand to keep things civil. On the whole the opposing extremities of Rowland Sinclair's social world seemed to regard each other as curiosities more than sworn enemies. As the night wore on, they may even have guardedly shared a drink.

Rowland was in the grounds watching the fireworks display, when Edna found him. She pulled him down and spoke directly into his ear so he could catch her words over the noise. "Rowly, Wilfred's here."

"Who?" he asked, sure he had misheard over the whirring squeal of a Catherine Wheel.

"Wilfred… your brother, Wilfred."

"Oh." He allowed her to lead him away from the noise a little. "Where is he?"

"He's waiting for you in the library."

Rowland straightened. "I'd better go and see him then."

Edna grabbed his sleeve. "Rowly, he's really angry."

Rowland put an arm around the sculptress. "I'm not afraid of Wil, Ed. It'll be fine."

"I'm coming with you."

"No, you stay here. There's no reason we should both miss this party… You haven't seen Humphrey, have you?"

"I don't think so." Edna wasn't interested in Humphrey Abercrombie at that time. "Wilfred's really angry, Rowly. I've never seen him so…"

"What did he say to you?" Rowland asked, frowning now. "Was he…"

"No… nothing like that… he was perfectly civil to me, but he looked like he wanted to kill you."

Rowland laughed. "He looks like that a lot, Ed. Don't worry. Stay here… keep an eye out for Humphrey and I'll deal with Wil."

The door was shut when Rowland reached the library. The party immediately outside it was getting a little uninhibited. A couple of shapely young ladies were performing some kind of cabaret in the drawing room, accompanied by Joynton Smith on a concertina. Robert Packer seemed to have left.

Rowland watched regretfully for a few moments. He wondered how much of the party he would miss while Wilfred made his feelings on this matter, and probably a couple of others, clear. Inhaling deeply, he walked in, closing the door behind him.

The library, largely unused since his father's time, was the room Rowland liked least in his home. It had been from this room that Henry Sinclair had controlled his empire and his sons. It was to this room that Rowland had been summoned as a child when his father was displeased. Its solid traditional furniture, dark colours and stately style all spoke of power—but that power had never been his. Just briefly, it occurred to Rowland that Wilfred always chose the library in which to bring him into line.

Wilfred sat in their father's chair, smoking. Rowland saw now what had so concerned Edna. His brother's face was pale with an intense simmering fury. Still, Wilfred had been this angry with him before. He couldn't quite remember when, but he was sure he had been.

"Hello Wil," Rowland said steadily.

"What the hell is this, Rowly?"

"A party." Rowland stood his ground.

Wilfred crushed his cigarette into the ashtray beside him. He stood up and advanced so quickly that Rowland stepped back reflexively. Wilfred poked him in the chest. "Damn it Rowly, are you trying to get yourself hanged?"

"I didn't know having a party was a capital offence."

Wilfred exploded, pushing Rowland back against the wall. "Do you have any idea who's in your house? What the hell are you trying to prove?"

"Proof?" Rowland retorted. "Since when did you need proof? I don't remember you asking Hardy or Middlemiss for proof."

For a moment Wilfred held his gaze. "What happened at *Oaklea* was unfortunate… but I'm starting to think that Hardy has a point."

Rowland stared at him.

Wilfred snorted. "You need not look so bloody wounded. Why would you invite every flaming Communist in Sydney to *Woodlands* if that wasn't exactly what you wanted me to think?"

The door to the library was pushed open and Edna walked in. She ignored the tension in the room. "Rowly, there you are! Detective Delaney was looking for you."

Wilfred stepped back in disgust. "I expect all your parties end with the police being called."

"Delaney's a guest," Rowland said coldly, hoping that the detective was in fact trying to find him for social reasons, and not because he needed to arrest someone.

Wilfred glanced darkly at Edna. "Would you excuse us, Miss Higgins. We're not quite finished."

"Rowly…" Edna looked uncertainly at Rowland.

Rowland kept his eyes on his brother. "Wil and I will be done in just a minute, Ed. Let Colin know I won't be long."

Edna hesitated, but in the end she left them alone again.

Rowland sat down. "Just say what you came to say, Wil, and let me get back to my guests."

Wilfred sat opposite him. He opened his mouth to begin and then he stopped. He shook his head.

Rowland waited.

Wilfred stood and left the room.

Rowland flinched as the door slammed. He sat in the silence for a minute. Then he rubbed his face, and groaned. This latest war had gotten out of hand. "Wil, wait!"

Rowland started after his brother, but the hallway outside the library was crowded with people who wanted to chat, to slap his back and thank him for his hospitality. Consequently, it took him several minutes to reach the front door. As politely as possible, he fought his way free of guests, hoping that Wilfred's car had not yet pulled away. In truth, Rowland wasn't sure what olive branch he could offer, or even if he really wanted to offer one. He was still cut by Wilfred's mistrust… but he didn't want to leave it like this.

The evening air outside was significantly cooler than within. The driveway was teeming with people and vehicles. Partygoers climbed in and out of cars both coming and going. Rowland looked for Wilfred.

A black Rolls Royce started up several feet away. Rowland recognised it. An older model, it had been originally purchased by his father. It was garaged at *Woodlands*, maintained and driven by Johnston, but Wilfred used it and the chauffeur whenever he was in the city.

Rowland sprinted to reach it before it pulled out, flinging open the back door and jumping in.

"Wil…" He stopped, falling back with the momentum as the Rolls accelerated out of the driveway. Wilfred's security men waved them through the gates without a second glance—they were watching for those trying to enter *Woodlands*, not those trying to leave.

"Humphrey!" Rowland stared at the Englishman, bewildered. Wilfred sat stiffly between them. "What the hell…?"

"Keep your head on, old boy," Abercrombie said. Then he spoke to the chauffeur. "You know where to go."

Rowland noticed the chauffeur now. "Michaels? Where's Johnston?"

Michaels ignored Rowland and continued to drive.

Rowland turned to Abercrombie and Wilfred, confused, and a little annoyed. "Stop the car. What's going on? Wil?"

Wilfred didn't move. He spoke calmly. "He's got a gun, Rowly."

Humphrey Abercrombie dusted the lapel of his jacket with his free hand, and he shifted the revolver into view. "Problem with white, you know," he muttered. "Shows every speck of dirt."

Rowland gasped, outraged. "What are you doing?" He reached out to seize the gun from the Englishman's grasp.

Abercrombie reacted quickly, placing the muzzle of the weapon against Wilfred's temple. "No further, Rowly. Shooting Wilfred here would make rather a mess." He eyed Rowland coldly. "Just sit back, there's a good man. There's no reason for this to get uncivilised."

Rowland sat slowly back in the seat, stunned. He wondered if Abercrombie had suffered some kind of mental breakdown.

"What are you doing?" He was careful to keep the anger from his voice.

Abercrombie smiled. His entire manner was unrecognisable.

Wilfred's face was tense, his eyes furious.

"I'm kidnapping you, you idiot."

"Why?"

"Because the buffoons I hired can't seem to manage it."

"They were working for you? Why would you want to kidnap me? Surely you don't need…"

"The money?" Abercrombie laughed. "No, Rowly, I don't."

"Then what the hell do you want with me and Wil?"

Abercrombie regarded him contemptuously. "I don't really want anything from either of you, I'm afraid."

Rowland swore, barely controlling the urge to swing at Abercrombie. "Then what do you think you're doing, you bloody fool?"

"Rowland," Wilfred said tightly, "you would do well to remember that your old chum has a gun pressed to my head."

Abercrombie laughed. "Well said." He lowered the gun to Wilfred's chest. "Your brother understands the situation, Rowly. Strikes me as a rather clever chap... he's certainly showing me a great deal more respect than you ever did."

Rowland shook his head in disbelief.

"Didn't you think I noticed?" Abercrombie said quietly. He spoke to Wilfred. "Rowly was quite the champion, you know. Stepped in I don't know how many times to save me from those well-bred thugs from all the best families, with whom I was incarcerated at Pembroke. I often wondered why." The Englishman looked at Rowland now. "Let's be honest, old boy, you didn't have much time for me yourself."

Rowland didn't respond. He felt a strange sense of guilt that he hadn't tried harder to like Humphrey Abercrombie. It seemed clear the slight had sent the man completely over the edge. Still, it was too late now.

"Of course, I did learn a lot at Pembroke," Abercrombie continued. "I saw firsthand the kind of men the upper classes unleash on the working man—the exploitation of power, the cruelty, the complete indifference to the suffering they inflict. It was a valuable lesson."

Rowland rubbed his face in his hands. "What on earth are you talking about, Humphrey?" He glanced at Wilfred who was still pinned back by Abercrombie's firearm. "Look, if this is over something I did fourteen ruddy years ago, why are you pointing a gun at Wil? Let him out and we'll settle it between us."

Abercrombie snorted. "Good Lord man, I didn't come halfway around to the world to address some schoolboy tiff." He pointed at

Rowland. "I remember you too well, old chap. You'd take a bullet before you'd let poor weak, helpless Humphrey Abercrombie hold you at gunpoint... but you're not going to allow me to shoot your brother."

Rowland smiled. "You overestimate me, Humphrey. I'm in no hurry to be shot myself... you don't need Wil."

"I think I'll keep him anyway."

"So what is this about, Humphrey?"

"For pity's sake, Rowly," Wilfred said through gritted teeth. "Mr. Abercrombie is a member of your beloved Communist Party. I presume that's why you asked him to move into *Woodlands* with the rest of your unemployed Lenin-loving freeloaders."

Rowland shook his head. Wilfred felt the need to hold the Communists responsible for everything. "That's ridiculous. Not that I'd care if Humphrey was a Communist, but Milt would know him if he was with the ACP—there's not that many of them."

"Of course I'm not with your local Australian Communist Party," Abercrombie scoffed. "There're more Fascist spies in the ACP than there are party faithful. In fact, I've had a time of it avoiding those few members who have enough international connections to recognise me when they're sober."

Rowland glanced out of the window—they were in a seedy part of the city now, driving through Oxford Street. A thought occurred to him. "How long have you been back in town, Humphrey?"

Abercrombie shrugged. "I didn't come back when you sent me home, if that's what you mean. I returned from the mountains a few hours before you did."

"You killed Moran."

"Yes."

"Why?"

"We had an arrangement. He couldn't keep up his end. He could identify me. A necessary precaution, I'm afraid."

"What arrangement?" Rowland asked, aware that both he and Wilfred could now also identify Abercrombie.

"We both had reason to want you out of the way for a while, Rowly. I wouldn't normally work with men like Moran."

"What reason?"

"In my case the Lister franchise. We would like to see the vote defeated."

"Who's we?"

The Rolls Royce pulled up in front of a dilapidated terrace. Rowland thought they were in Surry Hills, though he couldn't be sure. A decaying knee-high fence marked out the few square feet of bare dirt attached to the building. There were no streetlights but the moon cast enough light for Rowland to see the rotting weatherboards and broken windows. The adjoining terraces were in no better repair. Abercrombie ignored Rowland's question. "Now gentlemen," he warned. "I have a number of colleagues waiting in this salubrious residence. We are going to walk in. If either one of you does anything other than comply completely, I'm going to shoot. As I plan to have my gun pressed into Wilfred's back, it's unlikely I'll miss. Do we understand each other?"

Rowland glimpsed a movement of curtains. Abercrombie's colleagues obviously knew they'd arrived. The Englishman directed them into the terrace with a friendly hand on Wilfred's shoulder, and a gun in his ribs. Michaels walked up front with Rowland.

The door was opened by a woman, small and hunched. A half-dozen men were smoking in the front room. Two wore suits, the others sat in shirtsleeves. At least some of the accents were European. They stood when Abercrombie and his prisoners entered the room, and voiced approval and congratulations.

Abercrombie gave orders. Wilfred Sinclair was to be taken "upstairs" and secured. Three men pushed Wilfred up a narrow staircase, leaving Rowland with Abercrombie and the others. Abercrombie did not introduce his companions. He pulled out a chair at a small wooden table and motioned for Rowland to sit.

Rowland didn't move.

Abercrombie waited. "You don't have many choices, Rowly."

Rowland sat, his eyes glittering resentfully. "What do you want?"

The Englishman sat opposite him. "You know, Rowly, I had expected to find that you were no different to all the other selfish well-heeled morons we were at school with."

Rowland said nothing, regarding the man suspiciously.

"But after renewing our acquaintance and meeting your friends, I wonder if there is another way…"

Sullen, restrained silence.

Abercrombie gazed at him thoughtfully. "When I was at Cambridge, Rowly, I had the good fortune to join a group of men who had a vision for the world—a fairer world than we know today."

"I've read Marx too, Humphrey."

"Then you'll understand. We're trying to loosen the choking grip of capitalist power, old boy… destabilise it." Abercrombie leaned forward, looking directly into Rowland's eyes. "Do you know what's happening in Germany, Rowly?'

Rowland held his captor's gaze. He had visited Germany the previous year. Admittedly, it had disturbed him.

Abercrombie spoke for some time after that—of the Communists and intellectuals being detained and tortured under the direction of Germany's new chancellor, of the seemingly irresistible rise of the Fascists and the failure of democracy to stop it. He ranted about the exploitation of workers in Britain and of colonial injustice. Rowland had heard these arguments before and he was to some extent sympathetic... but he was not a Communist.

"You're not in Germany, or Britain—you're here," he said evenly.

"Rowly, I know you can see the truth in what I'm saying. Democracy is not going to survive in the face of the Fascists. Our only hope is to throw our lot in with the Communists. Join us—help us build a better world."

"And how exactly do you want me to help you, Humphrey?"

"You could vote against the Lister franchise and you could work with us."

Rowland laughed. "You want me to be a spy?"

"I am aware of your dealings with the New Guard, Rowly... It seems you've spied on the establishment before."

"That was personal not political."

"There's information you could give us. You have an insight into this country that we don't, as well as connections. With your access to funds and people we could strike a real blow against the capitalists. You could tell us how best to undermine the government, to give the working man a chance at managing his own destiny."

"That's treason."

"Not if your loyalty is to mankind and the greater good."

"So why the charade, Humphrey... all this bloody hysteria? What good could it possibly do your cause to annoy the hell out of everyone around you?"

Abercrombie was taken aback. He looked almost hurt. "I'd not expected you to be enlightened in any way, I'm afraid. I assumed I'd be dealing with a committed member of the capitalist establishment and, frankly, I was rather staggered to find you openly consorting with the Left." Abercrombie signalled to one of his comrades who brought glasses and a bottle of Scotch to the table. The Englishman poured two drinks before he went on. "If you recall, I did try to get you away from your companions—to remain at Caves House in my suite—but you refused to go anywhere without Isaacs and Jones."

"And the caves? You sounded like you were terrified?"

"We started the panic," Abercrombie explained. "But in the darkness, I needed a way to help the boys find you—of course you just accepted it as poor old blithering Humphrey."

"You seem to be offended that I believed you a fool when you took great pains to act like one."

Abercrombie stopped, and then he smiled. "You make an interesting point. Perhaps I am being a bit precious. I suppose Rowly, as much as I could see that being the Humphrey you remembered would give me the perfect cover, some part of me wanted your respect. You were the closest thing to a friend I ever had at school. Perhaps some part of me hoped you would see through all that."

Rowland shook his head. "All you did was alert me to the danger."

Abercrombie laughed. "You were already alert to it, Rowly. All my actions did was make you determined to ignore any danger… because of course you're nothing like me." His voice was bitter. "It served my purpose." Abercrombie pushed a glass of Scotch towards Rowland. "Initially, the plan was simply to make sure you were not at the Dangars board meeting. Once I realised I could appeal to your better nature I hoped that eventually I could count on you for more than that."

"By sending Moran to kill me?" Rowland bristled. "He was going to kill Ed, for God's sake!"

"Believe me, Rowly, I didn't sanction that. He was just to hold you till my men came out to get you. Moran had his own agenda. I apologise, Rowly." He said it so fervently that Rowland was almost convinced of his sincerity. "I would not have Miss Higgins hurt for the world."

"So why didn't you talk to me at *Woodlands*? You've been living in my house for the past week."

Abercrombie shrugged. "Tactical decision. Perhaps I lost my nerve. I wasn't sure I could bring you round." The Englishman sipped his drink and glanced at his stone-faced co-conspirators. He lowered his voice. "Look Rowly, the Lister operation is only a small part of a greater putsch. I'll admit that your presence on the board caused me to take rather a more personal interest than I probably should have. In doing so, I may have taken things too far."

"I noticed," Rowland said tersely.

Abercrombie went on. "It occurred to me at *Woodlands* that I could achieve the same thing by simply convincing you that Dangars was not in a financial position to take on the Lister franchise. Of course you chose to take counsel from Mr. Jones on the matter instead."

"And so you decided to kidnap me and Wil, because being held at gunpoint is going to convince me that yours is a reasonable point of view? Bloody oath, Humphrey, you're an idiot!"

Abercrombie's eyes flashed dangerously. "Careful Rowly, I'm not the cowering buffoon you remember."

"No, you're not. Now you've got a gun."

Abercrombie sighed. "I'd really hoped that we could forge a new friendship, as equals. Or is it that you can only befriend those who rely on you, so that you can lord it over them… is that it, Rowly?"

Rowland bit his lip. "I should have let them drown you," he said quietly.

Abercrombie laughed. "But you didn't. You jumped in fists flying. You did that rather a lot back then—quite the angry young man. What happened to you, Rowly?"

"I grew up."

"Rather a shame, really. There's a lot to be angry about now. Inequity, oppression, persecution—you could be so valuable to the cause, Rowly. Don't you want to have some purpose—have your life mean something?"

Met only with simmering silence, Abercrombie stood and brought his chair around the table. He placed it beside Rowland's and sat down again. "I need your help, Rowly," he whispered. "Everything that could possibly go wrong, has. I must bring them something... If I could just show them that an institution like Dangar, Gedye and Company could be destabilised, they'd see that revolutions need not be bloody." He brushed some lint from Rowland's lapel and straightened his tie. "Help me, Rowly, just once more."

Rowland stiffened, unnerved by the closeness that Abercrombie was imposing on him. He tried to reason with the man, struggling to soften his voice. "My vote won't make a difference, Humphrey. All the other directors are for the Lister franchise."

The Englishman's face darkened. For a moment he looked away, and then without warning, he turned and struck Rowland. "You're a liar," he said. "A coward and a liar!"

Rowland's head snapped back with the blow. It took him a moment to focus again, and for a few seconds he simply stared at Abercrombie. It was when the Englishman smiled that Rowland exploded and launched himself out of the chair.

He landed two punches before Abercrombie's comrades dragged him off.

37

UNDERWORLD RAID

---◆---

Police Offer No Evidence

SYDNEY, Tuesday

Joseph Dudley Prendergast (21), Albert Runnalls (32), Fred Lee (42), who were arrested in connection with the alleged raid on the shop of Kate Leigh, at Surry Hills, were charged at the Central Court today with having broken and entered the premises and assaulted Kate Leigh with intent to murder her.

All were discharged, the police having no evidence to offer.

The Canberra Times, 1933

Wilfred was sitting on a low cot when the trapdoor rose open and his brother was heaved through the opening. Rowland lay groggy on the floor of the small airless attic.

"Rowly!" Wilfred pulled him to his knees as the bolt clicked into place again.

Rowland coughed, groaning as he struggled to get up. It was black. The attic was windowless, dark though it was now morning. It smelled of mice. Wilfred flicked open his cigarette lighter, holding it up to see by the dim wavering light.

"Bloody hell, Rowly... for God's sake, sit down!" He eased Rowland onto the cot.

"I'm all right, Wil," Rowland said, grimacing. "I used to box, remember."

"You don't look like you were very good at it."

"I meant that I know how to take a punch," Rowland returned indignantly.

Wilfred put a bottle of lukewarm water into his hands. "Here, drink."

"Don't waste the lighter fluid." Rowland spluttered over a mouthful of the tepid stale liquid. "We'll need it to find a way out of here."

"What happened?" Wilfred's hand remained on his brother's shoulder.

"They wanted me to vote against the Lister fanchise." Rowland tried to pull himself together. "Humphrey completely lost his rag... he's gone somewhere, so we have a little while, I think." He tried to stand again.

Wilfred stopped him. "Just take it easy for a minute, Rowly."

"We have to get out of here, Wil. Humphrey's trying to save face... When he gets back, they'll start on you. He wants something to show that he's not a complete moron." Rowland tested the bruise on his left brow gingerly. It was sticky with blood. "Let's be honest, they can't just let us go now."

"Give yourself a second while we figure out what to do." Wilfred sat beside him. "I take it your friend is some kind of international insurgent."

"Believe me, he's not my friend anymore," Rowland muttered, thinking of the perverse pleasure Abercrombie had taken in belting him senseless while he was restrained from fighting back. Now more than ever, he wished he'd left him in the pond.

"He did this?" Wilfred's voice was hard.

"I'm starting to realise that Humphrey doesn't take rejection all that well."

"God, Rowly." Wilfred took a deep breath. "What the devil did you do to him?"

Rowland swore as he shifted too quickly. "Apparently, I humiliated the bastard."

"When you were schoolboys?"

"Yes, then... and now it seems." Rowland was fed up with Abercrombie's wounded feelings. "Humphrey's been so obsessed with me, he's cocked up his part of this grand operation."

"So the Dangars vote is just part of a general campaign to destabilise the country?" Wilfred handed Rowland his handkerchief.

Rowland soaked it with water and applied it to his head. "Humphrey seems convinced that economic recovery will cement capitalist dominance and allow the Fascists to march in." He sighed. "I can't say I'm altogether happy about the Fascists either."

For a moment Wilfred said nothing and then, "What exactly were they trying to get out of you?"

"In the end nothing. Humphrey was just angry... settling some old scores while he had some friends to help him. I wouldn't know anything particularly useful anyway."

"Of course."

"I wouldn't have told them if I did, Wil."

"I know that Rowly. How are you feeling?"

"I'll be all right. Nothing's broken." Rowland moved his battered body tentatively to make sure that was the case. "We have to get out of here. Humphrey's got it into his head that you might have some sort of information or influence he could use... I don't think he'll be long."

Wilfred stood. Flicking open his lighter he surveyed the attic. He flinched slightly when he looked at Rowland again in the light.

"Some of this wood looks quite rotten. We might be able to break through it and kick out the tin."

"It'll make a hell of a noise."

"We'll have to risk that."

Rowland nodded. "Okay then. Let's get started." He removed his dinner jacket. "It's bloody hot up here."

Wilfred dragged the iron cot over the trap door. "That should slow them when the noise starts."

They found a patch low in the sloping ceiling that had been particularly affected by white ants. The lining boards came away without difficulty and they were able to breach the bearers to which the roofing iron was secured. Light streamed in through large holes of corrosion. Wilfred inspected the area carefully. "This looks jolly rusty, Rowly. We might be lucky. I think it'll give with a decent kick."

Rowland stood back and allowed his brother to do the honours. Wilfred went about the task with his customary force and efficiency and soon there was an opening in the roof large enough to allow them through. Rowland draped his jacket over the jagged edges of tin, blanching in the sudden brightness of the morning. Already they could hear scrambling on the floors below.

"We're going to have to make our way up the roof and along," Wilfred said, as he climbed out and offered Rowland his hand. The cot started to buck as the trapdoor was pushed from below. Rowland grasped Wilfred's arm and hoisted himself onto the roof. He took a moment to find his feet on the slope before they clambered up the steep corrugated face to reach the ridge capping.

"Rowly!" Wilfred seized the back of Rowland's shirt as he slipped. Rowland grabbed the chimney.

"Are you all right?" Wilfred asked.

Rowland nodded, impressed by his brother's pragmatic calm. He looked along the adjoining roofs for some way to safety.

Wilfred followed his gaze. "If we shimmy along the ridge cap to that one," he pointed to a terrace house with a verandah at the back, "we might be able to slide down and drop onto the verandah roof without breaking our necks. We can drop down from there."

There was a crash beneath them.

"That's the cot," Rowland said, swinging his leg over the peak of the roof. "We'll have company soon."

They wasted no further time, working their way along the rusted ridge caps. Three men emerged through the hole in the tin.

Both Sinclairs turned when they heard the scream. Rowland saw the man grab desperately for the chimney. He missed and slid down the roof and over the edge. There was a splintering thud as he hit the ground, and more screams from the street.

Rowland swore, horrified.

"Keep going, Rowly," Wilfred commanded. "If we're lucky someone will call the police."

"Shouldn't we just shout for help?"

"We don't know who's here. The whole flaming neighbourhood could be Red for all we know."

The remaining men in pursuit were now shouting that the Sinclairs were burglars. The roofing iron was already starting to heat, and sections of it were rusted and jagged. Rowland gritted his teeth and tried to keep up with his brother in the precarious, awkward scramble towards their planned escape route. People from the street joined the shouting.

Wilfred reached the roof of the terrace with the verandah first. He'd just turned to speak to Rowland when the missile caught him unawares—a half brick hurled from the street.

"Wil!" Rowland's arm shot out as Wilfred overbalanced. He grasped Wilfred's elbow and, for a moment, held the weight. But he too was off balance and the result was that they both fell down the steep corrugated incline and then onto the roof of the verandah. Although the verandah had a gentler pitch, it was not wide enough to halt the momentum of their fall and they plunged headlong over its edge.

"Rowly?" Wilfred got to his knees first and nudged his brother.

Rowland pulled himself up onto his elbows. The ground was soft. They'd fallen into a vegetable garden, flattening a rather splendid crop of silverbeet. He glanced over at the staked tomatoes in an adjoining bed. All in all, they'd been lucky.

Wilfred hauled him up. "Come on."

An elderly gentleman wearing a wide straw hat burst out of the terrace, berating them in Italian and waving a tea towel. Rowland tried to calm him, to explain why two men in dinner suits had fallen from the sky into his silverbeets. His words fell on ears too angry to hear them.

"Rowly, tell him we need help," Wilfred said, pulling his brother under the verandah.

The old man was bemoaning the destruction of his crop. Suddenly he turned and threw his towel at them. Rowland ducked the gingham cloth, and then the straw hat, and then carrots pulled straight from the ground.

"I don't think he's going to help us, Wil."

The door into the house opened to reveal a quite substantial, roughened woman who had squeezed through the opening to investigate the commotion. She wore an oversized hat and, despite the heat, a silver fox stole. Bejewelled and bedecked she glared at them with small eyes set in a broad red face.

"Madam, please don't be alarmed. We mean you no harm," Wilfred started.

The woman answered with profanity, loudly and consecutively. Wilfred stepped back, appalled.

"Look sweetheart, it's not the first time some stuck-up ponce has thought he could put one over on me—but Katy Leigh didn't come down in the last shower…" She rummaged in her purse and pulled out a gun. "Now, just suppose you tell me what Matilda Devine sent you two gents to my joint for."

Wilfred frowned. "I assure you, Madame…"

"You shut up," Kate Leigh snapped. She pointed the gun at Rowland. "You talk. Who the hell are yer?"

"Rowland Sinclair."

The woman's eyes narrowed. "What are yer trying to pull? Sinkers is dead. I knew him well… a good bloke all things considered."

"My uncle," Rowland said uncomfortably. He was aware that Rowland Sinclair the elder had always had a fondness for the seamier side of life. Indeed, the old man had left him a half-share in one of Sydney's most notorious sly-grogeries… it had been an unwelcome legacy. But now it appeared that illicit nightclubs were not the extent of his misbehaviour.

Wilfred looked completely mortified.

Kate Leigh stepped closer and stared intently at Rowland. "Well my giddy aunt, you're that kid old Sinkers would take to the track! Gawd, aren't you just a chip off the old block!"

Rowland wasn't quite sure how to respond. His uncle had taken him to the track several times as a child, but he had no recollection of this very large, very loud woman.

"You don't remember old Katy, do yer? I was in my prime back then, a good sort." She laughed, a harsh uncouth cackle which exposed a halfpenny-sized gap between her two front teeth and a great deal of gold between the others. "You share your uncle's tastes then? Don't worry sweetheart, Katy'll take care of yer."

Admirably, Rowland managed to keep the horror from his face. Wilfred turned purple.

"Might have to clean yer up a bit first," she went on, looking a little distastefully at Rowland. She winked and adjusted herself to lift her ample bosom. "The first time will be for old Sinkers... after that it's two quid."

Wilfred looked like he was about to choke.

Rowland decided he'd better say something. "Actually, we're here on another matter."

"What other matter?" Kate Leigh asked suspiciously.

"We were escaping, to be honest."

At that point a young woman in nothing but a slip rushed out of the house. "Kate! The police are at the door, Kate!"

Kate Leigh's congeniality evaporated. Still brandishing the gun, she fished a razor from her pocket as she exploded. "Sneaks! Sneaks and spies. If you fellas have brought the ruddy constabulary to my joint, I'll cut you ear to flaming ear!"

Wilfred grabbed Rowland's arm and pulled him back as the woman waved the razor threateningly. "Miss Leigh," he said firmly. "If we were to meet the constable at your front door then I presume there would be no need for him to set foot in your... establishment."

She squinted at them, her eyes becoming slits in her bloated face. She flicked the razor shut and dropped the gun to her waist. "Go on then... I'll be right behind you. If that copper comes in you're both dead men."

38

CACHE OF LIQUOR FORFEITED

SYDNEY, Monday

The forfeiture of 1,001 bottles of beer, 84 bottles of whisky and one bottle of wine, found under the floorboards at the home of Kate Leigh, in Surry Hills, was today ordered by Mr. Bliss, S.M., in the Licensing Court. The magistrate said there was no doubt the liquor was on the premises for illegal sale.

The Canberra Times, 1933

There were several policemen standing outside the side door to Kate Leigh's Surry Hills grogery when Wilfred opened it. They seemed ready for a battle.

The first constable looked Wilfred up and down, clearly concluding that he was one of Kate Leigh's more well-to-do customers. The officer informed them that he was investigating a burglary in one of the adjoining houses during which a man in pursuit had fallen from the roof and died.

"If you wouldn't mind if we stepped inside, sir, I'd like to..."

The gun clicked behind them as Kate Leigh readied to make good her threat.

"There's no need, constable," Rowland said, pushing in front of Wilfred. "We're the men you want. We've been trying to hide out in this... home... but we can see now that the game is up. We're quite happy to come quietly as it were..."

The officer studied him. "That's very good of you, sir."

"Well, a man's been killed, constable. Giving ourselves up seems the decent thing to do... right, Wil?"

"Quite," Wilfred agreed, looking anything but agreeable.

"Shall we then?" Rowland smiled brightly. "It's about time we stopped imposing on Miss Leigh's hospitality."

The police officer seemed dubious, but with both suspects surrendering outright, there was really nothing he could do but allow them to walk into his custody.

And so the Sinclair brothers were arrested.

Detective Sergeant Colin Delaney handed Rowland a cold compress. Superintendent Bill Mackay sat behind the desk watching him thoughtfully.

"So who exactly is this chap Abercrombie working for?"

"Some Communist group he met in Cambridge—classicists probably, they were always a bit mad." Rowland glanced at his brother. Humphrey Abercrombie had confirmed all of Wilfred's paranoid tirades about the insidious plots of Communists. Instinctively he reacted against it. "I doubt the ACP even knew about this scheme of his."

Wilfred snorted.

"You can't really be sure of that, can you, Mr. Sinclair?" the superintendent said, scowling. "After all, you didn't even realise you were harbouring a spy. Only Mr. Abercrombie knows who his masters are."

"Well, why don't you just ask him?" Rowland snapped. His head ached, his entire body was bruised and he hadn't slept.

"I'm afraid we haven't apprehended him as yet," Mackay said tightly.

"We can't find him," Delaney admitted.

Mackay glowered at his detective.

"What about the others?"

"Well, one of them's dead... broke his neck in the fall. We have three of the others. A German and two Irishmen—all here illegally. No links here as far as we can tell."

Rowland felt vaguely vindicated.

"I'm not sure I understand Abercrombie's connection with this chap, Moran." Delaney took the hard-backed chair beside Rowland's. "Don't tell me your stockmen were Communists."

"It wasn't a real connection," Rowland replied, rubbing the back of his neck. "I mentioned Moran to Humphrey. Must have approached him—mutual benefit I suppose. When we got away, Moran started making demands and Humphrey shot him... to be honest, I wouldn't be surprised if it was in self-defence. Humphrey's more likely to kill a man in panic than cold blood."

"Well, one thing's clear—this Communist vermin, Abercrombie, was trying to take advantage of your past acquaintance," Wilfred said angrily. "I've always said your so-called friends would ruin you."

"He wasn't a Communist back then for God's sake," Rowland muttered. "He was the bloody Honourable Humphrey Abercrombie. If he hadn't been a chap, you would have wanted me to marry him!"

Delaney coughed.

Mackay cleared his throat. "Senator Hardy has taken charge of the prisoners for the moment—national security." The superintendent was clearly unhappy with his authority being overridden. "Some special committee looking into the matter."

"I've met them," Rowland said contemptuously.

Mackay stood. "We should allow you gentlemen to get cleaned up. Don't worry, we'll find Mr. Abercrombie."

"His mother," Rowland asked, remembering suddenly. "Lady Abercrombie... he said she was visiting a cousin in Melbourne. Does she exist?"

"We'll find out," Mackay assured him. "Don't worry, Mr. Sinclair, he won't give us the slip."

Rowland lay on the couch in the main drawing room of *Woodlands House* staring idly at the ceiling rose. He could feel his muscles stiffening in the wake of the exertions and trials of the last twenty-four hours. He hadn't yet caught up on the lost night's sleep.

He leafed through the handwritten manuscript which rested on his chest. Sarah Brent had sent him Aubrey's novel, along with a letter which outlined her expectations for the illustration of her monkey book. As much as he wanted to read his brother's writings, he was not able to concentrate.

A long hot shower had washed away the remnants of the vegetable garden into which they'd fallen, and Wilfred had once again summoned poor Maguire from his Macquarie Street surgery to patch up his brother. Milton had taken such great delight in his friend's embarrassed account of Kate Leigh's invitation that Rowland, too, had come to see it with amusement rather than horror. But

Abercrombie was still unfinished business and the whereabouts of the Englishman played on Rowland's mind.

Edna left Clyde and Milton to play the next hand without her, and came to sit by Rowland. She picked up the compact she had left on the side table and opened it, posing, admiring it quietly in the light. It was a handmade piece, engraved silver with her initials inlaid in seed pearls. A gift from Rowland to replace the compact which they had turned into a makeshift surgical instrument.

Rowland smiled as he watched her. Edna had been playing with the compact all day. She'd always been like that, taking such a singular and childlike delight in every new acquisition that giving her anything was a joy.

She closed the compact and placed it carefully back onto the table. "Where do you think Mr. Abercrombie is, Rowly?" she asked, sensing what was troubling him.

"I wish I knew, Ed," he said frustrated.

"They'll catch up with him." Milton spoke from behind his cards. "The Party's none too happy with some Lord Muck from the mother country interfering with things here without consulting them. Harry Garden's put the word out. Abercrombie won't have many friends in Sydney."

Rowland sat up. Friends in Sydney. "Babbington," he said slowly.

Clyde put down his cards. "The bloke from the caves. You think he's in league with Humphrey?"

Rowland nodded. "It explains why Babbington was so keen to defeat the Lister franchise. He must have known the numbers added up... and he was staying at Caves House." He stood, retrieved his jacket from the back of the couch and slid it on.

"Where are you going?"

"Wollstonecraft... I think I'll call on Babbington."

"Don't be silly, Rowly, just phone the police." Edna tried to pull him back.

Rowland shook his head. "Here's the thing," he explained, scouting around for his hat. "Perhaps I'm wrong. Perhaps Babbington has got a bee in his bonnet about Lister for some reason completely unrelated to world domination. If that's the case, the last thing I want to do is tell the police I think he's a Communist spy—it could ruin him."

"Has it ruined you?" Edna asked sceptically.

"God, I hope so. I'm still counting on them throwing me off this flaming board."

Milton and Clyde stood now as well.

"We'd better come, don't you think, Rowly?" Milton looked at him sternly. "Just to make sure you don't end up falling into another brothel."

Rowland laughed. "In Wollstonecraft? I'd be lucky."

"Still," Clyde said, "We wouldn't mind a word with old Humphrey ourselves."

Edna put on her gloves. Rowland looked at her. "You're not coming, Ed."

"Well I'm not sitting around here waiting for Wilfred to turn up so I can explain why you went looking for the man you only just escaped."

Rowland was immoveable. "If Humphrey is at Babbington's, I don't really want a lady present when I talk to him."

Despite herself, Edna giggled. "You don't want me to come because you want to swear?" She flopped into the couch and pulled off her gloves. "Oh Rowly, you are old-fashioned."

"Even so."

She rolled her eyes. "All right... go and act like men then, but if you're not back in an hour I'm phoning Colin Delaney and Wilfred."

39

WORKERS BEWARE!

The Friends of the Soviet Union in Australia is appealing to Australian workers for funds to send another delegation to Moscow.

Certainly the workers can do much better with their money than provide a jaunt or overseas picnic for four or five Communists or spies for the Red Internationale.

This organisation is well known as a revolutionary agency and is outlawed under the latest Commonwealth legislation. The wonder is that the Federal Attorney-General does not put the law into operation.

Sunday Times, 1933

The Babbington residence in Wollstonecraft was set well back from the road, built high to take advantage of harbour views. The driveway swept up to a Spanish Mission styled residence. A full summer moon lit the grounds with a monochromatic brightness that was almost equal to day. They all spotted the black Rolls Royce parked by the house.

"Right," Rowland muttered. "No need to knock then."

"Perhaps we should call the police, Rowly," Clyde suggested.

"I'm sure Babbington has the phone on," Rowland replied.

He stopped the Mercedes well before they reached the house. As they climbed out, Milton handed him his gun.

"What's this for?" Rowland asked, alarmed.

"Take it, Rowly. You're the only one with a licence for it."

"I have no intention of assassinating anybody, Milt."

"He was armed before, Rowly," Milton reminded him. "He probably still is. You should be too."

"You don't have to fire it Rowly," Clyde added. "Just wave it around like you might."

Rowland shook his head, but he took the Webley Mark II and, checking the safety, slipped it into his hip pocket. "Fine, we're armed. Shall we go?"

As they passed the Rolls Royce, Clyde signalled them to wait.

"Just give me a minute," he said, quietly opening the hood and shining a torch onto the engine.

"What are you doing?" Milton asked.

"Removing the distributor cap and dizzy… just in case he tries to make a run for it."

"That's not a bad idea."

"There, got it." Clyde tossed the parts into the shrubbery.

"Steady on," Rowland protested. "This is still my car."

"We'll find it later," Clyde assured him as he closed the bonnet. "After the police have taken Abercrombie away."

"I'm afraid that won't be happening."

Rowland spun towards the voice. Humphrey Abercrombie faced them from the doorway, arm straight, gun held high. He gripped a torch in his other hand, which he directed into Rowland's eyes.

Instinctively, Rowland pulled out his own gun. He cursed, recoiling as a bullet caught his weapon and ripped it from his hand.

Milton swore. "You all right, Rowly?"

Rowland nodded, glancing at the revolver which now lay on the lawn well out of his reach.

"Lucky thing, old chap," Abercrombie said, his gun still held in line of sight. "I was aiming for your hand."

"Humphrey, you don't need…"

"For God's sake, Rowly, shut up. I've got nothing to lose by shooting you." Abercrombie's voice was high, tense. "If I'm caught, I'll hang one way or another."

Rowland didn't move. "You don't need to make it any worse, Humphrey… your family…"

Abercrombie swore at him. "You're pathetic, Rowly!" he spat. "You play with the Left when it suits you, but you're not man enough to take a stand."

"Because I didn't join you in your insane scheme?"

"We could have been part of something great, Rowly." Abercrombie licked his lips and laughed. "Well, it's all been a bit of a cock-up, hasn't it? There'll be hell to pay I suppose… I'd better get back and sort things…"

"And how do you propose to do that?" Rowland asked, perhaps a little recklessly.

"Well I won't be using the Rolls I guess." Abercrombie's hair was damp, perspiration plastered it to his forehead, and his voice was shrill and unsteady. He moved his arm to point the gun at Clyde. "Before you contemplate moving, Rowly,' he said, without taking his gaze from Clyde, "Consider whether you're willing to risk Mr. Watson Jones. He does present a rather large target."

"We're not moving, Humphrey. You don't need to involve Clyde in this."

"I rather think he's involved himself, old boy. Now tell me, where is your car?" Abercrombie walked forward to rest the muzzle of his gun against Clyde's head.

Rowland told him where the Mercedes was parked.

"Righto, then." Abercrombie pushed Clyde in front of him. "Mr. Watson Jones is coming with me. At some point I will either let him out or shoot him, depending on whether I believe I'm being followed. Do you understand, Rowly?"

"Yes, but…"

"Once Mr. Watson Jones and I have departed, you may go into the house. You will find Mr. and Mrs. Babbington in there. The old chap lost his nerve after this morning's unpleasantness. I've shot them both, but not fatally… you may yet be able to help them."

"My God, Humphrey, have you lost all decency?"

"I'm not shooting you Rowly. A kindness in memory of our past camaraderie… perhaps you should not have dismissed me so easily, old chum."

Rowland said nothing more, sickeningly aware that there were two people possibly bleeding to death inside the house and that there was a gun against Clyde's skull. Afraid any move would panic the Englishman into shooting, he and Milton stayed where they were as Abercrombie and Clyde walked away.

The Mercedes roared to life and turned back down the driveway. Rowland hesitated for only a moment before running into the house with Milton on his heels.

"I'll look upstairs," Milton said when they found no-one in the drawing room.

Rowland nodded, beginning his search of the lower floor for the wounded Babbingtons. When a search of the drawing rooms, dining room and study proved fruitless, he headed to the back of the house, to the kitchens and servants' quarters. It was then he noticed the banging. He located the source quickly—the large pantry bolted from the outside. He opened the door to the cowering forms of two domestic servants. They screamed when they saw him.

He tried to calm them. Milton burst into the kitchen having heard the initial screams. On sight of him, their shrieks began anew. It took a couple of minutes to talk them out of hysteria and then finally Rowland was able to ask about the whereabouts of the Babbingtons.

"We don't know," the older woman sobbed. "We've been locked in that pantry all day. The Master and Mrs. Babbington aren't due back from the mountains till tomorrow."

Rowland glanced at Milton. Abercrombie had tricked them again. He'd be well away now.

"Are you able to phone the police?" Rowland asked the younger servant, who was the less distraught of the two.

"Yes, sir."

He and Milton wasted no further time, running back to the drive and scrabbling in the shrubbery for the parts Clyde had thrown into them. They had just found the distributor cap and dizzy, when Clyde came wheezing up the driveway.

"Bloody hell, Clyde! What are you doing here?"

"He let me out just down the street," Clyde gasped. "Ran back… a little out of breath…"

Rowland clapped him thankfully on the back.

Milton opened his arms wide. "And hast thou slain the Jabberwock? Come to my arms my beamish boy…"

Clyde took a step back.

Rowland shook his head. "Lewis Carroll." He handed Clyde the parts they'd retrieved. "We're glad to see you, mate… Now, would you put these back?"

"Why?"

"We need to go after Humphrey."

"Are you mad—he's got a gun."

"He's got my car."

Clyde groaned. "Fair enough. I think he was heading towards the bridge."

The Rolls was returned to working order quickly under Clyde's expert hands. Rowland got behind the wheel and they set off in pursuit of Abercrombie, passing an approaching police vehicle as they drove out.

"Did he say anything when you were in the car, Clyde?"

"Quite a lot actually... daft blighter's on some kind of personal crusade." Clyde shook his head. "He sure had me fooled. I thought he was just another one of your poncy school chums, Rowly. Turns out he's some kind of international insurgent. Must've taken some nerve to try to pull off this scheme of his."

"Crazy bloody scheme though—destabilising the country's economy to bolster membership."

"I dunno," Milton ventured thoughtfully. "The Depression has been good for party numbers. When people have jobs they have more to lose by speaking out... I can see his reasoning."

"You don't...?"

"Of course not. When the revolution comes here, it'll be the ACP leading it—not some bored English Lord playing Bolshevik on his hols!"

Rowland smiled. "He's not a Lord, you know... just Honourable."

They were approaching the bridge. It was nearly midnight now and there was very little traffic. The yellow Mercedes stood out from some distance away, parked just outside the Milsons Point pedestrian access to the bridge.

Rowland pulled up, leaving the headlamps on. There was no movement from his motor car. Abercrombie had apparently abandoned her.

They all stepped out cautiously. Rowland could hear sirens approaching. Whether it was the police they had passed leaving Babbington's house, or officers called to investigate the abandoned car on the bridge, he could not be sure. In any case he did not wait for them to arrive. Abercrombie had to be somewhere nearby.

They checked the Mercedes first. It had been parked and the headlamps turned off.

Clyde pointed to the stairs which led onto the bridge. "He must be on the footway."

They started up the stairs. Like the road, it was virtually deserted except for the occasional soul who had decided to sleep there, huddled against a pylon, visible only as a pile of clothes in the shadows. They began to sprint, caught by a sudden feeling of urgency. Abercrombie had a decent lead timewise, but perhaps he had not expected they would follow so quickly. Once he crossed the bridge, who knew where he would go from there.

It was Clyde who first spotted the shoes, placed neatly by the rail, near a streetlight, the jacket folded beside it.

"Rowly, Milt!"

Rowland looked down at the shoes. They looked expensive, an English label embossed on the inner sole. For a moment he stared mutely.

"Damn it! He wouldn't..." Rowland pulled himself up to lean out over the rail and looked down. The harbour was dark. The odd craft still traversed its waters but it was impossible to make out anything.

Milton grabbed Rowland's shoulder as a sudden rise in the wind challenged his grip on the rail. "You can't fish him out this time, Rowly."

40

For selling *Lady Chatterley's Lover*, a banned book by Mr. D. H. Lawrence, the English writer and painter, a bookseller at Cambridge, Massachusetts, was sent to prison for a month and fined £100. Copies of this book were ordered, by a London magistrate, to be destroyed last July.

The Mercury, 1930

Rowland rubbed a dilute solution of burnt umber over the surface of the canvas. The colours darkened and mellowed as he intended. The shadows about the river Styx, before which Psyche wept, deepened. He stood back and surveyed the result critically. Miss Martinelli was unarguably beautiful but he was glad she was gone. These finer finesses could be completed without a model and so he had been able to conclude their session early. Clyde was driving her home in the Mercedes. Rowland had done all that he could, all that could decently be asked of friendship. Now it was up to Clyde, and Rowland Sinclair could go back to painting in peace and quiet. Still, he had not forgotten Norman Lindsay's part in all this.

"You're ageing the painting?" Edna said, as she came into the room with a tray of tea and crumpets.

"Painting it aged me," Rowland replied.

Milton snapped closed his book and saw fit to contribute his poetic insight. "An aged man is but a paltry thing, a tattered coat upon a stick."

"Yes... Yeats," Rowland replied, without looking up from his work.

"Come and have some tea," Edna smiled. "How did your board meeting go yesterday?"

"Slightly less tedious than usual, considering recent events." Rowland pushed Lenin off the couch to take a seat beside Edna. "Without Babbington, the option on the Lister franchise was approved unanimously." He shrugged. "I wonder who would have voted against it, if Babbington hadn't been disgraced?"

"Was he a Communist then?" Edna asked.

"Hard to tell... certainly not a member of the ACP, but who knows. He has a degree in the classics too—perhaps plotting world domination is what they actually do."

"I had always wondered," Milton murmured, opening his book once again.

"Poor Humphrey," Edna said quite sadly, as she curled her legs up onto the couch. "I can't believe he... I really wish it might have ended differently."

"It would have ended badly even if he hadn't have jumped, Ed," Milton reminded her. "He killed a man aside from everything else. He was facing the noose."

"I know," she sighed. "But I was just beginning to like him."

Rowland didn't say anything.

Lady Abercrombie had returned to Sydney and, in her grief, retained solicitors. She had identified the shoes and jacket as belonging to Humphrey Abercrombie, but it seemed she was more than willing to litigate against any postmortem allegation that her son was a Communist. The Harbour Police hadn't yet recovered

Humphrey Abercrombie's body. And those of Abercrombie's associates who had been caught were saying nothing. Rowland wondered if they might all be underestimating the man again.

Edna wriggled around till she was facing him. "Did you finish reading Aubrey's manuscript?" she asked, obviously deciding the subject needed to be changed.

"Yes."

"And? Did you like it."

Rowland smiled. "Aubrey's my brother, I'm predisposed to like it."

"Of course. What's it about?"

Rowland laughed. "Have you read *Lady Chatterley's Lover*?"

"Which version?" Milton asked.

"The banned one—there's a copy in the library…"

Edna gasped. "Aubrey's book… really?"

Rowland nodded solemnly. "Like Lawrence with a sense of humour."

"Always thought *Sons and Lovers* could have used the odd punch line," Milton muttered.

Edna giggled. "Who would have thought…? Aubrey was more like you than Wilfred."

Almost unconsciously Rowland glanced at his father's portrait. Henry Sinclair's image seemed none too pleased with the idea.

"Sounds like Aubrey's manuscript might be worth the pain of having to illustrate Sarah Brent's monkey book in return," Milton ventured, grinning.

"Oh, I'm not doing that." Rowland folded his arms resolutely.

"Surely you didn't refuse?" Edna asked, dismayed. "Sarah had her heart set on illustrations…"

"Not to worry, Ed. I've sorted it."

41

VANDALISM IN GARDENS

... the following quotation from the monthly report of the Curator (Mr. E. W. Bick), to the City Council: "There has been considerable wilful damage caused by vandalism recently. Two automatic machines were forced open, and two locks forced, one of the latter being on the animal enclosure. Eight monkeys were liberated, and a great deal of trouble was caused in catching them. If the object was theft, it may be pointed out that any person removing an imported animal from the Botanic Gardens, a quarantine area, in addition to prosecution for theft, could be charged with a breach of the quarantine regulations, and would be liable to a heavy penalty."

Brisbane Courier, 1933

Norman Lindsay stormed into the sunroom at *Springwood*. Rose Lindsay looked up, startled. She was used to her husband's artistic temperament, but this mood was darker than most.

"Whatever is the matter, Norman? Has something upset you, dear?"

"That woman's impossible!" he exploded. "My monkey doesn't look intelligent enough according to her." He threw down a folder of fine, detailed drawings, on which he had already spent countless hours. "Apparently the simian in question is bloody brilliant!"

"Now Norman, calm down… it can't be that bad…"

"She wants me to start again. Suggests we hire a monkey so I can get a better understanding of the creatures!" The great artist put his head in his hands and pulled at his hair. "Where the hell am I supposed to get a bloody monkey?"

Rose Lindsay stroked his back sympathetically. "Why on earth did you commit to the project?"

"I was tricked!"

Rose laughed. "Oh come now, Norman, who would want to trick you into such a thing?"

"You know, Rose," he said bitterly, "Rowland Sinclair is a complete and utter bastard!"

Epilogue

Humphrey Abercrombie's body was never recovered. With none of his compatriots willing to say anything, no charges were ever laid against him, posthumously or otherwise.

Following the Reichstag fire of the 27 February 1933, the Nazis under the leadership of Adolf Hitler as Germany's new chancellor, passed a decree which rescinded most German civil liberties, including habeas corpus. Jews, communists, socialists, anarchists and other political enemies of the Nazis throughout the Reich were imprisoned in the Dachau Concentration Camp. In March 1933, the Enabling Act was passed conferring dictatorial powers on Adolf Hitler. By July, Germany was officially a single-party state, with the founding of any new parties banned.

Charles Babbington denied any knowledge of Humphrey Abercrombie. The rumours did however ruin him. He was allowed to resign from the board of Dangar, Gedye and Company. Mr. and Mrs. Babbington left Australia permanently in 1935 to take up residence in London.

Dangar, Gedye and Company went on to flourish, due in no small part to its association with Lister, which through its pumps, engines and other plants, powered rural Australia.

———————◆———————

The Rules Point Guesthouse was demolished in the 1960s. Until then it operated at various times as a guesthouse, pub and fishing lodge. There are still people in the High Country who remember the Rules Point Sports Days and dances.

———————◆———————

August Eichorn continued to stage his snake handling shows and purvey his Snakebite and Blood Poisoning Cure for the entertainment and good health of the people of the Riverina and surrounding regions. So confident was he of the efficacy of his cure that he encouraged some of Australia's most dangerous snakes, including tiger and brown snakes, to bite him, sometimes simultaneously. He eventually died in 1944 from blood poisoning.

———————◆———————

The Cassidy brothers were finally apprehended in Victoria. To this day, the proceeds of the Eugowra Stage Coach robbery, otherwise known as Glover's gold, have not been found.

———————◆———————

In 1933 Endeavour Press published *Bring the Monkey*, a light novel by Miles Franklin, illustrated by Norman Lindsay.

Acknowledgments

Miles off Course may have been a description rather than a title, if not for the following people who have kept me from becoming hopelessly lost in the literary wilderness. I am deeply and sincerely grateful.

My husband Michael, who can't always see the road, but whose internal compass is pretty true. Who, in the beginning, drew me a map of the 1930s and let me go.

My boys, Edmund and Atticus, who never stay on the path, who wander off to find places that no-one else knows and who are fearless in their exploration of this world.

Leith Henry, my life-long friend, whom I call when I have no idea where I'm going. Whose support from the beginning has made me much braver than I might otherwise have been.

My father who will still drive out in the middle of the night to pick me up, if I find myself stranded.

My extraordinary sisters, Devini and Nilukshi, who long ago set the pace.

The Greens—John, Alison, Jenny and Martin—and the team at Pantera Press. I would need to write a hundred books to even start to acknowledge the support, the generosity, the faith and warmth of my publishers.

Sue Bulger, and Aunty Flo Grant who shared their language, their insight and their humour to help me breathe life into Harry Simpson, a Wiradjuri man. Mandaang guwu.

Michael Schulz, my friend and colleague, a German Irish Australian, and a gentleman.

Laurie Keenan, master of all trades, statesman and local hero, who despite how I may have used his name in this book, probably hasn't shot anyone... yet anyway.

Rex O'Brien, Shamus O'Brien, and Petrina Walker, who patiently answered what must have seemed quite impertinent questions about what one actually does with cattle in the High Country.

My dear friends, the Kynastons, the Wainwrights, the Marshalls, the Henries, Wallace Fernandes, Alastair Blanshard, Dick Thompson, Rebecca Crandell, Angela Savage, Lesley Bouquet and Cheryl Bousfield, who are an infinitely rich source of advice, support and (perhaps inadvertently) material.

My colleagues at the Murrumbidgee Catchment Management Authority who have tolerated a fiction writer in their midst without undue alarm.

My editor, Deonie Fiford, with whom it is a pleasure and a comfort to work, who doesn't miss anything, who can see the way I wish to go and keeps me on that path.

Sofya Karmazina who wraps my words in the perfect image and who takes author requests like "please insert a monkey" in his stride.

Desanka Vukelich, Graeme Jones, Karen Young and all the extraordinary professionals who bring their talents to the production of my books.

Harry Hill, John Merritt, Klaus Hueneke, Colin Hoard, John Winterbottom and all the local historians of the South West Slopes who have preserved a past which might otherwise have simply slipped from living memory. The people of Batlow, Adelong, Tumut and Tumbarumba who are my neighbours, my friends and, quite often, my inspiration.

And finally, the greater community of reviewers, bloggers, booksellers and especially readers who have made it possible for me to be a writer. Thank you.

If you liked *Miles Off Course* then look out for
the next book in the Rowland Sinclair Series

PAVING THE NEW ROAD

It's 1933, and the political landscape of Europe is darkening.

Eric Campbell, the man who would be Australia's Führer, is on
a fascist tour of the Continent, meeting dictators over cocktails and
seeking allegiances in a common cause. Yet the Australian way of life
is not undefended. Old enemies have united to thwart Campbell's
ambitions. The clandestine armies of the establishment have once
again mobilised to ensure that any friendship with the Third Reich
is undermined.

But when their man in Munich is killed, desperate measures are
necessary.

Now Rowland Sinclair must travel to Germany to defend
Australian democracy from the relentless march of Fascism.
Amidst the goosestepping euphoria of a rising Nazi Movement,
Rowland encounters those who will change the course of history. In
a world of spies, murderers and despotic madmen, he can trust no-
one but an artist, a poet and a brazen sculptress.

Plots thicken, loyalties are tested and bedfellows become strange
indeed.

Please enjoy this excerpt from
PAVING THE NEW ROAD

PROLOGUE

"No! For God's sake, no! Rowland Sinclair cannot be trusted." Freddie Middlemiss was adamant and furious. His lips puckered and pressed into a disconsolate line. "The man's a disgrace. We still can't be sure he's not a bloody Red." He stubbed out his cigarette, agitated. "If I had my way, we'd shoot him and be done with it!"

"What Charles is suggesting may be tantamount to shooting him," Maguire observed. It was hard to tell if the surgeon was necessarily unhappy with the proposition.

Senator Charles Hardy pushed his fingertips together as he considered the warning. The select meeting of loyalists waited for his response in the private meeting room of the Riverine Club. A dozen men sat around the polished board table, ashtrays and scotch within easy reach. The air was heavy, a smoky, conspiratorial fog. It was a testament to Hardy's growing influence that the venerable men in attendance had travelled to Wagga Wagga at such short notice, and that they had done so without the knowledge of Wilfred Sinclair.

A throat was cleared. Frederick Hinton tapped the table impatiently, his chin dimpling as he dropped it into his fleshy jowls. Sir Adrian Knox mopped at his brow with a handkerchief as if he were searching for the judge's wig under which his balding crown was so often hidden. Even Goldfinch pulled restlessly at his moustache. Only Maguire remained rigid, unmoving.

"I believe Rowland was cleared of suspicion," Hardy said finally. "And the Sinclairs have always been true to King and country."

A general murmur of agreement.

"There is not a man here who would doubt Wilfred," Middlemiss returned. "He's a decent chap, but Rowland is another matter entirely. I doubt even Wilfred trusts him."

"Rowland has skills that could be very useful," Hardy said, sensing the mood was against him. It would take a great deal to convince these men to act against Wilfred Sinclair. "Rowland is fluent in French, Spanish and, most importantly, German. Not to mention the fact that the very associations which cause some of you to doubt his loyalty may make him privy to valuable information."

Frederick Hinton's round face puffed. "Surely you are not suggesting that we should endorse his enlisting the Reds to help…"

"No, of course not," Hardy said hastily. "But his ability to move among the vermin may be useful. Let us remember, gentlemen, why we need to place a man in Germany."

"We have not forgotten, Charles." Knox pointed at the Senator. "It's why we need a man we can trust, who is unimpeachable. It's why Wilfred is our man… whether or not he speaks German."

"One should also remember that the ability to speak German didn't really help Peter Bothwell in the end," Goldfinch added.

Hardy pulled the unlit pipe from his mouth. He spoke carefully. "You may be right, gentlemen. But let us not deceive ourselves—this operation is not without risk and Wilfred is both very valuable to and inextricably connected with our movement."

"What are you saying, Hardy?"

"I am simply making the observation that if things were to go wrong, Wilfred is inseparable from this organisation… he is closely linked to every man at this table. Rowland Sinclair, on the other hand, is a known renegade—there was that business last year between him and Campbell and then that nonsense with the

Theosophical Society. No-one will doubt that he was acting of his own accord."

Hardy's proposal was considered. The Senator waited.

It was Maguire who first broke the pensive silence. "Wilfred won't like it. He won't allow it."

"He could be made to appreciate the wisdom of it if we were resolved. We really can't risk a good man like Wilfred."

"And how do you expect to get Rowland Sinclair to agree?" Maguire asked. "You have hardly endeared yourself to him."

Hardy did not flinch. "Leave young Sinclair to me. I'll make him see the sense of taking his brother's place. Needless to say, I shall have to speak to him before Wilfred suspects our purpose."

Maguire folded his arms, tilting back in his chair. "Wilfred will not take kindly to this plan of yours, Charles."

"I suppose he won't," Hardy replied. "Regardless, it will keep Wilfred out of harm's way."

"By putting his brother directly in it."

Middlemiss snorted loudly. "Wilfred may thank us for it. Rowland's been little more than an embarrassment for years."

Maguire's beard moved with the clench of his jaw. "Rowland Sinclair is his only surviving brother. You're a fool if you think Wilfred will tolerate any proposal to send Rowland into danger!"

"Steady on, Maguire," Knox protested. "All we're doing is replacing Bothwell."

"And may I remind you, Sir Adrian, that Peter Bothwell is dead."

The room fell again into an uneasy silence as the inescapable fact settled on the consciences of the Old Guard leadership.

Hardy's voice was brittle. "All the more reason we should send Rowland Sinclair."

1

ERIC CAMPBELL

NOW IN LONDON.
FASCISM URGED FOR N.S.W.

LONDON, March 7

Mr. Eric Campbell told a press representative he was seeing Sir Oswald Mosley regarding organising Fascism in New South Wales. He proposes to visit Italy, Germany and Poland. Mr. Campbell added the time was never so opportune as now for Fascism in New South Wales. Not only Lang and his Communist friends need watching, but the Stevens Government was paving the way to Socialism and Communism.

The Townsville Daily Bulletin, 1933

It was a particularly inconvenient time to call.

The smoke was thick and the blaze in real danger of getting away. A misshapen, one-eared greyhound barked madly at the flames as it tried to warn its master of the peril.

"Lenin! Calm down!" Rowland Sinclair relinquished his shovel reluctantly. No doubt it would be another irate neighbour demanding to know why he was trying to set the street alight.

"Who is it this time, Mary?" he asked the housekeeper, who had personally ventured into the gardens of *Woodlands House* to bring him the message. He patted his thigh to call his dog to heel beside him.

Mary Brown sighed, conveying all manner of frustration, disapproval and concern in a simple exhalation of breath. She had been employed at the Sydney residence of the Sinclairs since well before its current master was born, and although she had run Rowland's household for several years, she did not condone his lifestyle. Of course she would never utter what it was not her place to say... and so she sighed again. "A Senator Charles Hardy, Master Rowly," she said, addressing him with the title she had used since he was a child. "The Senator is most insistent that he speak with you now."

"Hardy?" Rowland stopped, frowning as he unrolled his sleeves and rebuttoned his waistcoat. He and the Senator were hardly friends. Why would he call unannounced? "Ask the Senator to wait in my studio, please, Mary. I'll be along directly."

"What is it, Rowly?" Edna shouted over the crackling roar of the fire. The young sculptress for whom they had built the small inferno tossed an armload of split logs into the flames. She wore overalls, as she always did when she was working. Her auburn hair was caught back from her face beneath a headscarf and her cheeks were streaked with smoky residue. Rowland paused to enjoy the dishevelled picture of her. There was something particularly enchanting about such a beautiful creature, being so at home in overalls and soot.

"Rowly?" Edna prompted, rolling her eyes. She had become accustomed to how easily men were distracted in her company... or perhaps by it.

"Just an unexpected visitor," Rowland said finally.

"Who?" Edna persisted. She knew him too well to dismiss the hard glint in his dark blue eyes, and she was too curious by nature to let it pass.

"Senator Hardy, apparently," Rowland replied.

Milton Isaacs looked up from his book. The poet had taken refuge in the gazebo upwind of the fire, unwilling to risk his immaculate cream jacket in the smoke. "And they were enemies: they met beside the dying embers of an altar-place," he said loudly, looking pointedly at the fire.

"Byron," Rowland shouted back at him. Milton's posture as a poet was the ill-gotten product of his talent for quoting the works of English bards at will. That the words were not the creation of his own poetic inspiration was a detail that escaped most people... except Rowland Sinclair, who felt obliged to make the attribution his friend so conveniently omitted.

Milton snorted contemptuously as if it were Byron who had, in fact, stolen his words.

Clyde Watson Jones leaned on his own shovel, a wary eye still on the fire. He was not the eldest of them by many years, but his face was already mellowed, weathered but comfortable, like a well-worn pair of boots. The time he'd spent in the luxury of *Woodlands House* under Rowland's generous patronage had not erased the map of care etched by years on the wallaby, scrounging for work and dignity. "What would Hardy want with you, mate?"

Rowland's face darkened further. "I'm sure I'll find out." His last encounter with Charles Hardy had been anything but pleasant. The Senator had essentially accused him of treason... some cockeyed notion that Rowland Sinclair, the youngest brother of Wilfred Sinclair— that bastion of conservative respectability—was a Communist spy, a traitor to King and country. Rowland might have found it funny if it had not seemed that his brother was standing with the accusers.

Retrieving his jacket from the garden seat on which he had tossed it when they had first begun the task of digging a pit for Edna, he dragged it on. Edna reached up and straightened his tie, and used her sleeve to wipe a stray smudge of black from his cheek. Unfortunately her sleeve was not itself pristine and her efforts were less than successful.

Rowland smiled as he attempted to rectify the extra soot she had left on his person. It was just cursory... let Hardy take him as he found him... cinders and all.

He entered the house through the conservatory. Lenin padded quietly after him.

Rowland's studio, in which Hardy waited, had once been the grand mansion's main parlour. It was a large room with high, ornate ceilings and ample light afforded by bay windows. It was this light that made it an excellent studio space. That using it in such a way stamped his stewardship of *Woodlands House* absolutely did not displease Rowland either.

Charles Hardy was standing before the larger-than-life portrait of Rowland's late father, the pastoralist Henry Sinclair. His gaze, however, was on the painting which graced the opposite wall—a nude of Edna seated in the armchair which Rowland now invited his guest to take.

The Senator smiled broadly. "Just admiring your father's portrait... a fine, loyal Australian, a real Briton," he said as he approached Rowland with his hand outstretched.

Rowland accepted the handshake cautiously. Aside from the fact that he doubted Hardy had been concentrating on his father's portrait, the Senator was no more than thirty-five. It was unlikely he'd known Henry Sinclair, who had died in 1920.

"Of course, I didn't have the pleasure of meeting him personally... but I knew him well by reputation. A man to be reckoned with, I'm told. He was taken too early, as I suppose the best men are."

Rowland glanced at the glowering likeness in oil, and said nothing. He had been fifteen when his father died.

In the silence, Hardy's eyes fell upon the greyhound. The dog ignored him and stretched out at Rowland's feet. "Good Lord! Your dog?"

Rowland nodded.

"What do you call him?"

"Lenin."

Hardy changed the subject. "Been barbequing, I see."

Eager to ascertain the purpose of Hardy's unexpected visit, Rowland offered the Senator a drink. He allowed Hardy to make small talk for the minimum time that courtesy would allow before asking quite bluntly, "What can I do for you, Senator Hardy?"

"Please... Charles," Hardy said. He studied Rowland over his glass of whisky. "Look, Sinclair, I'd like to bury the hatchet, as it were... I misjudged you... I admit it and I apologise."

Rowland watched him suspiciously. "Thank you."

"Good... good... no hard feelings, then." Hardy didn't wait for Rowland to reply, and Rowland didn't make any attempt to do so.

The politician glanced back at the portrait of Henry Sinclair. "I should have known that despite your unusual social connections, the Sinclairs have always been King's men. Your father would have brought you up with love of country and Empire." He paused in his rhetoric. "I was hoping that I could rely on that now."

"Rely on it for what, exactly?" Rowland knew full well Hardy had not called merely to apologise.

"I hoped to enlist your help on a matter of national security."

Admittedly, Rowland's interest was piqued. "National security? Are you sure it's not Wilfred you'd like to talk to?" It was Wilfred who now wielded the power of the Sinclairs—influence born of wealth and political connections. Rowland had instead claimed the role of black sheep, a part which suited him and which he thought he played rather well. That the Senator would seek his help on any matter, let alone one of national security, was, at the very least, a little surprising.

Hardy sipped his scotch and let the silence settle dramatically before he answered. "No, it's you… Can I depend on you, Sinclair? Can your country, your fellow Australians, depend on you?"

Rowland raised a single brow. Hardy had always had a predilection for theatre. "What do you want, Senator Hardy?"

"I really must insist you call me Charles," Hardy said, placing down his drink. He leaned forward with his elbows on his knees. "I need your word as a gentleman, Rowland, that what I am about to tell you will not go outside these walls."

Rowland nodded impatiently.

"I understand that you are acquainted with Eric Campbell."

"I believe he is a mutual acquaintance," Rowland replied. He wasn't going to allow Hardy to deny his own involvement with the fascist group.

Colonel Eric Campbell was the commander of the New Guard, a right-wing movement of citizens which had once sought to overthrow the New South Wales government of Jack Lang, whom they decried as a Communist-coddler. Over a year ago now, Rowland had infiltrated the movement for his own reasons and, in the process, come to know Eric Campbell and the machinations of the New Guard quite well. But the whole affair had ended rather badly, destroying his reputation in certain quarters, enhancing it in others.

Hardy studied him piercingly. "The Riverina Movement was not a part of the New Guard," he said tersely, defensively.

Rowland did not resile. Led by Hardy himself, the Riverina Movement was to Rowland's mind not so different from the New

Guard. Indeed, Campbell and Hardy had been tentative allies against what they regarded as a common evil. Of course, now Charles Hardy was a respectable member of His Majesty's parliament and Campbell considered an extremist crackpot... in some circles, at least.

"What is Colonel Campbell up to, then?" Rowland asked.

"Abroad... he's abroad," Hardy replied, "on an educational tour of Europe. Right now he's in Britain consorting with Sir Oswald Mosley. In a couple of weeks he'll be in Germany meeting members of the Reichstag, perhaps even Hitler himself, making contacts and allegiances with, we believe, the intent of bringing European fascism to Australia."

Rowland laughed. "Last year you were all sure Stalin had his eye on New South Wales—now it's Hitler and Mussolini?"

Hardy waited until Rowland's grin subsided. "This is not a matter for jest, Sinclair... surely you are aware of the changes Hitler has already brought about in Germany... She is no longer a democracy. Hitler's latest manifesto speaks of *Lebensraum*... room to live. His agenda has become expansionist."

Rowland frowned. Germany did indeed disturb him. Only the previous year he had taken his friends there in search of the avant-garde, bohemian Berlin which had nurtured and inspired so many artists. But things had changed. Many of the painters and sculptors he had known and admired were under attack... their work labelled as degenerate. Rowland had called on his old friend Jankel Adler at the Art Academy, to find the revered painter persecuted and in fear of his life. Adler had since fled to Paris. It was hard to believe that such things could happen in the modern world. Clyde and Milton kept him apprised of what they learned through their links in the Communist party.

"And what has this got to do with me?"

"I'd like you to go to Germany."

Rowland choked on his drink. "You what?"

Hardy opened a leather briefcase and took from it a cardboard file of documents. "You are a scholar of languages, I believe—you speak German like a native."

"The natives might disagree."

"You also speak French, Spanish and Italian."

"I've not had call to do so recently," Rowland said carefully, wondering what exactly the file held.

Hardy sat back in his chair. He frowned. "I wonder if you might have read about Peter Bothwell?"

Slowly, Rowland nodded. The Sydney papers had reported the death of Bothwell, a grazier from Cootamundra. He had drowned, though the reported details had been noticeably vague. Bothwell had been in Germany at the time of his death. "Yes, I did read something. Did you know him?"

"I'm godfather to his boys." Hardy sighed. "Indeed, Peter and I have… had been friends for many years. We served together. You couldn't find a better chap or a more loyal Australian."

"My commiserations." Rowland wondered where the Senator was leading.

"The fact is, Rowly, Peter wasn't in Germany on holiday. We'd placed him there to wait for Campbell's arrival. He was a vital part of our operation to keep an eye on Campbell."

Now Rowland was intrigued. "The Federal Government sent this chap Bothwell to Germany?"

Hardy shook his head. "No, this was never official." He dropped the file onto the occasional table beside him as he tried to explain. "Let's just say Peter Bothwell was sent to Germany by men who have our country's, and arguably the Empire's, interests at heart… who are concerned to ensure that Eric Campbell's star does not rise the way Hitler's has in recent years."

"I see... but what has this got to do with me?"

"We have another man in Campbell's party... travelling with him—a little like a spy."

"A lot like a spy, I'd say."

"Blanshard is Campbell's interpreter. He speaks both Italian and German—and a couple of other languages besides. He will be assisted by other operatives in Italy, but Peter was to be his contact once Campbell arrives in Germany. With Peter's passing, Blanshard is isolated."

"So bring him back."

"That would be suspicious and he is the last man we have left within the New Guard. If we lose him we'll have no idea what Campbell's up to."

"And you want me to go to Germany to do what, exactly?" Rowland asked.

"We would like you to assist Blanshard, see what you can find out about Campbell's connections to the Nazi government." Hardy paused before adding, "I would like you to look into Peter Bothwell's death."

Rowland put down his drink. "I'm not a detective, Senator Hardy."

"No, but you do speak German and you are familiar with the country." He handed the cardboard file over to Rowland. "I'd like you to read this. It contains all the communication received on the matter of Peter's death as well as newspaper clippings, letters from Peter himself... that sort of thing. You read it and tell me if you think his sudden demise isn't suspicious."

"You want me to swoop in like some colonial Sherlock Holmes and solve the case?" Rowland didn't bother to hide that he thought the proposition ridiculous.

"I want you to find out what you can while you're assisting Blanshard in making sure Campbell doesn't bring Nazism back here."

"I wonder why you think I'd be interested in—let alone humanly capable of—doing what you want?"

"Because you more than anyone know how dangerous Campbell can be… the fanaticism he is able to incite. I believe the New Guard nearly killed you once."

"If I recall, Senator Hardy, the good men of your Riverina Movement seemed keen to shoot me too."

Hardy looked at him blankly and Rowland wondered if it were possible that the man was unaware of the excesses of the mobs he had incited to violence.

"Look, Sinclair." Hardy sat forward. "Do me the indulgence of hearing me out."

Rowland raised his glass. "Be my guest."

"I assume you are aware of the organisations of patriotic men who have the defence of democracy and our way of life as their purpose."

"I am aware of a number of organisations who claim that is their purpose," Rowland said carefully.

"And you are aware of your brother's involvement with the Old Guard?"

Rowland stiffened. The Old Guard was the vehicle of the establishment, a clandestine conservative militia, the leadership of which included Wilfred Sinclair. Beyond that he knew little about the movement. "What has Wil got to do with this?"

"The Old Guard is becoming increasingly uneasy with Campbell's attempts to forge allegiances with the European fascists. Our information is that he proposes to float a political party… to work within the democratic system to wrest power from it."

Rowland nodded. The parallels to the German Chancellor's recent rise to power were unmistakable. He frowned. "Our? You've been recruited to the Old Guard?"

"In times of need, like-minded men will join forces," Hardy replied. "The underlying tenets of the Riverina Movement were never at odds with those of the Old Guard."

Rowland shrugged. So Hardy was now with the Old Guard... it was inevitable, he supposed. He was a Senator.

"The Old Guard is concerned enough about recent developments to have installed a man within Campbell's inner circle and to have sent Peter Bothwell to Germany to ensure that he didn't receive too warm a welcome." Hardy spoke slowly now, ensuring his next words had maximum effect. "Now that Peter is dead, Wilfred himself will go to Germany in his place."

Rowland sat up. "Wil?"

Hardy sat back, noting Rowland's alarm with satisfaction. "Of course I was struck by the similarities between Wilfred and Peter... both good men with loving wives and fine young sons. Wilfred has two boys, I believe?"

"Yes."

Hardy spoke urgently now. "Wilfred is prepared to go to Germany, Rowland. In fact, he'll leave within the week. Your brother is a capable man, but he does not have your flair for languages and he does have a family."

"Why hasn't Wilfred mentioned this to me?" Rowland said, his eyes moving to the framed photograph of his young nephews which stood among the others on the mantel.

"Perhaps he doesn't trust you."

Rowland knew full well that Charles Hardy was playing him, but he couldn't prevent his response. "I doubt that's the case," he said coldly.

"You must understand, Rowly, Wilfred's in a difficult position. This is a matter of national import. The Old Guard are necessarily cautious men. If you'd seen service they would have proof of your loyalty, but unfortunately…"

Rowland glared furiously at Hardy.

"Perhaps if you were to assume this task for your brother, for your country and fellow countrymen… well, your loyalty would be beyond question, regardless of your associations."

"I'm not a fool, Hardy," Rowland said, his eyes flashing dangerously. "And I'm not interested in proving myself to the Old Guard."

"Of course, if you went, Wilfred would not need to." Hardy looked over at the picture of Wilfred's sons, leading Rowland's eyes and mind to the same.

"Is Wilfred aware you're here?" Rowland asked.

Hardy shook his head. "Rescuing you has become something of a habit for your brother. I expect he will object most strenuously to your going anywhere outside the bounds of his protection."

Rowland's eyes darkened. Hardy watched closely, clearly gauging the effect of his words.

Rowland rubbed his face, aware that he was reacting just as Hardy intended and irritated that he could be so easily and obviously manipulated. He stood and walked over to the mantelpiece.

"Peter Bothwell's younger son is barely two years old. He won't even remember his father." Hardy pressed his advantage. "Our only chance to prevent Wilfred doing this is for you to go in his place. Surely, man, you're aware of Campbell's extremism, his ambition…"

Rowland picked up the picture of Wilfred's boys. "Fine," he said quietly. "I'll go."

Sign up to The Crime & Mystery Club's newsletter to get the eBook of *Paving the New Road* for FREE.

bit.ly/PavingtheNewRoad

Why not try Robin Paige's Victorian Mystery series?

Meet journalist Kate Ardleigh as she investigates her first case with amateur detective Sir Charles Sheridan in this popular series sure to delight fans of Sherlock Holmes and Agatha Christie.

'An intriguing mystery… skilfully unravelled' – Jean Hager, author of *Blooming Murder*

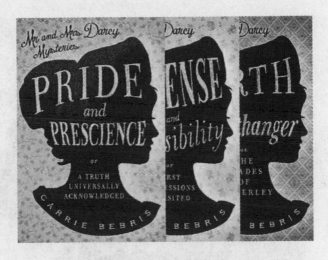

If you enjoyed this Rowland Sinclair mystery, you may enjoy Carrie Bebris' Mr and Mrs Darcy Mystery Series!

In the best Austen tradition with Regency backdrops, moody country houses, and delightful characterization – plus an added twist of murder and mayhem...

Pride & Prescience
Suspense and Sensibility
North by Northanger

Sulari Gentill is the author of the award-winning and best-selling Rowland Sinclair Mysteries, the Greek mythology adventure series The Hero Trilogy, and winner of the Best Crime award at the 2018 Ned Kelly Awards, Crossing the Lines.

She set out to study astrophysics, graduated in law, and then abandoned her legal career to write books instead of contracts. Born in Sri Lanka, Sulari learned to speak English in Zambia, grew up in Brisbane and now lives in the foothills of the Snowy Mountains of NSW where, with her historian husband, she grows French black truffles, cares for a variety of animals and raises two wild colonial boys. Sulari also paints, but only well enough to know she should write, preferably in her pyjamas.